Daughter of the Reich

Daughter of the Reich

A Novel

LOUISE FEIN

wm

WILLIAM MORROW
An Imprint of HarperCollinsPublishers

With grateful acknowledgment to the following source for song lyric translations: *Thesis: Lieder, Totalitarianism, and the Bund Deutscher Mädel: Girls' Political Coercion Through Song.* Source: Library and Archives Canada/OCLC 57575010.

P.S.™ is a trademark of HarperCollins Publishers.

HarperCollins books may be purchased for educational, business, or sales promotional use. For information, please email the Special Markets Department at SPsales@harpercollins.com.

FIRST EDITION

Designed by Diahann Sturge

Title page and part title art © dmitroscope / Shutterstock, Inc.

Library of Congress Cataloging-in-Publication Data has been applied for.

ISBN 978-0-06-296405-2 (paperback)
ISBN 978-0-06-301912-6 (hardcover library edition)
ISBN 978-0-06-302886-9 (international edition)

20 21 22 23 24 LSC 10 9 8 7 6 5 4 3 2

To my remarkable parents, who are with me always.

Those that fail to learn from history are doomed to repeat it.
—WINSTON CHURCHILL

Prologue

Leipzig
Summer 1929

The lake is silky smooth, lapping gently around the legs of the jetty. The knobbly planks beneath my toes are thick and warmed by the sun. Karl is on the bank, wriggling into his shorts under the towel Mutti is holding around him.

"Careful, Hetty," Karl shouts. "The water's deep out there."

"I'm just looking," I call back. "I want to see the big fish."

I shuffle right to the very end and curl my toes around the edge. Crouching low, I peer into the water. I can't see the bottom of the lake. Maybe there isn't one. Perhaps the dark green water goes all the way down to the middle of the earth where savage monsters lurk, waiting.

Walter swims toward the jetty. He splashes his arms around then floats on his back, pale toes bobbing up out of the water. He pops up again, grinning at me, pushing his wet hair off his face. I wish I could have swimming lessons like Karl, then I, too, could glide like a fish, instead of splashing about in the shallows, stubbing my toes on jagged stones and slipping on slimy weed.

From my perch, I watch Walter swim farther out into the lake. He disappears from sight, hidden by the solid wooden pillar of the jetty. I move to try to see him, but I lean too far and topple forward. My hands fly out, clawing at empty space, and I'm falling, down, down, down.

Belly first, I crash onto the stone-hard surface. I gasp with the iciness, but instead of air, there is only rancid lake water.

"Help!" I splutter, splashing hopelessly, blinded by blurry flashes of light and dark.

"HELP," louder now, but the water boils and churns, closing over my head, and the monsters suck me down to their deep, green lair.

Gripped by panic, I scrabble and kick, fighting back up to the surface. I manage a breath. There are voices in the distance. I thrash wildly, but it doesn't keep me up, and I'm swirling, round and round. The voices fade as I'm dragged down again, lungs screaming, but the water—sickening, cloying, heavy—fills them and I'm drowning.

Darkness folds in.

Something scrabbles at my swimsuit and scratches my back. There's a tugging, and I'm pulled up to the surface. Someone is holding me and I'm retching and coughing in the lightning-white sunlight until I think my insides are going to spill out. With a rasping choke, air surges into my lungs, and water pours from my nose. The person holding me is kicking hard, keeping both of us up, panting and grunting with the effort. The hands turn me onto my back and there's a strong body beneath me, keeping my head above the water.

"Don't struggle, you're safe now." A voice in my ear. Walter's voice. "I'm swimming you back to the shore." He wraps his hand around my chin and tugs.

I try to lie still, but water laps in my ears and I wobble as he jerkily swims on his back, huffing with the effort of keeping me up until we reach shallow water. Dimly, I hear cries and shouts from nearby. Walter's body is solid and safe. He begins to wriggle out from under me, but I cling desperately to him, our tangle of legs sinking to the lake floor.

"It's all right, you can stand now," he says, propping me upright. The mud squishes between my toes as I try to stand but I'm shaking, and my legs collapse beneath me. Walter holds me, and I lean against him. My throat stings from the coughing. Water trickles from my nose.

Mutti runs through the shallows, soaking her skirt, but she doesn't seem to care. She lifts me up, hugging me tight against her body, and we stagger back to shore. She wraps me in a warm towel.

"Hetty! Are you okay?" Karl is here, too, patting me on the back, peering at my face. "I told you to be careful!"

"Oh my poor darling." Mutti sinks down with me still in her arms. She rocks me back and forth as though I were a baby, not a big seven-year-old. My ear is pressed to her chest and I can hear her breath, ragged and fast, in her throat.

Walter stands close by, watching us, silent and dripping. Mutti turns to him.

"You saved her life, Walter. Thank heavens you're such a strong swimmer. If you hadn't been there so fast . . ." She begins to cry.

"It was no problem," Walter says, quickly looking away.

"I'm going to tell your mother how brave you've been."

"There's no need. Honestly." He grabs his towel and begins to dry himself.

Mutti wipes her eyes and helps me to dress. The back of my nose and throat are rough-raw, as if I have swallowed concrete.

"Perhaps Hetty should have swimming lessons," Karl says into the silence.

Mutti sniffs and nods.

She bustles around, laying out the blanket and picnic things. I've managed to stop shaking and try some raspberry pfannkuchen and milk from her flask.

I finally gather the courage to look directly at Walter. His wavy blond hair is half dry, half wet. He's saying something to Karl, but then he turns and looks at me and his face breaks into a smile.

His eyes are the warmest, kindest blue.

LATER THAT NIGHT, Mutti tucks me into my narrow bed, pushed against the wall in the bedroom I share with Karl.

"Good night, my darling." Mutti kisses my forehead. "You are all right, aren't you?"

"Yes, Mutti."

"Good." She smiles and strokes my hair.

She turns out the light and closes the door gently behind her.

I keep my eyes open. Through the gloom, I make out the

lumpy shape of the wardrobe against the wall and Karl's empty bed below the windowsill. With him in the room, the menacing shadows can't harm me. Each time my eyelids droop I'm back in the lake and the water is sucking me into its murky depths, choking and clogging my lungs. My heart thrums and my eyes ping open. *Stay awake. Stay awake. Stay awake.*

The door creaks sooner than I expect.

"Karl?"

"Hetty? You're still awake."

"Can't sleep."

"I wondered. Listen, I have something for you. To make you feel better. I was saving it for your birthday, but I want to give it to you now. I'll get you something else for your birthday." He snaps on the light and I blink at the sudden brightness.

Karl scrabbles under his bed and emerges with a brown, rectangular paper bag.

"Here," he says, placing it on top of my blankets as I push myself up to sit. He perches on the edge of my bed. His cheeks are pinched and his forehead wrinkles beneath his dark fringe.

"I wish I'd saved you today, Little Mouse," he says, "but I was too far away." I know he means it because as he looks into my eyes, I can see straight into his soul. The worry has made his pupils huge and black and I can tell he's crying inside, like me. I nod so he knows I understand.

"At least Walter was there. And he is your best friend."

I look at the paper bag, bulky in my hands.

"Open it then," he urges.

The paper crackles as I uncurl the folded bag. I slip my hand inside and my fingers brush the hard cover of a book. It's a journal, the type a grown-up might have. The front is covered with a rich patchwork of shapes in different shades of browns, oranges, and blues. The paper inside is creamy white.

"It's beautiful," I whisper. "Thank you, Karl."

"There's something else in there too." Karl smiles.

Resting at the bottom is a silver-and-blue fountain pen.

"I thought you could write all your secrets in there. Or stories you make up with that wild imagination of yours," Karl says, searching my face.

"I'll try and write some really good ones. But maybe not about drowning." I smile at him. I want him to know everything is okay.

As I settle my head back on the pillow, I know that it *is* okay, but some things are changed.

I nearly drowned and Walter rescued me.

That makes everything different.

Part I

One

August 7, 1933

*M*etamorphosis!*" exclaims Dr. Kreitz. "That's what the English call this book," and he waves its pages in the air with a flourish. "Can anyone tell me what that word means?" He leans on the teacher's table, shirtsleeves pulled up to his elbows. Not one of us makes a sound from our wooden benches in my new classroom at the gymnasium.

No more dusty, higgledy-piggledy volksschule for me. The small, black cinder playground and rough children are a distant memory from before the long summer break. The gymnasium is all high arches and echoey corridors. In its center, a great hall with a high beamed ceiling beneath its grand, red mansard roof. Here, the teachers are taller, smarter, stricter. I might have gotten better marks in the entrance test than Karl did three years ago, when he sat for them like me, at eleven; but now I'm here, I don't feel very clever at all.

"Does it mean transformation?" Someone at the back breaks the silence. I twist around and glimpse a small girl with frizzy black hair, a little like my own.

"Name, please," Dr. Kreitz says, his head popping up, eyes bulging out, reminding me of a frog.

"Freda Federmann," says the girl in a confident voice.

"Wonderful. Yes, Freda," Dr. Kreitz enthuses. "Transformation. Rebirth. Conversion. From the Greek *metamorphoun*, meaning 'to transform.'" He begins to pace. "Studying the Greeks and Romans," he says, "will teach us all we need to know about the human condition."

"Freda Federmann is a *Jewess*," I hear someone hiss to her neighbor from the row behind me. It's loud enough for the professor to hear, but he shows no sign of it. He picks up a book from the table as he passes by.

The professor has narrow shoulders and a potbelly. Part of his shirt hangs from his trousers and his tie is askew. This school, famous for its classical education, clearly picked him for his knowledge and superior brain, not for his appearance.

"Franz Kafka," he says, staring intently up at the ceiling, as though he might see the author perched on top of the rafters. "What a brilliant, and amusing, man he was. Listen." He vigorously flicks through some pages, his hair flopping wildly. He begins to read, treading a slow circuit of the room. He tells us, in a mesmerizing voice, the story of Gregor, the traveling salesman who awakens one morning to find himself transformed into an enormous insectlike creature.

Light filters through the long, rectangular windows set high up on the classroom wall. Adolf Hitler stares serenely down at us all from his vast portrait above the blackboard. Dr. Kreitz's voice rises and falls, fades and resounds. As I look at the portrait, Hitler's face appears to swell and move. He gazes at me, unblinking, but I'm certain his lips have moved, twitched, as if at any moment he might smile and step down from the picture, saying *ha ha, what a joke, I have been here all along.*

He doesn't, of course, and I tear my eyes away. Karl says I have too much imagination. My heart jumps and I wonder if he's right.

Dr. Kreitz reads on. I avoid looking at Hitler's picture and instead study the profile of the girl sitting next to me. Tall and elegant, she has long auburn hair that hangs either side of her shoulders in two smooth plaits. Her pale face is so perfectly formed, it could have been chiseled from the finest marble. She holds her chin high as she watches Dr. Kreitz travel around the room. Feeling my gaze, she turns and fixes me with sloping green eyes.

"Hello," she whispers. "My name is Erna Bäcker." A smile flickers on her lips.

"Hetty Heinrich," I reply, excruciatingly aware of my frizzy dark hair, big eyes, and too-round cheeks.

Erna Bäcker is simply the most bewitching creature I have ever seen in my life.

A knock on the classroom door stops Dr. Kreitz's reading abruptly.

"Herr Hofmann . . ." He addresses the tall, thin man, wearing a waistcoat and bow tie, who enters the room.

"Heil Hitler," Herr Hofmann greets the class.

"Heil Hitler," we echo back.

"Headmaster"—Dr. Kreitz clears his throat—"delighted you can join us."

Herr Hofmann sweeps to the front of the class.

"Welcome to our wonderful gymnasium," he says, smiling around the classroom. "You've all done extremely well to get here. But this is only the beginning. During your time at this school, with hard work and exemplary behavior, you can become exceptional. This is true not only for the boys, but for you girls, too. In the fullness of time, you shall go on to become wonderful members of our great new Reich. I am sure you will make both your parents and our school proud. Best of luck to you all."

I smile back at him. My dream is to become a doctor, preferably a world-famous one. I feel that, being here, at this great school, is one step closer to achieving my ambition. I shall try my very best at all my lessons. Always.

Herr Hofmann turns to Dr. Kreitz. "What are you studying this morning?"

Dr. Kreitz silently shows him the cover of *Metamorphosis*.

A look of horror passes over Herr Hofmann's face. "Dr. Kreitz, have you lost your mind?"

He shrugs. "It's a wonderful text, Herr Hofmann. Perfect for introducing the themes we are studying this year: symbolism, the metaphor, the absurdity of life—"

"We will discuss this later," Herr Hofmann says brusquely. "In the meantime, as well you know, this is not an appropriate text to be studying. Ensure you choose a suitable *German* author next time. Good day, children," and he sweeps from the room, banging the door shut behind him.

Dr. Kreitz shrinks.

His hand trembles as he returns to his desk and slides *Metamorphosis* into his bag. He licks his lips and stares at us, as if not sure what to do next. Chatter breaks out among the class and he makes no attempt to stop it.

Again, he reminds me of a frog, but this time, one that has been squashed and flattened on a busy road.

TOMAS IS WAITING for me when I come out of school. Long-legged and skinny, he leans nonchalantly against the trunk of a large tree on Nordplatz. Before I can make a run for it, he spots me and rushes over, bumping into me with a crooked smile.

"What's it like then?" he asks, looking over his shoulder at the school. We fall in behind a noisy group of older pupils streaming across the grassy square toward Gohlis.

"It's still school. Just . . . smarter and stricter, that's all."

Tomas looks a little wistful. He'd go there in a shot, if only his parents could afford the fees. He's clever enough to pass the test.

"It's odd, you not living in our block anymore," Tomas says. "Emptier," he adds after a pause.

"I'm not far away."

"I guess." He's breathing heavily as we walk, pausing to cross Kirchplatz. "What's your new place like then?"

"Just wait till you see it." I laugh. "After the flat, you won't believe . . . Come on," and I break into a run, a bubble of excitement rising inside.

Our vast new house on Fritzschestrasse has a pointy roof and two chimneys sticking up like thick fingers toward heaven. There are four layers of windows. We could have a whole floor each.

"It's the biggest house in the street," Tomas says as he

stares up in awe at the handsome building, all sandy brick and trimmed with black. His tawny hair is disheveled and his eyes insect-big through the grubby lenses of his tortoiseshell glasses. He screws up his nose as he surveys its vastness.

I stand taller.

"Does it have a garden out back?"

"Of course it does! That's my room." I point up at the window with the balcony overlooking the road on the second floor. There's a beautiful old cherry tree growing beneath it. Its branches extend over the iron railings and the pavement on one side and under the balcony on the other. From my special seat in the window, I can see the junction with Berggartenstrasse and nearly the whole of Fritzschestrasse until it bends around to the right, near Walter's flat. I watch him come and go.

"It must be very grand inside." Tomas presses his face right up against the iron railings. "Bet it's got two staircases. And a cellar. Maybe it's even got a dungeon with prisoners' bones in it!"

"Don't be stupid."

"Can I come in?" asks Tomas.

I steal a sideways look at him. Even though it's only been a few weeks, it feels like a different lifetime when he and I played in the street behind the flat we used to live in. It was the *old* me who kicked a ball around and slid down the muddy embankment to watch the trains puffing in and out of the station.

"Not today," I hear myself say. "Sorry. Maybe another time," and I push my way through the sturdy iron gate. It opens with a creak and when I let go, it shuts Tomas out with a loud and satisfying clunk.

In the echoey, wooden-floored hall I put down my satchel and remember the day we moved here in June.

"I'll need a cook, and full-time maid," Mutti had said, standing in this very spot, looking around in wonder. I can almost still smell her flowery wafts of Vol de Nuit. "I can't possibly manage this house without *help*," she'd said, her hand on her chest.

Vati, cool and relaxed, dressed casually in slacks and an open-necked shirt, had tousled my hair and said, "The most desirable residence in the whole of Leipzig. Or at least one of them."

"I love it," I remember saying, smiling into his baggy face.

"Who would have thought it, eh, Schnuffel? Who would ever have dreamed it?" he'd said, as he picked up a box, kicking open a door off the hallway with his foot. "My study," he'd said in a satisfied voice and disappeared inside.

"Can I pick a bedroom?" Karl had asked, eyes gleaming at the thought of a room all to himself.

"Why not?" Mutti replied, and I'd followed her as she'd carried out an inventory of the furniture and artwork the previous people had left in the house.

It'd be hard to forget the first time I saw the red-gold dining room; the bright afternoon sitting room with big patches of sunlight on the carpet and the grand piano; the pale-blue morning room with a gramophone in one corner; and the glass-domed garden room filled with wicker furniture and jungle plants. Our old flat would have fitted neatly into the hallway alone, with room to spare around the edges.

A surge of happiness now fills my chest like a swelling balloon and I run across the hall, my footsteps reverberating, through the stone-floored passageway, past the big kitchen and washroom, and out into the glorious sunshine of our triangular-shaped garden with its grass in the middle, flowers around the edge, and huge oak tree at the bottom. There's no railway line here like there was behind the flat. I won't miss the trains that shook my bed as they rattled and screeched their way to who-knows-where in the middle of the night.

I walk to the end of the garden and stare up through the dappled leaves and branches of the giant, old oak tree. Even though we no longer go to church—Vati says it detracts from our greater cause, and besides, Herr Himmler wouldn't like it—*I* know that God has smiled on me. He has given me this, because I'm special: a treehouse. Real. Solid. With a proper roof and walls. A narrow rope ladder dangles down from a hole in the middle of the wooden floor.

Just wait until Tomas sees *this*. He'll be mad with envy. I picture his face and laugh out loud.

Two

September 17, 1933

From my window seat, sitting in a nest of comfortable cushions, I keep watch on Fritzschestrasse. With luck, Walter might appear, hands shoved in his short-trouser pockets, scuffing his shoes, looking for Karl. But the road stays resolutely empty. Through the branches of the cherry tree, I see an old couple emerge from one of the elegant white town houses across the street. They have a shaggy-haired black dog with them. His tongue lolls from his mouth, giving the impression he's smiling. In the flat, we had no room for a dog, but Mutti can't say that anymore. I go in search of her.

Bertha is in the kitchen, wiping floury hands on her apron. "Your mother has a headache," she explains. "She went to lie down."

"How can anyone want to go to bed in the middle of the day?"

"I certainly wouldn't mind." Bertha sniffs, kneading a mound of dough. "Anything I can help you with?"

"We should get a dog. A big house like this *needs* one."

"I see. Well, that can wait until your mother gets up. Besides, she might not want a dog." She stops kneading and pounds the dough on the board. The muscles of her forearms flex beneath her mottled skin.

"Shall I wake her, do you think?"

"No, Fräulein Herta. I don't think."

I sigh and wander out onto the street. The old couple are shuffling across the road in the distance. I catch up with them.

"Good morning. May I stroke your dog? My name is Hetty. I live in the big house across the street from you."

The old man is dressed in a brown day suit and tie with a Homburg hat perched neatly on his head. The woman, tiny and frail, in a thin coat despite the warmth of the day, flickers her eyes at her husband.

He clears his throat and says quietly to her, "She's just a child, Ruth." He turns to me. "Of course. His name is Flocke, and I am Herr Goldschmidt."

Flocke wags his tail so hard that his body snakes and twists.

"Aren't you friendly?" Crouching down, I giggle as he jumps his two front paws on my knees and tries to lick my ears.

"Perhaps I could take him to the park for you?" I look up at the Goldschmidts. They really are very old and Flocke can't ever have a proper run. "I'm good with dogs. I shan't lose him or anything." I stand and look responsible.

Frau Goldschmidt answers this time. "You can't take the dog." Her tone is hard and sour, as though she has just swallowed lemon pips. "I won't allow it, after what happened."

I take a step backward. Perhaps she doesn't like children.

"Come on now, Ruth. There's no need for that. Let's go."
Herr Goldschmidt tugs on his wife's arm, but she doesn't move
and her dark eyes narrow into snake-slits.

"Your father"—she sounds like she's hissing the words—
"forced them out. Those trumped-up charges. The campaign in
that paper of his. It was criminal . . . all lies and falsehoods . . ."

"Ruth! Please!" Herr Goldschmidt shakes her arm, but she
is unstoppable, trembling and spitting her words at me.

"The Druckers were good people. Successful. But that cre-
ates jealousy, doesn't it? Envy from lesser folk. And now there
he sits, like a lord, in his stolen house . . ."

"*Ruth!*" Herr Goldschmidt's voice is high and sharp. He
turns back to me. "I'm sorry for my wife's words, she's not
herself today . . ."

But by now I'm certain the old woman is a witch and I'm
running hard and fast away from them, before she can spray
me with poisonous spit. I don't stop until I'm safely inside
my iron gate, my heart thudding like racehorse hooves in my
chest.

A car is parked outside in the street, and I find a young
woman standing in the hallway wrapped like a fat bockwurst
in a tight brown suit. She has chubby cheeks, a snub nose, and
the thickest lips I've ever seen. Her hair is the color of a paper
bag, plaited and so fiercely wrapped around the top of her head
that the skin above her ears is taut and red. She gives me a
surprised look.

"Hello," she says in a kind voice. "I'm Fräulein Müller. And
you must be Herta?"

Vati, big as a bear and smart in his stiff Schutzstaffel uniform, appears from the study. He hands a couple of thin document folders to Fräulein Müller.

"Hello, Schnuffel. I'm afraid I must leave you for a couple of days. I have to go to Berlin, on SS business." He hugs me, pressing my head into his chest. The hard buckle on his leather chest strap digs into my cheek. "Where's your mother? Hélène, *Hélène*!" His voice reverberates in his chest.

"Franz?" Mutti, wearing a wide-brimmed straw hat and a floaty dress, evidently recovered from her headache, glides in from the back garden, a bunch of flowers in one hand, scissors in the other. Karl trails in behind her. "What are you doing home so early?" Mutti asks in surprise.

"Ah, there you are. Hélène, this is Hilda Müller, my new secretary." The young woman smiles and nods at Mutti. "Listen, I have to travel to Berlin. It's urgent—more trouble with the Communists." He sighs. "But I must also finish my weekly editorial for the *Leipziger* this afternoon so the copy is ready for tonight's deadline. Fräulein Müller will accompany me to organize that." He stops suddenly and rubs his hands over his face, kneading his eyes with the tips of his fingers. Poor Vati is exhausted with his two jobs.

"Will you stay with Oma Annamaria?" Karl asks.

"Not if I can help it," Vati replies swiftly. "What I meant to say," he adds, "was I shall visit my mother if I have the time, but I'm likely to be far too busy." He turns to Mutti. "I'll telephone this evening," he says, taking her hands and kissing her on the cheek. "Good-bye, Schnuffel," he says to me. "Be good for your mother."

"Yes, Vati." I look up to his face, framed by slicked-back, fair hair. I search his pale eyes for affection and hope he sees only goodness in mine. But he is already looking at his watch.

"We must go." He turns to Karl. "I'm leaving you in charge, young man. Take care of your sister and mother."

We stand at the front door and watch Vati and Fräulein Müller climb into the waiting sleek black car. The woman's skirt is so tight it scrunches up around her thighs as she gets in. Her behind is large and round and she waddles like a goose.

"Mutti," I say, once they have gone, "the Goldschmidts, who live across the road, told me Vati stole this house. But how can you steal a house?"

Mutti whirls around and stares at me. "They said what? Why were you talking to them?"

"They've got a little dog. I just wanted to stroke it. Can I have a dog now we live here?"

"You mustn't talk to such people."

"I only wanted to pet the dog."

"But they are *Jews*, Hetty."

The word sends a shiver down my back. How was I to know? Karl wrinkles his nose and says, "Dirty pigs, Jews."

"They have nothing better to do than spread evil lies," Mutti says, her voice firm. I watch her put the flowers in a vase and fill it with water. "That is what these people do. It's very important you don't speak with them again. These are difficult times. That's why Vati does all this work for the SS as well as running the newspaper. They must protect Hitler and ban all the parties who seek to oppose him. Pick your friends carefully, Hetty. Stick only with *good* Germans, like us. Do you understand?"

"Yes, Mutti."

I follow her back outside, not wanting to be on my own. I look around the bushes and flowers at the edge of the garden. Everything looks calm and friendly, but I can feel the evil hovering outside the safety of our iron railings, and I shudder. I imagine a great big guard dog, patrolling the garden. Just the idea of it makes me feel safer.

Three

October 8, 1933

There's a knock at the front door.

"Who can that be, at this time on a Sunday morning?" Mutti frowns. Tall and willowy, dressed in peach chiffon, she bobs down the stairs. A strand of hair works its way loose from the dark sweep of her chignon and she threads it behind her ear.

I pull open the heavy front door. Walter stands on the doorstep, hands in his pockets. I throw the door open wider and breathe in, willing myself taller.

When Walter was a small boy, he would have looked like one of those chubby, blond cherubs that float about among the clouds in paintings of Mary and baby Jesus. Now he's fourteen, he still has blond curly hair and blue eyes, but he isn't chubby anymore; he's long and lean like a half-grown horse. A boy-man.

"Karl!" Mutti calls. She stands, holding the smooth knob of wood at the end of the banister as if she is afraid to let go.

"Good morning, Frau Heinrich," Walter says politely, stepping through the open door. "I wonder if Karl might be free?"

"Come up," Karl calls, his grinning face appearing at the top of the stairs. "We can chat in my room."

"Hi, Walter," I say.

He bends down to untie his shoelaces and doesn't seem to notice me at all.

"Do you want to come out to the treehouse?" I try. But he runs up the stairs after Karl.

Vati appears from his study, his hands on his hips. He scowls at Walter's back. "*That* boy again," he mutters, glaring at Mutti. "You've not told him, have you?"

"Come on, Franz." Mutti sighs, her hands dropping to her sides, shoulders sagging. "Please, not this again."

"Just because he once rescued . . ." Vati throws me a look and I know he means the Almost Drowning. "I don't like it . . ." He turns and the study door bangs shut, abrupt and loud.

Mutti and I stand staring at each other, alone in the hallway. Invisible fingers crawl up my back.

"What doesn't Vati like?" I whisper.

Mutti sighs again. "Go and wash your face and hands. We're going to visit the soldiers' home today."

"But—"

"Just for a couple of hours. It will be good for you."

"Do I have to?"

"You do," she says firmly. "Community work is . . . holy. It brings us closer to the Führer. It's very important that we look after each other."

"I'd rather play with Karl and Walter."

"Young ladies," Mutti says crisply, "need to learn the meaning of *obedience*."

A little knot forms inside as I stomp upstairs.

THE SOLDIERS' HOME is on Hallische Strasse, set well back from the street. The building is hundreds of years old, once a hospital, now given over to care for the brave soldiers who were badly injured fighting for our nation. A Home for Heroes. It has a pleasant garden and a wide terrace on one side, with a few wheelchairs lined up in a row. The men sit so still, staring wordlessly out across the lawn and the flower beds, that I wonder if they might have dropped dead already.

Mutti marches us up the front steps and rings the doorbell. We're greeted by a neat nurse who ushers us into a hall smelling of wood polish and bleach. She introduces herself as Lisel. Blond hair peeks from the front of her white cap.

"Heil Hitler. How lovely to see you again, Frau Heinrich," says the nurse.

"Heil Hitler. This is my daughter, Herta."

"So good of you both to come. Our residents very much look forward to your visits, Frau Heinrich."

We follow Lisel along a dark passageway, past a ward, and I glance in. Eight iron beds all neatly made and empty of occupants, who, Lisel tells us, are in the dayroom. I try not to breathe too deeply as beneath the smell of bleach is a pervasive odor of urine and something else unpleasant.

". . . Some of our inmates are war heroes, Herta, who have

no family. They deserve a fitting place to live out their days in comfortable surroundings."

"Yes, they deserve that." I nod.

"They certainly do. But we need more funds . . . It's very difficult . . ." Lisel says with a frown.

"I'm arranging a fund-raising lunch," Mutti offers with enthusiasm. "And my husband could draw attention to your plight in the *Leipziger.*"

Lisel smiles. "We are very lucky to have a patron like your mother," she tells me. "Working tirelessly for the good of others."

I glance at Mutti in surprise. To me, she is just Mutti. But now I see she is something else besides.

In the sitting room, three old soldiers are parked in a semicircle in their wood and wicker wheelchairs. I know I shouldn't stare, but I can't help it. The sight of one makes me sweat. Half his face is missing; the rest of it, a twisted mess of flesh. A small hole is approximately where his mouth should be, but a great chunk is gone from the cheek area. One eye is missing altogether, and the other stands proud from the shrunken flesh, white and cloudy. His face reminds me of the mangled parts of a half-eaten chicken.

My stomach curdles and I fear I'm going to be sick. Mutti grabs my arm and jerks it, hard.

I take a deep breath. If I'm to be a doctor, I cannot be squeamish.

In comparison, the other two, one with missing legs from the hip down, the other with half a leg and a missing arm, are easier to look at.

I watch Mutti, standing in the center of the dreary room, surrounded by this human horror show, and suddenly she looks like the most beautiful creature in all the world. Her sparkling eyes and charming smile flicker only momentarily as, radiant in her peach dress, she splashes color into the room and works her charm on the patients.

Lemon tea and cakes are brought in. Lisel administers tea to the mangled man through a straw poked into the hole where his mouth should be. It slurps back out when she removes the straw and dribbles down from the mottled flesh, once his chin, onto his shirt. She wipes up the spillage and comes to sit next to me.

"What happened to them?" I whisper.

"Injured by shelling. There are some even worse off than these." Lisel pauses. "It's a terrible thing, war."

"I've never really thought about it."

"And why on earth would you? You're only a child. Perhaps another time you might stay and read to the men? Your mother tells us how clever you are. They would love that. A pretty young thing to brighten up the place from time to time."

I look at Mutti with surprise and she smiles indulgently at me. A flush of warm pleasure at Mutti's words of praise washes over me.

"Of course," I say, meaning it with all my heart. "I would love to."

The nurse pats my knee and gets up to wipe the badly injured man's face again and to offer water.

Later, we wave good-bye to Lisel on the doorstep. I take

deep gulps of delicious fresh air and curb the urge to run away at top speed.

"Those men are shockingly injured, Mutti."

"These are the lucky ones, receiving such good care."

We walk slowly, savoring the late afternoon sun. Everything around me is in sharper focus, and more dear than ever before. I've not appreciated enough the beauty in the spreading branches of a tree; pure, sweet birdsong; or the perfection of my own limbs. I realize more clearly than ever before that I want to become a surgeon. To make them better. I vow to work harder at school.

Please don't ever let there be another war. Keep us safe: Mutti, Vati, Karl, and me.

"There won't be another war, will there?"

"Let's hope not. We are fortunate to have Hitler, because he is a peace lover and wants harmony in Europe. Sadly, the same can't be said for other countries. Look at what harm they did to us at the end of the war. Those disgusting reparations. So many injured men, so many unemployed, such poverty. They taunt us. *Want* us to suffer and suffer until we say No More and fight back for what is rightfully ours."

"But *who*? Who are *they*?"

"Our enemies, Hetty. There are many who want to destroy us. They want to kill, to maim, to rid us of everything we hold dear. They want to destroy our very way of life."

Little fingers of fear creep slowly across my skin.

"But *who* are these enemies?"

Mutti squeezes my hand.

"Oh, they are many and varied. But behind them all are the

Jews. They want to take over the world for their own benefit. But you mustn't worry yourself, my darling," she says in her bright voice. "With Hitler at the helm of our new Germany, we have nothing to fear. Those who seek to harm us will be quaking in their boots!"

Four

October 11, 1933

"Sorry, I can't today," I tell Freda, the Jewess, when she asks me to be her partner in gymnastics. Her shoulders droop in disappointment and I feel a stab of guilt. I search the playground frantically for another partnerless person to avoid being shoved together anyway. Gerda shakes her head at me and grabs Ava's hand, in case I should be in any doubt.

"Hey, would you like to be my partner today?"

I spin around and there is Erna, long and lean in her white gym-slip. A half smile flits across her lips.

"Okay." I attempt nonchalance, but my heart is pumping in my ears as we stand side by side.

Erna need not know where I used to live. She need not know that, at my old school, I had only one friend, Tomas. Our family is rising in the world; that's what matters.

"Girls!" Fräulein Sauber claps her hands for attention. "Listen carefully and follow my instructions. With your partner and your batons, you will work on the routines I taught you last week. Concentrate on reaching high with your arms, and the graceful placing of your legs and feet. Your partner will point out any errors. Find yourselves a space."

We position ourselves near the back steps of the building.

"Now"—there is a glint in Erna's eyes—"show me your best twirl, and don't forget to lift that baton high and point your toes." She mimics Fräulein Sauber's high-pitched voice, and suddenly I'm laughing and the two of us swirl and sway, waving our batons and pointing our toes in a vastly exaggerated fashion. With Erna at my side, I couldn't care less if I get into trouble with the squeaky fräulein.

I glimpse Freda, once, practicing her moves on her own in the far corner of the playground. She looks sad and lonely, but I mustn't feel sorry for her, because she isn't one of us. I make sure I don't look at her again.

"One, two, three . . . Heil!" Erna whips her baton across her top lip and extends her right arm up into a stiff salute.

"Erna!" I hiss at her daring, but I'm laughing so much my face aches.

"Class." I deepen my voice, to sound like Dr. Kreitz. I stick out my belly and throw my arms out wide. "Take note of this author you must learn nothing about! He is great, he is brilliant, and he is banned!"

Warmth at the sight of Erna giggling at my joke spreads like hot chocolate. Everything is suddenly possible and within my grasp. I only have to reach out and take it.

The lesson ends all too soon and we must go inside.

This time, I squeeze onto Erna's bench. We have a new

lesson each day, slotted between other classes. The Life of the Führer. We are to learn about the great man, Adolf Hitler, Frau Schmidt explains, by studying his struggles, his courage and fortitude. Frau Schmidt is herself misty eyed as she speaks of his suffering, and of his wisdom. We shall, she tells us, once we know everything, admire and love him just as much as she does. And then we sing.

Belting out the "*Horst Wessel Lied*," I glance out the window. The older classes are on their break. I scan the heads and find Karl. At the center of the crowd, he throws his head back in laughter. I smile as I watch him, then turn my gaze to a solitary figure sitting far from the others on a bench, legs crossed, one foot swinging lazily back and forth. His blond head is bent over, engrossed in a book. Walter. How funny he is! While Karl and his other friends show off and compete with each other, Walter does the opposite. He shuts himself away with his books. My heart expands as I watch him.

Our singing comes to an end with our daily chant of gratitude:

Führer, my Führer given me by God,
Protect and preserve my life for long.
You rescued Germany from its deepest need.
I thank you for my daily bread.
Stay for a long time with me, leave me not.
Führer, my Führer, my faith, my light
Hail my Führer.

MUTTI IS OUT fund-raising when Karl and I arrive home from school in a downpour.

"Once you're dry, you can have lunch with Ingrid and me," Bertha tells us, setting out four places at the big oak table in the flagstone-floored kitchen.

I climb the stairs to change my clothes. It was so different when we lived in the flat. Just Karl, Mutti, and me since Vati was often working. We were a little unit of three. Eating together; Karl and me sleeping together. We'd shop with Mutti and help her prepare meals in the kitchen. She would sing French songs and tell us stories from her childhood in France, before she came to live in Germany. She had more to do back then, because we didn't have a cook and a maid, yet oddly, she seemed to have more time for us. Now she rushes here and there doing her charity work and seeing friends, often leaving us in Bertha's care. I wonder if she sometimes forgets we even exist.

I click on the smart new wireless Vati has given me, which sits on top of my writing desk. They are replaying the speech Dr. Gross, head of the Nazi Party's Racial Policy Office, made last night to the youth of Germany. Karl and I had sat and listened to the whole thing dutifully before dinner.

". . . science teaches us that inherited characteristics are more important than environmental influences . . ." I slip off my soggy skirt and blouse. ". . . when we are no longer alive, our inheritance will live on in our children and children's children. When we grasp this, we see that great river of blood flowing to us through the centuries, and that is in truth the German people. Each generation is a wave that rises and falls, replaced by the next one. As individuals, we are a droplet in this stream. Unlike the liberal minded, we do not see ourselves as the center of the world." I pull a clean blouse, pullover, and skirt from my wardrobe and put them on. ". . . such understanding makes us modest. Unlike the liberal minded who acts as though he has achieved all his accomplishments by himself, we know that everything we accomplish is not because of our own abilities, but due to our inheritance. We are the proud carriers and guardians of German blood . . ."

I click the radio off. I know what he will go on to say. That every race is different. Simply by educating the Negro, it can never turn him into the superior Nordic. As I walk back down the stairs, I can feel the pure, precious power of my good German blood, at least from Vati's side, pulsing through my veins.

Bertha serves steaming bowls of goulash, each with a large, doughy bread dumpling. Just as we are finishing, Walter's head, glistening and wet, appears at the door.

"Ah." Bertha smiles at him. "Just in time for some pflaumenkuchen. Did you smell it? Come in, don't dither on the doorstep," she chides, clearing our bowls away.

He sits next to Karl. I smooth my hair and straighten my back.

"Have you written your history essay?" Walter asks Karl.

"No." He groans. "I'll have to do it tonight. What was it again?"

"To what extent can you draw a parallel between the symbolism of struggle and heroism in the medieval poem 'Nibelungenlied' with the current-day struggle of the German Volk?" Walter takes a mouthful of plum cake. "This is delicious, Bertha."

Bertha beams. I rest my head against the wall and imagine a time when Erna might be here, too, and the four of us—Walter and Karl, Erna and I—would sit around gossiping about school, or this person and that, easy in one another's company. I'm telling a story, and all three of them have their eyes fixed on me, nodding, listening, and smiling at my amusing anecdote.

"You coming then?"

"Hmm?"

"I said, are you coming to the treehouse with us?" Walter's looking at me expectantly. "I have Riesen caramel," he adds, shaking a paper bag at me.

I spring from my chair and follow the boys down the passageway, out the back door, and into the garden. The rain has stopped, and I breathe in the rich smell of wet earth. I watch them climb up the narrow ladder; then, holding fast to the slippery rungs, I clamber up after them, pushing myself through the hole in the floor that straddles the trunk and the main fork of the tree. I roll over and swing my legs through. As I do, my skirt rucks right up to the top of my thighs. Quickly, I pull it down. But Walter isn't looking.

He walks to the window and peers out.

"We're so high up," he comments, looking back at Karl and me. He grins. "Can a kangaroo jump higher than a house?"

Karl rolls his eyes. "Not one of your awful jokes."

"No, a kangaroo can't jump higher than a house," I say, thinking of our tall roof.

"Of course it can," Walter exclaims. "A house can't jump!"

Karl groans, but I giggle and Walter gives me a wink. He looks out the window again.

"You can see all the way to Rosental from here," he says. "Ouch!" He whips his hand from where he'd rested it on the sill and shakes it, then examines his finger.

"Let me see." I jump up. The dark line of a splinter slices diagonally into the soft padding at the top of Walter's index finger. It's in too deep to pull out without a tool. "I'll get my tweezers."

Hurrying down the ladder I hear Karl laughing as he says, "Watch out, she'll be amputating that. She has some ludicrous dream of being a surgeon . . ."

I grab my kit bag from my room. Back when we lived in the flat and I roamed the streets with Tomas, I'd bring my medical kit, slung on my back, and keep an eye out for injured creatures that might need help: the odd stray dog, which Tomas would hold still (getting bitten once or twice) while I treated patches of mange with borax; the next-door neighbor's cat with an injured tail that I bandaged, much to its disgust. I once even tried to glue the legs of a daddy longlegs back on, but it died anyway.

I run back to the treehouse and carefully pull the splinter out of Walter's finger with my tweezers. I give the hole a squeeze and it bleeds, so I know all the wood is out. Dabbing the wound with iodine, I tell him not to get it dirty to avoid infection.

Karl has spread a blanket on the floor and lies on his side, propped up on one elbow.

"She even reads books on medicine," he comments, watching me. "So dull."

"They are not."

"Anyway"—Karl sighs—"you do know, women can't even be doctors."

"That's not true!"

"Ask Vati if you don't believe me. However much you don't like it, Hetty, you're a girl, and you should start behaving like one."

His tone is not unkind, but I burn hot as I pack away the iodine bottle and close my kit bag. I feel the boys' eyes watching me as I fumble with the straps and buckles. Women can't even be doctors. Is he right? A hole opens inside me.

"Well, thank you, Dr. Heinrich," Walter says into the silence. "Nothing wrong with holding on to a dream." His words soothe like ointment on a wound. He winks at me for a second time. "I should pay you for your trouble," he continues, furrowing around in the paper bag and pulling out a large piece of caramel.

"The biggest piece, just for you, little Hetty." He smiles, holding out the sticky piece of caramel, and my heart flick-flacks wildly.

"Thank you." I take it and sit down, my back resting against the wall.

I pop the caramel in my mouth and chew the sweet golden lump, but it's large and hard and protrudes through my cheek, refusing to get smaller. Dribble escapes from the corner of my mouth and I quickly wipe it away with my sleeve.

"Very fetching," Karl says, laughing.

Walter sees and begins laughing too. "Here, have another piece."

I press my lips closed and shake my head, blushing red.

"Hurray!" Karl chuckles. "You've found a way to keep the girl quiet. Congratulations, my friend!"

A hard ball forms in my throat and I'm on my feet, bolting down the ladder before I allow myself to properly cry.

The boys' laughter follows me all the way back to the house and the cozy visions of my future life shatter like glass into a million multicolored fragments.

Five

February 10, 1934

Augustusplatz is packed. The vast square has been transformed into an unrecognizable film set. Up here, from our special platform, reserved for local dignitaries and their families, I feel like a film star, waiting to go out in front of the cameras.

I shiver, wrapping my fur stole closer around my neck. Powerful, blinding lights flood the expanse of the square and huge swastika flags hang from the tall buildings all around. Below our platform, members of a film crew slouch and smoke next to their tripods and cameras, stamping their feet and hugging their coats tighter as they wait for the main event. I look down at the pale, upturned faces of the crowd and the thousands of hands waving their tiny flags.

Mutti grips my hand tight. "It's Karl's turn," she says.

Karl steps forward, uniformed and serious. He grips the flag with his left hand, the right pointing to the sky, three fingers extended straight as an arrow toward heaven. His chin is raised and he stares straight ahead, unblinking.

"Adolf Hitler," he chants without quiver, "you are our great Führer.

"Thy name makes the enemy tremble.

"Thy Third Reich comes, thy will alone is law upon the earth.

"Let us hear daily thy voice and order us by thy leadership,

"For we will obey to the end and even with our lives.

"We praise thee! Heil Hitler!"

My throat closes and heat rises from somewhere deep in my soul. Karl, the dearest of all brothers in the world, dark haired, dark eyed, and beautiful, is initiated in the Hitler Jugend. Hitler owns him now.

Karl accepts the coveted dagger and returns to the rest of his *schar*. The next boy steps forward and repeats the oath. When the last new recruit has been initiated, the boys troop off the stage and join the other squares of HJ boys at the front of the crowd.

The film crew check their cameras. A man comes onto the stage and tests the single microphone standing in the middle. A loud crackle comes from somewhere. We wait for the main event, still to come.

And we wait. My fingers and toes slowly become numb. I try wriggling them, clapping my hands, and blowing on them, but it doesn't work.

At last the band strikes up Franz Liszt's fanfare. A hush comes over the crowd and almost as one, a thousand heads turn. I glimpse the open-topped black Mercedes crawling down one side of the square. I forget the numbing cold, the

unforgiving hardness of my chair. It really is *him*. The greatest
of all men, my brother's new father.

The car pulls up in front of the platform and the Führer
climbs the stairs, passing me so close I could reach out and
touch him. Vati is clapping hard and fast, smiling broadly.
Small and nimble, in the flesh, Herr Hitler is terribly good-
looking. He wears a brown suit and a swastika armband. His
hair is very dark, like mine, and is swept elegantly to one side.

For a few moments, he surveys the crowd. He raises a fist
skyward, then clutches it to his chest. The crowd goes wild,
crying "Sieg Heil! Sieg Heil! Sieg Heil" until the Führer holds
his hands out and, as one, they are silenced, without him utter-
ing a single word.

"Heil, my German Youth!" he cries at last. "It is our will
that this Reich shall endure in the millenniums to come. We
can be happy in the knowledge that this future belongs to us
completely!"

Mutti is gripping my hand so tightly it hurts. Her eyes fill
with water. The Führer pauses and looks around. His eyes, the
color of the deepest ocean blue, sweep over our little group of
local dignitaries, pause, and lock with mine.

I can't breathe, and my head reels.

"In you, my youth," he says as he looks at me, "there must
be no weakness. I want a brutal, domineering, fearless, cruel
youth. A youth before which the world will tremble. It must
bear pain. There must be nothing weak or gentle about it."

Why does he talk directly to me? I can't hear his words anymore because there is a strange roar in my ears and a mist

comes down over my eyes. I watch his mouth move and his hands gesticulate; a little section of hair comes loose and flops over his forehead.

He isn't looking at me anymore, he is gazing out over the thousands down there, but that stare, that *connection* has lit a white-hot fire in my soul. He singled me out.

He saw that I am special. I can be *someone great.*

"That is how I will create the New Order," the Führer is saying, a fountain of spit spraying from his mouth, his body reverberating with the force of his words. "That is how victory will be claimed!"

Words pour from his mouth, building like a thundering wave around the square. He speaks of a brilliant future with no more poverty, no more class divisions. Just one great, unified nation that will be the envy of all the world.

"A world that will one day be ruled by *you*, my German youth," and he points at the formation of HJ boys.

He is a magnet, impossible to resist, pulling me toward him. When he finally finishes his speech, my eyes, too, are filled with tears.

We stand together, we Germans.

Us against the world.

I am floating. High above the platform and the crowds. High over Augustusplatz and the great city of Leipzig. High over Germany itself. Higher and higher until I can see the great planet Earth as God sees it, spinning through space and time among the planets around the sun, and there in the center of it all, this blessed land, with its swaths of deep forests, rich farmland, and lakes teeming with fish. Its factories and coal mines and its army. I can see its people: good, honest, and hardworking, cruelly downtrodden for so long, rising together and turning to face the outside world. To show them who we truly are and to take back what is rightfully ours. It is a power; a force, like gravity, which cannot be resisted.

The band strikes up again, only this time the drumbeat is like that of an ancient warrior dance. It beats and pulses through my body as the mighty Führer leaves the square, standing in his car like a victorious Roman emperor in his chariot. Behind him marches an army of torchbearers. The lights in the square are dimmed, and through the sudden darkness the flames appear to flow like a river of fire through the center of Augustusplatz.

MUTTI AND I walk home from the city center in the dark, freezing night. Vati had to return to his office, and Karl stayed with his new group, his Hitler Jugend schar.

"When can I join the Hitler Jugend, Mutti?" I ask, my breath dense as smoke in the light of the streetlamps. The ceremony has burned an impression on my soul, like a footprint. I feel that Hitler has called to me and I must answer. He wants *me* to play a role in Germany's great and glorious future.

"Don't be silly, the HJ is for boys."

"But there is a girls' section, the Jungmädelbund."

"Vati doesn't approve of that sort of thing for girls."

"Why not?"

"Because girls should concentrate on home things."

"But I don't like home things. I want to go camping and play games and sing songs and march, like Karl will get to do. Besides, I'm *twelve*!"

"And Vati would say that is even more reason why not."

"But it's not fair! All my friends are joining the Jungmädel-bund. What will they think if I don't?"

"Don't exaggerate." Mutti hunches her narrow shoulders. "Many people don't think it is right for girls. Even Herr Himmler *himself* doesn't agree with it. He says the idea of girls marching about in uniform with backpacks is ludicrous and it makes him sick. Oh, *do* come along, Hetty."

Trailing behind, I say no more the rest of the way home.

You can't stop me. I'll find a way.

I climb the stairs and get ready for bed.

My limbs ache with weariness as I lie there, but sleep won't come. I hear Karl arrive home and Mutti's muffled voice from the hallway.

"My darling! How proud we are . . . The very *best* of boys . . . Will go far in this life, I know it . . ."

Karl's bedroom door bangs shut, and I hear Mutti's soft step on her way to bed. A heaviness settles over the house, but my bed becomes an unbearable mess of twisted sheets and blankets. I wrap a warm shawl around my shoulders and creep into my window seat, gazing out over the dark street.

All is quiet and still, the limbs of the cherry tree etched motionless against the night sky. A few wispy clouds scud in front of the moon. Soothed, I lean back against the wooden shutters and turn to peer through the dark at Hitler's portrait above my mantelpiece. Mutti's mutterings about enemies just make me afraid but *He* gives me courage. Whether I join the Hitler Jugend or not, I'm certain I have a part to play in this great new Reich. *He* doesn't mind that I'm a girl, and nobody, not Mutti, not Vati, not Karl, can stop me.

A little niggle eats away at the back of my mind. Until now, I'd been sure my destiny was to become a doctor. But what if Karl is right? I think back to the ceremony, to the moment I met the Führer's eyes and he spoke his words, those incredible words *directly to me*. And then I know it. I know what I must do.

I run to my bookcase and retrieve the journal Karl gave me so long ago, and in the moonlight, I write:

> *My Hitler, I devote my life to you. Make your plan for me clear, because from now on, everything I do, it is for you and you alone. I will make you proud that I'm your child. Oh great, great Führer . . .*

I wake up with a start, my legs curled and stiff beneath me. The shawl has dropped from my shoulders and cold seeps into my bones. The soft purr of an engine rises from the street below. I look out my window. Vati!

He climbs out of the car and I raise my hand to bang on the window, but pause, knowing he'd be angry I'm not asleep.

Vati walks around to the other side of the car and opens the door. Another figure climbs out, a woman, her face obscured by her hat. They stroll together along the pavement and stop just below the streetlamp. Vati turns to face the woman. Slowly he places his arms around her waist and draws her into an embrace. She tilts her face up and in the circular glow cast by the lamp I clearly see Hilda Müller's pale, round face. She closes her eyes and opens her mouth, a thick, red circle of lips. Then Vati, *my* Vati, bends down and kisses that horrible mouth. A long, slow kiss.

Pinned to the window, I can't tear my eyes away. When finally it's over, Fräulein Müller climbs back into the car and it pulls away. Vati stands for a moment watching it travel down the road, his hands in his pockets. Then he turns toward the house. The iron gate creaks shut behind him.

MY HEAD THROBS as I wake to strong morning light. I'd forgotten to close my shutters last night before crawling into bed. Coming downstairs, I see that I've missed breakfast and Mutti has gone out. A new worry awakens. Should I tell Mutti what I saw? The thought sends a wave of horror through me. Bertha makes me some warm milk and hands me a plate of sausage and bread from the store cupboard.

"Morning, sleepy," Karl says as he comes into the kitchen.

"I need to talk to you about something," I whisper when Bertha moves toward the sink. "In private."

"Okay. Treehouse?" He raises his eyebrows.

We sit on the floor, sharing the bread and sausage, a blanket wrapped around our shoulders. Despite the temperature, it's cozy in our secret nest, just the two of us.

"Should I tell Mutti?" I ask quietly, after recounting what I saw.

He shakes his head. "You must have dreamed it, Hetty. You have a crazy imagination."

"But I was awake, Karl, I saw them. It was horrible."

"You're being ridiculous. It was the middle of the night. You fell asleep in your window seat and had a bad dream. Besides, why would Vati want to kiss Fräulein Müller? She looks like a heifer with those massive hindquarters." He begins to laugh. "Moo," he says blowing out his cheeks and making his eyes all big.

Perhaps he is right. I could have dreamed it. Suddenly, I have a picture of a brown-patched cow with Fräulein Müller's round face and fierce plaits where its ears should be.

"Moo," I say, giggling.

"Moo, Herr Heinrich, how about a kiss?" Karl laughs and curls up his top lip, just like a cow smelling the air.

I'm laughing so hard my eyes begin to water. Karl digs me in the ribs with his elbow.

"See?" he says. "See how silly it all is?"

Our maid Ingrid's fair head appears at the base of the tree.

"Walter Keller is at the door to see you," she calls up to Karl. Racehorse hooves thud in my chest.

Karl's forehead creases. I expect him to throw the blanket off his shoulders and bolt down the ladder, ending our private chat. But his body is completely still.

"Tell him I'm not here," he shouts down to Ingrid. To my astonished face he explains, "I have to go out soon anyway. Meeting some of my HJ friends."

His serious face cracks into a smile and he pushes me onto the dusty treehouse floor, tickling me hard under the armpits.

"Stop it! I don't want to play that game," I yell, fighting him off.

"What's the matter?"

"Why did you send Walter away?"

Karl shoves me in the shoulder and sits up.

"What does it matter to you?" he asks gruffly. "He was my friend, not yours. I've got new friends now. I don't need Walter."

He gets up and begins climbing down the ladder.

"See you later, Little Mouse."

I sit for a long time, legs dangling through the hole, getting colder and colder.

Does this mean I won't see Walter anymore? How can that be?

Well, Karl, just because you have new friends doesn't mean you have to lose your old ones. I'm going to make sure I keep mine. Because friends are precious. Like jewels.

Six

The gray streets of Leipzig are hidden beneath a deep layer of crystal white. Delicate ridges line every branch and twig of the cherry tree, transforming it into the sugar-coated world of *The Nutcracker and the Mouse-King*.

It's the first day of the school winter holidays and Tomas, thinly dressed for the weather, hops from foot to foot on the doorstep. His lips are tinged blue.

"Come out with me," he says. "I hardly see you these days." He wrinkles his nose and pushes his glasses up.

"I've a lot more homework now." I hold fast to the doorframe. His eyes are too big for his thin face, and they protrude, like an owl's. Behind me, the house is warm and Bertha is making zimtsterne cookies; the smell of hot sugar and cinnamon drifts from the kitchen.

"We could build a snowman in Rosental." His breath fans and coils above his head. I think of how Karl has ditched Walter and how I vowed not to do the same with my friends.

"All right, I'll come," I say, and as he smiles, his eyes crinkle and disappear.

I pull on my boots and coat. Selecting a pair of warm gloves, I think of Tomas's bare hands. There's always a whiff of mold about him. A faint hum of sweat, grime, and misery. But we were once poor, and I mustn't hold it against him. I pick up a second pair of gloves and a woolen hat, too.

"Here, you can use these." I hold them out for him. "It doesn't matter if you don't give them back," I add.

He takes them and strokes his fingers across the wool.

"Thanks, Hetty," he mumbles, looking down. He pulls the hat over his ears and then puts on the gloves. "Warm as a hot potato now," he says, clapping his hands together and giving me a shy smile.

Snowflakes peacefully float from a low granite sky, drifting onto the mounds piled against the railings. We cross Pfaffendorfer Strasse and walk toward the big iron gates at the entrance to the park. On the side of Tomas's temple is the large, mottled, yellowy-green remnant of a bruise. I wonder, like an apple repeatedly dropped to the floor, if he is all brown and rotten on the inside, too.

"My father lost his job," Tomas says as we kick our way through the fresh, untrodden snow.

"Oh dear. Has he got another?"

"There's none to be found." Tomas runs my glove along the top of a railing, the snow mounding in front until it falls off the end. "We've had to move in with my uncle's family above his cobbler's shop on Hallische Strasse. We couldn't pay the rent for our old flat, so we got kicked out."

"He could join the Sturmabteilung," I say, remembering how Vati had talked of a big SA recruitment drive not so long ago. "The Brownshirts always need loads of men," I tell him confidently.

Tomas half chokes, half laughs. "He'd rather we starve than join the SA. He'll have nothing to do with those *thugs*." He spits out the word. "Even though they have a uniform and *weapons*, like a proper army." He looks wistful now, at the thought of weapons.

There's trouble with Röhm, I recall Vati recently saying to Mutti. *Two million hungry men. Out of control. It'll need to be dealt with* . . . If only I'd listened properly.

"What does your mother think he should do?"

"She doesn't care, provided he puts food on the table. And he's not even doing that at the moment. Just slouching about, like a good-for-nothing." He sucks in a long breath.

We cross the road and walk between the tall stone pillars marking the entrance to the park. The wide expanse of Rosental stretches away so blindingly white, it hurts my eyes.

"Can't he even get a job in a factory?"

Tomas shakes his head. "I told you. There's none to be had. You're so lucky to be . . . Wow, this snow is *thick*." He kicks at it and ventures off the path into untrodden snow and sinks to the top of his boots.

We try to run and stumble. Laughing, we gather armfuls of the fluffy white powder.

There's a swooshing noise and a snowball hits Tomas in the back of the neck with savage force. Gasping for breath, he scrabbles at the lump of snow and ice wedged between his bare skin and the collar of his thin coat. A second one, stingingly accurate, hits the side of his head.

"Ow!" He rubs the spot where it hit. Mouths open, whooping and yelling, four boys run from behind shrubbery, pelting us with hard lumps of gritty snow. I recognize the Brandt brothers from our old school. They've always had it in for Tomas. Just our luck to bump into them now.

The boys surround Tomas, nudging me out of the way. I stand outside the circle while they murmur in low voices. One of them kicks lumps of snow at Tomas's skinny, bare knees. A knot of anger forms in my belly. There's four of them and one of him. How's that fair?

"Poor baby Tom Tom," Ernst Brandt says. "His vati won't let him join the Jungvolk." He laughs. "He'd never survive it if he did. He'd get beaten for wetting the bed!" The other boys laugh too.

"I don't wet the bed, stupid," Tomas says, throwing his shoulder against Ernst, trying to shove his way outside the circle.

Ernst is on him in an instant, the other boys yelling encouragement. He's twice the size of Tomas and anger boils in me, red-hot fury at the bullies who *always* pick on scrawny Tomas. In my mind, the months fall away and I'm back on the street behind our old block of flats with Tomas, when it was us two against the dirty swine who beat him to a pulp just for the fun of it.

I launch myself at Ernst's neck, digging my fingernails into the soft flesh beneath his chin. The three of us drop to the ground, Ernst beneath me but reaching back to grab some part of me. He lets out an almighty yell and tries to push me off, but I'm clawing wildly at his face.

"STOP THIS AT ONCE!" shouts a woman's voice, fierce and loud. Hands grip my shoulders and pull me away from Ernst. I'm spun around and the hands let go.

"Fräulein Herta! Fighting with boys like a dog! You should be ashamed of yourself." Bertha, her cheeks blotchy purple, eyes looking like they might pop out of her head, stands in front of me. "What on earth would your mother think?" Her chest rises and falls as her breath puffs out like steam from the big, black kettle on the range.

Ernst and Tomas disentangle themselves and slowly get up, covered in snow. The other three Brandt brothers stand still, gawping at Bertha.

She shifts her gaze to Ernst and gasps. His face is a mess. My nails have dirt and bits of his bloodied skin beneath them. Tomas scrabbles in the snow, finds his broken glasses, and shoves them, lopsidedly, back on.

"Look what you've done to that boy's face!" Bertha exclaims. "You've drawn blood!"

"But it was Ernst who started it, Bertha." My mouth forms the words slowly, as though chill and shock have made it work at half speed. "He attacked Tomas. *I* was trying to save him. That lot"—I point at the other brothers—"they yelled encouragement and would've joined in, if I hadn't . . . The odds were unfair."

Bertha looks at Tomas. "Is this true?" she asks crisply.

Tomas nods and stares at the ground.

Ernst dabs his bloodied cheek with his handkerchief and says nothing.

"Hmm," she says with a grunt. "You should know better than to fight with a girl," she goes on, looking at each of the brothers in turn. "You'd better get off home before I cuff the lot of you."

Ernst thrusts his shoulders back and juts his chin out as he saunters off, his brothers trailing behind him.

"You're pathetic," Ernst hisses at Tomas as he passes. "Need a *girl* to fight your battles for you." He spits on the snow.

Bertha watches him go, her arms crossed over her chest. She looks at me, her face softening. "That was brave, fräulein," she says, "to stand up for a friend. But silly all the same. You're a young lady, and young ladies do not go in for fighting. That's all there is to it. Now, off home with you."

Tomas and I, unlikely friends thrown together long ago through lack of alternatives, walk slowly back to my big house on Fritzschestrasse. From there he will carry on to the tiny flat above his uncle's shop on Hallische Strasse.

"Thanks," he mutters, when we reach my iron gate.

"S'alright."

"See you tomorrow?"

"Maybe . . . Bye, Tomas."

"Bye, Hetty."

I take the steps two at a time and close the front door behind me. I lean against it for a moment, knowing Tomas is still standing outside my gate, looking at the air I just ran through.

Hoping I'm going to come back.

Seven

April 20, 1934

Happy birthday," I whisper to the Führer's image as I pad across the floor to throw open my shutters and let in the morning sun. The cherry tree has exploded with pink-tipped blossoms, reminiscent of candy floss. I open my window wide so I can hear the birdsong and climb back into my bed, snuggling under the covers where it's still warm. I lean against my propped-up pillows and lock eyes with Hitler as he stares out from his position above the fireplace opposite my bed.

There's a bang on my door and I jolt.

"Hurry up, Hetty. You'll be late for school," Karl yells.

"Almost dressed. Coming!" I climb reluctantly out of bed.

Downstairs, everyone is already eating breakfast, the early morning news playing on the radio.

". . . Hermann Göring will today transfer the administration of the Prussian State Secret Police, the Gestapo, to Reichsführer Heinrich Himmler . . ."

Mutti looks up at Vati. "Did you know about this?"

Vati raises his eyebrows and stops chewing for a few moments, listening intently to the radio. ". . . *In Austria, eighty-one men, opponents of the government, have been incarcerated in Wöllersdorf . . .*" Vati loses interest in the story and switches the radio off.

"There was nothing in Goebbels's news briefing this morning. It's all been kept quiet."

I help myself to a cup of warm milk, salami, and pumpernickel and take a seat next to Mutti.

"Now things will become interesting," Vati says. "I wonder what Göring will do next." He looks at his watch. "I'm late this morning. I must send a journalist to Berlin to get the scoop. If we're quick, we'll have something in time for tomorrow's print run." He leans back in his chair. "Mark my words, this will be a change for good. There's chaos out there, on the streets. Stirred up by Jewish conspirators and Communist thugs. Himmler and Heydrich will bring them to heel. This is good news, Hélène. Good news indeed. *Every* German citizen should be working for the good of the Reich. And these are the men to make it happen."

Vati wipes his mouth with his napkin and pushes his chair back. "I must be on my way." He kisses Mutti and ruffles the top of my hair on his way out.

"What does he mean?" Karl asks after he has left. "What chaos on the streets?"

I glance out the window. Fritzschestrasse is all peace and calm. Perhaps the trouble is in Berlin, or Halle, or Munich. I hope it doesn't spread to the respectable streets of Gohlis.

"People are starving, Karl," Mutti says, her forehead wrinkled up. "Even though, since Hitler has been in power, things are getting better, there is still no work for many, many people. Hungry, idle men make for trouble. And worse, they listen to the lies and empty promises of our enemies. We have problems that have been brewing for many years. One man cannot solve them all at once. People must be patient. But some are too stupid to trust. Others simply have evil intentions to be rid of him. A strong leader is what we need right now, and we are lucky we have one."

I stare at the food on my plate. *Thank you, Hitler, that I'm not one of the starving.*

"Is Vati in danger?" I ask, vaguely aware of his special duties in the SS to protect Hitler and the Party. I picture him, face-to-face with ugly thugs on the streets of Leipzig, many against one, just the way it is with Tomas.

"Of course not," Mutti says quickly. "But he has an important job, through the *Leipziger Tageszeitung*, to make sure the citizens of, at least this city, know truth from *lies*. The lies of the doubters, and the bad-mouthers," she adds firmly.

"But what exactly *does* he do when his puts on his Schutzstaffel uniform?"

Mutti smiles. "He's a senior officer, Hetty." Then she laughs. "He does a lot of organizing and paperwork. Now, enough of this, both of you, you'll be late for school, and I must visit my blessed old soldiers today."

I swallow the rest of my milk and follow Karl into the hall to gather our coats and satchels.

"Bye, Mutti," I say, kissing her cheek.

"Come on, funny Little Mouse," Karl says, holding the front door wide for me to pass through. "I'll take care of *you*. Always."

AT THE END of school, I wait for Erna just inside the big double doors. Students pour out of classrooms, congregating in the corridor, before passing out into the bright light outside. Walter appears in the throng. He walks apart from the chattering groups. I try to catch his eye, but his head is down. There's a pressure in my chest as he passes. I long to reach out and touch his shoulder, ask him what happened between him and Karl. But my arm stays limp at my side and the opportunity is gone.

Outside school, my heart sinks when I see Tomas waiting. Erna nudges me as he walks toward us.

"Who's this?" she asks with a giggle. "Is he your sweetheart?"

"Don't be silly. It's just Tomas. From my *old* school," I whisper out of the side of my mouth, because he's within earshot. He looks so scruffy and rough. Like a battered old coin next to shiny new ones. I have the urge to grab Erna and run away, but it's too late.

"Hello, Tomas, from Hetty's old school," Erna says with a smirk, as I hang back.

"Hello." Tomas looks uncertainly from me to Erna and back. He pushes his ugly glasses up his nose. A thin line of mucus tracks its way down from one of Tomas's pink nostrils and reaches his top lip. His tongue flicks out and licks at it.

Erna turns away. She hitches her satchel onto her shoulder and gives me a little wave. "See you tomorrow, Hetty," she says, leaving me with Tomas.

I set off fast for home and Tomas trots to catch up.

"How've you been?" he asks.

"All right. You?"

He shrugs.

I remember the conversation over breakfast this morning, and my heart softens a little. "Your father got a job yet?"

"No."

"He could become a policeman. Or work for the Party."

"No way. He'd rather die."

"That's stupid. Why?"

"Because he's a Communist and he hates the Nazis."

I stop walking. Tomas's words rise and mingle with the spring breeze ruffling our hair. They hang there, heavy and shocking.

"He can't be. You're making it up."

"I'm not." We begin to walk again, Tomas dragging the heels of his too-big shoes along the pavement. "He has meetings in my uncle's flat with this Polish man, Bajek. And other men he used to work with from the factory. I've listened through the door."

"What've you heard?" I sidle closer to him, dropping my voice to a whisper.

"They talk about this person and that person and how they've suffered. About the National Socialists bullying and roughing people up. How they aren't allowed to meet anymore, but it won't stop them. It's that Bajek. He's the main one."

"Communists are *traitors*," I hiss.

"I *know* . . ." he hisses back.

We've been studying Hitler's early life at school. His longing to be an artist. His early struggles against his parents and how, if things had been easier, he would not have been where he is today. We've learned about his misery in the 1920s, how he was tried for high treason and imprisoned. But these hardships only made him stronger. His quest for the German people seemed impossible, but he continued to fight, and win he did. We must all be like the Führer and fight, even if it means risking our lives. A vision of his face floats. *Help me.* He wears a solemn look, but then one ice blue eye winks. *My child*—his voice is firm and resonant—*you must do the right thing. It is your responsibility to be a leader and show the way. Tell Tomas, I, too, went against my parents' wishes. Show no weakness, Herta. You must be fearless in all that you do* . . .

The vision fades but my skin prickles. So *this* is what He has planned for me. *Not* being a doctor, but someone who guides others along the path to righteousness. I see clearly the mangled shapes of the men in the soldiers' home, maimed so cruelly by our enemies. I know what must be done.

"Come home with me, Tomas. My parents won't mind. You can have lunch and stay for the afternoon if you like."

"Really?" Tomas's eyes flare.

"Yes, really."

Ahead, I glimpse the humped shapes of two people shuffling toward us from the direction of Berggartenstrasse. An old man leaning on a stick, an old lady holding on to his arm.

My heart jumps at the sight of Flocke, silently padding at their side, blacker than black.

I point at them and whisper to Tomas, "They're *Jews*." He looks around and wrinkles his nose in disgust.

"Let's get a bit closer," he says, eyes lit with something I've not seen before.

We walk toward them. We get quite close and Tomas shouts, "Eww, there's a nasty stink around here!"

The Goldschmidts stop and stare at us approaching.

"Say something." Tomas nudges me.

I open my mouth to speak but no words come. They both look so old and frail.

"Go on," Tomas urges. "Show them who's best." He turns toward them and spits, the white globule landing on the pavement between us and them. My stomach turns over.

He nudges me again.

This time I manage to push a few words out. "It's the smell of swine," I say, but my voice is barely a whisper.

"Louder," Tomas says. We're just a few feet from them now. *Frau Goldschmidt was unkind*, I remind myself. *She shouted at me and wouldn't let me walk Flocke. She deserves this.* I try not to look at Herr Goldschmidt.

"*Jewish* swine," I say, my voice firmer than before. Frau Goldschmidt is trembling and Tomas laughs. It makes me braver. "Disgusting—who would want to live among pigs?" I don't look them in the eye and the words come easier. They start to flow like vomit, sour and choking. "Sheds. Pigs should live in *sheds*, not houses!"

I'm light-headed and Tomas and I both double up with laughter as we run away from them and cross the road.

But the look on Herr Goldschmidt's crumpled face and the trembling of his wife's hand on his arm as we pass them leave a sickness swirling in my belly.

You can't be a leader if you don't believe in what you do. Hitler's voice echoes in my ears. I pull myself taller and nod in agreement. He's right. I mustn't be weak; I have a job to do, and only I can do it.

WE STAND TOGETHER, shoulder to shoulder, in Vati's study. I squeeze Tomas's hand to encourage him. He's completely mute.

I look around the room and see it for the first time as Tomas must see it. The huge leather-covered desk. Vati's imposing armchair and the floor-to-ceiling bookshelves filled with files and the paperwork of authority. Vati himself, with his slicked-back blond hair, massive and commanding in his black uniform.

"Well?" He raises a pale eyebrow, peering at us over the top of his half-moon reading spectacles. The air is fusty with old cigarette smoke and the acerbic tang of whisky.

Tomas is still struck dumb. I'm scared he is going to change his mind or Vati will become impatient and throw us out.

Show no weakness. A youth before which the world will tremble.

"Vati . . ." My voice comes out louder than I expect. "You remember Tomas? He wants to report something, but he is afraid and doesn't know who he should speak to, so I thought you might hear him."

Vati puts his pen down and leans back in his chair.

"Well, speak then, boy."

Tomas clears his throat and at last finds his voice. "It's . . . about my father. Well, about this Pole, really. Bajek. I think he might be a Communist."

Vati sits up straighter in his chair. Tomas glances at me. I nod encouragement.

"And what makes you think that, son?"

"I heard him. And he's got my father into it, too. Also, I found some leaflets . . ."

"What leaflets?" Vati asks sharply.

"Propaganda leaflets."

I smile at Tomas. He's doing really well.

"They have discussions. They say Hitler is an idiot. They say it's only a matter of time before people see sense. They talk about different men they know and which side of the fence they sit on."

"Do you remember any names?" Vati asks.

"I think so. Some." Tomas shuffles his feet. "Sometimes when I'm out playing with my brothers, I sneak back to listen. They talk about victory of the working man and revolution and about the wrongs of rich people and things. But I forget . . ."

"Don't worry about that." He pushes a sheet of paper toward Tomas and hands him a pen. "You write me that list of names."

We watch as Tomas scratches a couple of names onto the paper. Thinks a moment, then writes a couple more.

He looks up at Vati. "These are the only ones I know."

Vati rises from his chair, comes around the desk, and shakes Tomas's hand.

"You have done the right thing, my boy. You will be re-warded. What Jungvolk rank are you?"

"My parents won't let me join up," Tomas says. His head and shoulders droop with the shame of it.

"What? But you must join immediately!" Vati looks out-raged. I give him a hard stare, but he pays me no attention.

"I'll take care of that. How do you fancy becoming a stan-dard bearer, eh? That's a real honor. You are a true son of Germany; you've done a brave thing. Now, not a word to your mother and father, you understand? You leave all this to us. We will take care of everything, yes? Good boy."

"What'll happen to him? To my father?" Tomas asks in a small voice. "Will he be arrested?"

"Of course not. You mustn't listen to idle gossip. We will take your father into protective custody, for his own safety. Do you know what that means?"

Tomas shakes his head.

"It means that we take him away to look after him. To *protect* him. Germany has enemies, Tomas. You must keep a lookout for them. Always have your eyes and ears open. Anything, however small or insignificant, you must report it. It's your duty. To me, or to your HJ superiors." Vati returns to his chair. "Now, you mustn't worry. I will take care of your vati. Not a word, mind. This is of utmost importance."

Vati turns to me. He smiles and winks. "Well done, Herta, my girl," he says. "You are growing up, Schnuffel. I'm proud of you."

His words are delicious. Perhaps there is hope of a change of mind from him about the Jungmädel, after this.

"Now," he says briskly, "I must make some telephone calls. Tomas, it might be best if you stay with Herta for a little while. Have some lunch with us."

I smile into Tomas's pale, drawn face. He is finally going to join the Hitler Youth, and his father will be *protected* from the evil of communism. Perhaps the Gestapo might even find him a job.

It has all gone so much better than I ever imagined it would.

Eight

August 19, 1934

Look!" Erna points up to the top of the monkey enclosure. "We're in luck!"

We prop our bikes next to a bench behind the zoo, where it backs onto Rosental park. A small group of the flat-faced gray creatures sit close to the side of the cage, high up on wooden poles. One of them swings down onto a platform where pieces of fruit are scattered. It grabs a slice of apple, and, clasping it tightly in its little fist, the animal climbs back onto the pole. There it sits, nibbling while its friends squawk and chatter with one another like a bunch of old ladies.

In front of us, small children play on the flat grassy expanse of Rosental in the warm August sunshine and dogs bound in great, loopy circles. From my bag I take out the two slices of linzertorte, wrapped in brown paper, and offer one to Erna. We sit and eat in silence.

A monkey couple crouch apart from the rest, close together, preening and checking each other's fur. The quiet, gentle movements are broken from time to time as one or the other finds something, a flea or a louse perhaps, and, swiftly grabbing it, pops it into its mouth.

"Imagine if people did that." Erna suddenly giggles at the monkey couple and wrinkles up her nose. She nudges me with her elbow. "Imagine *you* doing that with *your* sweetheart when you get one."

I almost spit out my mouthful of sweet pastry and jam.

"Erna!" I splutter. "Shhh . . ."

She turns and looks at me, wickedness flickering in her eyes. "Perhaps you already have someone in mind," she says, nudging me again.

"Don't be ridiculous. We're only *twelve*."

"I'm *nearly* thirteen. Anyway, what about Karl?" She looks at me sideways.

"What about him?"

"He's awfully handsome."

"Karl?" I laugh. "He hardly ever washes and almost never changes his pants and vest." Something quivers in my belly. A snake flickering its tongue. I carefully lick the jam off my fingers. "Reenacting famous battles. Airplanes. Football." I count them off. "That's what Karl likes."

I study Erna's profile while she chews and watches the monkeys. The delicate sweep of her nose. Her high cheekbones and smooth, milky skin. She really is impossibly pretty.

But Karl's not interested in girls.

She lets out a long sigh and scrunches her paper bag into a small ball.

"I told my father about you," she says, turning the ball round and round in her hands. "He said not to be friends."

"Why not?" I stare at her in surprise.

"It's not *you* he doesn't like," she says hurriedly, "it's your father."

"But he doesn't even know my father!"

"I probably shouldn't say," she says, squeezing the ball to make it flat. "It's only because he's wrong. I *should* be friends with you, and whatever *he* says won't change a thing. You'll always be my best friend, won't you, Hetty?"

And everything for a moment stands still. Like the most perfect picture. The sun is gloriously golden and warm. The birdsong is brighter and sweeter than ever before, and the monkeys at their most playful and full of joy.

I try to look unruffled, as if people declare me to be their Best Friend every day. "Of course," I say, barely breathing, and I can't help smiling. "Always and forever."

We sit for a moment in contented silence.

"What is it that your father doesn't like about mine?"

"Honestly. Don't worry about it."

"He shouldn't say things about people he doesn't even know." How odd to think of Vati being discussed in other people's living rooms.

Erna takes a breath. "Something to do with the way he took over the newspaper," she says in a rush. "But he's probably got it all wrong."

Frau Goldschmidt's wrinkled crone face swims into focus. *Your father . . . forced them out . . . all lies and falsehoods . . .*

Jealousy. That's what Vati said it was.

"It's all lies and gossip. People are jealous of my father's success, that's all."

I meet Erna's eyes and she looks away.

"Yes. That must be it." She digs a hole in the gravel with the toe of her shoe. "My father's a silly old fool for listening."

"He should be more careful."

The monkeys have eaten most of the fruit and begin a game of chase, swinging from pole to pole. The grooming couple saunter off and disappear into the covered enclosure.

"I'm going to join the Jungmädel," Erna says. "Will you come too?"

"Vati won't let me. He thinks the HJ should just be for boys."

"But everyone else is. Surely you can persuade him?"

"You don't know Vati. When he's made up his mind, it's impossible to change it."

Perhaps Erna will find a new Best Friend in the Jungmädel. I scan the flat, green expanse of Rosental stretching out toward the woods in the distance. The sun is suddenly too hot, and the glare hurts my eyes. I can feel a headache developing in my temples.

Erna gently touches my arm. Her eyes are stretched wide open.

"Please don't tell your father what mine said, will you?" she whispers.

"Of course I won't."

"I can trust you, Hetty, can't I?"

"Erna"—I look straight into her catlike eyes—"I'm your best friend. You can trust me to the ends of the earth. I promise you that."

Nine

September 10, 1934

"D id you hear they got rid of Dr. Kreitz?" Erna whispers. "When?"

"Friday. And other teachers too."

She nods at the solemn-suited wall of authority at the front of the main hall where we are gathered for assembly. There are definitely some new faces among them.

"Quiet!" Herr Hofmann's voice booms. "Silence for our new science teacher. Herr Metzger, the floor is yours."

A slim young man in a brown suit and bow tie strides to the front of the stage. His young face is round and shiny. A smattering of white pimples covers the rough, red skin of his chin. He can't be much older than Karl.

He pulls a cord that unfurls a large white banner on the front wall. A poem is displayed in large black letters:

Keep your blood pure,
It is not yours alone,
It comes from far away,

It flows into the distance.
Laden with thousands of ancestors,
And it holds the entire future!
It is your eternal life.

"Eugenics. The beautiful science of race and genes," Herr Metzger begins in a soft, syrupy voice. "Human progression is on the brink of a new era. The possibilities of a superrace, free from crime, free from hereditary diseases, and free from insanity, is within our grasp. This is the essence of scientific advancement."

The floorboards creak as he walks back and forth in front of us. His fair hair is greased back, and his light blue eyes twinkle.

"The result? A population of the best. The fittest, bravest, the most beautiful, clever, and robust. The epitome of Darwin's theory. A people who will be superior in every way and who must spread their influence throughout the world. *This* is the vision behind the science. And who would not dream of such a world?" He stops and scans our faces. I lock my knees together, sit up straight.

"He's rather a dish, don't you think?" Erna whispers in my ear.

"Shh."

"All right, teacher's pet." She giggles.

I dig her in the ribs.

Herr Metzger talks of population projections and the societal cost of supporting growing numbers of physically disabled people, not to mention the insane, the epileptics, and the feeble-minded. He shows us the different races, and their place on a Darwinian scale of advancement. Nordic at the top, Jews at the bottom. The French, thankfully, are not too far below the Germans. Lucky Mutti is from near Paris. The population in the South of France has been infected by North Africans and can no longer be considered racially pure.

The hall is hot and Herr Metzger removes his jacket. Erna is all attention now. She giggles at his informality.

"It is vital," Herr Metzger goes on, "that Aryans breed only with other Aryans. Interbreeding with inferior races will ultimately cause the fall of Western civilization, just as it once did to those ancient civilizations of Greece and Rome. For those with hereditary diseases, sterilization is essential. It is not the *fault* of those unfortunate individuals. But they cannot be permitted to pass their . . . *afflictions* on to future generations. For the good of all mankind, this is an inviable truth."

I think of how Hitler sometimes speaks to me, so very clearly, inside my head. Not for the first time, I wonder with a pang if I have some kind of madness. People say, if you hear voices . . . I can feel my armpits are damp with sweat; my back, clammy.

Is sterilization painful? I stare at Hitler's portrait dominating the big wall behind the teachers sitting at the front.

Am I mad?

No, Herta. I have chosen you.

But I'm a girl!

I need girls, Herta. Boys will fight to win the war, but girls . . . you will be future mothers. Mothers are to be honored. Worshipped. Because without mothers, without girls, we cannot succeed.

Sweat beads on my forehead. I glance at Erna but she is watching Herr Metzger, transfixed as he click clacks, back and forth, in front of our bench. The silence in the hall is unnerving. Not a rustle, nor a twitch.

Herr Metzger consults a piece of paper he pulls from his pocket. "Freda Federmann, Walter Keller. Join me at the front, here."

Walter Keller.

Time slows as Freda shuffles off the bench behind me. I twist around and see Walter stepping over the knees of his classmates several rows back. Karl sits at the end of the row and catches my eye. I can't read the expression on his face.

I watch Walter walk slowly through the middle of the grand hall, smart and upright in his dark suit and tie. Sunshine flows through the long windows and a million tiny dust particles are illuminated by beams of light. Walter passes through them and in his wake the dust shoots skyward and swirls crazily, before re-forming and slowly descending once more through the diagonal shards of light.

Herr Metzger towers over Freda with something I can't make out in his hand.

"A Jewess," he says, and a shudder ripples through the hall. His words, unexpected and chilling, creep down my back.

"Observe her frizzy black hair," he murmurs. His voice is soft. The words seem to slither from his mouth and slide, serpentlike, around the hall. He leans over Freda as if she were a zoo specimen. It is almost as if the teacher and the girl are alone and he has forgotten the rest of us are here.

Walter arrives level with Herr Metzger. He approaches slowly and deliberately, then stands right next to Freda. My brain is locked in confusion.

"This is awful," Erna murmurs.

"But what's Walter doing there?"

Erna shakes her head and says nothing.

Herr Metzger barely seems to notice Walter's arrival. He lifts the instrument in his hand and I see now it's a pair of metal calipers. He dangles them in front of Freda's face.

"Her eyes are too close together," he announces. "A clear sign of a clever but untrustworthy nature."

Nobody makes a sound. There's a sour taste in my mouth.

"See this oversized, lumpy nose? You will notice it's shaped like an upside-down nine. A classic characteristic of the Jew."

Herr Metzger slowly moves the calipers around Freda's face. Her lips are too thin. Her ears stick out too far. Her hair is too wiry. Tears begin to flow silently down her cheeks. She is trembling. One tear, then two, fall to the floor.

Walter sidles closer to Freda. Next to her Jewish features, Walter is blond, blue eyed, and perfect. It suddenly dawns on me why he is there. Herr Metzger wants to contrast the Aryan with the Jew.

I watch Walter take hold of Freda's hand and give it a squeeze. He doesn't let go. They stand there, the two of them, hand in hand until Herr Metzger, with his calipers, sweeps them apart.

"Now look at her frail, undersized body. The Jew is unsuited to, and incompetent at, sport. She is lazy by nature." He spits out his words and saliva sprays in front of him. Freda flinches as it hits her face.

He takes a step back and points at her feet. "Inside that girl's shoes you will find big, flat, ugly feet. These make her clumsy and unable to run well."

Freda's face is stricken and I can't bear to watch anymore. I look down at my hands folded in my lap.

"Why doesn't he stop now?" I hear Erna say quietly, as if to herself. "He's said enough . . ."

A flash of movement and I look again. Herr Metzger whips around and grabs Walter's shoulder, jerking his head up. With a face twisted in disgust, he pokes at him like a side of beef hanging in a butcher's shop. "This Jew," he says harshly, "has thousands of years of trickery and treachery bred into him. His only care is that of self-advancement. He will stamp others into the ground to get his own way. He is rotten from the inside out. He will cheat and . . ."

The room lurches. A thousand needles prick the back of my neck. *It cannot be true.*

"No!" I shout, half choking on the word as it escapes me. Several heads turn and stare, then just as quickly swivel back to the stage.

I want to yell at them, *You're wrong!* But I can't. There's an urge to run. Far, far away. The wooden bench remains hard beneath me and I'm frozen and useless as I watch.

With his attention focused on Walter, it takes Herr Metzger a few moments to notice what's happened. The smell of urine is strong and unmistakable. It trickles down the inside of Freda's legs, soaking her stockings and pooling around her shoes. A tremor of sniggers and stifled laughter breaks out behind me.

"Dear God . . ." Erna exclaims out loud.

Realizing the bottom of his trousers and shoes have been splattered with Freda's piss, the teacher drops Walter's shoulder like a hot coal.

"Get out," he says, his voice low and tremulous. "Neither of you need bother coming back."

Walter winds his arm around Freda's heaving shoulders. She waddles toward the exit, leaving a trail of wet footprints behind her. The door swings, and they are gone.

A moment of stillness, then Herr Hofmann leaps to his feet.

"My dear Herr Metzger . . ." He says something we can't hear, and Herr Metzger swiftly leaves after Freda and Walter. "You two"—the headmaster points to two girls at the other end of the front row—"fetch a mop and bucket and clear this mess up. The rest of you, back to class. The entertainment is over."

Filing out of the hall, I'm numb. My mind is refusing to accept what I just witnessed. How can it even be *possible* that Walter is a Jew? Wonderful Walter, the boy who saved my life, a dirty, stinking Jew? It cannot be possible. They've made a mistake. He looks nothing like one. But then I remember Vati's words, *Not that boy again*, and his look of displeasure whenever he used to find Walter in our house.

My classmates push past me, chattering in excited voices as they turn left toward our classroom. To the right, the heavy front doors are ajar. Walter and Freda must have walked through them only a few moments ago. A thin strip of light pierces the darkness of the corridor.

"Hetty . . ." Erna's voice, far away. "Hetty!" Her face is a frown and she says, "Don't. Think of the trouble you'll be in . . ."

But she fades as I feel Walter's strong hands pulling me from the mouths of the monsters in the lake. His kindly blue eyes and warmest of smiles hover in my mind, and suddenly I'm bolting, hurtling along the corridor, punching through the doors and into the bright, blinding daylight.

I tear across the grassy slope of Nordplatz. Around the far corner of the church, I see them.

"Walter," I call. He's holding Freda's hand, half turned toward her, saying something. I catch the sound of her strangled sobs. "WALTER!"

They both turn, openmouthed at the sight of me.

I stop in front of them, panting hard.

What am I doing here?

"I just want you to know . . ."

Freda's eyes are puffy and red. Her skirt and stockings have dark wet patches on them. Up close, she stinks.

I look at Walter's face. Tears well in my eyes. How *can* he be a Jew? How could I have been so stupid not to have known? I finally understand why Karl doesn't invite him home anymore.

"Go back to school, Hetty," Walter tells me in a flat voice. "You shouldn't be here."

"I don't care," I tell him. "I don't care that you are a Jew. *I* will always be your friend," I vow. "*Always and forever.*"

I turn before he can reply and run fast, back across Nordplatz, toward school.

Hitler is trying to speak with me, but I close my mind to him.

There. I've said it. My words are free, floating through the fresh air of Nordplatz.

Even if I wanted to, I can't take them back now.

Part II

Ten

May 31, 1937

I prize open my eyes, slowly, one at a time. Rolling onto my back, I stretch each limb out fully. My foot hits a hard, warm lump at the bottom of the bed.

"Kuschi." I smile at the curled black shape. "What are you doing in here? If Mutti catches you . . ."

The dog raises his head, looks at me, and thumps his tail on the bedcover. He yawns and goes back to sleep.

"Cheeky." I laugh, reaching down to stroke his soft shaggy coat. He must have escaped from the kitchen when Ingrid went down in the early morning. "You love me, don't you, Kuschi Muschi?" His breathing is soft and even. No hint of the trauma he suffered last year.

"Flocke," I call softly. What might he remember of his old life? He opens his eyes and I sigh. "Well. This won't do, will it? Let's go and have some breakfast."

I wash and dress. Karl's door remains firmly shut as I pass by.

In the dining room, Vati, unusually, is at home having break-fast. More and more he is away, his SS duties taking his nights as well as eating into his days. He looks deep in thought. He holds Mutti's hand where it rests on the polished walnut table, his thumb drawing soft circles on her skin. He says something quietly to her and she throws her head back and laughs, her hair rippling down her back. The floor creaks as I hesitate in the doorway.

Vati looks up and drops Mutti's hand like a guilty secret.

"Ah, good morning, young lady." He pours himself coffee from the tall pot, its giraffelike neck long and elegant.

"First day of the holidays, eh?" He gives me a wink. "I hope you have some worthy plans."

"Yes, Vati. I have lots of Bund Deutscher Mädel commitments, and the summer camp, of course. Plus I shall see my friends, help Mutti, you know . . ."

He grunts and watches me spread *frischkäse*, creamy white, on a slice of dark rye bread.

"You could spend the summer working on a farm, like the Käfer girl up the road," he suggests.

"Franz!" Mutti exclaims. "What are you suggesting . . . you know half those girls come back impregnated by the Hitler Jugend boys they send to the same farms. What a dreadful idea . . ."

"Don't worry, Mutti. There's no way I'm spending my summer working on a farm. Virtuous and valuable though, I know. Summer camp is quite enough for me. I'd rather stay here with you and help at the soldiers' home."

Vati chuckles and nods.

"Well, they do adore you, Hetty," Mutti says, then turns to Vati. "But you should take a holiday, too, Franz. You work so hard."

He reaches for her hand again and gives it a squeeze. "I know, Hélène, and I would love nothing better than to take you, Karl, and Hetty away, but it's impossible at present. Tensions are running high, and I can't leave the paper at the moment."

"What do you mean?" Mutti asks, lighting a cigarette, then leaning back in her chair, head cocked to the side.

"We have too many foreigners in Leipzig," Vati says bluntly. "We must *do* something. They take jobs, houses, *food* away from Germans. They bring bad manners." He waves a hand. "Habits. They smell. And"—he shoots a look at me—"*worse.*" He shifts in his seat. "And this looming possibility of war. Look at the trouble in Spain! Only this morning we've been carrying out reprisals for attacks on our boats. I fear where it may lead."

Mutti taps ash into the tray. "You *really* think we are heading for war. Again?" She shakes her head, cheeks pinched.

"England has a new prime minister. But I think it would be foolish to assume he, or any other leader, will be sympathetic to German interests. Word is, he's weak. Malleable. Time will tell."

Mutti blows smoke from the side of her mouth. I wave it away with my hand.

War. Such a small word for something so unimaginably big. I think of Karl's plans to join the new flying force, and the room chills.

"If it comes to it, Hélène, I'm certain that victory will be

swift and decisive. As for me, I must concentrate on *this* city."
He frowns. "If we stick to our principles, the future is positive.
We can't be complacent. I must use the *Leipziger* to further
our cause."

"How?" I ask.

"A newspaper, Schnuffel, is a powerful weapon. Of course,
our Herr Goebbels guides us with his daily press releases. It
is our duty to shape the opinion of the masses and ensure the
Fatherland's values and best interests are always in the fore-
front of people's minds."

I chew my bread and cheese. At school, we are studying
Mein Kampf. Everyone knows the Jews stabbed our army in
the back at the end of the last war. With the help of Fink's new
book, *The Jewish Question in Education*, I can identify a Jew
just by looking at a person's features. If I see one, I cross the
street, just like everyone else, and I never look them in the eye.

"Franz, these things will still be there if you take a few days
off to go to the beach. Besides, you *are* the boss. You must have
people who can run things while you aren't there?"

Vati shrugs. "I only appointed Josef Heiden as editor two
weeks ago. I can hardly go off and leave him at this stage . . .
Besides, with my SS commitments ever increasing . . ." He
pauses. "If Karl wasn't so busy flying gliders this summer, I
could have him work with me at the *Leipziger*. He would be
such an asset. And think what I could entrust to him in the
future, which I can't to anyone else."

"If you could get him to work with you over the summer,
before he leaves . . . I wish with all my heart he'd change his
mind. I worry sick about him going."

Vati shakes his head. "The Luftwaffe arranged it. It's vital flying experience before moving on to the real thing. Besides, he's determined to go. I think, in time, he'll come back to the *Leipziger*. He's a young man, Hélène. He must find his own way. He wants to do his bit for the Reich and it's only right and natural that he should." He drains his coffee cup.

"I want to do my bit for the Reich, too," I blurt out. "Perhaps I could work at the paper this summer, Vati? I'm a quick learner."

Vati looks at me, narrowing his pale eyes. In the strong sunlight, his skin is pasty and sags with fatigue.

"That's a kind offer, Herta," he says slowly. "But your place is here, with Mutti. Help her with her charity work. It's more important, too, that you learn how to run a home than understand the inner workings of a newspaper."

"But, Vati—"

He scrapes back his chair and the discussion is over.

"Now, I must get to work."

He leans across to peck Mutti's cheek and plants a kiss on the top of my head. Mutti hurries out of the room after him, just as Karl arrives, unshaven and sleepy eyed. I ball my fists beneath the table.

"Morning, Little Mouse," Karl says as he sits heavily on the chair opposite. "Did I interrupt something?"

"No, not really." I sigh. "Just the same old argument. Vati wants you to work at the paper and Mutti doesn't want you to join the Luftwaffe."

Karl helps himself to some bread and spreads it with butter. He places two layers of leberwurst on top, humming a little tune under his breath.

"Why so cheery?" I pour us both some tea and plop a slice of lemon in each cup, plus two scoops of sugar in mine.

"I'm excited!" He smiles broadly and takes a large bite of bread and sausage, chewing vigorously. "No more school and I leave for the Luftwaffe in only a few weeks."

"Are you that keen to leave home?"

I try to imagine life without Karl. His empty space at the dinner table. The silence without his step on the creaky floorboards. No more *us*.

"I will miss you so much."

"Of course you will. And I shall miss you, too, my Little Mouse, but . . ."

"Will you stop calling me that?"

"What? Little Mouse?"

"Yes, that."

"No."

"*Arschloch*."

"I'll tell Mutti you used a bad word." He mimics my voice and we laugh.

"But really, why *do* you want to go? Vati could have you straight into the SS, and the *Leipziger* will be yours one day. You'd make a great reporter. With your charm, you could get anyone to tell you *anything*."

"But, Hetty," he says, leaning toward me, his eyes shining, face animated. "Can you imagine anything more exhilarating, more exciting than being a pilot? The Luftwaffe will be the envy of the world. And I'm right here, at the start of it. Why would I want to join those stuffy Black-shirts? No disrespect to Vati. It's just *for me*, I couldn't live without being airborne.

No feeling like it in the world. And after all these summers of flying gliders, I've got a dreadful taste—no, an insatiable appetite—for the rush of it."

"It sounds awfully dangerous."

"And you sound like Mutti. It's a terrific thrill, that's all. Our aircraft are the most advanced in the world. Other nations will soon give up, faced with our Luftwaffe. Perhaps one day I'll be able to take you up flying, Little Mouse. You'd love it."

I watch his face as he chews, reaching a hand up to sweep his hair back. His bicep swells under his shirtsleeve. Without me noticing he has reached manhood, and now he needs to break free. Become his own person, away from Vati's dominating presence, away from Mutti's fussing. Perhaps even away from me. The thought is a physical pain, and for a moment I see how it is for Mutti.

"Come on, Hetty, cheer up," Karl says, his face earnest and kind. "Let's make the most of this last summer holiday together, eh? We'll have some fun, I promise."

Eleven

July 25, 1937

There's barely a cloud in the cerulean sky. A lark hovers overhead, a tiny black dot against the sun. Its song, pure and strong, rises and falls, immersing me with its pure, sweet joy.

The long grass tugs at the bottom of my skirt. I lift it high and pick my way, careful to avoid thistles and stinging nettles hidden in the lush pasture. Kuschi leads the way, like a dolphin beneath the waves, his whereabouts revealed only by the disturbance of the grass heads and occasional glimpse of his tail.

"Let's head for the riverbank, Kuschi Muschi," I call to him. "It'll be easier walking up there."

Reaching the top of the bank, I stop to catch my breath. It's not yet seven, but there is already heat in the sun's rays, forewarning another sweltering day. We follow the path along the course of the Weisse Elster, as it winds its way through the vast stretch of allotments spread out before us. I walk slowly, past fruit trees, rows of baby cabbages, canes of runner beans, and tomato plants. In the far distance, the low roar of a car engine starts up and a distant clanking of machinery floats from somewhere beyond the allotments.

"Hetty? Good God, is that you?"

I start in surprise.

A young man, of medium height, approaches from behind a plum tree. He has an athletic figure and is well dressed in dark slacks and a cream shirt. He's carrying a woman's basket filled with fruit and vegetables. He peers at me from beneath the wide brim of his hat, his face in shadow.

"Yes . . . it really *is* you!" he exclaims.

Kuschi, who'd been engrossed with an interesting smell some distance away, rushes toward him, barking furiously. The man removes his hat, revealing a mass of blond curls, and looks hurriedly about.

"Shh!" he says to Kuschi, holding out his hat as if it were a shield. "Shush, or someone'll hear you!"

The hair gives it away. He's changed, but not entirely. A rough sketch that has been painted over to faultless accomplishment, its lines developed with painstaking, intricate brushstrokes.

"*Walter?*"

I'm eleven again, watching my brother's friend with adoring eyes, willing him to notice me.

He steps closer, eyes uncertain, a hint of a smile. It's been more than three years since we've seen each other. Since *that* day.

"Quick," he says, "let's get out of here. Someone may have heard the dog."

He covers his basket with his free hand and runs for the gate to leave the allotments.

"Why?" I call after him, glancing around. "Aren't dogs allowed in here?"

Walter falters, half turns. "Best not wait to find out," he retorts over his shoulder, picking up his pace to a run again.

I follow with Kuschi bounding and snapping at my ankles, excited by this new game of chase. Managing not to trip over him, we scramble through the gate and don't stop until we reach a line of trees where the ground once more slopes up into a steep bank. The path runs behind it, right next to the river. On the other side of the bank is a little-used lane, and in front of us is an old humpbacked bridge leading to Trachenbergstrasse, which joins Hallische Strasse, and onward, toward home. We take the path by the river, out of sight now of anyone in the allotments or the lane, and Kuschi leaps straight into the water.

Laughter dances in Walter's eyes as he looks back at me, hooking his basket into the crook of his arm.

"Wow," he says. "Little Hetty, all grown up . . ."

Under his gaze, something double flips inside and I feel my face flush.

"So . . ." I can't meet his eyes. "You're all grown up yourself."

And you are a *Jew*.

Unformed thoughts swirl, refusing to fashion themselves into words. He catches my awkwardness and is silent too.

Kuschi explodes from the river, shakes himself at the water's edge, and runs to me, rubbing his sodden body against my calf. I shriek, shaking the hem of my skirt.

"What a marvelous dog," Walter remarks.

He crouches down and pats Kuschi's wet side. The dog wags his tail so violently, it hits Walter in the face. He screws up his nose and teeters backward. Kuschi turns and licks his ear avidly, as though he were a tasty piece of meat, making Walter laugh.

"He's a character, isn't he?"

I shouldn't be with a Jew.

But this is *Walter*.

My mouth is dry. I lick my lips. "He used to belong to the Goldschmidts," I mumble. "They lived across the road from us. Jews . . . But one day, they left their apartment and abandoned him. I found him in the snow, shivering and starved." I think back to that day. Vati didn't want a Jew's dog in the house. I had to treat him for fleas and scrub him clean. Eventually he relented, but he insisted I change his name from Flocke. "How could anyone be so cruel?"

Walter strokes the dog and doesn't reply.

Something in me pings open, like a spring releasing. Long-buried feelings rise up and words flow out, full of shaky emotion.

"What happened, Walter? I mean . . . where did you go, after that day?"

He flashes me a look and waves a hand toward the bank. "Shall we sit for a few minutes? There's so much I want to say to you."

You cannot sit with a Jew. Hitler's voice; Herr Metzger's; Vati's. I can no longer distinguish. They swirl and merge together. I look around; the empty lane, the grassy bank and river. The allotments stretching into the distance. Nobody is about, but what if someone comes?

He looks at me expectantly. His face has altered: a man's jaw, a hint of stubble on his cheeks. Like Karl, he's eighteen, almost nineteen. But the warm blue eyes are the same. A breath of wind lifts his hair from his forehead. I clutch Kuschi's unattached leash tight in my hand. An invisible force takes hold, and I'm sitting next to him on the bank. Not too close. I draw my knees into my chest, wrapping my arms around my shins.

"What you did that day, what you said . . ." His voice is low and buttery. "It was very courageous. And generous."

"I got into awful trouble for bolting out of school, but I meant it, at the time." I speak to my knees.

Then I did, but I'm older now. Wiser. In the three years since that day, I've come to understand the threat, the danger posed by the Jewish race. Now I understand the character, the *essence* of the Jew. But I don't tell him.

"I'm sorry to hear that. I never got the chance to thank you."

"There's no need."

A sound in the lane: bicycle wheels. I clutch the leash tighter. It passes by.

"No, Hetty, it was brave, to run out of school like that. To say those words to Freda and me. Especially after Karl cut me off. It meant . . ." He takes a long breath. "So very much."

I shrug. I was just a child. I had no concept of what I was doing, at the time. I didn't want Walter to be a Jew. But he is.

"I mean," Walter is saying, "especially coming from your family. It must be hard. To think differently." He looks at me and I meet his gaze. That flipping sensation again. Electricity pumps through my veins. "You do still," he says quietly, "think differently?"

His eyes pull me in and I'm nodding.

Herta Heinrich. Do not forget who you are. Those who serve Adolf Hitler serve Germany. Those who serve Germany serve God.

I look away. My hands tremble.

"What *did* happen to you?" I ask out of curiosity. "I never saw you again. Or Freda."

Walter sighs and picks at some grass, letting it fall to the ground through his fingers. "We had to move. Someone daubed *Out with the Jews* over our front door. The landlord said we had to go. Didn't want to risk his windows being smashed in. Besides, we couldn't afford the rent when he raised it. Business isn't exactly booming for my father."

"A lawyer, isn't he?" I ask, remembering. It was only Walter, his mother and father. I met his father once. He was small and thin, compared to Vati, at least. Quiet-spoken. Bookish. He'd been reading the day I met him. *What a useless occupation*, I remember Vati commenting, although now I wonder if that was in relation to the reading, or the lawyering. I recall feeling sorry for Walter. No siblings and quiet parents; no wonder he spent so much time with Karl and me.

"He was. Banned in thirty-three. Since then he has worked in my uncle Josef's fur trading company on the Brühl. I work there, too, in the warehouse. Not really what I want to do, but there's no choice. It's a struggle—nobody wants to buy or sell from a Jew. The banks won't lend to us. We still have the remnants of an export business, but it's hard going."

"Where did you go to school, after the gymnasium? What about university?"

The questions fall out.

"Me?" He laughs and shakes his head. "There's no opportunity for someone like me, Hetty. I went to the Jewish school—the Ephraim Carlebach School. I've left now; Freda's still there. As a Jew, I wasn't permitted to take the Abitur, so I've no qualifications. We live in my grandmother's house on Hindenburgstrasse together with Josef, his wife, and three children. It's a large house, and luckily my grandmother owns it, so we can live rent-free. It saves the cost of three homes."

I turn my head. Take him in. I think of the pictures in Fink's book. Walter bears no resemblance to any of them. If I saw *him* in the street, I wouldn't need to cross it. The open-necked cream shirt with his blond hair curling over the collar; a patch of pale skin at the neck. Legs stretched out and crossed at the ankles. Nevertheless, where once I thought him almost part of our family, now he is a stranger.

He oozes Otherness.

Jew.

Repelling, yet strangely compelling.

Silence stretches between us, thorny and uncomfortable. I spot the basket brimming with produce at Walter's feet.

"Do you have an allotment?" I nod at the basket. Something safe to discuss.

He shakes his head and looks a little sheepish.

"It isn't easy these days. If our livelihood is taken away, how are we supposed to earn money for our keep?"

"You *stole* those?"

"I only took one of each. Just a few things to keep us going. They won't even notice."

"But . . . those allotment owners work hard. They are decent, honest people. They're not rich. Why do you think *you* deserve their things?"

"We didn't *deserve* to be in this situation in the first place," he snaps, then takes a deep breath, as though he'd like to say more, but doesn't dare.

So this is what he's become. A little adversity and he transforms into a thief. True to his nature. Looks are deceiving, blood and breeding can never lie.

I shouldn't be here.

I feel the weight of his eyes. My throat is tight. The image of a hook-nosed, curly-headed lout, ravaging an innocent, pretty girl, dances in my mind.

"It's been nice to see you, but I must get back for breakfast." I stand in a rush. "Come on, Kuschi, we need to go home."

"Wait, Hetty. Please."

Walter's hair droops over his forehead and his eyes are the color of a tropical sea. He is beautiful, desperate, tragic.

If something bad was going to happen, it would have already. Again, I wonder how he doesn't look remotely like the evil depictions of the Jew in *Der Stürmer*. The contrast is laughable.

I sit down again, Kuschi pressing his warm, damp body against my legs.

"I'm sorry you think badly of me. Fact is, life here has become pretty intolerable for us. I wish I could leave Germany, like so many others have done," Walter says, looking out over the river toward the trees on the opposite bank. "But my father refuses. Over his dead body, he says, will he let Hitler take what our family has worked so hard for." I watch him carefully. Isn't the reverse true? It's the *Jews* who have stolen from hard-working Germans.

"I've written letters all over Europe trying to get an apprenticeship or a job of some sort. But I've had no luck. Jews aren't welcome anywhere, it seems," Walter continues.

This is making my head ache. People only ever talk of getting rid of scheming, thieving Jews. Nobody mentions where exactly they should go, other than Palestine. I stare at the basket and wonder what to say.

"I'm sorry for you, Walter, truly, but *stealing*?"

"Hetty . . ." He touches my hand; the shock of his skin on mine is electric. He looks hard into my eyes. "The bakery will no longer sell us bread. The greengrocer refuses us entry. Haven't you seen the signs, NO JEWS, outside so many shops? They permit dogs, but not us. I don't want pity; I just want you to see how it is. The truth is, we are barely getting by."

"But . . . There are Jewish shops. And department stores. What about those?"

"Yes, but most have been taken from their Jewish owners, or shut down. If I go there, I risk being set upon by SA thugs." His jaw is set and his eyes become angry. He laughs harshly, his face red. "And you berate *me* for stealing a few vegetables?"

His anger hits me like a fist in the belly, and I shrink from him.

"I'm sorry." He stretches his hands toward me. "I didn't mean to . . . God, you're the last person I want to think badly of me." And there, suddenly, is the Walter who saved my life, open and honest. Not angry at me, but at life. His face crumples. "We just have to hope these times will pass, and things will become . . . normal again."

Can it be so wrong to take a few vegetables if you are denied the ability to buy any? whispers a tiny voice. I silence it.

"I really must get back now." I speak into an uncomfortable silence. The temperature is climbing and Kuschi pants gently at my side.

"Of course." Walter glances around and then looks at his basket. "Me too. This is rather conspicuous."

We stroll back to the humpbacked bridge where we will go our separate ways, me across the river back to Gohlis, and Walter, right, toward his grandmother's house on Hindenburgstrasse. I'm strangely aware of my body: the shortness of my legs, the messiness of my hair, my thin arms, the fat feel of my tongue in my mouth, a strange tingling sensation on my skin.

"How is Karl?" Walter asks suddenly. "He must have his Arbitur by now and be off to university soon?"

"Yes. He did well, but Karl is going to join the Luftwaffe." It's impossible to keep the pride from my voice.

"A pilot, eh? He'll do well, I'm sure."

"He reached a high rank in the Flieger-HJ. The Luftwaffe recruited him because he was so well thought of."

"Remember the games we used to play, Hetty? Cowboys and Indians? We always argued over who would have the pistol, and who the bow and arrow." He shakes his head and smiles to himself.

"You used to let me be the doctor-squaw. I'd scrub your feet and treat your war wounds. Afterward I'd make you mud pie dinners!"

"Very delicious they were too." Walter laughs.

We reach the bridge. He opens his mouth to say something, then closes it again. We stare at each other and I shuffle my feet. The silence stretches. Not taking his eyes off mine, Walter reaches out for my hand and solemnly shakes it. I feel a flicker of illicit excitement at his touch and don't want to let go.

"Well, it's been very nice to see you." He slips his hand away. "I'm sorry things are as they are, but I wish you well. Goodbye, Hetty." He smiles and gives a half wave of his hand as he turns, shoves his hat on his head, and walks away.

I watch him walk three steps.

"Wait! When will I see you again?" I burst out. Then I shrivel and bite my lip.

Walter stops and turns.

"You really want to see me again?"

"Only if you want to. I know it's probably not a good idea."

"You can say that again!"

"I mean, we shouldn't."

"We definitely shouldn't." He leans against the rough wall of the bridge and slides his free hand into his pocket, crossing one leg in front of the other. "It would be very dangerous. Especially for me. A dastardly Jew caught with a beautiful young German woman? I know of a Jew who was recently dragged from his house and beaten for being too friendly with the daughter of a tax inspector."

Beautiful. Young woman.

Can he really think me beautiful?

"But you're worth the risk," he continues with a broad smile. "How about we meet at seven, next Sunday morning, here by this bridge?"

"I'll be away at camp with the Bund Deutscher Mädel. My parents never wanted me to join, but after it became compulsory last December for all Aryan children, they had no choice but to let me."

"In two weeks' time then?"

"In two weeks, yes."

"But not a word to anyone." Walter waggles a scolding finger at me, his face stern.

I nod and walk quickly away over the little bridge, turning toward the slowly waking city.

"Come on, Kuschi," I call, looking back over my shoulder. Walter is walking away, square shouldered, basket at his side. He glances back and grins when he sees me looking. My heart skips and I am weightless, all the way back to Fritzschestrasse.

Twelve

August 3, 1937

E rna's tread crackles on the rocky path behind me.
"Isn't this glorious?" she asks. Her face shines with perspiration but her plaits are still neat, her uniform tidy.

The boulder-ridden path rises steeply ahead. The glory in these Bavarian hills has begun to pall after walking uphill for hours in a heat wave. I can smell my own rancid sweat. I wipe my handkerchief around the back of my neck, lifting away damp clumps of loose, frizzy hair from the remnants of my plaits.

"My feet are in shreds," I reply. "New boots. Should have broken them in before we left," I add, wincing with each step.

"Good for the soul. It'll strengthen your character."

"My character was doing just fine *without* blisters, thanks very much." Tears prick at the back of my eyes.

Erna glances behind her, but the rest of the girls in our BDM schar are spread out and the leaders are up ahead, so there is no one to witness my moment of weakness. "Come on, Hett, we must be nearly at the top. Just one last push and we can set up camp. Remember, Herr Hitler wants us girls fit, brimming with health and vitality."

"When we get there, I just want to lie down."

"You are funny, Hett." Erna laughs.

"I'm not joking!" With every step, the backs of my boots rub the raw skin on my heels.

"Come on, you moody old thing. Look happy; Fräulein Ackermann is up ahead. She might even award you a badge, if you put in some hard work and give her a dazzling smile or two . . ."

I follow Erna's strong back as she strides up the narrow path. My tongue sticks to the roof of my mouth and I'm certain my breath is as sour as my mood. Not for the first time, Erna appears to read my mind and in her crisp, clear voice begins to sing "*Wanderlied der Jugend.*"

> *When we stride along side by side and sing the old songs*
> 　　*that echo in the forests,*
> *We feel it must succeed: with us, a new time comes . . .*

The joyful melody lifts my spirit and my feet begin to move in time with the familiar beat that plays in my mind along with her words.

> *Birch leaves and green seeds.*
> *How the old mother earth, as if with pleading gestures,*
> *holds out her full hands to humanity, so that it becomes*
> 　　*her own.*

We scramble up the last steep slope, arriving at the top with heaving chests and sweat dripping down our backs.

"Good work, you two." Fräulein Ackermann beams at us as we pass. "There's a surprise up ahead. I'll give you a clue; it's refreshing and wet!"

"A waterfall." Erna smiles as we leave her to hustle the rest of the girls to the top.

The campsite is on a wide, flat ridge. Grass grows sparsely between the rocks. The ground slopes down toward a large pool. Erna is right; it's fed by a beautiful waterfall.

In dribs and drabs the rest of the group arrive. On the flattest part, after clearing away the worst of the stones, we pitch our tents, dig a hole for a latrine, and fetch water for cooking and preparing the food.

"Resilient. Tough. Independent. Girls worthy to be the mothers of the master race. That's what our Führer wants you to be." Fräulein Ackermann drills us once the work is done and we are all assembled, dusty and tired. "And never forget the BDM principles: purity, cleanliness, virtue, obedience, and compliance. Now, go and take a dip in the pool. You've earned it!"

Yes, and a good German girl never questions or complains. She always acts for the good of her community. Girls must be tall and strong and beautiful, without enhancement. We must be clean and look after our hygiene. We must be modest and demure. Above all, a girl must always put menfolk first and support them in their struggle. However tired we are, however hard we have worked, their needs must come before our own.

Our duty is to serve the Führer, Germany, and our future husbands. Boys learn to govern and be leaders; we must be compliant. The demands are constant; there is no time to follow my own path.

I cannot help but feel the essence of *me* is slowly being sucked out.

We gather our towels and hurry down the rocky slope, following the sound of rushing water.

Doing the right thing means personal sacrifice. Give up what you want, for the good of all.

I shake my head, try to clear it. Still He lives inside my skull. The Führer who sees everything. My deepest fears, my hopes and dreams. And some of the thoughts I've had since that Sunday, I really don't want him to know.

"Look around you, Hetty. We are truly on top of the world," Erna says.

All around us are hazy mountains and deep green valleys. The glassy black curve of a lake lies in a basin thousands of feet below. Above, craggy rocks jut skyward, and thin strips of white cloud float lazily in a clear blue sky.

This is the land of the gods. There is something cleansing in the scenery.

"It's sublime," I admit.

"Now let's swim," she says, and I watch her as she walks toward the pool, her auburn plaits flickering gold, her back long and shoulders strong. She is the sun, a beautiful, golden orb drawing everyone toward her. I'm in her shadow. A little planet sucked into her orbit, resentful of her power, and yet I can't help but love her. Her purity and honesty. Her positivity.

She is so much better than me.

I wish I could tell her about Walter. Ask her advice. Just five more days until we are due to meet on the bridge.

A dastardly Jew caught with a beautiful *young German woman . . .* I can see his mouth form the words. His lips pursing, eyes taking me in.

I cannot tell her. Or anyone. I promised not to. But it's so hard. Boys only ever notice Erna. Never me. And Walter isn't just *any* boy. He has good looks. He is brave, manly. He could be the epitome of the Aryan ideal. It would be so easy to forget what he really is.

I pretend he isn't a Jew and imagine us together, figures lit up as if in a movie. There's an intense look in his eye, then his lips are on mine. He says to me, *Hetty, please be mine. I have never felt this way about a girl before.* His hands are around my waist, but he begins to slide them lower and I say to him, *Walter, stop. I am not* that *sort of girl.* And, of course, he does stop, because he loves me, but—

"*Hetty!* What on earth are you waiting for? It's so refreshing in here!"

Erna is treading water, her hair slick and dark as spray from the waterfall falls on her head like a torrential downpour.

"Coming!" I remove my boots and wriggle out of my skirt. The other girls fling off their clothes, right down to their undergarments, and leap into the water, shrieking and squealing, chattering and laughing. I peer into the black depths. *You are a strong swimmer now.* I remove my neckerchief, unbutton my sweat-soaked shirt, and pull off my woolen socks one by one, carefully folding everything and finding a spot to place them neatly on the rocks. *You have no reason to be afraid.*

I stand in my underclothes, puny and exposed, at the edge of the dark water. The granite rock, warm beneath the soles of my feet, is reminiscent of that sun-warmed jetty all those years ago. Terror hovers and my legs begin to quiver. I cannot let anyone know I'm afraid. I close my eyes and launch myself off the rock, far out into the center of the pool.

The shock of the icy water takes my breath away, as it once did before, and I plunge downward. I uncurl, fighting the panic, kicking frantically for the surface.

I shoot up into the light, taking huge gulps of air, still kicking hard. I can almost feel those strong hands, pulling me up, away from that hideous watery end.

"Hey! Move out of the way down there!" someone shouts from above. I look up, pulling my body vertical. Erna and three others are seated high up on a rock next to the waterfall, ready to jump. I swim out of the way and watch the four girls plummet through space and crash into the pool. The water swallows them, bubbling in the place they entered. A second's pause and they shoot to the surface, laughing, gasping, and wiping water from their eyes. They have no fear, and suddenly I hate my own.

I flip onto my back and float, gazing into the azure sky, trying not to think about the terrifying volume of water between me and the solid earth. It laps around my head and seeps into my ears. The cold numbs and soothes my aching limbs. What I would give to be having a long soak in a mineral bath, then to fall naked into Walter's arms . . .

Hell! What depraved thoughts are these? *Give me strength, oh Führer, to banish this evil from my mind.* My heart beats in double quick time.

The personification of the devil as the symbol of all evil assumes the living shape of the Jew. Hitler's words rattle through my mind. *By defending myself against the Jew, I am fighting for the work of the Lord.*

It's so hard. Dirty visions spring, unbidden, into my head. They are grubby and wrong.

I try to focus on the white clouds drifting high above me. A movement in the distance catches my eye. Three black dots in a "V" shape, traveling low and fast across the sky. Fighter planes. Perhaps they're off to join the war in Spain. Deep in the peace of the countryside, that real war, happening so far away, is surreal. And what of this bigger war that Vati alludes to? One right here in Germany, and all over the world. A war to right the wrongs of Versailles and to restore Germany to its rightful place as leader of the world. A war to crush the ambitions of the Jews. My stomach twists.

"Erna," I say urgently, "I need to talk to you about something. It's private." I glance at the bevy of girls bobbing nearby.

"Of course. Come on, let's go and get dry. I don't know about you, but I'm freezing."

We dry ourselves beside the pool and dress quickly under the late afternoon sun.

"So what's eating you, Hett? I knew you weren't yourself."

I check there is no one in earshot. Most of the girls are still in the pool. The few that are out are already dressed and making their way back to the campsite. Now is the time.

"The thing is . . ."

I remember my promise to Walter that I wouldn't tell a soul. Erna is a BDM leader. Even if she didn't *want* to report us, she has the duty to do so. And knowing how seriously she takes it . . . she would see Walter just like everyone else.

As the enemy.

"Hetty?"

"Oh. You know. It doesn't matter anymore. It's . . . well, no, I've changed my mind."

Erna spreads her wet towel, slip, and panties on the warm rock to dry.

"All right then. Suit yourself." There's hurt in her voice. "If you change your mind *again*, you know where to find me. I'm going to supervise the cooking."

She strides toward the campsite and doesn't wait for me.

Give me strength, oh great Führer, to resist temptation. I'm sorry for my depraved thoughts. Show me the way, and I will follow. Wherever that takes me.

I will not go back to meet Walter on Sunday. Consorting with a Jew is against every law and principle in the land. If we were caught together, Walter would risk being sent to a dreaded concentration camp, or worse, he might face a firing squad. Besides, I want to be good, honest, and pure. My thoughts about Walter are disgusting. They sicken me. I want no more of them.

LATER THAT EVENING, we sit around the campfire and sing songs. I sing with gusto, louder and louder, surrendering my soul to the music, closing my mind to all thoughts but the rhythm and words. By the time we reach the last, I feel cleansed. Refreshed. Filled with new vigor to be a better person and put the weakness I suffered earlier behind me, forever.

> *We all stay in solidarity under our shining flag.*
> *There we find ourselves as one people.*
> *No one goes alone anymore.*
> *We all stay in duty to God, the Führer, and the blood.*
> *Firm in conviction of faith, happy in work that each does.*
> *We all want to be as one: Germany, you shall stay alight.*
> *We will see all of our honor in your bright light.*

Thirteen

August 7, 1937

Erna lives on the top floor of an apartment block just off Kirchplatz. The flat isn't large, but it is light and airy.

"I'm so glad you could come!" Erna grabs my hand and pulls me straight up the stairs to her bedroom. The ceiling slopes on both sides and four little dormer windows are punched through, peeking out under the overhanging eaves. I glance out at sweeping views over the treetops, roofs, and chimneys of Leipzig.

Erna flops onto her bed and holds herself up on one elbow, her chestnut hair falling like a curtain behind her. She beams at me.

"I'm in love, Hett!" she announces, her cheeks flushed. "Madly. I've not told anyone else, but I had to tell you!"

"So who's the lucky man?" My heart beats a little faster as a vision of Walter's keen blue eyes flashes unwanted into my mind.

"His name is Kurt. He lives on the other side of Leipzig. He's a *total* dish. Impeccable manners, *and* he's rich."

"Heavens. He sounds perfect . . . does he have any friends?"

Erna laughs. "Maybe. But don't tell anyone. Please. No one can know."

"Why not? What's the problem?"

"My parents would have a fit. They're very old-fashioned, and I'm only fifteen. They wouldn't approve of me cavorting around on my own with a boy. And he's older—eighteen." She sighs. "But oh, I'm bursting with happiness, Hetty. It's the best thing that's ever happened to me."

Really. And such things always happen to you, Erna.

When she's run out of things to say about the perfect Kurt, we go to inform her father, a round pebble of a man in the sitting room, that we are going to meet friends in town. He's drinking a cup of coffee and reading a newspaper—not the *Leipziger Tageszeitung*, but the *Völkischer Beobachter*, a national morning newspaper. Erna chooses not to mention that the friends are boys from the Hitler Jugend, even though they are just that. Friends. On the front cover of his newspaper is a full-page spread devoted to the seven-hundred-year anniversary celebrations of the city of Berlin. Pictures of the parades and displays of the mighty German army take up half the broadsheet page. He doesn't look up.

"Listen to this, Erna." Herr Bäcker chuckles, smoothing a hand over the shiny skin of his bald head. He reads out a section about the tour of a group of men from a place called Worcestershire in England who have traveled to Berlin to play a game called cricket. "The English team claim the Germans have been unsportsmanlike. They complain about German gamesmanship," he says, wrinkling his forehead, "and yet they enjoy all the delights of the famous Berlin nightlife."

"Vati . . ." Erna scolds. "You shouldn't say such things . . ."

He ignores her and continues talking as he scans the print with the paper held out above his ample belly. He doesn't seem to have noticed me. "What did we expect? To make friends with the British over a game of cricket, a beer, and a Berlin prostitute? Ha! The insanity of our leaders, beggars all belief—"

His words are so shocking I freeze in the doorway.

"*Vati!*" Erna tries again.

But Herr Bäcker rants on. "Still, I suppose if you put a bunch of stupid, crazy, drunken madmen, who have failed at all else in life, in charge of running our country, what else can one expect? Ruination and disaster, that's what."

Erna's eyes are wide with alarm. "Vati, you mustn't . . . Please stop."

"Damned Nazis. Bloody Hitler," Herr Bäcker says fiercely to the newspaper, shaking its pages in anger.

"*Vati!*" Erna's voice cracks like a whip around the room. At last he looks up from the paper, openmouthed in surprise, and sees me standing there before him, in my BDM uniform. "You must not talk so," Erna says more softly and tips her head toward me. "You remember my friend Hetty?"

"Eh, er . . ." He clears his throat and begins to fold the paper. "I . . ." He laughs nervously and peers at me through narrowed eyes as though I'm fuzzy and out of focus. "You're a friend from school, are you?"

"Yes, Herr Bäcker," I reply quietly, but my heart thrashes wildly and a sweat breaks out.

Who is this man spouting such vile talk? Is this what the

enemy looks like? Not a red Bolshevist pushing the cause of Communist revolution. Not a rich, hook-nosed, pig-eyed Jewish conspirator. Just an ordinary, middle-class, nondescript nobody. The father of my best friend. In how many other houses, behind closed doors, are such attitudes held and whispered? How can we ever hope to overcome the treachery of ignorant fools like this?

"Hmm. Well, apologies, Helga, my tongue runs away with me sometimes."

"Hetty," Erna corrects him. "Hetty *Heinrich*."

"Hetty Heinrich," he repeats slowly, wrinkling his brow. He clutches the newspaper more tightly. "Ignore me, Hetty. I'm just . . . I don't mean any harm by it, do I, Erna?"

"No, Vati." Erna's voice is low with shame.

There's an awkward silence. Herr Bäcker smooths and folds the paper.

"We're going out, Vati. I'll be back in time for lunch, before this afternoon's BDM meeting," Erna says and shoos me from the room.

Out on the street, her face is pinched and pale. "My father doesn't mean what he says. He's old and silly. I don't think he even knows *what* he is saying most of the time." The air is stiff. We walk slowly, and in time. Heel, toe. Heel, toe, our rubber-soled shoes quiet on the pavement.

"It's okay, Erna, there is no need to explain."

. . . *Insanity of our leaders. Damned Nazis. Bloody Hitler.* The words jolt and jar in my brain. Is this what Erna has grown up listening to? Why has she never said?

"He's just a stupid old man," she cries out. Her words

stop me in my tracks. Her face is puffy, red. She's angry. Or humiliated. Probably both, but I've never heard her speak in ugly terms about anyone before, let alone her own father. Poor Erna. "Look, Hetty." She turns toward me, pleading. "I know you, well, *we*, are under a duty to report such talk and all that, but . . ."

How can she, Erna the Enviable, the Perfect, say *nothing*! I think of Tomas and how brave he was to speak up about *his* father. Perhaps, if Erna doesn't have the guts, I should do it myself. It wouldn't be hard. Vati would be pleased with me. I picture him telling Karl and Mutti about how I am a true child of the Reich. But the glow is quickly extinguished by the thought of losing Erna forever as my friend. How bleak, how meaningless life would be without her.

I place my hand on her arm. "I won't say a word."

"He doesn't really mean it . . ."

"Your vati's secret views are safe with me, I promise," I add, giving her arm a squeeze.

Her face relaxes and she flashes me a quick smile.

We say no more about it, walking in silence until we arrive at the tram stop where a man and woman wait. I sense there's been a power shift between us. She isn't so perfect after all. She's been holding things from me. Her father's allegiances are clearly not with Hitler, and she's kept quiet about it. She isn't as pure of heart as I'd thought. Does that make us equal? I wonder how many other clandestine secrets we each hold inside. Insidious truths hidden from each other like festering wounds, blackening our hearts and keeping us from the honest purity every good German girl should strive for.

Perhaps *this* is the reason she remains my friend. She's not too good for me, after all.

Forgive me, Führer. I know what I should do, but this is Erna and she is my best friend. I can't hurt her.

I picture the Führer's vivid blue eyes staring into my own, searching my soul and seeing that my intentions are good.

Do not worry, he announces, *this man is not of importance. I have bigger enemies to fight. Together, we shall beat them all.*

WE MEET TOMAS and three of his HJ friends at a table outside Coffe Baum on Kleine Fleischergasse. The weather is still balmy as we sit and watch the people of Leipzig stroll along the narrow, cobbled street. A waitress brings a tray of water, hot coffee in silver pots, warm milk, and sugar.

Erna sits next to me. She is quiet and withdrawn. I feel her neediness. Her reliance on me to keep quiet. *Wissen ist macht.* Knowledge is power. It's a new sensation, a reversal. I'm the witty one this morning, filling the air with chat and laughter. The boys are reveling in *my* company.

"I've started my apprenticeship at the machine tool factory," Tomas tells us in a lazy drawl. "Only two weeks in and I'm bored as pig shit already. Pardon my language," he says, looking at me. "I've barely set eyes on a tool, just swept the floor for fourteen days straight. Only three years of this before I get released to do my two years with the Wehrmacht. Can't wait for that. Just hope the war hasn't been and gone before I get there. Knowing my pig-sucking luck, it will have."

Every boy's dream is to fight for Germany.

"Surely it can't be that bad. I mean, you won't have to sweep floors for three whole years, will you? That wouldn't be much of an apprenticeship," I say, generously ignoring the second swear word. Inevitable, I suppose, mixing with foulmouthed factory workers.

"They like to start you at the bottom. So you feel like you're working your way up. You know, from the toilet pit, to the rim, so to speak. I'm not staying there forever, though. I've got ambition. I'll do better in the Wehrmacht."

"Did you hear about Dr. Kreitz?" Erna suddenly asks.

"Haven't heard his name in a long time." I shake my head, remembering the crazy old literature teacher. "He was a teacher at our school," I explain to the boys. "He got kicked out, ages ago. He made lessons . . . fun, interesting. There are no teachers like him left anymore."

"Committed suicide," Erna exclaims in a rush. "Hung himself by the neck!" She clasps her own throat and demonstrates the facial expressions of a dead Dr. Kreitz.

"Oh, but that's terrible! Why would he do such a thing?" I picture Dr. Kreitz, all disheveled and enthusiastic. How could he be dead?

"Couldn't get another job. Apparently, he and his wife were starving to death. The SS were after him, on account of his *suspect* political views." There is discomfort in her eyes.

"That's sad," I reply carefully. "I liked Dr. Kreitz."

Hermann, a sallow-faced boy with pockmarked skin, shrugs. "I hear loads of people are finishing themselves off these days. Especially Jews. They want to avoid a *worse fate*. But what could be worse than killing yourself?" He takes a sip of water and stares at me. There's an uncomfortable silence.

"The SS must do their job, and they do it bloody well," Tomas suddenly growls. "I've personal experience of that, right? We should keep our noses out of their business."

We all look at Tomas in surprise.

"Sorry, didn't mean to offend," Hermann says with a sniff.

"Anyway," adds Tomas gruffly, "who gives a damn if a few Jews or other wastrels top themselves? A few less of the swine to worry about." He glances at the clock on the wall of the tall building opposite. "We should go. We don't want to be late for our HJ meeting."

The other boys agree and there's a shuffling and scraping of chairs as they make to leave.

Tomas's eyes linger on me a little longer than necessary, then he turns his back and I watch him and his friends walk toward the tram stop on Markt. Poor Tomas, taller now, but still awkward and skinny, he's hardly the Aryan ideal. But the way he just spoke up for me then, it seems he looks out for *me* now, the way I once looked out for him.

"He's sweet on you," Erna remarks, watching him go. "What a catch!" She giggles for the first time since we've been here. "Secret sweethearts, eh." She elbows me, teasingly, and I swipe her arm away, angrily, heat rising to my cheeks.

"I should go too." I turn away. "I'm having lunch at home before this afternoon's meeting. Sorry, Erna, I shan't walk. It'll be quicker on the tram."

I hurry toward the tram stop with an odd sense of deflation. It's an irritation, a discomfort. It could be Karl's imminent departure. Or the revelation about Erna's father. Or the news of Dr. Kreitz. Or Erna's teasing about Tomas being my sweetheart. Or perhaps it's because I decided I'm not going to meet Walter in the morning. Maybe it's just the hot weather.

The carriage is crammed with sweaty workmen in overalls traveling home after their shift, through the city center toward the main train station. They've come from the factories and warehouses in Plagwitz and Lindenau. I squeeze into a space near the door and hold my breath as my nose slots under the armpit of a fat, hairy man hanging on to one of the leather straps dangling from the roof.

"Hey, miss!" calls a voice from farther inside the carriage. "There's a seat just here, next to me by the window, if you fancy it?"

"It's okay, I'm only going a couple of stops," I reply, politely. The man is youngish. Dirty looking, with hungry eyes.

"Fine. Suit yourself." His voice, tinged with anger, carries the clipped tones of a Berlin accent. There are more and more harsh Prussian voices around Leipzig these days. Compared with the lighter, softer Saxon, their accent grates on the ear. As Vati wrote recently in the *Leipziger*, the burgeoning industry and wealth of Leipzig is enticing all sorts of people from far and wide to come, sniffing the possibility of a sound job and prosperity. But they bring with them bad morals, crime, and disease.

I wish I'd walked after all.

"Girls aren't what they used to be," the man moans in a loud voice to another, standing in the aisle. "All full of their own self-importance, now they're wearing uniforms. Girls in uniform? Pah! How *ridiculous*."

The other man glances over at me. I stare at my feet, feeling my face turn the color of beetroot. My blue BDM skirt swings as the tram lurches around a bend. The men laugh and another says, "BDM . . . it doesn't stand for *Bund Deutscher Mädel*. It stands for *Bubi Drück Mich!*"

Squeeze Me Laddie. How dare they?

"Let me give you a squeeze, girl, eh?" The first man, with the Berlin accent, laughs.

The other joins in. "I heard it was *Bund Deutscher Milchkühe!*" *League of German Milk Cows.* Half the carriage is laughing. I'm sweating now, burning with indignation, but I'm locked in a metal box with these dreadful, rough men. I peer out the window, trying to work out how far to the next stop, glad I'm still close enough to the door to make a quick getaway. Are these the sort of men Tomas works with? Please don't let him turn into one of them.

"Girls these days. Take last night. Group of girls in the bar, alone, no men with them. I politely offered to buy a young lady a drink. She laughed in my face! Just because she's in a uniform. They *all* laughed at me. Pff! Who the hell do they think they are? Young ladies? Nah, sows, the lot of them." The man with the Berlin accent again.

"Hey," he shouts to me, "you should be looking for a husband, girl, not strutting about in that stupid Nazi uniform!"

I long to yell something back at him. Something to put him in his place, like *I wouldn't choose* you *as my husband if you were the last man on earth* . . . but I don't dare. I just stare at my feet, willing the tram to go faster so I can get off it sooner.

"Oi." The fat hairy man, whose armpit is in my face, addresses the other men. "Watch your tongues," he says gruffly, "and leave the little lady alone. She's only a youngster." He turns and dips his big, round head toward me. He smells of beer and cigarettes. "You okay, girl?"

I nod, absurdly grateful to this rough gorilla-man for standing up for me. The tram slows for the next stop.

"I'm getting off here," I say quietly, not wanting the others to hear. "Thank you."

I jump out as soon as the tram screeches to a halt, thankful none of the men follow me. I take a long, deep breath of fresh air, delicious after the stale odor of male sweat and beer in the carriage. My legs are weak and I grab the spokes of a metal gate in front of me to steady myself.

I look up and see I'm standing at the entrance of a small Jewish cemetery. Someone has defaced a few of the gravestones. "Jewish Swine" is daubed over one. Another has been smashed into pieces. A third reads: "The only good Jew is a dead Jew!" and the one next to it, "Spill Jewish blood—the only way to solve the Jewish Problem." Hairs stand up at the back of my neck.

I think of the whispers of a Jewish conspiracy. Of not knowing what they plan, and when. Because this is the way they work, underhand and secretly, through the medium of foreign governments. Through revolutionary movements and unrest. Dividing and unsettling. Maneuvering themselves into power in all spheres of life. A bead of sweat tracks down my spine. Hitler *will* lead us to victory. He must.

I hurry away from this ill intent among the gravestones.

A vision of Walter floats in front of me as I walk. His soft, curly blond hair. His warm blue eyes. That smile. How polite and proper he is compared to those brutes on the tram. And they have the audacity to call themselves *German*.

Walter is *not* a normal Jew. He cannot be.

I'm certain he isn't part of this Conspiracy of International Jewry.

Where is his hooked nose and shifty eyes?

He is kind, handsome, and funny.

Perhaps he isn't a Jew. Maybe he is a *mischling*, a mix with Aryan blood, too. This would explain his looks. Maybe he doesn't even know it himself.

I turn into Fritzschestrasse and the thrill of rebellion suddenly flows through my veins. I *shall* meet him tomorrow morning. Just one last time, to say good-bye, and tell him we can't meet again. Nothing terrible happened last time, and no one will ever know.

To simply not turn up would be rude.

And I have been brought up to have good manners.

Fourteen

August 8, 1937

I am standing on a high, narrow rock. Behind, a meadow of lush grass and wildflowers. Ahead, the rock falls steeply away into a deep emerald valley. Tight bands of conifers grow vertically on the steep slopes. At the bottom is the winding silver strip of a river, shimmering in the sunlight.

A tiny figure stands on the riverbank, waving both arms above his head. He is urging me to come down and join him.

Walter.

The breeze tugs my hair and the sun is warm on my face. The tang of freedom is in the air, and I'm giddy with it. I close my eyes and tip forward until I reach the point where I cannot change my mind. I begin to fall, slowly at first, then faster; the air rushes and roars. I'm arching forward, but something isn't right. I open my eyes and Karl is there, in a glider, sailing toward me, blocking my way . . .

I wake with a start. Pushing myself upright, I peer at the hands of the clock on the mantelpiece, but it's only five thirty-five. I flop back onto the pillow, the vividness of the dream still with me. It isn't too late. I could stay here, and everything will be the same. Or I can go, and everything will be different.

Be a good girl. Clean of mind and body. Don't stray into the path of evil. Be meek. Act only for the welfare of others. That's what *He* would tell me. I lie still and wait for his voice. Nothing. I prop up my pillows and recline against them, looking toward Hitler's portrait over the mantelpiece. It's fuzzy and unclear in the half-light seeping around the edges of the closed shutters. Still nothing.

My mind is blank. Empty. Quiet. Blissfully quiet. Could that be permission? Really, what harm can there be? It's just a walk with an old friend. Nothing more.

I'M EARLY OF course. Ridiculously so. What will Walter think? That I'm too eager? I hope my long skirt, high buttoned blouse, and shapeless jumper will convince him otherwise. God forbid that he should know what thoughts have really crossed my mind.

I throw a stick for Kuschi. He brings it back, drops it at my feet, and whines until I throw it again. I hurl it into the river and he bounds in, swimming hard against the current to grab it before it floats away. He has no fear of water.

A sound on the road: a stone clipped by a shoe, scattering across tarmac.

It's him. Striding up the lane with his hands in his pockets, hat pulled low over his forehead. He looks up and smiles.

A million butterflies flutter in my belly.

"You came," he says.

"So did you."

He laughs, I laugh, and everything melts. My insides, the nippy air, the trees and the hedgerows, the road, the bridge— all soften and bleed together, warmed and muted, running like wet paint on a canvas.

"Let's walk," he says, and we fall into step on the path. We follow the river through a wood where the roofs of scattered houses can be glimpsed through a dense tangle of branches, marking the edge of town. From here the river flows out into wide, undulating farmland. With each step, we put distance between us and Leipzig, and I feel a rising, glorious sense of liberty.

"How was summer camp?" he asks.

"It was okay." I pause, unsure of how much I should reveal of the BDM to an outsider. A possible enemy of the Reich. We step in time with each other on the path.

"You don't seem very enthusiastic." He laughs. "But that doesn't surprise me."

"Why not?" I decide to go along with his misinterpretation.

"Because you always were different. Special different, I mean. Like how you ran out of school that awful day and chased after Freda and me . . ." He swallows hard.

"It was a long time ago, Walter," I say quietly. "I've changed."

He continues as though he didn't hear. "I always admired that about you. Your independence of mind. Your spirit and passion. The way you dreamed of becoming a doctor, even though it was impossible. I knew you were smart, questioned things. Definitely not a blind follower of rules." He pauses. "I can tell that you, of all people, see the truth behind the rhetoric."

I glance at him. His words make my skin feel hot. No one has ever spoken so openly to me. Besides, he makes flaws like independence and questioning of rules sound like *good* qualities.

"How could you notice all that, when you never took the slightest bit of interest in me?" I ask.

"Who said I never took any interest in you?"

"You barely noticed I existed."

He shakes his head and smiles. "Well, that's where you are entirely wrong, Miss Herta," he says with a wink. "I noticed much more about you than you might imagine."

I feel my cheeks redden.

"So what do you plan to do when you leave school?" Walter asks, changing the subject.

"I'd like to go to university"—I sigh—"but Vati doesn't want me to. Besides, it's terribly complicated to get to university these days if you're a girl. And Vati would need to approve. Of course, I've had to give up that silly dream of being a doctor. How I wish I'd been born a boy."

"I'm rather glad you weren't." I feel his eyes on me and my skin burns even hotter. "I think you would make an excellent doctor," he adds.

"And how on earth would you know that? You haven't seen me since I was twelve."

Herr Metzger's warnings flicker through my mind. Should I be wary of these compliments? Is he trying to ingratiate himself?

"People don't change," Walter is saying, "not deep down. You're still the same girl inside, I'm sure of it. Anyway, do you want to know the thing I *really* used to like about you?" He's smiling again.

"What?"

"You laughed at *all* my jokes. However bad they were, and some were truly dreadful. That's earned you a special place in my heart."

I smile. "And do you still tell terrible jokes?"

"Of course!" He puts his head to one side and looks at me. "Did you hear about the dog who used to chase people on bikes?"

I shake my head.

"In the end," he says, looking deeply serious, "they had to take his bike away!"

"Oh, you tease!" I laugh. "I see the jokes haven't improved. And are *you* the same boy you always were?"

"Absolutely."

"Oh? So do you still strip down to your underwear in front of girls before you swim in the lake? And do you still get cross and stamp your feet when you can't be the cowboy with the rifle, because you have to be the Indian with just a bow and arrow?"

"Yes. Most certainly. And what, Miss Herta, is wrong with that?" He swipes playfully at my arm. "Everyone knows it's much better to be the cowboy with the proper weapon. And besides, it will be a very lucky girl who gets to see *me* in my underwear!"

Blushing furiously now, I begin to run so he can't see my face. I call over my shoulder, "Race you to the big tree!"

Kuschi barks with excitement and shoots off down the path

ahead of me. I focus on the tree, chin up, pumping my arms and legs. But his feet thump closer and closer behind me. In a flash, he is overtaking and accelerates away, finishing lengths ahead. I might as well have been walking.

He waits by the tree, hands on hips, chest rising and falling. "As I recall," he says with a wink, "you never did beat me at running."

"Well, you obviously haven't learned when it's polite to let a girl win!"

"And if I had? I'd've let you win on purpose, and you wouldn't have liked that, either."

It's just like being twelve years old again.

I march straight past him and he runs to catch up. "See?" he says. "I've proved my point. People don't really change as much as they think they do."

He's right, of course. I would have felt cheated. I give him a lighthearted thump, and without really understanding why, we are both laughing once again, and I'm glad he won. He is the boy, after all.

We follow the course of the river through a field of ripening yellow wheat. It's waist high and grows right up to the edge of the path. Kuschi dives into it, chasing something. He disappears, reemerging farther up the path, tongue lolling from his mouth.

There is not another soul to be seen, and the city is far behind us. Walter's presence is bedazzling. So easy, but alarming. Like being with a rare and magnificent tiger. It seems tame, and I'm enthralled by its beauty, but it has the power to destroy me.

"Is it true," I ask quietly, "what they say? About this Con-spiracy of International Jewry to take over the world?"

"Well, if there is one, I'm certainly not a part of it. Nor anyone else I know."

I laugh at my own stupidity. Of course he wouldn't tell me, even if he was part of it.

"Seriously, Hetty, you can't *really* believe these lies?" He looks at me with worried eyes.

I think carefully before speaking. *He* might be different, but the rest of his kind are to be feared.

"We've suffered. Us Germans, I mean. Ever since the punishment of Versailles. So much poverty and hardship as a result."

"You say *us Germans*," Walter says, plucking a head of wheat and pulling it apart, dropping the pieces at his feet as he walks. "Can't you see that I'm German, too? That is all I am. I'm more German, even, than you!"

"What on earth do you mean by that?"

"You have a French mother. My family have lived in Ger-many for generations. I've always been proud to be German. My father was decorated with the Iron Cross for his bravery in the war, fighting for *Germany*. And how has he been re-paid? By being stripped of his citizenship and his livelihood! We are *aliens* in our own country." His eyes are wide and he waves his hands with passion. He frowns and taps his temple. "Remind me. I forget—was your father decorated for bravery in the war?"

"No. He *was* brave though . . . He was overlooked for a medal. It was a travesty."

"Really. Well, he's doing all right now, isn't he? We, on the other hand, have seen our business destroyed, our lives turned upside down. Just imagine, for a moment, how that is, will you? Imagine your country wants to be rid of you. A devoted German citizen, yet you have nowhere else to go."

Satan is clever and has a way with words. Do not believe all that the devil seeks to tell you.

"What do you mean, stripped of your citizenship and livelihood? You're not making sense . . ." I imagine what Vati would say, were he listening to this.

Walter takes a deep breath. "They have taken away our passports, Hetty. If we want to leave the country, we must pay something called an exit tax."

"What's that?"

"Essentially, it's an exorbitant amount of money we would have to pay the government. We'd have to give them everything we own." Walter speaks slowly, patiently, as though I am a small child. "Our house, our valuables. They tax our business on its value back in 1930 when it was worth ten, twenty times what it is now. Being a Jewish business means banks, if they lend to us at all, charge us interest rates five times higher than any other business. And nobody will buy from us, other than a few loyal customers, mostly foreign ones. They have strangled us almost into bankruptcy. It's simply sheer determination not to be beaten that has kept my uncle and my father going these last few years."

"I think you are taking it all too personally," I find myself saying. "The Nazis have rescued the nation. I think you've forgotten the *dire* state we were *all* in after the war. You can hardly blame the Party when it was *the Jews* who were behind the shocking terms of the peace treaty that resulted in all our suffering—"

"Do you *really* think a bunch of conniving Jews forced the hands of those governments who signed that treaty?" Walter's face reddens as he speaks. He's angry. I have prodded the tiger. "According to our Führer, Jews are the instigators behind the tyranny of capitalism AND communism. Two opposing ideologies. Why? Ask yourself, Hetty. The Jews behind everything that is bad? It's simple and easy to blame us for all that is wrong. And people believe what they *want* to believe, whether the evidence is there or not."

His words sting, and I squirm beneath the force of them. But he's being unfair. *We're* not personally responsible for *his* family's bad fortune.

"Well, none of this is *my* father's fault. People have always been jealous of his success."

Walter stops walking. His eyes search my face. "You don't know, do you?"

"Know what?"

"How you came by your home."

"What do you mean? What's this got to do with anything?"

And now there he sits, like a lord, in his stolen house.

This is not how this morning is supposed to go.

"You *really* don't know, do you?" he repeats.

"Well, what then?" I shout at him. "If you know something, tell me! How can you blame me for not knowing something if I've not been told?"

"I'm sorry. I just thought . . ."

"Please tell me," I repeat, quieter now.

Wissen ist macht. Knowledge is power.

We walk again, side by side, along the dusty path.

He takes a deep breath. "The family who owned the house you now live in were Jewish acquaintances of my parents. They were much wealthier and better connected than us. Herr Drucker was the ultimate boss of your father. He owned and edited the *Leipziger Tageszeitung.* But the National Socialists don't like Jews controlling newspapers. So a number of people, your father and the mayor among them, got together and concocted stories about Herr Drucker to oust him. Corruption, tax evasion, that sort of thing. All made up, of course. The whole case went to court, heard by Judge Fuchs, a big supporter of the Nazi Party, who was only too happy to oblige with a favorable judgment against Drucker."

"These are terrible accusations!" I cry. "Why should I believe you?"

"You don't have to. But it's the inconvenient truth." The look in his eyes is honest. His expression hard. Is this the truth? Or what he *has been told* is the truth?

I look out across the wheat-gold field and remember the day we moved in. The fancy furniture, the artwork, the crystal and silver all left in the house. Like fitting pieces of a puzzle together, a picture emerges. Why would anyone leave such treasured things behind?

"So what happened to the Drucker family?" I ask. "Where are they now?"

"I've no idea. My guess is they left Germany."

"How could you know all this?"

"I remember it so well. The day my father told me what had happened. It was the very first time I felt fear. And shame."

"Shame?"

"I wanted to be like everyone else. Like Karl, I wanted to join the Hitler Jugend and do my bit for Germany. I didn't see why I should be excluded."

I look at him, and our eyes meet. I want to believe him.

I look away.

But I don't want to believe him. With all my heart, I don't.

Something twists in my chest and I want him to stop. "You're giving me a warped version of the truth. Vati got to where he is by sheer hard work. He's not some kind of . . . lazy criminal. You have to be wrong, Walter. You've been fed lies."

"Why would I tell you something so serious if it were wrong, Hetty? I have nothing to gain and everything to fear by telling you this. Think about it."

I watch the river flowing between the grassy banks.

"You must know, better than most," Walter adds, "where they send people who speak up against the authorities. Concentration camps. Without a proper, fair trial. Hard labor, terrible conditions. For indefinite periods of time. Rumor has it, they even carry out executions there. There's no doubt people are shot if they try to escape. The SS have recently opened another camp not so far away—near Weimar. Why would I risk telling you a pack of lies? You only need to say one word to your vati and—"

"Oh, Walter. I'd never do that," I interrupt. "Besides, I didn't know about these camps. Vati rarely talks of such things. To me, anyway."

Kuschi appears from the edge of the wheat field and nudges his nose into my palm. I scratch his ears as he walks beside me, then he dashes off again, disappearing beneath the waving wheat heads.

"If you knew all this at the time, why didn't you say something?" I ask. "Why did you stay friends with Karl and continue to visit?"

Walter sighs. "Because I was an idiot. I never told my parents I was around your house all the time. They'd have gotten mad at me if they knew. I was so ashamed to be Jewish. I didn't tell anybody, and I don't think Karl realized, not for a while, anyway. I don't look like the stereotype, so I suppose he had no reason to suspect . . . I desperately wanted to be like any other normal, patriotic German boy. It was only after he joined the Hitler Jugend, and I didn't, that he figured it out. One day, he just cut me off. He never explained." He presses his lips together and kicks at the ground. "He didn't need to."

We walk on in silence. I think of our big house, of which I have always been so proud. And Vati. Vati, who calls me Schnuffel and loves me. Vati, who tells us *all the time* how far he has come in this life. How honest, hard labor reaps great rewards and how Germany can be great once the selfish, dishonest Jewish race is banished and the terrible morals of inferior foreigners are wiped out.

And here he sits *in his stolen house*? Could it be true?

Walter looks at his watch. "We should head back," he says. "It's not that I want to, but . . ."

We've reached the end of the field. The path winds into the relative darkness of the woods that lie beyond.

"Yes. Me too."

We turn around and retrace our steps. Kuschi lollops past, long pieces of wheat heads sticking from his collar. He looks comical with the yellow fronds waving as he runs. We laugh at him, and the tension is gone. The air is peaceful once more and the morning floats with the sound of birdsong and the ripe, sweet smell of late summer.

Back at the bridge we stand facing each other. I run my fingers back and forth over the rough surface of the stone wall.

"Well. I guess this is it then," he says softly. "It was lovely to see you again."

"Yes. It's a shame . . ." I look into his face at last.

Those fine blue eyes.

The world tips, just a little.

"Let's shake hands and hope that sometime in the future we can be friends again." Walter extends his hand; his grip is warm and strong. I fight an urge to step closer and take a breath of him. Shaking hands is too formal.

"Walter," I begin, staring at my feet and his, facing each other on the dirt path. "Heaven knows what you must think of me, and I know it's mad and stupid, and wrong, but can't we meet here again, like this? There is no real harm, is there?"

"Hetty . . ."

His eyes are snug and warm, like home.

"It would be a total secret. I've told no one. I know how dangerous it is for you. I would never tell a soul, I promise. Please, Walter, can't we?"

He looks away and shakes his head.

There is silence for a long time.

At last he says, "Hetty, I would love to see you again. I would love to see you every day. Since we met two weeks ago, I have thought of nothing but you. But how can it possibly be? Your father is a high-ranking SS officer, for heaven's sake. I can't let you put yourself in any danger. As for me, I'd be completely done for if we were caught together. Let's put a stop to this before we get into anything . . . too hard to get out of."

He might as well stab me in the heart.

He takes my hand again, and this time, very lightly brushes his lips along the back of it.

Polite.

Old-fashioned.

Somehow, just right for Walter.

"Fine," I say, pulling my hand away. "But just in case you should change your mind, I shall walk Kuschi here at first light, every Sunday morning from now on, even in winter."

He stares into my eyes and with a sad smile says, "Good-bye, Hetty."

I turn quickly and cross the bridge without looking back, Kuschi a comforting presence by my side. And all the dull and tedious way home, I feel the lingering touch of Walter's lips on my skin.

Fifteen

I long to tell someone what's happened. But I can't. It's too dangerous and must remain a secret. I need to occupy my mind. I scan the bookshelf opposite my window seat. *Mein Kampf*, of course; *Volkstänze Lieder Spielmusik für Dorfabend und Fest*, my BDM song book; my unread copy of Hans Grimm's *Volk ohne Raum*. It should be read, I know, but it's over one thousand pages long. Within its covers lies the simple message that Germans, the cleanest, most honest and hard-working people in the world, do not have enough space to live a decent, honest life. More land is needed. An empire, no less. I'm sure the author could have given his message in half, or better, a quarter of those pages. There is a poetry collection by Agnes Miegel and several copies of the monthly magazine passed to me by Mutti, *Die Frau*, together with a few assorted school textbooks.

And there, nestled among them, is the journal Karl had given me the day of the Almost Drowning. I snatch it off the shelf. My only entry to date is the one I made three years ago,

when I devoted myself to Hitler's cause. I stare at my passion-
ate words. For one impulsive moment, I consider ripping out
the page. Instead, I turn it over, and on a new, blank page,
begin to pour out my heart.

*We couldn't stay away from each other. Two Sun-
days after you said we mustn't meet anymore,
you were there, standing by the bridge. I thought
it was a mirage, my imagination playing tricks.
But when I touched your arm, you were solid and
real and perfect. Last week, while everyone in the
house was still sleeping, I packed a picnic breakfast and we went to the fields. Thank goodness
Ingrid and Bertha had the day off! It was warm,
and we lay among the sweet-smelling, freshly cut
hay bales, completely alone, hidden from view. For
a short time it was almost possible to imagine we
hadn't a care in the world. We talked and talked,
not about politics, we steer clear of that, but about
everything else. I'm amazed at the similarities
between us—we both love spargel, sauerkraut,
and brägenwurst. I couldn't believe that you eat
pig meat, but you say your family isn't religious.
Like us, I suppose. Being a Jew, I thought you'd
be more different. But then, as you said, you are
more German even than me. Everyone says Jews
can't be German. Now I'm not so sure. Until now,
I've only heard one story. How strange it is to hear
yours of hardships and restrictions. You know so*

much that I don't. You quote poetry and know about philosophers (not just German ones), and you've read books I've never even heard of, about things and places I didn't know existed. You talk of painters like Klee and Kokoschka and writers like Kafka and Mann. Everything about you is new and interesting and exotic and extraordinary.

After we ate, you folded your jacket into a pillow and lay back, eyes closed, arms folded across your chest. I watched as you drifted into sleep. The gentle rise and fall of your chest. Your eyes tight shut, sunlight playing over your skin. I could have sat and watched you all day, but suddenly you woke, your body tight, eyes wide open, tense, and, reluctantly, we both knew it was time to go home.

"Miss Herta?" A knock at the door. Ingrid.

I snap my journal shut and hide it beneath a cushion beside me on the window seat.

"Come in," I say, arranging myself as though all I'm doing is staring out my window, contemplating the view.

She opens the door and stands there, giving me one of her looks. The insolent one. The one she wouldn't dare give to Vati, Mutti, or even Karl. I wonder if she somehow senses I'm hiding something. She has a viper look about her: thin face, beady eyes, and a tongue she flicks out to lick her lips, a sort of nervous twitch.

"Yes, what is it, Ingrid?"

"Didn't you notice it's dinnertime? Your mother sent me to check you're quite all right."

"I didn't hear the gong," I tell her without moving from my seat. "Please tell Mutti I'll be right down. I have to wash," I add, waving her away.

"As you wish." She bristles at my words and leaves the room.

I tuck the journal under the mattress and push it as far in as I can. With my deepest secrets in there, I can't risk it being found.

AFTER DINNER, KARL goes into town for a dance organized by his HJ schar. We move to the sitting room where Mutti drinks strong, black coffee, and Vati cradles his cognac.

I sit at the far end of the sofa, away from Vati's armchair. Smoke curls upward in the lamplight as Vati puffs on his cigar, spreading a thin cloud across the whole room. The sickly sweet, choking scent of it stings my nostrils and the back of my throat, making me cough.

"I'm starting a new venture in the *Leipziger*," Vati announces, stretching out his legs and allowing his belly to expand as he leans backward in the chair. "I'm calling it *The Moral Crusade!*" he says, sweeping a grand arc with his arm. "While Hitler looks outward to expand our nation abroad, we cannot let the enemy take advantage and continue to corrupt our way of life at its very core."

"It's about time something was done about this lowlife," Mutti mutters.

"I don't see any lowlife around in Leipzig," I say swiftly. I think of those brutes on the tram, but I don't mention them. Vati might stop me traveling around on my own.

"The underground music and art, the prostitution, the immoral literature. It's not limited to Berlin," Mutti comments.

"But here in *Leipzig*?" I ask.

"Yes, there is a blatant disregard for the law," Vati says. "The local police know what goes on, yet they do nothing about it. They report to Party officials or the municipal government. Letters get sent back and forth, people can't agree, and so nothing gets done."

"What does Lord Mayor Schultz think about it all?" Mutti asks.

"He and I are totally in agreement on this. We need *action*. Decisive action."

"Against what, though, Vati?" I ask.

Vati puffs on his cigar. "Moral degradation," he says, blowing out a cloud of smoke. "Leipzig is now Germany's fourth-largest city. It's a sprawling metropolis with workers from all over Germany. Plus more than our fair share of Poles, Russians, Slavs, Jews. They openly sabotage our laws, corrupt our young girls, drink to excess. A Jew was caught *this week* openly swimming in the city pool."

"Is that really so bad?" The words are out and Mutti and Vati turn to look at me. I shrink back against the cushions and hold my breath. Walter's smile. Those eyes. *Dirty Jew.* Is that what he is? Would everyone think the dirt, the smell has rubbed off on me? Why should it be so wrong for them to swim in the same pool, walk in the same park?

"We want Leipzig to continue to be a safe place for you to travel around alone." Vati waves his glass vaguely in my direction. "We've afforded you a great deal of freedom. Perhaps too much. You go off walking that dog of yours, all alone in Rosental . . ."

"But I'm completely safe, Vati."

"Herta." Vati looks at me sternly. "Do you know how many Jews remain living in this district alone?"

I shake my head.

"Two *thousand*! In Gohlis alone. With their loud voices and dirty habits. Despite all our efforts to get rid of them, they persist. Like vermin."

And they have never done me any harm, I want to shout at him. I've never once been approached. From what I've seen, they just go about their business, like anyone else.

"How can we be sure you'll be safe?" Vati continues. "Berlin has managed to rid *their* parks of them, so there is no reason why we shouldn't too. After all"—he puffs up and prods his chest with his index finger—"*I've* succeeded in ending the Jewish stranglehold on the press, a much bigger problem, so surely I can get them out of our parks, and make sure the police do their duty."

And you've stolen their houses.

This house.

"So what exactly will you do?" Mutti asks, cocking her head.

"I shall run a weekly column in the *Leipziger* to highlight all the issues. I'll remind the public of the law. Perhaps a different one each week. I'll invite people to write in with any . . . behavior or issues the authorities are failing to deal with. Like this one." He taps the newspaper and I catch sight of the headline: "Jews Disturb Quiet Leipzig Neighborhood to Conduct Religious Meetings in Empty Washhouse!" "I shall encourage every good German to keep their eyes and ears open for any hint of corruption or anti-German behavior, and to report it. Our journalists will investigate all allegations." He smiles. "Otto Schultz is most impressed with my initiative. He's invited you and me for drinks next Wednesday evening, Hélène. Party officials from all over Saxony will be there."

"But that's excellent news, Franz."

"They'll come forward in droves," Vati says with a flourish. "Especially the women. Ha! Women and their petty jealousies. You should see the letters I get. Many have more than a grain of truth in them, but not all. Investigating keeps the men busy and employed."

My stomach plunges at the thought of someone reporting Walter and me to Vati's newspaper.

"Actually, Franz," Mutti says, pouring another coffee from the pot, "I have a plan of my own that I've been wanting to discuss with you. I'm hoping you'll be able to help," Mutti says briskly. "And Otto Schultz, since he's such a fan of yours . . ." He nods for her to continue. "I've been speaking with the Mothers' Union of Leipzig. It seems there are too many . . . unwanted children. Good Aryan children— perhaps the offspring of young girls who've had a summer dalliance with those HJ boys." She shakes a hand dismissively. "They are of good, pure blood and should be raised in the right way. The *German* way, rather than left to chance and sent to undesirable families." She pauses for breath. "Similar state-run children's homes are being established in other cities, Munich, for example. So I think we should provide a home for children of the Führer, here, in Leipzig. We can even add a school, all overseen by the SS, to ensure the correct procedures are followed. What do you say, Franz?" Her eyes sparkle with excitement. "The soldiers' home is running well, and I need a new project. What could be better than children? After all, they are the future of the Reich."

Vati nods his approval. "Good idea. Of course, we shall need to have each child tested for racial purity. Let's discuss it with Schultz on Wednesday."

I don't want to hear any more. I want to be in my bed, in the dark, with my mind closed to all this. I want to be alone and free to think of Walter. I only want to think of him.

Sixteen

September 19, 1937

I wait in the gray light of dawn on the bridge. Steady rain is falling and Kuschi and I are quickly soaked through. I turn up the collar of my trench coat and tighten my belt. Kuschi regards me with sullen eyes, his head bent low, tail tucked between his back legs. He isn't a fan of the rain and would have preferred it if I'd left him curled in a tight circle in his basket.

"Sorry," I say to him as I stroke his head, "but you're my cover." He gives my hand a half-hearted lick.

By the time Walter arrives, Kuschi and I are shivering. He kisses me gently on the cheek and brushes a damp strand of hair out of my eyes.

"You both look miserable."

"Better now you're here."

He smiles, and all the doubts crowding my mind are rinsed away.

"Let's find somewhere dry. I can see you need warming up . . ." He frowns in thought. "There's that old hay barn on the far side of our wheat field. We could shelter in there. On a morning like this, we'll be sure to be all alone."

The thought of Walter warming me up makes me giggle, and I no longer care about being soaked to the skin. What *is* it about him that brings this lightness, this frivolity, this down-right recklessness to my spirit? It's a side of me I never knew existed.

We take the path by the river. Around us, the trees and fields are distilled through a glistening, rain-wet filter as the morning light grows stronger. Everything appears more beautiful than before. I curb the urge to break into song.

We reach the barn and Walter pushes open the door. I hesitate in the entrance. There's a musty, damp smell in the air and it's gloomy inside. I make out some bales of old hay in one corner and piles of rusting farm machinery in front.

"It's fine, Hetty. I'm not going to . . . take advantage, if that's what you're worried about," Walter says softly. "I mean, we don't have to go in. I just thought it'd be nice to be out of the rain."

"Oh." I look down at my shoes, mortified that he should think that I might think . . . "I trust you."

"Good."

I follow him inside. *Take advantage.* Is that what it's called? But what if *I* want it too? Are those images of the two of us that play in my head *normal*? I'm not supposed to want it. Not the way a man does.

Walter climbs up on the hay bales and spreads out his coat. He leans down with a grin and offers me a hand, helping me up next to him. Kuschi whines at us from below.

"Oh come on, you, too, dog." Walter pats the hay next to him and in three bounds, Kuschi is up and nestling himself next to Walter. I sidle closer on the other side, and Walter slips his arm around my waist, pulling me in tight. "Relax." I feel him smile. "Are you warm enough?"

"Yes." I rest my head on his shoulder.

After a moment's pause, he says, "I never thought sitting on moldy old hay, in a falling-down barn damp from the rain, could feel like a piece of heaven. But it does. Anywhere with you feels like that."

I laugh. "Don't tease!"

"It's true. I can forget who I really am."

"What do you mean?"

The air stills. We breathe. In, out. In, out, in harmony with each other.

"I don't know where to start," he says.

I reach for his hand. "Start from the beginning."

"I miss our flat," he says. "I miss *home*."

I remember the first time I went to Walter's flat, not long after the Almost Drowning. Coming from our run-down apartment, where the stench from the outside toilet was so bad you could smell it from the street, Walter's flat had seemed like a palace. Behind the smart, white façade was an elegance beyond my then imagination. As a treasured only child, Walter had always been destined for the gymnasium. He'd befriended Karl, really because the two had been the brightest in the class at volksschule. Had Vati not done so well at the newspaper, enabling him to afford gymnasium fees, Karl and Walter's friendship might have ended there.

The atmosphere in the flat had been warm and welcoming. I can picture Frau Keller, petite and pretty, with her light blue eyes and fair hair, cut to just above her shoulders and neatly curled in a fashionable style. In the high-ceilinged sitting room, I'd perched on the edge of a big armchair, scared to touch anything that might break. Frau Keller even had a maid who brought lemonade and delicate biscuits on a flowery tray. I remember Frau Keller playing the piano and laughing, her fingers dancing over the keys and the jolly tune she played. She had asked if I wanted to have a go at the piano. But I was much too shy and I'd just buried my head in Mutti's chest, hiding my eyes. I remember following the boys to Walter's room. The shelves of books, his neatly made bed. The old-fashioned furniture and the tall clock that ticked and chimed in the quiet of the elegant hall.

"I mean, I love my grandmother, and my extended family," Walter is saying, "but we don't have our own space anymore. To make ends meet we have to take in lodgers—it's our only income, really, as the business makes no money anymore. So I share a small room with my three cousins. They're children, noisy and annoying at times. Not their fault, but it's hard. And my grandmother is always on edge about having things *just so* for the lodgers. Besides, we never really know the views of those staying. Most people are fine, but it only takes one to make some sort of official complaint. So we are rarely able to speak freely at home. Sometimes the strain of it is unbearable."

"That does sound . . . difficult."

"And my father, he's a shadow of what he used to be. It's like he's aged and shrunk. Given up. Sometimes, I hate him for it. Hate him for not getting us out while we still had the chance."

"Why can't you go now? Find somewhere better to live?"

His face crumples and for a moment I think he might break down. But he pulls himself upright. "It's impossible. Too damned late. No country will take more Jews. They all say they have too many. Besides, we can't afford the exit tax—I told you about it before. We can't get our passports back without parting with a lot of money, which we don't have, even if we could get a visa somewhere else."

"And your mother? What about her?"

"She's the strong one now. She keeps going, even though my father's lost his will. And my grandmother. Without them . . ." He sniffs. "I'm not sure where we'd be. Everyone just keeps hoping and praying things will get better. But they're burying their heads in sand. They need to see the reality. Things will only get worse."

"Worse? It already sounds awful, Walter," I say, squeezing his fingers where they lie next to mine. "How could it possibly get worse?"

"We're being banned from more and more places. There's even talk that the city's Jews be banished to one area in just a few buildings—like a ghetto from the Middle Ages." He snorts. "People wonder how we got to this place, in just a few short years. But it's because we've let it happen. We've just sat back and taken it. Nobody has been brave enough to speak out. To stand up and fight."

I remember what Vati said about all the Jews who still live in Gohlis. How they persist, like vermin. Anger stirs inside me.

These are *people*, like us, not rats. We listen to the rain, thudding now, on the roof of the barn.

"I read letters from friends in London and New York," Walter continues. "The things they're able to do. And me? What sort of future do I have?" He tenses, turning toward me. "Oh, Hetty, if only you and I could leave tomorrow, on a steamship to New York. If only that were possible!"

"And then?" I whisper.

Walter paints a picture with his hand in the air. "We could live in a high-rise—one thousand feet tall. With a view over Central Park. Or Broadway. I'd work in a smart office, instead of a dirty old warehouse." He pauses. "We could go to restaurants and cinemas, theaters and libraries. *Together.* Nothing is banned. You can buy any book, listen to any music, watch any film. You can do any job, Jew or gentile, black skinned or white."

"Really?"

"Really."

"So . . . I could be a doctor. They have women doctors?"

"Probably. Certainly."

"And you could go to university too?"

"I could. And, better still, we'd be able to be together, openly, instead of having to hide in fusty old hay barns."

We both smile at the thought.

A place I could become a doctor.

But I gave that dream up years ago.

The barn door creaks and we jump. It creaks again, but we are quite alone. Just us, the rain, and the wind. We smile again at each other.

I try to imagine what that might be like, to live in a place like New York. The way Walter describes it makes it sound enticing. But I wonder if, in reality, it isn't just a little . . . frightening. With all that freedom, how do they control people? How do they stop criminals from wreaking havoc?

Perhaps Walter spends too much time with gloomy people. From what I gather, he creeps about all the time, on the outskirts of society. I need to show him that Germany *isn't* so bad. That it is also vibrant and growing and that Adolf Hitler, aside from not liking Jewish people, or pretty much any foreigners, has the *best* interests of Germany at his heart. He is doing *good things*, too.

"We can't go to New York," I say slowly. "But we could catch a train somewhere. Where we wouldn't be recognized. We could go shopping, stroll in the park. Nobody would suspect . . ."

He stares at me and I wonder if I've said the wrong thing. Have I been too forward, or would it be too risky? He's quiet for a few moments.

"You know, Hetty, you're right. Walking in the countryside with you is lovely, but it would be nice to do something more. I'm fed up with hiding in the shadows. Why don't we go into the city?"

"That would be too dangerous, Walter." I sigh. "We might be seen."

"It's not likely, though, is it? Especially at the moment. The Leipzig Fair is on. There's about two hundred thousand strangers in town. Everyone I know is busy working."

"Everyone I know *avoids* the crowded city center at this time . . ."

"Exactly!"

"But . . . Why would we risk being seen, even if it's only a small risk?"

I look into his pleading eyes. Such a trip seems foolhardy.

"There's something I want to give you," he says carefully. "We'd hide in plain sight. Nobody would suspect a Jew to brazenly parade so openly with a German in public. We'll be completely ignored."

I shake my head. "We can't."

"Look. We won't go to any of the places anyone you know ever goes. I promise. It'll make a lovely change from these fields." He grins at me. "I wouldn't risk this if I thought there was any chance we'd be seen," he encourages. "I should be able to take my girl out for a day of fun, if I choose."

My girl.

"We could go next Saturday," I find myself saying.

"Don't you have school?"

"I rarely go to school on Saturdays anymore. They prefer us to be with the BDM. I should be going on a hike, but there are six hundred girls going on this one. I'm not a leader, so they won't miss me. I'll get Erna to tell them I've hurt my foot."

"That's it. We can do this." He nods. "I'm fighting back. In a small way. But it feels good. It feels *so* good. Hey," he says as he nudges me. "How about a joke?"

"Okay." I sigh.

"This one's a bit naughty, so no telling your father, right?"

"Of course not!"

"So two men meet. 'Nice to see you're free again,' says one to the other. 'How was the concentration camp?' 'Great,' replies the first. 'Breakfast in bed, choice of coffee or chocolate, and for lunch, soup, meat, and dessert. We played games in the afternoon before coffee and cakes. Then a little snooze and a film after dinner.' The second man was astonished. 'That's great! Funny, though, I recently spoke to Meyer, who was also locked up there. He told a different story.' The first man nods gravely. 'Ah yes,' he says, 'that's why he's back in there again!'" Walter looks at me and smiles.

"You seriously think that's funny?" I stare at him in amazement.

"Ah well," he says, shrugging. "Maybe the dark Jewish humor takes a bit of getting used to."

He hugs me tight, tickling my ribs, and now we're both laughing. Kuschi catches the light mood and becomes playful, yapping and pawing, hopeful we shall be on the move once more.

Seventeen

September 20, 1937

T wo suitcases sit neatly side by side in the hallway.
It's come so fast. Too fast.

Karl appears at the top of the stairs. He wears a long gray coat belted around his slim waist. Neat tie, a glimpse of an eagle, a splash of red, his infectious smile and warm brown eyes that glow beneath a smart Luftwaffe cap.

How unbearable that he is leaving home.

Liszt's Hungarian Rhapsodies blare from the sitting room. Mutti is trying to be cheery. The volume is at its highest.

Karl runs down the stairs putting his finger to his lips.

"Don't spoil the surprise, Little Mouse," he says with a wink. "I'm going to give her my best twirl." Ingrid sidles next to me, throwing admiring looks at him.

"Hi, Mutti," I call above the music. "I'm home from school."

Mutti appears in the doorway, slender and beautiful. She's dressed in emerald green and wears the rich red lipstick she would not dare to wear out of the house. Earrings dangle and sparkle in her ears, and a single diamond pendant glitters at her throat.

"You look wonderful, Mutti," I tell her, but she neither hears nor sees me. She only has eyes for Karl and slaps her hand to her mouth as tears well up in her eyes. She opens her arms and a sob escapes as he steps forward to hug her.

Later, when Vati is home, we eat dinner in silence, the only sound being that of a knife on fine china and the clink of a glass as it's set down. Bertha has prepared Karl's favorite meal, fried chicken with onion and roasted potatoes.

I can hardly believe this is our last meal as a family. Now, lunches and dinners will be without him. School will be without him. The house, vast, echoing and empty.

Stolen.

The walls lean in, oppressive and gloomy. Does Karl know how our father got this house? Would he even care? After all, it was Karl who turned his back on his friend. Or perhaps he simply had no choice in the matter. He *had* to give him up.

I stir the greasy chicken and potato around my plate. The smell of it is nauseating. I push the potato to one side and quietly slip some chicken to Kuschi, lying beside my chair, who thumps his tail on the floor in thanks. I stroke the soft fur on his head.

"Herta?" Vati's voice slices through the silence. "I do hope you are not feeding that dog under the table."

"No, I was scratching my leg." I give Karl a pleading look, and he immediately turns to Vati. After a lifetime's practice, he's a master of diversion.

"How soon do you suppose they will let me fly?" Karl asks.

"I have no idea about the inner workings of the Luftwaffe, but you will have to work your way up from the bottom. They will need to toughen you up for a start. You've led a privileged life so far, my boy. They have to turn you into a man."

"Hey, come on! I've proved myself already in the HJ. You don't rise to the rank of Oberscharführer by being a soft layabout."

Vati nods his big head and leans back in his chair, wiping his greasy plate clean with a hunk of bread. He rings the little bell on the table.

"True, but believe me, you've seen nothing of the world yet, boy. The Hitler Jugend is merely children playing. This will be for real. One day soon there *is* going to be a war. You will have to be harder than you believe possible. Total brutality is the only way to win. Anything less will fail. And such a failure is unthinkable." He takes a wooden toothpick from the pot in the center of the table and pokes pieces of food from between his teeth.

Ingrid enters the room, and we fall quiet again. She stacks the plates and leaves.

"Well," says Mutti, breaking the silence once more with a false cheerfulness in her voice. "Let's not put the boy off before he has even started, eh?"

"I'm not put off," Karl says, his eyes fixed on Vati. "I'm more of a man than you think me, Vati, and I will make you proud. You'll see."

Vati grunts and Karl's shoulders slump a fraction.

"I want to play my part, too," I chip in. "Karl, do you remember how I dearly wished to be a doctor when I was younger?" Karl nods and smiles. "Well, I was thinking, if there really *is* to be a war, then surely we'll need as many doctors as possible, to treat the injured?" Mutti, Vati, and Karl all stare at me. "So"—my voice falters but I push on—"perhaps I could study medicine abroad?"

Vati's mouth tightens and Mutti raises her eyebrows. Nobody speaks.

"It's possible," I press on, "to do this in other countries, and my grades are good—"

"Don't be preposterous, Herta," scoffs Mutti. "That's absolutely out of the question."

"What Hetty means—" Karl begins.

"But why?" I cut in, frustration and anger surging up, like an unstoppable wave. "I want to do something *important*."

"It is *important*"—Vati's voice is caustic, silencing the rest of us—"that you learn to be quiet and know your place. No daughter of mine will have a job, let alone travel *abroad*. We will find you a worthy husband, but first you need to curb your tongue, or no man will want you."

"But—"

"*Hetty* . . ." Mutti gives me a warning look.

The air in the room thickens and it's hard to breathe. Perhaps I could run away with Walter. Out of this stifling house where Karl will no longer live, and away from Vati, his Moral Crusade, and his big, fat hands, squeezing the life out of me.

"A toast!" Vati says, lifting his glass of wine, blood red under the light of the chandelier. "To Karl, at the start of his career in the Luftwaffe."

"To Karl and the Luftwaffe," Mutti echoes, raising her glass, too, and they both take a mouthful of wine, their eyes never leaving their son.

LATER, KARL GOES out to say good-bye to a friend. Mutti suspects he has a secret sweetheart, but I know this cannot be true. He would have told me if he did. We've always told each other everything.

Except one thing.

I go to my room, pull my journal from beneath my mattress, and curl up on my window seat to wait for Karl to return. I draw a simple picture of a red heart, split and broken in loneliness. Still smarting from our conversation over dinner, I can't fathom the will to write anything. There is an enormous gulf between the possible world painted by Walter's optimistic strokes, and the one *I* know to be real.

Oh mein Führer, give me the strength to know right from wrong. Good from evil. Please help me.

Individualism is stupid and obstinate. His voice pounds my brain. *That path leads to ruination. Everyone must obey orders. I was an ordinary soldier for six years and I never once answered back. Each and every one of us must complete our own struggle. Provided you always have Germany at your heart, and you are pure of soul, you will know what you must do.*

I stare at his portrait. Usually it calms me, but not today. It's as though a tiny fraction of my soul has broken off and flies free with Walter and I'm certain I will never get it back. That part shall never obey. I finally understand that.

.   A couple of hours later, I hear Karl return and I creep into his room. I don't want to sleep, knowing he will be off first thing in the morning. I smell beer on him and wonder when it was that he started drinking. I lie on his bed and watch him collect his shaving brush and razor, alarm clock, books, and writing things and place them neatly in a small case.

"Well," he says, sitting down with me on the bed. "This is it. I shall miss you, Little Mouse."

"Me too. Just look after yourself, you."

"Oh, you needn't worry about me, schatz. It's you I worry about." He digs me playfully in the ribs.

"But will it really be as bad as Vati says? All this toughening up?" I don't want Karl to change. I want him to stay as he is. Kind. Protective. Gently teasing. All the things an older brother should be. I'm afraid of what he might still become.

"No, of course not. You know what Vati's like. He thinks everyone is a big softy. Not like they used to be in *his* day. *In the war.*"

"I suppose you're right. Let's hope your Luftwaffe superiors are not like Vati then."

"God forbid!" Karl rolls his eyes and laughs. I wrinkle my nose at his beer-laden breath. He pats my hand. "Shouldn't you be going to bed now?"

"I'm not tired yet. Karl—I need to ask you something." I swallow.

"Well, ask away."

"Do you ever think of Walter Keller? I mean, do you ever miss him?"

Karl's body stiffens.

"No," he says. "Why on earth would I?"

"You used to be so close. Inseparable. Surely you must—"

"That was years ago. I was just a kid. I didn't know anything back then. I had no idea he was a . . ." His voice peters out. He twists hand over hand.

"Jew." I finish his sentence for him. "Does it really matter so much? That he is one?"

"You are kidding me, aren't you?" He gives me a hard stare. "What's this all about? Why are you bringing it up now?"

He gets up and walks over to his case. Picks it up, puts it down again. He moves to the window, his back to me. "Have you seen him, Hetty?"

"No!"

"Then why are you asking these questions?"

"I just wondered, that's all." I change tack. "This house? Did you know . . . I mean, I heard a rumor, about how Vati came by it. Do you know that story?"

He turns to face me, crossing his arms over his chest.

"What did you hear? Who have you been talking to?"

"No one."

"So how did you hear a rumor then, if you've been talking to no one?"

"It was just kids at school. You know, chatter."

"What the hell! What were they saying?" He comes back to the bed and sits next to me.

"Stuff about how it was a Jew who lived here. How Vati took him to court on trumped-up charges to do with the newspaper, and then he got the house from him too. Is it true, Karl?"

Karl's face relaxes. "Oh, that old gossip again." He laughs. "The Jew part is true, sure, and the court case. But not the trumped-up charges. That's ridiculous. That is classic Jew-fed rumor. Look, they've been ousted from all their positions of power. They're bound to be angry. They've had their big fat noses put out. So what do they do? They choose a cowardly way of revenge. Rumors and falsehoods. Do not believe a word of it, Little Mouse. C'mon. You're better than that."

It sounds so logical when Karl puts it this way. But it seems every story has two sides. Which is the right one?

"Don't worry that pretty little head of yours one moment longer. It really isn't worth it. They have a nerve, those kids, speaking about Vati like that. Perhaps you should remind them of their duty, next time, eh?" Karl continues, patting my hand.

"Yes, you're probably right. You know, I think I will go to bed now, after all." I smile at him. Secrets, like a veil, float between us, translucent, but a barrier nevertheless.

"See you in the morning, schatz," he says, and I leave him to sleep one last time in his boyhood bedroom.

Back in my own room, I switch off the light and climb into bed, unease creeping like a cold draft across my skin. I pull the blankets closer around me, tucking them beneath my chin.

He has no reason to be suspicious.

Eighteen

September 25, 1937

We take a tram to the city center and sit near the door, squeezed together on the wooden bench, my leg touching his. The Reichsmarks I've been saving since my birthday sit heavily in my skirt pocket. He slides an arm around my shoulder. I freeze. Is this too much? I risk a glance behind, but most people in the carriage are staring sightlessly out the window, lost in their own worlds.

Walter convinced me it would be fine when we discussed it in the soggy, deserted barn. Now we're here, I'm not so sure.

"You look . . . beautiful," he says, sending a warm rush from my head to my toes. His breath tickles my ear.

An elderly lady, sitting behind us, tuts at Walter's outrageous attentions. I spring away, my heart pounding so hard I feel sick.

"Relax," he whispers, pulling me closer.

The lady huffs, louder this time.

He leans in, placing his mouth right up to my ear. "You must join in. Look like you're enjoying this, or she might become suspicious. Please." He speaks so quietly I can barely make out the words.

I swallow, then turn to look at him, forcing myself to smile. Our heads are close together and for an instant I think our lips might connect. The lady taps her stick on the metal bar at the back of our seat. We jump at the shock of the sound, but Walter just laughs and pulls me close again.

"Young people today, there is no *decorum* anymore," we hear the lady say to her neighbor.

My body fizzes. What the hell are we doing? How can Walter be so calm? He's staring out the tram window, humming a tune, tapping a hand lightly on his thigh. But his other hand holds mine, and I can feel his palm is clammy. *Act natural*, I will myself firmly, just like we agreed. Surely, in my BDM uniform, with this attractive blond young man at my side, nobody can suspect a thing. But my nerves remain on edge all the same.

We jump off the tram in Hindenburgstrasse, not far from the House of Nations. I exhale a slow breath of relief. Ahead, the huge building housing the fair is festooned with flags from every nation, flanked by tall flagpoles from which swastikas flutter in the breeze. It's a beautiful day and the square opposite is teeming with visitors. Tables and chairs have been set up outside and waiters in long white aprons rush from one customer to the next carrying trays piled high with tankards of beer, pretzels and sausages.

As soon as the tram has rattled away, Walter catches my arm. "Hetty, you must act like we do this every day of the week. That way we really won't attract attention. Remember,

we deserve to be together. Just like everyone else. Don't we?"
His jaw is fixed, his expression fierce.

"Yes. Of course we do. I . . . I didn't realize I'd be so nervous. How do you stay calm?"

"Because . . ." He swallows hard, and for a moment I think
he is going to cry. "This is *my* city, *my* girl, and I should have
as much right as the next man to walk about, out in the open
with her. I've thought about it a lot. I've spent too long creeping in the shadows. This feels like the *right* thing to do. It's
defiance against a giant wall of despair. With you at my side,
Hetty, I feel strong. You give me that."

People are bustling all around, but where we stand, his fingers
tight around my arms, there is absolute stillness. As though we
two, in the midst of this crowded city of strangers, are alone in
an invisible oasis of calm.

My thrumming heart slows. "It's going to be fine," I say
with a nod.

"Yes. It really is." He releases my arms and smiles. "Now.
I'm starving. Let's eat."

"We'll never find somewhere." I look around the busy
square. Every table is taken.

"All two hundred thousand fairgoers are here, getting
lunch," Walter observes. "Come on, let's go somewhere
quieter."

We walk south, threading our way through the throngs,
passing the imposing new government buildings and the law
courts. We turn down unfamiliar backstreets where it's quieter,
poorer. I'm reminded of the street outside our old apartment
block. Children play in the road, several without shoes. An old

woman sits on a stool in a doorway, shelling peas. A man pushes a barrow, knocking on doors, trying and failing to sell kitchenware. Skinny, mangy dogs sniff in the gutters.

"Time for a joke, I think," Walter says. He checks behind us, then speaks quietly, so nobody else can possibly hear.

"Hitler visits a lunatic asylum. The inmates are all lined up. He passes down the line and comes to a man who isn't saluting. 'Why aren't you saluting, like the others?' he barks. 'Mein Führer,' the man replies, 'I'm the nurse, I'm not crazy!'"

I swallow a snigger. "Walter, really, you shouldn't tell such jokes," I caution, "you'll be sent to a camp if anyone hears."

"Sometimes," he says, "a little humor is the only thing that makes it all bearable."

We turn into a wider, busier road. Across the street is a large department store. *Salamander's*, I read.

"Perhaps there's a café in there," I suggest.

We walk through the revolving doors. Just inside the entrance stands a board with a store guide. We look down the list of departments and sure enough, there is a café on the ground floor. A shop assistant points us in the right direction. We wander through the rug and curtain departments. The shop floor is quiet.

I try to ignore the creeping feeling that someone might be following.

"Hetty?" Walter studies my face. "Are you feeling all right?"

"Fine," I tell him, checking over my shoulder.

"Sure?"

"Absolutely."

I force a smile.

"Good," Walter says. He takes hold of my hand and gives it a squeeze, just for a moment, his skin warm and soft against mine.

The café has rows of square tables covered with bright red linen and cheerful prints on the walls. A counter stretches across one end with delicious displays of cakes and pastries. There are a couple of empty tables and we choose the one near the window.

I order kartoffelsuppe and Walter the goulash.

"So, fräulein," he says in a low voice when the waiter has gone. "Are you looking forward to the rest of our day?"

He leans across the table, smiling into my eyes. I bury my fears, wondering what it is he has in mind. Thoughts begin to bubble. His coat spread beneath a tree and us lying on it, kissing. Window-shopping, arm in arm, laughing and joking together. A visit to a museum, perhaps, or even to the fair. The day stretches ahead with tantalizing possibilities.

"Where do you want to take me?" I smile back at him.

"I've arranged to give you something. You are going to love it." And he rubs his hands together with delight.

The waiter returns to the table with our drinks, setting down two glasses of chilled apple juice. The background chatter from the other tables rises and falls around us. Nobody looks or stares. Walter watches me over the rim of his glass.

"Tell me! What will you give me?"

"You're going to have to wait. I want it to be a surprise." He winks.

The waiter returns with my steaming bowl of potato soup

and Walter's goulash and potato pancakes. The soup is deliciously salty; tangy, with chunks of bacon and sausage. We eat in silence.

I place my spoon in the empty bowl and glance around at the other customers while Walter finishes his meal. A noisy family; a couple smiling into each other's eyes; two ladies gossiping; the next table along by the window, a mother and daughter perhaps . . . I catch my breath. My eyes float back to the two ladies. One of them is vaguely familiar. Do I know her? Is she a friend of Mutti's? One of her charity ladies, I think. Could she have seen me?

"Shall we go? Let's get the bill," I urge, passing a handful of coins to Walter.

"Thank you." He wears a pained expression, shame, perhaps, as he slides the money across the table.

"Hurry," I urge.

"Are you okay?" He looks at me with concern and signals to a waiter.

"Couldn't be better. Just want to enjoy the rest of the day." I force myself to smile.

The ladies are having a disagreement about something. They shake their heads and gesticulate. Fortunately, this keeps them from observing their neighbors.

Walter counts out the cash for the waiter and I follow him out of the café. Once we are back in the crowded, narrow cobbled streets of the old town, I can breathe again. How stupid, how utterly reckless we've been. I long to be in the fields and woods where there is no chance of being seen. We head toward the outer ring road, where the old city walls would once have stood.

There's a chill to the air, but the sun is out, bathing the city in a rich amber gold that only autumn brings.

"Did I ever tell you how beautiful you are?" Walter smiles at me as we walk arm in arm.

"Frequently," I reply, wishing he would lower his voice.

We cross the tram lines and busy main road and he leads me into Gottschedstrasse, a quiet side street flanked with tall buildings and a few shops with awnings overhanging the pavement. We stop on the corner outside an imposing churchlike building, three stories high, with a huge iron door. Light shines from the glass windows above it.

"What . . ." I begin, but my eye is caught by the large, gold Star of David on the wall beside the door.

"The Community Synagogue," Walter explains.

I shrink away.

"Why did you bring me here?" I look at him in disbelief.

"It's okay." He smiles. "You don't have to come in. But hidden in here is the thing I want you to have."

"But . . . oh, Walter, that's not a good idea."

"Why not? You don't know what it is yet."

Why not? A million reasons why not, but I can't find the words. I look up and down the street. What if I'm caught, outside a *synagogue*?

"Walter—"

"Look, just wait here. I promise, I won't be a moment." His face is alive with excitement, and he jumps up the four steps to the door and hammers on it, looking around at me, grinning. I melt back against the wall of the building opposite. A few seconds later, a man opens the door and Walter is swallowed inside.

I stare at the iron door. What goes on behind it? Strange, alien prayers; foreign ways and an exotic language I don't understand? Or perhaps devil worship and evil plotting? There is a pounding in my head and the seconds stretch to minutes. Waiting is unbearable. I check the street countless times. I could run away, but my feet don't budge.

A man in an overcoat and hat suddenly rounds the corner. I panic. What should I do? I look so suspicious standing here in front of this *place*. I push myself off the wall and begin to walk slowly along the pavement toward the man. I cross the street and pass him with my head bowed. A few more paces and I dare to look back. He's gone. I exhale and slowly retrace my steps toward the synagogue.

At last Walter appears again from behind the iron door.

"Sorry! The rabbi wanted to chat . . . here." He runs down the steps toward me, smiling, and places a book in my hands. "I know how much you loved *Metamorphosis*. I remember. Hopefully you'll enjoy these stories just as much."

I stare at the mottled brown cover, slightly dog-eared at the edges, with *Franz Kafka, Betrachtung* stamped on the front.

"It's a rare first edition," Walter says with pride in his voice.

"But . . . what am I to do with it? What if someone at home finds it, or sees me reading it? Walter, how can I possibly take this thing home? Besides, I might lose it!" I hold the book out toward him. It feels dangerous in my hands, like a stick of dynamite that might explode at any moment. "Please, take it back," I whisper.

"Come on, Hetty! I risked . . . I *lied* to the rabbi—told him it was for an ailing relative. I thought you'd be pleased . . .

I'm sure you can find somewhere to hide it in your room. I remember how you loved to read, and these types of books, it's impossible to get them anymore."

"*Illegal*, Walter, not impossible."

"Well, true. But so many have been destroyed."

"I know, and it's kind and thoughtful . . ." I stare at his face, full of disappointment and hope; and my insides soften.

I hug the book to my chest, then slip it into my pocket.

"I'm sorry. I don't mean to be ungrateful." I reach for his hand and we walk away from the synagogue. "I will treasure it, I promise. You're so good to me."

"I'd give you the world if I could," he says tenderly.

Haltingly, he moves me back against the wall of the adjacent building. And then his arms are tight around my waist, drawing me in, and he kisses me properly for the first time. Slowly, gently, until everything fades away and I no longer care about anything but him.

Sitting in my window seat, I stare at the Kafka resting in my hands. *Betrachtung. Contemplation.* But will I be able to bring myself to read it? Perhaps I can skim it and then get rid of it. Walter really doesn't understand. He can't, or he wouldn't have burdened me with it.

I hear a knock at the door and quickly shove it behind my back as Ingrid's face appears. Her eyes dart about more than usual. There is a slight flush to her pale cheeks.

"I've come to lay the fire," she says. "Before you need to change for dinner . . ."

She kneels in front of the fireplace and sweeps yesterday's ash into a bucket.

"Your mother tells me I won't have to do this for much longer," she says cheerfully.

"Oh?"

"Herr Heinrich has ordered a special boiler that will heat the whole house," she tells me. "It's the new thing. For those who can afford it, anyway."

She puts the bucket to one side and begins to crumple up pieces of newspaper, arranging the balls in the grate.

"Imagine that! Automatic heating in every room in the house. 'Cept ours, I suppose," she adds.

"It's much colder in this house than it ever was in our flat," I tell her, glancing out through the almost-bare branches of the cherry tree, into the night.

She begins to pile kindling wood on top of the newspaper.

"Ah, but your heart must be warm, even if your body is not."

"Sorry?" I stare at her as she bends over, the nodules of her spine forming a bony ridge beneath her black dress. She places the kindling carefully around the edges of the grate.

"Love warms the heart, like nothing else can."

Panic seizes me in an icy grip.

"I don't understand what you mean."

"I mean," she says, straightening her back and turning toward me, her lips sliding down into a reverse smile, "wasn't it you I saw with a handsome young chap in Salamander's this afternoon?"

One beat. Two beats.

"You were mistaken," I say. Our eyes lock. "I wasn't in Salamander's this afternoon. Why would I go to a place like that?" I snort.

"How strange." Her brow knits. "I could have sworn it was you."

"Not me. Must be someone who *looks* like me. There's a girl, she used to be in my class, Freda. She looks a bit like me. Same hair. Must have been her you saw."

I grip the book tight in my fingers. Ingrid turns back to the fireplace. Strikes a match, cups her hand around the flame, and sets the paper balls alight.

I try to breathe, but my chest is so tight I fear I'm going to choke.

"I was with the BDM, marching in the countryside," I tell her, even though, as I say it, it sounds lame.

She rocks back on her heels watching the flames catch the paper and the kindling. The fire crackles and spreads.

She stands, picks up her tools and her bucket, and turns to me.

"My mistake then, Fräulein Herta. How silly of me. Ring the bell if the fire goes out. It's a windy night, and I had terrible trouble with the one downstairs just now."

"Yes. Thank you."

We smile at each other, but there is no warmth in the gesture. From either side.

She leaves the room and I'm alone with my thoughts. Terrifying visions of what she saw. Would she remember Walter? It's years since he came to the house, and he's changed so much. Besides, even if she *did* recognize him, would she even know he's a Jew? I rack my brain, trying to remember if there was ever a conversation at home when his Jewishness was discussed, but I can't think straight. Did she follow us and see me outside the synagogue, or even see us kiss? Why else would she have said the word *love?* Was it *so* obvious? I pace the room. What if she makes inquiries or tells Mutti? Should I have said something different? Well, it's too late now. I will simply have to stick to the story. She is mistaken, and it's her word against mine. I push the book under my mattress, next to the journal.

I think about a recent lesson with Herr Metzger. The one where he spoke of his relief at the implementation of the 1935 Law for the Protection of German Blood and German Honor. The law that will save the German people from the poisoning of our blood by the bacterium of the Jew. Before the Führer took power in 1933, the body of the German people had been severely ill. At last, the infection of minds and bodies is being cured. We are becoming racially healthy once more. The punishment for relations between Jews and Germans is severe. Racial defilement is a heinous crime.

Oh, Walter, what the hell have we done?

Nineteen

October 10, 1937

I have a terrible headache. A thick black snake has slid inside my skull, squeezing and twisting my brain until I could scream with the pain. It's been getting worse all morning, and finally, I give in to it, excusing myself from lunch to go lie on my bed.

I should have met Walter by the bridge last Sunday, as well as this morning, but the conversation I had with Ingrid after meeting Walter in town has rattled inside my head on and off ever since and I daren't go.

My throat tightens at the thought of him returned to Hindenburgstrasse not knowing why I didn't come last week or this. He'll be worried. Perhaps he'll think I don't want to see him anymore, after our audacious city adventure, and he won't bother to go back to the bridge next week. I toss and turn, doze and wake.

Damn the headache and damn Ingrid. After a couple of hours, the headache reduced to a dull throb, I go downstairs and find Mutti in the afternoon sitting room. In the days after

Karl left, she became abstracted, as if when he went, he took a chunk of her with him, too, and I began to worry if she was quite all right.

Now, to get over his absence, she's thrown herself with renewed vigor into getting her children's home up and running. She sits at the writing bureau, head bent, her pen scratching furiously as she writes letters to the Party, to the mayor, to the newspapers. A faint, rapidly speaking foreign voice comes from the new radio Vati has installed next to the gramophone. Sometimes, when Vati has left for work in the mornings, Mutti finds a French station and listens, as now, with her head inclined, a smile twitching on her lips. I cross the room and snap the machine off.

"What did you do that for?" Mutti jerks around and gives me a hurt look, as if I've roughly woken her from a pleasant dream.

"Vati will be angry and forbid it if he catches you."

"But he won't be back from Berlin until this evening." She sighs. "Working on a Sunday, too." She arches her back and stretches her arms out behind as though she's been hunched over her writing desk for many hours already.

"What about Ingrid? Is she here?" I stare at the doorway, in case she's hovering just outside.

"No, I've given her the whole day off. But what's Ingrid got to do with it?"

I sigh with relief. The book will be safe beneath my mattress, for now anyway. "Why don't we do something today, Mutti? Go out together. We could both do with some fresh air."

She looks back to the letters on her desk. "I must finish

these . . . Perhaps later." She gives me a quick smile. "There's so much work to do, setting up one of these ventures. All the paperwork. And finding the children. One must do it *right*."

"What do you mean, finding the children? If they're orphans, wouldn't they just . . . be handed in?"

"I should say, finding the *correct* children. It's sorting the desirable from . . . the others. They are developing tests, physical assessments, to check the purity of the children. They're very thorough—sixty-two separate checks to be made on each child. It's most rigorous. But it means we have to look far and wide to find appropriate children."

"What about the ones who don't pass the tests?"

Mutti regards me vaguely. "Well, they . . . go to other places. Oh," she says, turning to me fully. "I nearly forgot, that boy called for you early this morning. I told him you usually walk the dog in the park on Sunday mornings, but that today you are unwell."

"Which friend?" I ask, my breath catching. Walter called for me! He must have come here after I didn't turn up. What a risk he took . . . surely he wouldn't have?

"Oh, that sweet boy. The old friend of yours from volksschule, I forget his name. The unfortunate one," she adds, waving a hand.

"Oh, you mean Tomas." My heart sinks. How stupid. *Of course* Walter wouldn't call for me *here*.

"That's it. Tomas. What happened to him after . . . that awful business?"

"You mean with his father? His uncle threw his mother and all seven children out. They live in Plagwitz now. Tomas had to leave school and get a job. At least he has an apprenticeship now."

She tuts. "Well, he's scrubbed up all right. Looks as though he manages a wash and a decent meal. Always so underfed, as I remember."

Not Walter.

Just Tomas.

How wretchedly disappointing. Mutti's pen begins to scratch the paper again. I wander over to the sofa and sink onto it, curling my legs beneath me.

"Do you miss Karl terribly?" I ask.

Mutti sighs. "If my right arm had been severed, I would miss it less," she says wistfully. "The house is so quiet and empty without him." She smiles at me. "Thank goodness I still have you."

The unexpected intimacy is a warmth that spreads through me like soup on a cold day. It reminds me of how it used to be, before we moved to this house. Before she became so busy with her charity work, a satellite around planet Vati, and a distant presence to me.

"Still," she says, "it is the passage of life. We prepare our sons to set them free into the world. That is the point of it all."

"And your daughters?"

"Our daughters never really leave us," she says, laughing. "They may live in different houses, but they will always be around to share our grandchildren and take care of us when we are old."

"But what if I should want to work in another city? Or marry a man who lives far away, just like you did?"

"That won't happen. Besides, why would you want to?" she asks, her forehead folding into a little frown.

"I would like to travel the world. To do something more interesting and *important* than simply to marry and have children."

Mutti gives me a scathing look. "What can be more important for a woman than marrying and having children? Besides, you know Vati wants you to give up this notion of having a job. It isn't *appropriate* for a girl like you to get a job, let alone travel the world."

"And is that what *you* want for me, Mutti? To marry young and give you lots of grandchildren?"

"I would like you to be happy, Hetty," Mutti says as she looks out the window across the leaf-scattered lawn. "But what *I* think, or what *you* think or desire, doesn't matter. What you *have* to do is your duty. As we all do. First, to the Führer. Then to Vati, and one day, to your future husband. You are almost sixteen, I should hardly have to explain this." She continues to stare out the window and I study her profile. Always poised, refined, and elegant, she rarely speaks her mind. It seems almost preposterous that she is a person in her own right, with thoughts and opinions that might be different from Vati's.

What lies beneath her skin? How can I find a crack in her armor? An opportunity to pull the real Mutti out from behind her serene and composed exterior.

"You are a sweet girl, Hetty." She tears her gaze from the window and back to me. "You are clever and thoughtful, but you have much to learn. You know little of the world. You must curb your tongue and control your impetuous nature.

These are not good qualities in a woman these days. But my dear maman, she would have loved you." She smiles at the memory of poor, dead Oma Fabienne.

"Tell me some stories from your childhood in France," I beg. "When Oma Fabienne was alive, and you were little."

But Mutti shakes her head. "Another time, Hetty. I really am awfully busy." She turns back to her letters, and our conversation is over.

VATI TELEPHONES TO say he will be catching the four o'clock train, to arrive in Leipzig shortly after five thirty. Tomas also telephones, asking if I'm feeling better, and would I like to go to the cinema with him.

Not really. Not now.

Instead, I decide to walk to the Hauptbahnhof to meet Vati when his train arrives.

As I get close to the station, the pavements swarm with people, making it impossible to hurry. When I finally reach the main concourse, I see from the board that Vati's train arrived five minutes ago. I scan heads as people stream from the platforms but it's impossible to find anyone among the crowds and I can't see him anywhere.

I give up and edge my way out of the station into the flow of people heading slowly toward the city center. My shoelace is loose, so I stop outside Breuninger stores for a moment to tighten it. In the window is a display of new winter fashion. A little drab, color-wise, gray and navy blue, but the style is attractive: clean, slim lines, with nipped-in waists and belts.

I stand up, turn, and there is Vati, just a few feet away. He looks toward me, smiling and laughing. He seems so happy, all the stress and worry he normally carries wiped from his face; he is almost unrecognizable. But he hasn't seen me. He's looking at a woman with her back to me. I open my mouth to call out, but Vati flings his arms around the woman. They stand in a close embrace, their bodies pressed together, foreheads touching.

His name freezes in my throat, and I shrink back against the shop window. Everything blurs. Sounds merge and fade. All I can see is Vati embracing the woman. She shifts slightly, and I spot what I missed a moment ago. A little girl, perhaps two or three years old. She is propped up on the woman's hip, staring at me over her mother's shoulder. She has enormous bright blue eyes, and loose blond curls, fine as silk thread, tumble about her angelic face.

Vati says something to the woman, but I don't hear his words. He turns his attention to the little girl. She pulls her eyes from mine and reaches up toward him. He tenderly takes her in his arms.

How strange that Vati would want to hold a child. He's never been interested in children. I can hardly remember receiving so much as a hug from him.

The girl wraps her fat little arms around his neck and whispers something in his ear, giggling. Such an intimate thing for a child to do. It's as if she knows him.

All at once, in a terrible moment of realization, I understand. I slap a hand over my mouth to stop myself from crying out.

The woman wears a tight black skirt and although I can't

see her face, in that instant, I know who she is. The fat behind gives it away.

It never crossed my mind to wonder why Fräulein Müller had disappeared as suddenly as she arrived, replaced with an older, middle-aged secretary with glasses and a gray bun.

Fräulein Müller was pregnant with Vati's child.

I gag. Swallow the vomit in my throat.

No, no, no!

I cannot bear to see any more. Jaw clenched, I turn away before either of them notices me and merge into the crowd streaming in the opposite direction.

People, stinking strangers, press their bodies against me. There is no air. They're squeezing tighter and tighter and I'm suffocating. I elbow and push my way through, desperate to get out onto the street and away, far away, as fast as possible. I stumble out of the crowd and into the path of cars in the road. Horns honk and vehicles veer around me. I dodge a horse, and a man on a bike swears at me. The buildings close in. All I can see is the little girl's big eyes staring at me and the way she snuggled so comfortably into Vati's arms. I can't go home. How can I? Mutti will be sick with worry, and Vati angry that I'm not home for dinner, but I don't care. I will not go home and look Vati in the eye, not after what I just saw.

Mutti!

Poor, poor Mutti.

Can she know?

Should I tell her?

I walk and walk without any idea where I'm going, or what

I'm going to do. I pass through alleyways and streets, past churches, shops, schools, and apartment blocks. Daylight fades and the lights of the city illuminate my path. Time loses all sense of meaning. The shadow of Vati's contentment with that bundle of strange child in his arms hovers everywhere I look.

Finally, drained and bone-weary, I dry my tears and slowly make my way back home.

"WHERE ON EARTH have you *been?*" Mutti is crying, her eyes red-rimmed and puffy.

"I ran into a friend," I mumble. "We went back to her place. Sorry, I lost track of time."

"What were you thinking, Hetty?" She is shouting now, wringing her hands in despair. "Disappearing like that in times like these?"

What should I say to her? How can I possibly put into words what I witnessed?

Vati's face is blotchy red. Piggy eyed with soft, wobbly flesh. "We've been content for you to roam around this town with your friends. But if they are a bad influence or it leads you down the wrong path, we'll put a stop to it. Immediately. There'll be no more hanging around town with your friends. This is a warning, fräulein."

I *hate* you. I hope he sees it in my eyes.

A vision of the pretty, blond, curly-haired girl is etched in my memory. My sister! The word is alien on my tongue. *Schwester.*

"Sorry, Vati."

"You deserve a beating for causing your mother such alarm," he continues. "Go to your room. I don't want to set eyes on you until morning."

Gladly. I don't want to set eyes on you either. You make me sick. If I deserve a beating for causing Mutti alarm, what do you deserve for being unfaithful?

I turn and silently climb the stairs. I reach for my diary under the mattress.

> *I cannot tell Mutti what I saw. It will destroy her. It will destroy everything. It's clear, she can never, ever know. How I wish Karl were here. I can just picture him, his eyes kind, his head close. "Don't worry, Little Mouse," he would say. "I'll deal with Vati." But Karl is hundreds of miles away and I'm all alone.*

Walter takes me into his arms and whispers in my ear that he will make everything all right. *Leave your parents*, he urges. *Come and live in America with me.* I'm leaving the house for the last time, inexplicably wearing a Luftwaffe uniform. Mutti refuses to say good-bye and Vati is happy to see me gone. I turn back for one last look and see Vati, seated on the sofa, bouncing the cherubic, golden child on his knee. Only the child acknowledges my leaving, with a look of victory in her glacial blue eyes.

I snap awake, extinguishing the vision of Vati and the girl-child. I'm stiff and cold sitting on the bed, the diary open on the floor. My head swirls with exhaustion and a dull ache pulses in my temples. I pick up the journal, close it, and hide it away, climbing into bed without bothering to change.

But now I'm wide awake and the night crawls by, the darkness expanding and contracting. A stone lies in the pit of my stomach. A rock of pity for Mutti. A great slab of loathing for Vati. And all the while, the walls of the house pulse and throb in time with my beating heart.

Twenty

October 12, 1937

I sit at the back of the classroom as we are read *Mein Kampf* as a class. Frau Schmidt insists on it, ever since half the teachers at school were dismissed for using un-German texts. We studied it last year, too. Now we have gone right back to the beginning and started again. The book was long and slow going the first time. It's soporific the second. And now we must go through it all again, tedious chapter by tedious chapter.

Frau Schmidt no longer bothers to initiate discussion. Instead, blessedly, she skips chunks and then quotes salient parts out loud to the class.

"If we consider how greatly he has sinned against the masses in the course of the centuries, how he has squeezed and sucked the blood again and again; if furthermore we consider how the people gradually learned to hate him for this, and ended up by regarding his existence as nothing but punishment of Heaven for the other peoples, we can understand how hard this shift must be for the Jew."

Frau Schmidt plows on, appearing to neither notice nor care whether any pupil in the class pays attention or not.

"The black-haired Jewish youth lies in wait for hours on end, satanically glaring and spying on the unsuspicious girl whom he plans to seduce, adulterating her blood and removing her from the bosom of her own people. The Jew uses every possible means to undermine the racial foundations of a subjugated people . . ."

With every mention of the word *Jew*, Walter's beautiful face swims into my mind.

Could Satan really be crouching beneath his peachy skin?

"What if he isn't black haired, Frau Schmidt?" I ask when she nods at my raised hand.

There is a collective rustle as the class turns to look at me.

"I'm not sure I understand your question, Herta." Frau Schmidt pauses and removes her glasses.

"I mean, what if he has blond hair and doesn't look like a Jew at all? But he is one. What then?"

She stands looking baffled, as if not sure how to answer.

"What if he looks Aryan," I press, "and acts like one too? What if he has the best of manners and is courteous and brave? What if he believes in Germany just as we do? Is he still a danger then?"

Nobody makes a sound.

Thirty sets of eyes rest on me.

"Why would you ask such a question?" Frau Schmidt's voice is strained, her cheeks flushed. "Because of course, you know the answer, don't you? There is no difference, however the Jew may look. His true character will belie the outer casing. His blood cannot be anything but inferior. His mind can be nothing but flawed, and his intentions will have the same aim of self-betterment, whether he be fair or dark." She grips the side of the teacher's table until her knuckles turn white. "I hope I have answered your question adequately, Herta," she adds and replaces her glasses.

She's afraid I've set her a test. She knows who my father is and fears I will report her. These days, a teacher has more to fear from a student than the other way around.

"Yes. That is most clear. Thank you."

Erna nudges me in the ribs.

"What did you ask that for?" she asks, and I shrug, because I don't fully understand myself.

AFTER SCHOOL, BACK at home, I go to my room and retrieve my journal from its hiding place. Within its geometric covers, I can be entirely honest. It's my only true, trusted friend.

> *Oh, how I miss you, Karl! The house is different without you. The air inside its walls is stilled, as if frozen without your life to fill it with warmth and movement. Sometimes the floorboards creak or a curtain swishes in the breeze, and I think it's you. But there is no one there. Perhaps it's the ghosts of past inhabitants, their misery trapped, seeping out of the masonry, infecting our lives with bad luck. Please come home soon.*

The telephone rings in the hallway.

"Would you like to go to the cinema to see *Operation Michael*?" Tomas's voice is fuzzy at the end of the crackling line.

"I'm not sure I'm in the mood."

"Please come, Hetty. I've already asked Erna and she said yes. It's a war film," he adds, as though that would tempt me.

I suppose anything to take my mind off the girl-child and that revolting husband stealer, as well as Walter and the wretched Kafka that still lies unread beneath my mattress.

ERNA AND TOMAS are waiting for me outside the cinema.

"Hurry up, snail!" Erna calls, waving as I run from the tram stop. "It starts in five minutes."

Our seats are in the middle row. The lamps are dimmed and voices become hushed. Above our heads a shaft of white light from the projector cuts through the darkness, illuminating the big screen at the front. Clouds of cigarette smoke rise and curl through the beam.

The projector whirs into life. I settle back into my seat between Tomas and Erna to watch the newsreel. Tomas leans toward me and nestles his arm against mine on the velvet armrest between us. I glance at him but his attention is focused on the clip *Festliches Nürnberg*. His head is close to mine, but angles away so I can see the thousands of marching soldiers on the screen weirdly distorted through his glasses.

He turns and I feel his lingering gaze. He whispers, his mouth too close to my ear, "So many soldiers, it's a wonder there are any civilians left in Germany." His breath is hot and clammy on my skin.

I lean away and turn my attention to the Nuremburg Rally. Scenes of vast mines of coal and ore, of sprawling factories spewing gleaming cars, clothes, electronics, and appliances. The might of Germany. The inexorable advancement of the

German people. Germany, the narrator proclaims, is the envy of all nations. There are shots of endless cheering crowds, and a smiling, proud Hitler announces to the world he only wants peace in Europe. Then the sound of a hundred thousand marching boots. *Peace?* I think of the wrecked men in the soldiers' home. There are tanks and guns and the Luftwaffe flying in beautiful formation. My heart skips for Karl. Finally, there is roller skating, folk dancing, and a fire show. The cinema audience spontaneously erupts into cheering, clapping, and shouts of "Heil Hitler."

Tomas smiles in the semidarkness; carried along with the excitement, he moves closer. "I just hope the war doesn't start and finish before *I* can play a part in it."

"Why does everyone talk of war when Hitler claims only to want peace?" I whisper.

"Because we need to show the bastards what we're made of!" Tomas waves a hand toward the now blank screen. "The swine out there have to see Hitler means business. War is the only way to do that, so to get to peace, you need to have war, right?" He looks sideways at me.

"The Führer must know what he is doing," I say, thinking of Karl, vulnerable up there in a metal box with wings.

"Of course he does. He's the ultimate leader. God among men. He has a Master Plan for all this."

"Let's hope he's better at winning wars than he is at writing books." I soften my voice so nobody can overhear. Tomas thankfully laughs at my joke and the screen lights up again.

After the scenes from Nuremburg, the main film is something of an anticlimax. My mind wanders. Is Vati with his other daughter? He could, at this very moment, be tickling her round belly and making her giggle. I imagine him smiling at her mother, running his fingers tenderly down her cheek, praising her for giving him this lovely child. Bile rises and stings the back of my throat. The cinema is no sanctuary from my thoughts. Everywhere I go, I'm haunted by that vision of Vati. There is no escape. No respite. I shift uncomfortably in my seat and only now do I notice Tomas has my hand in his. I gently pull it away.

If only it were Walter here beside me, holding my hand.

But then, he wouldn't be allowed to come in here at all.

It's dusk when we get outside. We sit on a bench opposite Thomaskirche. Strains of the clear, high voices of the boys' choir flow from the ancient church across the cobbled square.

"My father is dead," Tomas suddenly announces, his voice a harsh monotone, breaking the amiable silence among the three of us. A bolt passes through me.

"What happened?" Erna gasps.

"He fell from a prison window," Tomas answers, his voice flat, devoid of emotion. "He was cleaning it, four stories up. Must've leaned out too far."

"That's just awful. How horrible," Erna says. "I'm so sorry."

"Well, I'm not," Tomas replies swiftly. "He was a terrible embarrassment. He didn't fight in the war. He was a Communist. He was anti-Nazi. Truth is, he was a traitor and he got what a traitor deserves." His cheeks are pink and his smudged glasses have slipped, just as they always used to, halfway down his nose.

Erna looks at him, wide-eyed with shock. "But you can't be happy that your own father is dead!"

"I'm not happy. Of course not. But he only had himself to blame. He was selfish and we all suffered because of him. Never earned a decent wage. Now we have to live in a shithole in Plagwitz, and my poor mother has to do the work of a man and a woman. Slaving all hours in that goddamn factory, while we live on crap food and factory fumes. You never knew him, Erna, or anything about it. Hetty understands, don't you, Hetty? We're better off without him, that's all."

I squirm on the bench. If I hadn't gone to Vati with Tomas, someone else would have, sooner or later. The whole family might have had to pay a price, so the reality is, I helped them.

"We did the *right* thing, Tomas," I say softly. "I know it's been hard for you. But everyone knows you are the hero here."

Erna looks from one of us to the other.

"I'm sure you did," she says at last. "But I hear that some of these prison deaths aren't as *accidental* as they might at first seem. There are rumors, awful rumors, about what goes on in these prison camps."

I close my mind to what Walter has said too.

"What sort of rumors?" I ask, irritation escaping into my voice. She's been listening to her father's rhetoric, I'm sure. It's rubbing off on her. The perfect Erna, perhaps becoming *less* perfect? Was it a mistake not to mention Herr Bäcker's views to Vati?

Erna's face clouds for a moment. Then, with a frown she says, "I'm not saying that those who've done wrong don't deserve to be in prison . . . It's just that, many of the people who were taken into *protective custody*, due to their political opinions, have been transferred to camps. The conditions are

apparently very bad. I heard that, when they are due to be released, those dates get pushed back, or there is a mysterious
death, or someone has tried to escape and died for it."

"And who told you this?"

Erna closes her mouth and gives her head a slight shake.

"Erna, you shouldn't listen to such talk. You know that," I say,
looking hard into her eyes.

"It's difficult to know what's true, and what's rumor," she
says carefully. "But surely Tomas's family deserve to know how
such an accident could have happened. It sounds suspicious—"

"What could you know about it?" I round on her. "Don't
make things worse than they already are for Tomas."

"It's all right, Hetty." Tomas frowns. "There are a lot of rumors flying about. You mustn't believe everything you hear,
Erna. Bastard enemies of the Reich. They just want to cause
trouble."

Erna is quiet for a moment. "Well, I'm sorry anyway, Tomas."

We sit in silence again, letting the news about Tomas's father
sink in. It seems like another lifetime when Tomas and I, aged
twelve, stood shoulder to shoulder in Vati's study that day. How
much has changed since then. Even little weedy Tomas is becoming a man. Lanky, square jawed, and low voiced.

Through the branches of a tall plane tree, I watch colored
light filter through the high, narrow windows of Thomaskirche,
while the boys' voices, honey sweet, crescendo to an impossible
high, then abruptly stop. A hush descends over the square.

Erna and I say good-bye to Tomas and walk home through
lamp-lit streets, hand in hand, friends again, after our disagreement over the camps earlier. Rain begins to fall, light

to begin with, then with full, soaking intent. There is a rich, earthy smell in the air. Cars swish through puddles and lights reflect on the newly wet black pavements.

"Everything is changing, but I want it to be how it was," I say suddenly, thinking back to how uncomplicated life used to be, before we had to watch what we say to each other; before Walter's family had to hide in the shadows. Before I knew about Vati and the girl-child.

Erna looks thoughtful for a moment. "Don't you think the future's bright then, Hett?"

"It doesn't feel like it, at the moment." How much to reveal? I wish I'd not been so defensive about Tomas's father. Have I made Erna wary?

"Why not?" she asks, her voice falsely bright. "We have loads to look forward to. The Gewandhaus concert. The BDM dance. How about a kiss with a good-looking Wehrmacht officer?" She nudges me. "What more could a girl want?"

She makes me smile, despite the melancholy that has settled deep in my being.

"Really, what's bothering you, Hett?"

"Oh. Nothing. I suppose I'm just missing Karl, that's all."

"Of course you are. How is he getting on?"

"Fine, I think. He doesn't write to me much."

"Bet you can't wait to see him when he's home."

"Heaven knows when that will be."

"Christmas, isn't it? That's what he said—" Erna stops mid-sentence.

"What?"

"I mean, I think it would be about that time, wouldn't it?"

She speaks quickly, rushing over her words, but her walking pace has slowed, and even in the dark and through the rain, I can feel she is blushing.

"You just said, 'Christmas. That's what he said . . .'" A mist descends. I stop walking. The sounds from the street are muffled, as though I am far away. Then, as if the fog has cleared, I see it. What I missed. How could I not have realized? Perhaps I did, but I didn't want to know it.

"Hetty . . ."

"How do you know when Karl is coming home?" I snarl. "And I don't?" Nausea stirs in my belly. The rain is soaking through my jacket, and my shoulders are damp. Water drips from my hair.

"Because Karl wrote it in a letter."

"A letter? How many letters has he written to you?"

"I'm not sure."

"Three. That's how many he's written to *me* since he's been away. Three. Is it more, or less, than *three*, Erna?"

"More than three," she mumbles. "I'm so sorry, Hett. I knew I should have told you. Karl thought you might be upset, so I kept quiet. It was the wrong thing to do, I know that now."

"Don't you *dare* blame Karl!"

We stare at each other through the wet darkness.

"I'm not blaming him, I—"

"Why would you keep this from me? Why would *Karl* want to keep it from me? We tell each other everything! *You and I* tell each other everything."

"Yes, we do. And I was going to tell you, honestly. I just couldn't find the right time."

"That's pathetic, Erna. You coward."

So it was Erna's idea. Karl would never have kept a secret from me. She has talked about it with him. Persuaded him. I imagine her whispering in his ear. Them laughing together, at my expense. Turning him away from me. *My own brother! My so-called best friend!*

"So you're his sweetheart then?" I try to keep my voice calm, even.

"Yes."

I feel a sharp pain in my heart. Karl is mine. I'm his Little Mouse. He kept it from me. *She* kept it from me. Excluded me. They don't want any part of me in this *thing*.

"How long?"

"Not that long. A few months, that's all."

"A few *months*! And you never thought to tell me? What about Kurt? It was all a lie, wasn't it? And you *begged* me not to tell your parents. For Christ's sake . . . What about our friendship? Does it mean so little to you? Were you just using me, to get to Karl?" Rain, spit, and anger, ugly and bitter, spew from my mouth.

Vati. Karl. Erna.

Three of the most important people in my life, and they've all betrayed me.

"I'm sorry." Erna's voice is pleading. Her sodden hair is plastered to her head, her face shiny and wet. "I never meant to upset you this much. We were going to tell you, but there didn't seem much point in the beginning, what with Karl due to go away; we thought it wouldn't last. Then, after the summer camp, it started to get serious, but the time never seemed quite right . . ."

"So you chose to lie about a made-up boyfriend. Why, Erna? What was the point of not telling me the truth?"

"I don't know. It was stupid. I *hated* lying to you. Truly, Hetty. I was just worried it would ruin our friendship . . ."

"Well, it damn well has now, hasn't it?"

I stare at Erna, her shoulders sunken in misery at my vicious words. I'm hurting her and it feels good. She's the easiest one to take my rage out on. I can't do it to Vati, or to Karl. But Erna? Eternally good and perfect Erna? I can get to her, all right.

But you haven't exactly been truthful either.

That is different.

Walter is a secret for his safety.

A different situation entirely.

"Go away, Erna," I say at last. "Just leave me alone. I hate you both. But mostly you. You're nothing but a lying *pig*."

I turn and run, hard and fast through the downpour. My chest hurts and I'm soaked to the skin, but it doesn't silence the torrent of voices in my head.

What have you done?

YOU are the villain, for falling for a Jew.

VATI is the lowlife with his secret family.

You've just lost the best friend you have ever had.

Hetty Heinrich, you are the biggest fool in the universe.

Twenty-One

October 14, 1937

Everywhere I go, Erna's there. She's at school. She's at BDM. She watches me with sad, puppy dog eyes. But I'm not giving in. I'm not ready to forgive her. The more I think it over, the more certain I become. I suppose it will make Vati proud of me again, not that I really care what *he* thinks anymore. Besides, Erna deserves it. Plus it's insurance. In case Ingrid speaks. They'll never believe Ingrid if I do this. There will be no doubt where my allegiances lie.

We have a big rally in Leipzig tomorrow. I need to be ready for it. I must feel cleansed. Deserving of the Führer's praise.

Vati is working at home. I press my ear to the closed door of his study. All is quiet.

"Come in," his muffled voice answers my soft knock.

"Please may I have a quick word, Vati? This won't take long."

He is a busy man. Two jobs *and* two families. No wonder he looks tired.

"Why, certainly, Miss Herta." He smiles as I enter the room, waving me to the chair in front of his desk. He squashes the end of his cigarette into an ashtray full of other recently smoked butts. Despite the open window, smoke hangs in the air, constricting my throat as I take a deep breath. "Is something bothering you?"

I stare at him for a moment. His round face and baggy skin. His so-familiar pale eyes. I want to scream at him, *You and your disgusting Fräulein Müller, and that child, that's what! Is she your Schnuffel now?*

"A little, Vati," I say instead. "Something has been playing on my mind for some time."

There is rot in my soul. I can feel it growing. Deep in my bones, seeping into my veins. But this will cleanse me. Put me back on the right path. The path of duty, correctness, and obligation. Hitler's path of selflessness.

I clear my throat. "It's about a friend of mine, Erna, and her father. I overheard something, and it worried me." The words spill from my mouth with ease.

"Go on."

"It's . . ." A shadow flits. The body of Tomas's father, falling from a high prison window. Was it an accident? Nobody will ever know.

"I'm never too busy to hear things that worry you, Herta. It's important you feel you can come to me," Vati is saying. "Without good girls like you, where would Herr Himmler and our beloved Führer be, eh?" He smiles again, warm and encouraging.

A ghostly Walter begs me not to do the right thing.

Bloody Hitler. Herr Bäcker's words echo in my mind.

"I heard . . ."

"And what did you hear exactly, Schnuffel?"

"I heard them say . . ." Erna's sloping green eyes swim across my vision. *You can trust me to the ends of the earth, Erna.* I swallow hard. Vati stares at me, waiting for me to speak.

A kaleidoscope of images flicker: Erna and me in the playground at school; lying on her bed talking endlessly; marching together in the BDM; sharing our deepest hopes and dreams as we huddle side by side in our tent on summer camping trips. Walter. Heavenly, Jewish Walter.

Vati is becoming impatient. He drops his pen onto the paper in front of him and grunts.

"Heard what?" he presses.

I sit up a little straighter. *A promise is a promise, Erna. You might have betrayed me, but I shall never do that to you.*

"Sorry, Vati . . . That try as they might, they cannot get front-row tickets for the Annual Celebration of the Hitler Youth." I feel a sweat break out on my forehead. "Herr Bäcker admires the Führer so very much. It would be the biggest *thrill* for them if you could, perhaps, pull a few strings and . . ."

I watch Vati's face change. He guffaws. "Is that all?"

It's the best I could do in the moment.

"Well, could you?"

"No, Herta. I cannot pull favors for your friends. The front row is reserved for men of importance and their families."

"That's a shame."

"He really admires the Führer, eh? And the daughter, Erna, isn't it? I hear good things about her. I asked your brother about this Erna, as you seemed to be spending a lot of time with her. He said she is very highly regarded in HJ circles. *These* are the sort of friends you should be spending your time with. Well, I could probably swing an invitation for the evening party. Leave it with me, I'll see what I can do."

"Thank you, Vati. They will be so grateful."

"Yes, yes, but no promises. Is there anything else?"

"Nothing else."

"Then you must let me get on. I've urgent matters to deal with." He waves a hand dismissively at me and goes back to the paperwork on his desk. I stare at the top of his head, bent over as he studies his half-written letter. He picks up his pen, the nib scratching as it moves across the page.

You failure, Herta Heinrich. You are no better than a worm, putting your own interests before that of the Fatherland. Once, you pledged yourself to me. And now? Are you a deserter?

A sickness settles at the base of my belly. The rot remains. And I know of only one way I can properly rid myself of it, for good, though I dread it.

Mutti has gone to visit a children's home in Burghausen. She hopes the SS-run home and school will be a model for her own venture. With Vati working behind the closed door of his study, there is no one; Karl's absence is stronger than ever.

Restless, I wander into the garden room. Outside, the colors of summer have gone. The huge tree has shed its leaves, exposing the great bulk of the treehouse I never visit anymore. For a moment, I ache to see Erna, but we've not spoken since my harsh words in the street over Karl. I should go and apologize. Come clean and tell her about Walter. But I can't, I'm not brave enough. I pick up today's *Leipziger* from the table and turn the pages, hoping for a distraction as I scan the headlines.

COUNTRY-WIDE TOUR FOR DUKE
AND DUCHESS OF WINDSOR!
NEW CAR COMPANY, VOLKSWAGEN, PLANS
AFFORDABLE CAR FOR EVERY MAN IN GERMANY!
BRITISH DELEGATION VISIT LEIPZIG, TO ADMIRE
SPEED AND EXTENT OF MOTOR-ROAD NETWORK

Then:

ACCLAIMED GERMAN ACTRESS SET TO ROT IN
JAIL AFTER CONVICTION OF RASSENSCHANDE

This catches my eye.

The well-known and previously highly regarded actress Dora Heck has been tried and convicted of the heinous crime of Racial Defamation. It is unusual for a woman to be convicted of such an anti-German crime, given that women are usually the victims of rape or sexual coercion by the perpetrator. In this case, however, the actress, who was close, our reporters believe, to some of those in the higher echelons of the Party, had traveled to London, under the guise of promoting her latest film. The Gestapo officers, who secretly followed her having received a tip-off from a concerned member of the public, discovered she was

having unauthorized sexual relations with a German
Jew now living in London. Upon her return, she was
arrested, tried, and found guilty. Before she was sent
to prison, Fräulein Heck was subjected to the humili-
ation of having her head shaved and being paraded
through the city center as a warning to others not to
repeat her mistakes . . .

Dear God. Panic rises and I drop the paper on the table
as if it had bitten me. True, Walter and I haven't had *sexual
relations*, but we've kissed. Does that count? I'm certain it
would. Imagine if Vati were to find out. What if Ingrid alerts
the Gestapo to follow me?

There really is no choice now, and I have no time to lose.

MUTTI AND VATI, resplendent in evening dress, wait in the
hallway for their car to collect them. Mutti is brimming with
enthusiasm after her visit to the children's home. She waves
a book entitled *Raising the Ideal German Child: A Guide for
Modern Mothers.*

"Full of advice on how to toughen the next generation. This
will be most useful for my orphans," she says. "Don't wait up
for us, Hetty. After an early dinner with Judge Fuchs, we are
going to the opera." There is a flurry of sliding on gloves, hats,
fur stole, and outdoor shoes, and then they are gone, leaving a
faint whiff of smoky cologne and flowery scent behind them.

I fetch the Kafka from beneath my mattress and stare at its
cover. Once, I would have delighted in this book. Devoured it
with hunger. I finger it tentatively, turning to the first page.

I try to read, but I can't concentrate. The words tumble over themselves on the page. It's evidence of my non-German thoughts. I must be rid of it. Fast. I snap it shut and slip it into my pocket.

I approach the kitchen to collect Kuschi, as always, my excuse to go out. Ingrid is talking.

"I saw it with my own eyes, Bertha, honest to God, it's true!" Ingrid's voice is high with indignation. Bertha's reply is quieter, mumbled so I can't hear. "Seriously, something should be done. I mean—"

I walk into the room before she can say more. She starts at the sight of me.

"Something should be done about what?" I ask. She's sitting at the table, her feet up on a chair, a cup in her hand. Bertha's at the sink, scrubbing potatoes.

"Sorry." She swings her legs down from the chair, slowly, as though trying to make a point. "I didn't mean to offend."

"What was it you were saying?" I probe. "Don't let me stop you."

Her cheeks flush and she looks to Bertha for help. Bertha shrugs and goes back to her scrubbing.

"It was just some silly gossip in the fishmonger's this morning, Fräulein Herta. People talk these days, you know. Everyone watching everyone else, you never know who's going to report on who. Anyone with a grudge. How do you prove it, if you *didn't* do anything wrong?"

I burn hot and walk across the room, taking Kuschi's leash from the hook, bending down to hide my face. I fix the leash to his collar with trembling fingers.

"No one will have anything to worry about if they abide by the law. Only those with something to hide have a reason to fear," I say at last, looking her straight in the eye. "I'm going for a walk with the dog. Not sure when I'll be back."

"What, in the dark?" Ingrid reacts.

"Oh, Fräulein Herta, I'm not sure your father would like that," Bertha cautions.

"I'm just walking around the lamp-lit roads of Gohlis," I tell her firmly. "What harm can come to me in a *respectable* neighborhood like this?"

I shouldn't need permission from a cook or a maid to leave my own house.

I walk quickly. Like an invisible magnet, I can't resist the pull of him. I have no real plan except to go to the place he lives. Walk the pavements he walks. Breathe the air he breathes. Aching with the knowledge of what I must do. Kuschi's paws click on the pavement at my side.

We cross the little stone bridge, the river flowing smooth beneath my feet. I stop for a moment and lean over the wall. I can smell its dank wetness as it gushes and churns around the ancient arches of the bridge. My head swims and for a second, I think I might pitch forward into its depths. I spring away and walk fast down the dark lane, anxious to be back on the main roads with their bustle and streetlights.

The northern end of Hindenburgstrasse is a wide, busy, tree-lined avenue. Large and imposing buildings line each side. I walk slowly past a little row of shops: a haberdasher's, a grocer, a café, and a butcher's. All are shut except the café and a florist at the end of the row, where a man and a boy wearing aprons are dismantling displays of flowers and taking them into the shop.

"That's all I can let you have this evening, I'm afraid," the man calls to someone inside. "I might have some more leftovers tomorrow, if you want to come by at closing then . . ."

They clear the door and someone wearing a hat pulled low over his forehead exits, holding a bunch of lilacs wrapped in brown paper. He strides away, the flowers tucked under his arm.

All other movement in the street freezes.

The pavement lists.

It cannot be.

"Walter?"

He turns, and stares, wide-eyed and openmouthed. Flashes of Ingrid, the Gestapo. I wasn't prepared to see him now. Should I run? But I'm frozen in time and space and he comes to me.

"Hetty . . . How did you find me?" He seems hesitant, restrained.

"I never thought I'd actually *see* you . . ."

"Oh . . ."

"I mean, what were the chances?" I whisper.

There's an awkwardness between us and he shrinks back, rests his shoulder against the wall.

"Why haven't you come the last two Sundays?" he asks after a beat, and suddenly I understand his distant reception.

"I wanted to. But so much has happened since we met in the city." I stop. We're so exposed, here on this main thoroughfare. "Is there anywhere we can talk? Properly talk? There's something you should know." I remember my resolve. But somehow, in Walter's presence, everything solid turns to liquid, and I feel it slipping away.

Walter nods and shrugs himself off the wall. "I know a place. My friend Lena, her family owns a café. She's completely trustworthy," he adds, turning and walking quickly down the street.

I trail after him. We turn off the main street and after a couple more turns, we're standing in a shabby backstreet with ramshackle old houses and a run-down-looking café on the corner. A bell tinkles as Walter pushes open the door. I tie Kuschi to a lamppost and follow Walter.

A solitary man sits smoking at one of the tables, his head hidden behind a newspaper. The only other person inside is a dark-skinned young woman of suspect racial origins, serving behind the bar. Walter indicates for me to sit opposite him at one of the tables.

"Good evening." He smiles at the girl. "Two teas, Lena, please," he calls.

"I'll be right with you," she answers, clattering around behind the counter.

Walter glances at the smoking man and leans across the table. His face softens. "Tell me, why didn't you come on Sunday?"

"I was afraid we'd been seen in Salamander's. Now I'm sure we were."

"Who saw us?" His words are calm, but his body tenses.

"Our maid, Ingrid."

"Shit."

"Yes." We stare across the table at each other.

"I don't suppose she remembers you. And even if she does, she doesn't know you're a . . ." My words fade out.

I think about my resolve. Now. *Do it now.*

"Actually, Walter." I take a deep breath. "I-I think we should put a stop to all this."

His face falls. I look away and squeeze my hands together in my lap. *Stay strong.*

I tell him about the story I read in the *Leipziger* about the actress.

Walter says nothing and picks at some loose skin next to his thumbnail.

"It's too dangerous, for both of us." I fish the Kafka from my pocket. "And I'm sorry, but I can't read this."

"Hetty . . ."

He slides the book across the table and shoves it into his jacket pocket. He looks at me now and there is so much hurt in his eyes. I let my fingers brush his hand lying on the table. A lump forms in my throat as I imagine a future without our Sunday mornings. Without the warmth of his hand in mine, the touch of his lips, or the smell of him. This and the events of the past week—first Vati, and now Erna and Karl—are suddenly an unbearable weight, crushing me.

Lena approaches the table carrying a tray and I pull my hand away. She places the teacups and teapot in front of us, giving me a sideways look with her dark eyes, and then retreats behind the counter. She begins to polish it, paying close attention to the area near to where we sit. Walter notices me staring at her.

"I promise," he says, "you can trust Lena with your life and mine. She has as much to lose as us. She'd never tell a soul."

I feel my shoulders relax. I try again. "Walter, you must know this isn't what I want . . ."

He gazes at me, then pours the tea.

Such a simple task, but I have never once seen Vati pour tea for Mutti. I watch Walter's hands move, strong yet gentle.

I take a sip of tea and meet his eyes over the rim of my teacup.

He looks away and I see the muscles twitching in his jaw. "You know," he says, his voice cracking. "We've had so much taken away from us. So much. I thought I'd found some happiness with you. I'd decided, damn them, the Nazis. I'll fall in love with whoever I choose. How dare they, with their disgusting laws, consider me inferior. How dare they declare me not good enough for you, if *you* consider me to be." He sits back in his chair. "And now it looks like they've won, after all."

"I'm sorry," I whisper.

He slumps in his chair, deflated. As though all the fight has gone out of him. I search for something to say, to break the silence.

"I've found out Vati has a mistress," I blurt out. "They have a child together. A little girl."

Walter puts down his cup.

"Oh God. That's awful."

"I saw them together."

He reaches out and strokes my hand, just once, with his fingertips, then leaves his hand on the table, close to mine. "Those Nazi Party bastards. They all have mistresses."

His words are like a punch in the belly and something scrunches up inside.

"Why do you think this has anything to do with him being a Nazi . . . Don't you forget, Walter Keller, I am one too!"

A foreign creature is in control of my mind, forcing the words from my mouth.

Walter rocks back on his chair. His eyes bore into me and I shrivel.

"I don't understand; whose side are you on?"

"Whose side? This isn't a question of *sides*. I'm on *our* side. Yours. No—I mean, I don't *know*."

I look around the café. The man has left, his newspaper folded on the table. No one else has come in.

"I went to Vati today. I thought that, if Ingrid finds out who you are and should let slip, well, it would be *her* word against mine, wouldn't it? There must be no doubt in my father's mind where my loyalties lie, so I decided to tell him that I'd once overheard Erna's father make an anti-Hitler rant only—"

"Hetty! How could you! Don't you make *me* an excuse for doing something so despicable!"

"Shh!"

He looks around. Lena is still behind the counter. And there is nobody else in the café.

"I'm not," I whisper, leaning toward him. "But I wanted to tell you the truth."

I begin to sweat. I was meant to be finishing things with Walter, not baring my soul and then falling out with him. Who exactly am I? A Nazi *and* a Jew sympathizer? Is that even possible? Is it just Walter, or all of them? Pain thuds again in my temples.

"I don't understand," he says, his face contorting. "You call yourself a *Nazi*. Yet you seem happy to meet with me, to listen to what *I* think of the Nazis. To *kiss* me. Then you defend them. Have I totally misunderstood you, Hetty?" A fire is lit behind his eyes. "Are you going to tell your father of *my* opinions too?"

"Of course not!"

"How can I be sure? Why do you make an exception for me?"

My skin feels hot.

"You haven't misunderstood me. The truth is, and I want to be entirely truthful with you . . ." I place my hand on top of his, but he pulls it away. "I don't agree with everything Hitler says. But if you think about it, lots of it makes sense, too. To put the good of all before individual self-gratification. Our nation, our future, is the most important thing. Isn't he, being 'married to Germany,' the very epitome of that? No class divisions, prosperity for all, law and order—they are all good, aren't they? Taming the chaos in the world, eradicating disease and mental illness. Controlling it. Science to make us better, to further our advancement. How can any of it be wrong? Besides, he is the first man in history to recognize the equal importance of women, to recognize the mother and housewife as a profession in the highest order—"

"But these are just *words*, Hetty. Manipulative, deceitful, duplicitous *words*. Look at his actions, at the consequences. Don't listen to his poison. Think about it. It's all too simple!"

I don't know, I want to scream at him. *I don't know anything anymore!*

"Think of what is happening in *reality*." Walter presses on.

"All this *fear*, the informing, nobody trusting their friends. There is no freedom anymore. Freedom to speak, to think, to feel. He wants to control it all. He insults 'the masses' by doubting any capacity for intellect. He sees only one way: to crush, to force, to divide, to dictate. And you women? Oh, he celebrates women. He speaks of your crucial role in the Thousand Year Reich, and yet, that role can *only* be as mother and homemaker. You are not permitted to be anything else. You are certainly not expected to use your mind. Preferable if you don't have one at all. And you, Hetty, with your deep thinking, your quick wit, and your independent spirit. You will be utterly wasted."

"Stop it." My head is swelling. Hotter and hotter. The thudding in my temples is growing to a thunder. "Just stop," I say again, putting my head in my hands.

Walter is watching me. Waiting. His face is twisted. He's angry with me.

"I don't want to hear any more of this," I say. "I'm leaving—"

He grabs my hands. "Just imagine how it would be to live in a free country. One where nobody watches you to see if you are having un-German thoughts. Where you could say anything you like."

"It would be chaos," I say, spitting the words at him. "There would be violence and street fighting, like the mobs who used to roam the streets before the Führer—"

The door jangles and an elderly couple come in. Walter and I freeze in silence, bodies stiff with conflict. The waitress reappears from the back.

"Good evening, Lena, my dear," says the bespectacled lady as she removes her hat. "We were hoping for a nice slice of your apfelstrudel if you have some."

"Of course. Take a seat, anywhere you like," Lena says, giving us a quick glance.

Walter pours some more tea from the pot. It's lukewarm when I take a mouthful.

"It doesn't have to be like that," he says quietly. "You could be whatever you want, Jew or non-Jew. Scientist. Lawyer. Doctor. Friends with whoever you want. Marry who you want."

His words are seductive, just like Hitler's. Different words. Different promises. I feel like a butterfly tossed in a stiff breeze.

"I've never been away from here. I have no idea what it would be like. Have you?"

"No." He shakes his head and slumps in his seat.

Who is right? And who is wrong?

Lena is back.

"Can I get you anything else?" Her dark eyes are troubled.

"No. All fine, Lena, thank you," Walter says without taking his eyes off me.

I stare back into Walter's flecked and beautiful eyes. The seduction of them. They pull me in so irresistibly, but I *must* resist. I have to stop this before I fall, completely.

"I should go." I push my teacup to the center of the table and stand up.

I try to see Walter for what he is. No ordinary boy, but a Jew who has tried to seduce me.

"Yes" is all he says, sweeping a hand through his unruly hair.

"I probably won't come on Sunday. I think it would be for the best."

"Yes," he says again, not meeting my eyes. "As you say. It would probably be for the best."

"And just so you know," I whisper as I pass him by, "I never did tell Vati about Erna's father. I didn't have the guts."

Twenty-Two

November 3, 1937

I know I shouldn't care. I shall probably never see you again. But I hate that you should think badly of me. Why does it even matter so much? You're a Jew. You have no right to my heart. I'm worth more than you could ever be. You are pigheaded. You see things only from your side. You're underhanded and devious, the way you have wriggled yourself into my heart and soul. Into my head. I can think of nothing but you, and how I'm desperate to be with you, but know I shan't ever be again. You turn everything I've ever known on its head, and you make me think about things I shouldn't have to think about. I was happy, before. I knew right from wrong. Now everything is confused and broken. I want to hate you for it, Walter Keller. But I can't. Could it be that I've fallen in love? Is this how it feels?

When I arrive at the afternoon's BDM gathering, the first person I see is Erna, rolling bandages. She sees me, too, and quickly looks away, rolling with great attention to her work. It will have to be me who makes the first move. What to say? *I have missed you dreadfully, dearest friend. I've been such a fool. Oh, and I've kept a much worse truth from you than you kept from me. Can you forgive me?*

"Hello, Erna. How have you been?"

She looks up at me. Her green eyes lack their usual sparkle; her skin is paler than ever.

"Oh, Hett . . ." She glances around her, lowering her voice. "I've missed you so much. Have you forgiven me?"

"Have I forgiven *you?*"

"I'm so sorry for not telling you about Karl and me."

"Oh, Erna. *I'm* the one who should be apologizing. I totally overreacted. I've been so silly . . ."

She shakes her head, her eyes moist with tears.

"I shouldn't have lied. I've been a rotten friend."

I think how close I came to informing on her father, and my insides curdle.

Erna places the rolled bandages neatly in the bandage box and closes the lid. She wipes her eyes and I see her hands are trembling.

I watch in silence as big fat tears roll down Erna's porcelain cheeks.

"Erna . . . we . . . none of us are perfect."

She gives a hollow laugh and blows her nose.

"Except you, Hetty." She slides her hankie back into her pocket. "You're pretty close to perfect."

"Me?" I choke. "I'm just about as far from that . . ."

"Yes, you are." She studies me with her green eyes. "You

never do anything wrong. You're clever and pretty and brave. You stand up for your friends, even if they haven't done the right thing, and everyone adores you. I don't deserve a friend like you."

"Oh, Erna, if only you knew. I'm not what you think I am . . ."

"What do you mean?"

"If I tell you, you must swear—"

"Of course, I swear!"

But the room is filling up. Too many ears, too close. My heart pumps hard. I'm so desperate to talk to her about Walter, but here it's too risky. Besides, since I shan't be seeing him again, it hardly matters anymore. Perhaps someday, in the future, when I stop hurting. Maybe we'll be able to have a giggle about it. One day.

"Not here," I say at last. "Not yet. Just not yet."

"Hett—"

Fräulein Ackermann appears in the doorway and the chatter in the room fades.

"Heil Hitler." We salute.

"Heil Hitler," she replies, smiling broadly as she opens up her first aid case.

ON SUNDAY MORNING, I'm awake before dawn. The house sighs with the rhythms of its sleeping occupants. I'm not going to meet Walter, so why do I lie here, wide awake? I toss and turn, but sleep is not going to return. I might as well walk the dog since I'm awake.

I creep through the frigid, silent house to fetch Kuschi, wrapping myself in my coat, hat, and gloves and head out through the iron gate into the darkness. Kuschi makes the decision, tugging on the leash, leading me toward the river. I try to pull him the other way, but then, as Walter won't be there anyway, I give in to his demands.

As I approach the bridge, the eastward sky is beginning to lighten. I pause on the ancient hump and lean over the stony wall as I've done so many times before, to watch the dark water flow beneath. A movement in the road makes me jump and Kuschi stirs at my feet, thumping his tail against my legs.

He arrives, moments later, shoulders hunched inside his coat, the sound of his footsteps lost beneath the rush of the water. We stare at each other through the low morning light.

"I thought you weren't coming."

"Then why are *you* here, Miss Herta?" Walter's voice carries a hint of amusement. Irritatingly self-assured.

"I'm walking my dog."

"Of course you are. Of all the places in Leipzig you could walk your dog . . ."

"I like walking here. And you? What's your reason for being here?"

"I came to see you."

He stands close, leaning over the wall, and for a moment I long for him to put his arm around my shoulders, but he does not.

"What made you so certain I would be here?"

"Just a hunch." He turns toward me, the warmth of his breath on my face, a self-certain smile on his lips.

"Why do you think you're so clever, Walter Keller? Why are you so arrogant to think that I want to spend my time with you?"

He shakes his head and looks at the river. "I'm not in the least bit certain," he says. "I took a chance. I admit, I'm pleased to see you here. I can't deny that. I can't deny I'm attracted to you. That I enjoy your company, despite our differences, and all the danger. No, more, I *love* your company. But if you look me in the eye, now, and tell me you never want to see me again, then I shall go away and never bother you again."

He turns around to face me. It's light enough to see him properly. I square up to tell him exactly that: Leave me alone. I have no need of you. You are dangerous to me and I want you out of my life. *Give me strength, mein Führer.*

But the words fail me.

We stand close, staring at each other in silence, the water swirling beneath us.

"You can't say it, can you?" he murmurs. That hint of amusement again.

My heart burns and I want to hit him. Beat him hard on the chest with my fists. But I long for something else, too. I want to climb right inside his skin and know him completely.

So I say nothing at all.

A fraction of movement and his lips, warm, lighter than air, brush mine. I freeze. The shock of it. The air around me contracts. Then he is kissing me, properly. His tongue parts my lips and he pulls me toward him, passing his arms around my back. I'm lost in him, in this moment.

Then I remember my vow and pull away.

"I'm sorry," Walter says. "I shouldn't have."

"No. You shouldn't."

"I won't—"

"I . . . I like it though. I like it when you kiss me. But we can't . . ."

"Let's just . . . make the most of things while we can. Who knows what will happen in the future. Perhaps"—he grabs both my hands—"you and I should just run away together. I can't fight the urge to be with you. I don't *want* to fight it. So let's just go and live in sin."

I laugh, because I don't know if he is joking.

"It's lighter now." He looks around. "People will soon be passing by—let's walk."

We leave the bridge and take the path between the bank and the river. It's narrow and we have to walk in single file for a short distance. When the path widens, he comes alongside me and takes my hand. Our step is in time. Easy and natural, it's as if we've been walking step by step together for a thousand years.

"I'm sorry," I say, "about the other day. I don't want to argue, and I hate that you think badly of me. It's so hard to know what to think about . . . everything."

"I'm sorry too. I was angry. Things are . . . hard . . . I took it out on you, and I shouldn't have. It's not your fault. And I could never think badly of you." We walk on a few more paces in silence. "Do you remember that day I fished you out of the lake when you couldn't swim properly?" he asks suddenly.

"The day you saved my life, you mean. How could I possibly forget?"

"You were quite small." He laughs.

"You don't forget almost dying, Walter, nor the person who rescued you."

"I remember it like yesterday. I relived it enough!"

"What do you mean?"

He looks away, as if embarrassed.

"I dreamed about it afterward. Nightmares, really. That I didn't save you. I kept diving down, looking for you, but you weren't there. Or I did get ahold of you, but you'd slip through my fingers and I'd watch you sinking down, staring up at me, fingers outstretched, but I just couldn't get to you."

"Oh, Walter, that's horrible! Why didn't you say?"

He smiles. "It was silly, really, because I *did* get to you. I suppose it shows just how much you meant to me, even then."

I pass my arms around his waist and squeeze him tight.

"And I thought you never even noticed I existed."

There is a deep sense of peace in the air.

"You were right, the other day," I say, sighing. A confession. "About Herr Bäcker. I mean, he shouldn't have said the things he did, but it was right to keep quiet."

He gives me a squeeze this time. "I was shocked, when I thought you'd reported him. But I shouldn't have doubted you." He smiles again. "I knew you would never do such a terrible thing."

Kuschi rushes off ahead, chasing rabbits in the woods, his black shape flashing between the trees. The shadow of Tomas's father crashes to the ground.

You don't know what I once did.

The trees begin to thin as we reach the edge of the fields. Walter's face is illuminated as he walks through a patch of sunlight. His eyes are full of hope.

If only it could just be him and me in the world. Adam and Eve. Beginning afresh.

"Do you really think we could?" I ask on a whim.

"Could what?"

"Run away together."

He laughs.

"Where would we go?"

"Paris . . . or New York. Switzerland. It wouldn't really matter, would it, if we could be somewhere together. Properly together."

"We could check into swish hotels."

"Or a cozy guesthouse."

"Or rent a chic apartment on the Champs-Elysées."

"I would fetch you breakfast in bed and then go make my fortune writing love poems." We laugh at that idea.

"We'd have to take Kuschi," I say after a pause. "I couldn't leave without him."

"Sure—why not? Do you suppose he speaks French?"

I dig him in the ribs and he wraps his arms tight around me.

"If we were to run away together, Hetty Heinrich, I should never, ever let you go. Not for a single minute."

WE PART AT the bridge and only then do I glance at my watch. It's almost ten already—damn. I run with Kuschi all the way back to Fritzschestrasse. Gasping for breath, I slow down when I've rounded the corner past Walter's old flat and only then do I notice the figure leaning against the railings beneath the branches of the cherry tree. All gangly arms and legs. Tomas. What's *he* doing here?

His face lights up when he sees me. "Ah! There you are. I was hoping to catch you before you went out. I should like to walk with you today, or one Sunday, if you would like to, that is." His Adam's apple rises and falls visibly through the skin of his throat as he swallows.

"It'll have to be another time—I've already walked this morning."

"You're flushed." He peers closely at my face.

"I've been running," I reply quickly. "I'm late, and I'll be in trouble if I don't go in now."

"Or we could just talk? We don't have to walk—we could go to a café or—"

"Another time, Tomas. Today just isn't convenient. Next week perhaps?"

I don't give him time to answer as I pull Kuschi through the gate and up the steps, leaving him standing on the pavement, watching me as I close the front door.

There are two sides, or more perhaps, to every thought. Every action. We only ever want to see one. But you alone, Walter, you make me see there can be another. Or another. Or another. You make me see the world is so different from what I thought it was, from what I have always been taught it is. I know you were only joking when you talked of running away, but I can't help but think of it. You asked me once to imagine life in a free country where I could be anything I want to be. I can picture so vividly being in some foreign city. I imagine the streets, the houses, the people and the way they might behave. But most of all

I imagine living with you, darling Walter. It is a place where nobody knows or even cares that you are a Jew. They don't care if we walk hand in hand in the street or sit at the same table or watch the same films or dance together, shocking and free. Would that really be so wrong? And I can't help myself, but I imagine living in sin with you, doing all the things lovers do together. The idea is both exhilarating and terrifying. But I know it will never happen, so instead, I write it here, in my journal where nobody but I can see.

Twenty-Three

I dig my hands deep inside the fur-lined pockets of my coat and hurry toward our meeting place. It's nearly the shortest day of the year and, as yet, it's barely light. A keen wind lifts my hair and numbs my face.

He's there, waiting, hunched inside his coat on the low wall of the bridge. As soon as I reach him, he gathers me into his arms.

He enfolds me inside his coat, and pressed against him, I'm safe and warm. He kisses me gently on the lips.

"I've been watching the sun come up," he says, waving a hand in the direction of the glow in the sky behind him. His face is so close I can smell his peppermint-scented breath. "Beautiful," he murmurs, looking at me.

Kuschi begins to whine at my side. He pauses and whines again, louder. I pull away from Walter and bend down to stroke his head.

"Let him go," Walter says, holding his coat open. "He can run around and have some dog fun. I need you in here. With me."

I unclip Kuschi's leash and he ambles off on the path by the river, waving his tail in happiness. What simple pleasures a dog has.

If only it were so with humans.

We walk, hip to hip, arms wrapped around each other. The wheat field ahead of us is winter bare, dark earth lying inert in frigid furrows and ridges, waiting for spring to warm and waken the hidden life slumbering deep inside. Beyond the field, slim skeletons of leafless beech trees extend away into seemingly endless forests. Kuschi's moving shape merges and disappears against the black furrows.

Then Walter kisses me and the outside world fades.

It's just his body against mine. The hard ground beneath my feet, and the smooth lining of the inside of his coat against the back of my hands.

Lost in his touch, the sound of a cough rips me from my entrancement.

"What was that?" I whisper.

"What?"

"A noise." I'm frigid with fear.

Walter looks over his shoulder. Nothing moves.

"I didn't hear anything." He turns back to me.

I scan the landscape. The grassy bank. The empty path. The line of trees. We hold our breath.

Crack. The unmistakable sound of a twig breaking underfoot. Then movement on the riverbank.

Suddenly Kuschi's running back from the field, barking furiously, as he disappears over the other side of the bank.

Walter's eyes are wide.

"Who's there?" he shouts.

No reply. No barking. Only the wind rustling dying leaves in the treetops and the river flowing behind us.

"Stay here," I whisper, and, throat tight, I climb up the bank. On the other side is the little lane. My knees give way at the sight of a tall, gangly figure in a dark jacket with his collar turned up, walking briskly away. Kuschi runs in circles around him, inviting him to play. This is no stranger.

Bile rises in my throat.

"Get away, stupid *bastard* dog." The figure bends and pushes Kuschi roughly. He half falls but goes back for more, perhaps thinking this is some kind of a game. The boy straightens and looks back. My eyes lock with his.

"Tomas," I croak, but he doesn't hear.

He shouts gruffly again at Kuschi and aims a kick at him. Then he turns and breaks into a run, his jacket flapping at his sides.

I stumble and trip back down the bank to where Walter is pacing.

"It was Tomas. He saw us—"

Walter's face is drawn and pale. "We're finished. Both of us."

"No, it'll be okay. Tomas wouldn't . . ." I try to convince myself, as well as him.

"Heaven knows what'll happen to you, but I'll be convicted, Hetty, for sure."

"Now you're overexaggerating," I say, but my throat tightens despite my confident words.

"Am I?" He clenches his jaw. "I don't believe so." He begins to follow the path back toward the bridge. He turns to me angrily.

"You of all people must know what happens to Jews who seduce Germans. And don't pretend you don't."

"Wait—" I run to keep up with his fast pace.

Back at the bridge, his face is tight, eyes full of fear. "I'm sorry, Hetty. I've been so stupid. I should have been more careful. Must get home. Must think."

"Please. Try not to worry. I'll make it okay. Tomas is a friend. You'll see."

I try to call out for Kuschi, standing on the bank, tail between his legs, but I have no voice.

Of all the people in the world, why did it have to be Tomas?

I DROP KUSCHI at home, then take a red-and-yellow tram south through the center of Leipzig. It screeches and winds its way around the edge of the old town and past the grand government buildings. Near the law courts I change trams and head west, out into the industrial grime of Plagwitz. Row upon row of grim tenement blocks with a few straggly trees and rough patches of grass punctuate the cityscape. Redbrick chimneys and the high rooftops of solid factory buildings tower over blocks of flats.

At the tram stop I pull the map, with Tomas's address scribbled in the top corner, from my pocket to double-check the route. It's not far. I find the tenement block, one of several identical ones, just off Karl-Heine-Strasse and across the road from a two-story factory. A truck rolls out of the high iron gates with SA guards on either side. The barrier is lowered once the truck has passed through.

I turn and stare up at the flats. Beneath each small, square window hangs a swastika. For the first time, I see menace, not glory, in the rows of black, white, and red fluttering benignly in the breeze. I shudder and push the door open into a dreary entrance hall.

The caretaker, a shriveled old man with cloudy eyes, directs me to the third floor of the building, flat number eleven. The stairwell smells of urine and cigarette smoke. I climb the steps slowly.

I hesitate at the door of flat eleven. Faded red paint clings in patches to the dark wood. I scrunch my hand into a fist and knock firmly on the door.

I wait and the silence deepens.

The door opens a fraction and a young boy peers around at me.

"Is Tomas in?"

His head disappears and the door swings wide open. Tomas is silhouetted in the doorway, the room behind him dimly lit. Several of his siblings stare at me with big, questioning eyes. He steps into the corridor and quickly pulls the door shut behind him.

Anger radiates from him like heat.

"Tomas—I can explain. Can we talk?"

He shrugs and gives me a raw, hard stare.

"Please."

"There is nothing to explain. I saw all I needed with my own eyes." He folds his arms over his chest. "I watched you for a long time."

The smell in the corridor is nauseating.

"Can we go somewhere else to talk?" I plead. "I can't explain here." I imagine ears being pressed up against the thin walls of the surrounding flats.

Tomas turns and leads the way downstairs without another word. Thoughts tumble: Tomas's hand on mine in the cinema; his tawny eyes, owl-big through his smudged glasses, always watching me; his occasional calls to the house; his gentle, unwavering friendship. Tomas knows my movements. My early morning walks with Kuschi on Sundays. Stupid, stupid of us not to have varied our routine.

Out on the street, Tomas heads in the direction of the tram stop. A truck rumbles by and a group of chattering women emerge from behind the factory gates, fanning out into the street on their way home after a shift.

Say something. Anything.

Suddenly Tomas turns to face me. The fury in his hazel eyes is magnified by the lenses of his glasses. "What the hell are you up to, Hetty? I thought . . . Shit. It doesn't matter what I thought." He hunches his shoulders and hurries away again.

We pass a dingy block of flats. A window on the ground floor has been broken and a fraying, filthy net curtain flutters pathetically in the breeze. I jog to keep pace with Tomas's long stride.

"It does matter, Tomas," I try as I come level with him. "But you see, Walter is just an old friend of my brother's. There's nothing in it. Nothing happened, nor will it ever—"

"I know *exactly* who he is. And I know that you must be out of your sane mind."

"I didn't plan it, honestly . . ."

"But you *enjoyed* it, didn't you, Hetty? You enjoyed that kiss. I saw"—he spits out the words—"the wonderful Hetty kissing a filthy Jew. You *disgust* me. How dirty, cheap, and *low* can you get?"

For a moment I think he is going to hit me and I recoil. He lets his fists fall to his sides. I take a step away from him, wipe my hand across my brow. It comes away damp.

Be brave.

"Have you . . . told anyone?"

But he just stares at me, pink cheeked and hostile.

"What will you do?" I press.

"Is that all you care about?" he snaps. "You just don't get it, do you?"

He kicks at a trash can propped against a wall with such force it lands in the middle of the road with a loud clang. The lid clatters and rolls along the pavement.

"Get away from me, Hetty Heinrich. Go away and you'd better hope I never see your face again. You have no idea what you've done. No idea . . ."

And he runs, hard and fast, up the middle of the street, dodging a car and a bicycle before disappearing around the corner.

I collapse into a heap on the pavement, my back pressed against the brickwork, slouched in the dust and filth. What have I become? Tomas is right. I strayed from the path and look what I have turned into. But it's too late now. I can't go back, we're doomed. I finally allow the tears to come, self-pitying, tension relieving. Perhaps running away isn't such a bad idea, after all.

Twenty-Four

December 20, 1937

Groggy from lack of sleep, I fumble in my drawer for warm stockings. Somehow, I have to let Walter know about my disastrous meeting with Tomas. Perhaps I should go to the café, ask Lena where he lives.

There's a knock at my door.

"Yes? Mutti, is that you?"

Ingrid pokes her head around the door.

"I've a message for you." She holds out a small, sealed envelope.

"Thank you, Ingrid." I take it, as though I receive hand-delivered messages like this at seven o'clock in the morning every day of my life. I drop it casually onto my bedside table.

Ingrid hovers, eyeing the envelope. "The delivery boy is waiting. He says you might want to send an immediate reply." She cocks her head and stares at me long and hard.

I feel my face redden and turn my back on her.

"Oh. Right. I'd better read it now then," I say lightly, tearing open the envelope with trembling fingers. I keep my back to her, shielding the note with my body.

My darling,

I'm in such a desperate state I had to get in touch. I hope it doesn't make things worse for you. I'm sorry I was angry with you yesterday. I was just so afraid—I acted harshly. I hope you can forgive me. I'm worried for us both. How did you get on with our friend? Could we meet early in the morning, somewhere safe, to work out what to do? I was thinking perhaps the station? Can you get there at six a.m.? It would give us more time. We could even jump on a train somewhere away from all the prying eyes. Let me know if it's possible.

All my love,
W xx

P.S. You can trust the messenger boy—he's Lena's son.

I ball up the note and put it in my dressing gown pocket. "I do have a reply, actually, Ingrid. Just one moment." I hastily scribble my own note.

My dear,

I tried to speak with our friend, but his mind is made up to cause trouble. I am afraid for us both. Of course I forgive you. You were right to be angry and upset. Yes,

*let's meet at the station tomorrow at 6 a.m. I will bring
provisions and money.*

Till then,

xxx

I seal the envelope, and, after a moment's thought, I write "Lena" on the front.

Ingrid can barely contain her curiosity when I hand it to her. She fingers it as though she might work out its contents through her fingertips.

"It's just a message to a school friend," I tell her. I don't like the gleam in her eye.

"Of course, Miss Herta," she says primly. "I'll give it to the boy right away." She leaves the room without bothering to hide her smirk.

I stare at the closed door after she's gone. Wringing my hands, I run to the window, stricken with paranoia. Is there really a delivery boy? But yes, a few moments later, the shape of a dark-haired boy of perhaps eleven or twelve passes beneath the cherry tree as he lets himself out onto the pavement. There's a flash of white in his hand, but it does nothing to unravel the knot of fear in my belly.

"Hello! Anyone? I'm back." Karl's voice echoes up from the hall. My journal lies open on the floor, the pen and a smudge of ink next to it on the rug. I must have drifted off.

I scramble up from my window seat, shove my journal

under the mattress. I run downstairs. Mutti is already there.

"I was having my afternoon nap!" she says, smoothing her dress. "How lovely that you're here at last! Now we can properly celebrate Christmas . . . I've no idea where your father is . . . some mysterious errand. Anyway, it doesn't matter, you're home!" She beams at Karl and he gives her a kiss.

"Ah, Little Mouse! Good to see you, oh scruffy one. What's happened to your hair?" He ruffles it and laughs.

"Shut up! I fell asleep, too. My hair got messed—"

"So did Mutti, but she doesn't look like that . . ."

"Karl—"

"It's okay, schatz, I'm only teasing. You look as lovely as ever. How about a drink?" He takes off his coat and throws it on the rack. "Ingrid? Could you fetch me a beer?"

We follow him into the afternoon sitting room where a fire burns brightly in the grate. I curl up next to him on the sofa while he drinks.

"Hauptmann Winkler is terrifying," he tells us. "Sometimes he carries out room raids at five in the morning. Our beds must be perfect, boots shining, uniform in good order. We have to be dressed and ready to fly in seconds. He'll shout orders and yell technical questions about Junkers and Messerschmitts and the weather and the most obscure aspect of flying or fighting when you're muzzy headed and half asleep . . ."

"He sounds awful . . ."

"But Kunz, Wolfy, and Greg—my good friends—we have each other's backs. You need to, with Hauptmann Winkler around." He finishes his beer. "It's good to be home." He smiles at Mutti and holds his glass out for Ingrid to refill it.

I am sleepy and warm in the fireside fug, and his voice washes over me like bathwater. But my stomach knots when I think of Tomas. I picture him with Vati, right at this very moment. *Herr Heinrich, I have reason to believe your daughter is having illegal relations with a Jew . . .*

"Hetty?"

"Hmm?"

Karl is staring at me. "I said, do you want to come with me to meet up with Stefan, Frank, Claus, and the others for a drink this evening? Erna will be there. We could go by the Christmas market. What do you say?"

"Sorry, I was . . . that would be lovely. Yes, please, Karl."

"Well . . ." He stretches and stands. "I must unpack and wash."

Mutti and I smile at each other once he has left the room. It *is* good to have him home, but even Karl's presence can't shift the fingers of dread creeping around my neck, threatening to strangle me.

LATER, I WANDER into Karl's room where he's stretched out on his bed, a half-drunk bottle of beer in his hand.

I sit on the end of his bed and he moves his feet to make room for me.

"So what's it *really* like in the Luftwaffe? C'mon. I want the real, not the Mutti-filtered, version. Is it all you dreamed it to be?"

"Oh, Hetty, it's . . . Well, yes and no. The flying is indescribably wonderful. Just me, and my machine, up there." He points out the window into the night sky. "The pure, raw *power* of it. Me at the controls, her responding. And boy does she respond! The speed, the maneuvers. It makes gliding seem like child's play, although now I understand the value of it. I've learned so much about the wind, currents, weather, physics. All valuable stuff."

"And what else?"

He swallows hard. "Truth is, it's pretty harsh. And because I went to a gymnasium, the superiors think I'm just an over-educated *arschloch*. I'm always singled out for punishments. For . . ." He stops, his lip quivers a fraction, then he closes his mouth tight and swallows.

"Karl?"

"It's fine. I'll get through it. I've a couple of decent friends now. They've got my back, like I said. And last week, Haupt-mann Winkler actually pulled me aside and grudgingly told me I'm a natural pilot. I just need to . . . make sure I'm *one of the boys*. That's all. I've got a handle on it. It's going to be fine."

I watch his face as painful memories appear to pass through his mind.

"Are you sure you're fine?" I ask, touching his knee.

"Yes, of course I am," he replies firmly. "But here, what's been going on at home? I want to know everything." He smiles.

How I wish I could tell him about Walter and Tomas. Ask his advice. Once I might have, but now I don't dare. Besides, it sounds as though he has been having a difficult time as it is.

"Come on, what is it?" he pushes me. "It's about you and Erna, isn't it? That letter you wrote me . . . You were pretty upset."

"I'm sorry. I was a goose," I say, hugging my knees to my

chest. I watch his face carefully to see if he's angry with me, but he smiles and slaps my knees playfully.

"Erna's been inconsolable—she thought she'd lost you as a friend."

"I feel such a fool."

"Typical of you, schatz. Shouted before you thought it through. I promise, we didn't set out to hurt you. It was . . . complicated. We didn't want to make it a big thing. Especially as it might not work out, with me going away and everything. And then when it got more serious, I couldn't risk Mutti and Vati knowing in case they told Erna's parents. They'd never have allowed her to have a boyfriend. It wasn't that we were trying to upset you . . ."

"I know that now."

"You've made up then?"

"Yes. We've made up."

"Great. I'm pleased. I'm really quite smitten, you know."

"That's good," I say, not able to meet his eye. How I wish I could talk about Walter like this.

"Hetty?"

"Yes."

"There's something else, isn't there? I know you too well. You can't hide anything from me, Little Mouse."

Well, I have hidden something. Something huge.

I sigh and instead tell him about the other plague on my mind, Vati, Fräulein Müller, and the girl-child. He listens quietly, his face solemn.

He is quiet for a few moments and stares absently out the window. He shakes his head and says slowly, "All you saw was

Vati greeting the fräulein and hugging a little girl. It might have been the first time he set eyes on her in years. Perhaps they bumped into each other and she was showing off her child?"

"I know what I saw, and it was not that."

"You know what you *thought* you saw. But you might be reading something into it that just wasn't there."

"Why don't you ever believe me? Besides, it proves I didn't dream up what I saw that night outside my window all those years ago."

"It proves nothing but that you have a vivid imagination, still working its magic, that's all."

"Karl . . ." There is heat in my throat and a desire to slap him. *Make* him listen.

"All right. Let's assume for a moment you are right. That you saw what you thought you saw. So Vati has a mistress. Big deal. Loads of men have mistresses. Especially important ones. Herr Himmler for a start. It's life. It's expected of successful men. Vati would never leave Mutti, I'm certain of that. And, so long as he is discreet, well, what's the problem with it?"

His words are astonishing. I stare at him with an open mouth. He thinks it's *okay* for Vati to have a mistress and a secret child?

"How can you say that!" I choke. I kick him with my bare foot. "What if it was a boy I saw Vati with, not a little girl. Would that bother you more, to think he had another son?" I take a deep breath. "Perhaps there already is one. How would you feel then?"

"You're being ridiculous, Hetty. It's not true."

"How do you know that?"

"Jesus. What's happened to you?" He takes a long slug of beer.

"What's happened to *me*? What's happened to you, Karl?"

"I'm not going to listen to any more of this nonsense, Hetty," he says, unfolding himself and getting up.

"Are you just going to deny it, then, that's it?"

"It's time to get ready to go into town," he says, ignoring me. "You can still come if you want." And with that, he leaves the room.

I stare at the door for a long time, my eyes filled with tears. How could he be so harsh? This isn't the Karl I know. I worried so much before he left that he would change, and he has. A deep, gaping hole has opened up inside. Vati has his mistress and new child. Karl has Erna. I cannot openly be with Walter, and Mutti is so involved in her new school project that she is rarely home, and when she is, her head is buried in paperwork. Besides, I can hardly talk to her about any of this.

And I have never in my life felt more heart-achingly alone.

Twenty-Five

December 21, 1937

I'm up well before dawn. I pack my knapsack with two outfits and my raincoat. With shoes in one hand, I tiptoe downstairs in stockinged feet.

I flick on the light switch in the kitchen. Kuschi is curled in his basket. He opens one eye and thumps his tail a few times.

"Go back to sleep, darling Kuschi," I tell him, scratching the loose skin on his neck.

I take some money from the housekeeping jar, solely meant for Bertha's use, and stash it inside the knapsack, hoping she doesn't keep track of her spending too carefully. I lift the bread from the bread bin and begin to cut slices for sandwiches.

The door creaks. Of course Ingrid would be up extra early this morning! I turn around to greet her, preparing an explanation, only it isn't Ingrid. It's Karl standing in the doorway, hair ruffled, still wearing yesterday's clothes. Even from here, he stinks of smoke and liquor.

He leans on the doorframe and curls his lip at me.

"And just where do you think you're going at this time in the morning?" His speech is slurred, accusing.

I turn away from him, my mind racing. I begin buttering the bread.

"I'm making sandwiches for the BDM. Where have *you* been?"

"None of your business."

"Weren't you with Erna last night?"

"Took her home nice and early so her parents wouldn't worry. Then some of the boys and me went for a couple more drinks . . ."

"A couple? A dozen more like," I say with a snort. "I wonder what Erna would think if she saw you like this?" I cut slabs of cheese and place them on the bread.

He weaves toward me and leans on the counter. "She loves me, whether *you* like it or not." Up close, I can see his eyes are cloudy and bloodshot.

"You should go to bed," I tell him. "Get a couple of hours' sleep before Mutti sees you. What would your Hauptmann Winkler make of you now? I can't imagine you'll last long in the Luftwaffe in *that* condition."

"What would you know about anything anyway?" Karl sneers. "Living like a spoiled princess. I always tried to protect you. Take care of my little sister . . . and what do you do? Huh? Abuse us all with your wanton *disregard* for everything—"

"What are you talking about? Go to bed, Karl, you're drunk."

"Oh no, I'm not going anywhere until *you* tell me what you're up to."

"I'm not up to anything."

"Word is, you have a secret lover boy."

The knife slips from my hand and clatters on the board. I snatch it up.

I slice off some butter and force my fingers to keep moving, trying to spread the butter but it's too hard and the bread crumbles beneath it. "Who told you that?"

"Doesn't matter *who* told me. That's not the point. The point IS . . ." He waggles his finger at me again. "The point IS, why's he a secret? Eh? After all the scrapes I got you out of . . . you owe me some honesty."

"There is no secret. There's no lover boy."

Karl fetches a glass and fills it with water. He guzzles it down and refills.

"Not good enough, Little Mouse," he says. "You need to tell me what's going on." He pulls out a chair and sits languorously on it. "See, I've got all morning. I'm not in any hurry."

Perhaps he's not as drunk as I first thought. What does he know? I wrap the sandwiches in newspaper. Whatever the case, there is a mistrust between us that was never there before.

"Whatever you've heard, Karl, it simply isn't true. There's no lover. Ask anyone, Erna, Mutti, Vati. You know I would never be allowed . . ."

I place the sandwich parcels at the top of the knapsack.

"You don't seriously think I'm going to let you go, do you?" he drawls. "You still haven't explained why you are making sandwiches at five o'clock in the morning."

"I told you. These are for the BDM. A . . . Christmas community thing. For those in need. I was awake. Couldn't sleep, so I thought I would do it now."

"All very virtuous, I'm sure, Hetty, but a couple of sand-wiches, wrapped in newspaper? Not very festive, is it? C'mon, I'm no fool." He stretches out his arms and folds his hands behind his head. "I tell you what, I shan't mention your early Sunday morning meetings with Lover Boy to Vati, if you make me a promise."

Something explodes in my chest. He knows. Damn Tomas!

I bend down to fiddle with the string at the top of my knapsack, tying and retying it, hiding my tears from Karl. "And what's that?"

"Give him up, and never see him again. If you don't, I'll have no choice but to do what I have to. I certainly won't pro-tect you anymore." His voice hardens. I don't answer and he says, "I'll know if you break that promise. I have my spies."

I wipe my eyes, take a deep breath, and stand.

"I'm not going anywhere this morning, Karl, and I have no idea what you're talking about. I have no lover boy, and I do not intend *ever* to get one. I shan't ever get married. One day I *shall* become a doctor, you'll see, and I'll travel, far, far away from here. Right now, I'm going back to my room, and I suggest you do the same. Until you look and smell presentable."

As I walk past him, he grabs my arm and pulls me to face him.

"Why risk it?" he says, his words lucid again, his tone plead-ing. "Don't play with fire, Little Mouse. A dance with the devil . . . it can only ever end in disaster."

I pull my arm away and leave the kitchen.

Closing my door, I throw myself onto the bed, pummeling the pillow with my fists. Hot tears soak the covers. I picture

Walter waiting in vain for me at the station, our plans in tatters. Walter's situation is perilous, and whatever happens to him, it will be my fault. An idea comes to me, and I rummage in my drawer for some writing paper and a pen. I will find a way to get this delivered when Ingrid and Bertha are up.

Lena,

I know we hardly know each other, but despite this, I hope you can accept me as your friend. I rather need your help and I have nobody else to turn to. Our mutual friend is in great danger. I cannot go to see this friend myself, for fear it will make things worse. I would be extremely grateful if you could warn him that things are very bad. This is why I couldn't be at our rendez-vous this morning. Please tell him that I truly cannot risk seeing him again, certainly not at this moment. Tell him, this is for the best, and that he means so very much to me.

Yours so very gratefully,
Herta

Twenty-Six

January 29, 1938

Tomas, hunched in a threadbare coat, blows on his hands to keep them from turning blue. Snow still lies on the ground. Winter is never going to end, or so it seems.

"Don't you have any gloves?" His fingers look an alarmingly blotchy red blue.

He avoids my eyes. "Stupidly left them on the tram. Wasn't thinking straight, you know, coming to meet you."

"Look, Tomas . . . come on, let's get you some gloves." I sigh. "I can pay. I think I should. You didn't have to come, but I'm glad you did." I lead the way across the road to the Breuninger stores. I have to find a way inside his head. Drill behind his skull into his mind. Tomas is a child of Hitler. He cannot ignore what he saw.

Since Lena wrote back that my message had been safely delivered, I've had no contact with Walter. I've not dared. At any moment I was ready with my rehearsed speech for Vati's interrogation, but it never came. It seems Karl was as good as his word. No more Sunday morning rendezvous, and he keeps his mouth shut. Since he returned to the Luftwaffe he has written once. A friendly, chatty letter, but between the lines, I sense a distance that wasn't there before.

"Men's outfitters, second floor," I read off the store guide.

We travel up in the lift without speaking. At the glove counter, Tomas takes his time sifting through the options, trying on the samples the shop assistant presents him with.

"I think I'll take these," he says at last, pointing to a pair of sheepskin-lined leather mittens. They are the most expensive option, but I don't flinch at the price, and I tell the assistant to put them on Vati's account. I'll tell Vati they were for my birthday, perfectly believable as I celebrated my sixteenth only last week.

"Now," Tomas says, walking out onto the street and brandishing his gloves with a flourish, "you must let *me* buy *you* a coffee."

"Absolutely. That would be lovely."

In a cozy corner of a coffeehouse off Nikolaistrasse, we sit opposite each other at a little wooden table, Tomas's tall frame hunched over the table. He thrums out a rhythm with his fingers until a waitress appears.

The coffee, when it arrives, is hot and bitter. I add two lumps of sugar and stir, smiling at Tomas, wondering how to start. Which words to use.

"I forgive you," he blurts out suddenly, his eyes finally meeting mine.

"Pardon?"

"I mean, as long as what you said is the truth, and you won't see that *arschloch* again, then I can forgive you."

He sits back in his chair as though a great weight is lifted, but there is tension in his jaw and his fingers twitch constantly.

"I haven't seen him again, honestly." I lean forward to emphasize the point. "And I won't. I meant it. I'm truly sorry. I would never want to hurt you, you of all people, Tomas." I place my hand on top of his, just for a moment. It flaps like a dying fish.

His face crumples. "It's tormented me, Hetty. Like living in some sort of hell. I thought I was going mad. But I get it now. I was wrong before. It wasn't your fault. He twisted you. I see that now." His face is shiny with perspiration. "He tricked you—forced you—into falling for him. It's what they do, the scum."

"Tomas—" I fight the anger rising inside me at his words. His hateful references to Walter. I want to tell him all of it was my own free will. Walter didn't trick me. He couldn't, he wouldn't. That all this about the evil, scheming Jews is made-up nonsense. But something stops me. I have to work out the consequences of everything I say. I can't risk him knowing how I really feel.

"No. Wait." The toe of his shoe drums the floor. "I need to know you aren't still in his hold—you know—that you're free of his *influence*. Then I'll try to forget what I saw. And I shan't make any trouble for you."

"Any more than you did already by telling Karl," I say before I can stop myself. Slow down. Breathe. "I mean, you had every right . . . But it's made things difficult for me. With Karl."

"What do you mean, telling Karl?" His shoe stops drumming. "I didn't tell him."

"You didn't?"

"No, Hetty, I've not told a soul. I swear it."

"Oh . . ." My mind is racing. I try to remember the details of that awful conversation in the kitchen. Karl never mentioned Walter's name. Neither did I. Perhaps he *doesn't* know. If Tomas didn't tell, well then, perhaps Karl *is* just guessing, and my mysterious "lover boy" could be anyone.

"I mean," he says, "I should report him. I want to. I'd love to see the filthy scum punished, but"—his face puckers—"I can't see how to do it without making trouble for you."

"Can't we just forget all this, Tomas? It was just a stupid kiss. In a moment when I lost my mind. I don't know what I was thinking . . . But I promise, I'd never do it again."

"That's good, Hetty, yes, that's good." He tap, tap, taps his shoe on the floor and nods his head. "It's been tearing me up, this whole thing. I couldn't bear to think . . . See, I thought of reporting him anonymously. Writing to the paper even, telling them what I saw him do. But, of course, he'd just deny it." He leans forward. "He'd lie. Do anything to save himself, including naming *you*. I couldn't take that risk."

We stare at each other across the table for a few moments. The pupils in Tomas's tawny eyes are huge and round, magnified as ever, through his glasses. I swallow hard. How do I reply to that? "Thank you," I whisper finally. I take a sip of coffee and hope he doesn't see how my hands tremble. A new worry stirs in my belly.

"So," Tomas says. "Let's talk of other things." His expression changes. "Hetty, I wanted to tell you"—he becomes animated, excited—"I've signed up to join the Heer, once my

apprenticeship is finished. The army will need trained me-
chanics like me. Loads of them. I'll have a job for life. What
do you think, Hetty, eh?"

"I think that's great. Yes, really great." I smile at him over
my coffee cup.

But if *you* didn't tell Karl about my secret Sunday morning
meetings, then who did?

Twenty-Seven

February 10, 1938

The snow is gone, but a dense fog settles over Leipzig during the night in its stead. As dawn breaks, I leave the house for school, stepping out into the damp gloom. The usual sounds of morning are muffled. Car headlights are dimmed, and the clip-clop of a horse's hooves are oddly detached from the ghostly dark shape that slowly emerges from the pallid mist.

It would be easy to let my imagination get the better of me. I start and turn at muted sounds, but ghouls and murderers remain hidden in the nebulous atmosphere. I pull my coat tighter around me and hurry across Kirchplatz and into Gohliser Strasse. A tram rumbles and screeches around the bend behind me, drowning all other sound, so when a figure emerges unexpectedly from a recessed doorway, I scream, wild with fear.

"For Christ's sake, hush!" hisses the figure, wrapped in a coat and scarf, hat pulled low. "It's me!"

"Walter? Jesus, what the—"

He grabs my arm and marches me quickly along the street. The tram rolls away. People pass us, heads down against the weather. Before we reach Nordplatz, Walter guides me across the road and down Prendelstrasse.

"Where are we going? I have to be at school in ten minutes!"

Walter continues to propel me in the opposite direction.

"You're not going to school," he tells me firmly. "You're going to spend the day at the zoo with me."

"This is ludicrous! What if they call my parents? Why did you come to find me? You know we can't see each other . . . Has something happened?"

I look up at him. All that's visible is a small section of pale, pink cheek between his black scarf and gray felt hat.

"Shh. All in good time." He turns toward me, and now, finally, I see the twinkling blue of his eyes and my stomach plunges.

"They'll think it odd if I'm not in school. I'm not like some who hardly ever attend anymore. It'd be out of character for me. This is dangerous, Walter."

He takes my arm again and we recross the road. A few yards away is a phone booth.

"Go in there. Call the school. Pretend to be your mother and say: Herta is unwell today. She won't be coming in."

"I *can't!*"

"Yes, you can."

His gaze is steady and I find myself pulling open the door. He puts a few coins into my hand.

Dry mouthed, I pick up the receiver, insert the coins, and ask the operator to be put through to the office at the gymnasium.

Through the door Walter, hands in his pockets, nods and smiles encouragement.

There's a ringing tone, then a click and "Good morning," in a stern voice, then silence as the woman at the other end waits for my reply. I stare at the dirty floor.

"Good morning," I say, in an unnaturally low voice. I try to mimic the soft inflection Mutti puts on certain words. I hope the line isn't too clear. "I would like to inform you, my daughter, Herta Heinrich, is unwell today. I'm afraid she has a fever and won't be able to come to school."

"Thank you for informing us, Frau Heinrich," says the voice. "We hope she will feel better soon."

"Yes, thank you. Good day."

The line clicks as the speaker at the other end disconnects. I replace the receiver and can hardly believe the brazen thing I have just done.

"It worked!"

I fling myself into Walter's arms and laugh. We shall have this whole morning together and nobody will know. Hidden from the road behind some rough shrubbery outside the zoo, we kiss, and kiss, and kiss.

"You make me braver than I could ever be on my own," I tell him. "I've missed you so much."

"I have missed you, too. And you make me reckless, Hetty. Reckless like I've never been in my life. Love makes us do crazy things, doesn't it?"

I laugh, my breath instantly cooling, hanging in the air.

Love.

He looks down at me and as his eyes lock with mine, there is such understanding between us. I would follow him anywhere. To the ends of the earth, if he asked me.

They're unlocking the gates to the zoo. Walter pays the entrance fee and we walk into the deserted grounds, linking arms as we head straight down the center path.

"I've been so worried, without any news from you." I steal a look at him.

"But you told me not to get in touch. I was certain they'd come for me. I didn't dare go out. My mother was so angry with me when I told her I'd been seeing a German girl. Couldn't tell her it was you, of course. She even made me hide in the attic for a couple of days. And all I could do was stay there, mad with worry about what might be happening to you. But nobody came, so I dared to come downstairs, then I dared to venture out. I can hardly believe it, but it seems Tomas didn't report us," he says, and we huddle together for warmth. "After a few weeks I crept about, like some sort of criminal, trying to see you. I spotted you a few times going in and out of school. It was unbearable watching but not being able to speak or hold you. Two months without you has been a grueling eternity. I couldn't take it anymore and decided to take the risk."

"I'm so glad you did," I whisper. "Tomas never said a word because I think he has a soft spot for me."

"What a genius you are." He winks.

"Still. We need to be extra careful."

"Absolutely." Walter looks serious. "We were reckless before, but we can be more clever about meeting, vary the time and place. We can use Lena. She is totally trustworthy. She's even kept our secret from my mother and father. She knows my parents would forbid it, if they found out."

"Isn't it an awful risk for her? Why would she?"

"You aren't the only one who has other admirers, you know." He winks again.

But the chill of the day intensifies when I remember Karl's words of warning, and I glance behind me into the shape-shifting fog.

There are aviaries on either side of the path. A bedraggled owl perches in one; small birds flit about in another, and in the largest are some wading birds, standing on the edge of a small pond sunk into the concrete floor. I check again over my shoulder.

"Relax, Hetty. No one is here. Tomas has done nothing, we're in the clear," Walter says, hooking his arm through mine. I nod, but I can't shake the sense that someone is lurking unseen in the amorphous shroud.

We carry on in silence, deeper into the zoo, past the otters and the North American beavers. The only other people around are zookeepers, handing out breakfast to the hungry inmates.

We watch a couple of huge hairy bison standing near the fence eating hay, then continue along the winding path until we stand in front of two vast grizzly bears pacing back and forth in their enclosure, passing each other without acknowledgment. They are silent on their dinner-plate-size paws, sniffing the air now and then with pointed, damp-looking snouts. They are magnificent creatures, and I pity them for being here, when they should be in a forest somewhere, wild and free.

The fog begins to thin; a ray of sunshine penetrates, dousing the swirling cloud in soft amber. Perhaps Walter is right. Here we are alone; I should make the most of this opportunity to enjoy his company.

I smile into his eyes and the tension I felt lifts, floating away with the mist.

"You know," he says, the bears padding back and forth in front of us, "when you smile, you are the most beautiful creature in all the world."

I poke him in the ribs. "Don't tease."

"I'm not teasing. It's the truth. I've thought it often enough, but I haven't dared to say. I figure, if I don't tell you this stuff now—"

"Shh." I put my finger to his lips. "Don't say you might never . . . Just, don't say that."

"Okay. I won't. But if I want to tell you how much you mean to me, and how beautiful you are, you can't stop me."

I feel my face flush under the intensity of his gaze.

"And you can feel free to tell me anytime," he continues, "just what a dashing chap I am, how you love my dazzling company, or how good my jokes are . . ." I giggle and we begin to walk on. "In fact, it's time for a little joke, now, I think," he says. He pauses a moment, then says, "Göring has attached an arrow to the row of medals on his tunic. It reads, *Continued on the back* . . ."

"You really do tell the *most* appalling jokes . . ."

He's smiling. "It's just what we do. It's sort of how we get by, I suppose."

Walter looks around, then pulls me behind the trunk of a large tree so we are hidden from view of the path. He slips his arms around my waist and we are kissing again, our bodies melting together, his hardness growing against me. It's both wondrous and terrifying, this power I have.

But, if I were to give myself to him, would the magic, the mystery, the wanting, all be over? After so long apart, I want him to want me. Above everything, and everyone. When the kiss is over, we stand for a long time, foreheads pressed together, breath mingling in the cold air.

"Do you ever think of doing 'it'?" I whisper.

"You are joking, aren't you? Do I ever *not* think of it?" He pulls me closer. "Would you want to?"

The air is still and quiet. Water drips from sodden leaves.

"I don't know . . ." But I do know. I desperately want it.

The weight of the idea, the vastness of it, hangs over us, heavy and penetrating as the fog, yet lighter than air. The impossibility. The idea of his bare skin on mine. The touch of his hands, the surrendering of myself to him.

The mingling of our blood.

"Hetty, it's okay. We don't have to. We shouldn't. We won't. I'd never do anything you didn't want."

And after that, we don't talk of it anymore. He simply holds me, and I breathe him in.

Twenty-Eight

May 13, 1938

I know I should end it. That day we went to the zoo—I was weak. I should have done it then, because now, it is so much harder. But every time I sneak away to see you, I'm terrified we'll be seen. I won't get a second chance from Tomas. And now he calls for me, once a month or so. To see a film, or to go for a walk. Sometimes I can make excuses, but mostly I don't. For your sake. Luckily his shifts at the factory are long, so he doesn't get many days off. Walter, I'm so afraid we'll be spotted together again. But today was a blissful day, warm and sunny, blossoms everywhere. With Mutti and Vati out celebrating Lord Mayor Otto Schultz's birthday, we had time to take the tram south to the Leipziger Auenwald, where nobody we know could find us. You told me you loved me, that you wish we could spend the rest of our lives together. Then we kissed. I could do that all day and never bore *of it. But now my heart aches with the bitter-sweetness of it all.*

I pull up the loose floorboard at the back of my cupboard and place my journal inside this new, safer hiding place. I return the floorboard, then cover it with piles of spare linen and blankets. It's early evening and Mutti and Vati are not yet back from their champagne lunch.

In the afternoon sitting room, I find the *Leipziger Tageszeitung* and flick through the news section. There are several national stories about zero unemployment and the country's industrial successes.

I skim the editorial articles and Vati's weekly section: "The Leipziger Moral Crusade." There is a feature on the capture of a number of known "asocials," guilty of the most foul moral degradation. I recall Vati mentioning that these people had been sent to Buchenwald Concentration Camp. The words *concentration camp* are rarely mentioned. When they are, people whisper them, as though, if you speak them out loud, you may bring bad luck and end up in one yourself. They are tucked away from view, hidden in remote places. It adds to their mystery, and the fear of them.

Vati says these are terrible rumors, caused by foreign newspapers printing false articles, stories supposedly gathered from inmates who've escaped from such camps. Foreign propaganda, he said, whipping up hatred for the German people. But now, I wonder. I think about Tomas's father, and I feel a rush of fear. It seems impossible. After all that Walter has told me, could it be possible that these disturbing stories are true?

I throw down the paper. I remember a time, a couple of years back, when Vati took Karl and me into the offices of the *Leipziger.* He was keen to show Karl the wonder of the place and convince him that one day he would want to take over the running of it. We had looked in on the bustle of the newsroom, phones ringing, journalists rushing in and out, people shouting at one another. Vati had explained the time pressure to get stories and pictures into the paper for each edition. We'd watched the huge printing presses in action, the laborious task of setting the metal letters in the frames, word by word, sentence by sentence, page by page. The whole effort—the working conditions, the sweat, the dirt, the heat and intensity—we had wondered to Vati, what was the point of all this when people would glance at the headlines and throw the paper away?

Vati was horrified. "This," he had told us passionately, "is the most important tool we have. With these inked words, we can shape our nation. There is no such thing as *news* per se. News is power, wrapped in a message, presented, told, and retold. With this newspaper"—his eyes were filled with pride—"*I* have the power to put into the world what I want, and in the way I would have the masses understand. Do you realize what supremacy, what *authority* that gives me?"

But Karl remained fixed on wanting to fly airplanes, and I had not properly grasped what Vati meant, until now. I think of how it is for Walter. How it is for all the "enemies" of the Reich. How it is for *me* being in love with Walter, knowing that, every minute we spend in each other's company, he is at risk of arrest. How many others are there like us? Simply because of who their parents are? Anger swells at the injustice. *I* see nothing inferior about Walter. Or, indeed, any of his kind. They, *we*, are all just people. And I see Vati's newspaper, finally, for what it is. Not news, but manipulation of thought and mind.

"IF THEY DON'T come back soon, the *schweinefleisch* will be burnt to a cinder, and I'll be blamed," Bertha mutters to Ingrid. The dining room table is set for dinner. Ingrid has decanted the wine, and my stomach rumbles with hunger at the delicious smell of roasting pork emanating from the kitchen.

"The crispier the better," I say, "I'm starving. Why don't we eat anyway?"

"I couldn't possibly! What would your mother say?" Bertha stands with her hands on her ample hips and her cheeks puffed out.

"Worked up a good appetite today, Fräulein Herta?" Ingrid smirks.

"What do you mean?" I feel my face flush beet red. "I went for a picnic with my friend Erna . . ."

"Ah! Is that what you call it—"

"Ingrid!" Bertha cuts in. "There's three vases I noticed—in the hall, the morning room, and the dining room—where the flowers have gone over. Get rid of them and order some fresh to go in. Better still, go down to the florist's now; they'll still be open, and bring some back." She turns angrily and begins scrubbing at the sideboard with her brush and soapy water from the sink.

I want to hug her for putting Ingrid in her place.

"Everything's so upside down these days," she says, once

Ingrid has left the room. "The order of everything. It was all clear in the old days. Parents and children. Master and servant. The bosses and the workers. The upper classes and the lower. Now it's all got muddled." She moves to scrubbing the top of the cooking range, slopping water onto the hot surface so it sizzles. She scrubs hard, rocking back and forth, both hands atop the brush. "Everyone telling on everyone. Trying to get one better on people. Children ruling their parents. Servants their masters. It's not right." She sniffs hard and I wonder if she's crying.

"I wasn't doing any harm today, Bertha, I was—"

She turns slowly to face me. "I don't want to know where you were or who you were with, Fräulein Herta," she says. There is fear in her wide eyes. In her tense shoulders. "What you do in your spare time is your business and nobody else's. And Ingrid would do well to remember that. But she thinks she knows better. She thinks because she has Karl's ear . . ."

"Karl's ear?"

Ingrid.

Bertha stares at me, eyes wretched.

"She likes to gossip, that one," she says. "Wants special treatment. Praise. She wants to get noticed. And by *gossiping*, she gets what she wants. But I know one thing." Bertha wiggles the brush, then plops it back into the sink. "It will end badly for someone. Her, in all likelihood. All I can do is tell her to keep her mouth shut." She shakes her head and purses her lips. "You shouldn't—"

But before she can finish her sentence, the front door bangs and Mutti's and Vati's voices fill the hallway. Bertha begins to bustle around, getting ready to serve the meal, and says no more about it.

Watching her, I wonder where her loyalties lie. With Hitler and the Fatherland? With the family, us, who she works so hard for? Or with her own folk, whoever and wherever they may be. Or perhaps, and the back of my neck prickles as I wonder, fleetingly, could it be that Bertha has some sort of secret sympathy with those excluded from this Aryan revolution?

Twenty-Nine

October 7, 1938

We walk separately, a hundred yards apart, past the soaring, classical structure of the university building, centuries old, solid and constant. I lift my face to the sun; a feathery breeze touches my skin. I glance back. He's on the other side of the road. The slightest tilt of his head as he acknowledges my look. However many times we do this, it's the same rush of adrenaline. Fear and excitement in equal measure.

I enter the small park beyond the university buildings. A park where Jews are forbidden. Thank God for Walter's blond hair and blue eyes. A young man passes on his bike, a bag of books slapping heavily against his thigh. An elderly man shuffles in the distance with a stick. Nobody else is in sight. It's as safe as it will ever be. I sit down and rest my back against the solid trunk of a tree. A couple of minutes later, he sits beside me.

"Hello, you." I lean toward him for a quick kiss. "I have one hour at most."

"Is that all?" His shoulders sag.

"I'm sorry, I'll have more time next week—"

"It's not that . . ." His voice falters. He looks wretched.

"Walter? What's wrong?" I touch his shoulder.

He looks at me and swallows.

"Hey." I rub his arm. "Not even a joke today?"

He shakes his head. He is deathly pale. "There's something I must tell you."

"What is it?"

He clears his throat. "My father finally accepted a few weeks ago that life here is intolerable. Hitler will take everything that's ours, whether we remain here or not. He decided we must leave Germany, at whatever cost. So every day he's been walking from embassy to embassy, queuing for hours on end, trying to get visas for the family. But, as I predicted, we've left it too late. We should have done this years ago. Now, like vermin, no country wants any more Jews." I wince at his words. "We're stuck," he continues. "Except . . ."

"Except?"

"There is one way." He sighs. "But it . . . I'm not sure I can go through with it."

"Why? But you must." My heart squeezes as I say it. The most important thing is that Walter is *safe*. So it's good news. Walter doesn't meet my eyes.

"It means me going alone," he says in a flat voice. "I'll have to leave my parents, my grandmother, all my family." He scrunches his fists tight. "Worse still, I can't bear to think of my life without you in it."

"I don't understand. Why is it that only you can go?"

He takes a long, deep breath. "We have good friends in England; the father is a doctor. They left Germany in 1933. They have a daughter who is a year older than me. Anna."

"And they can help?"

"They think I would be able to get a visa . . ." He swallows again. ". . . if I'm a relative, and they guarantee to support me financially."

"But you aren't, are you? A relative, I mean. How—"

"Hetty . . . oh hell." He looks skyward, then finally meets my eyes. With a jolt I see his are brimming with tears. "I have to become engaged to Anna. It's the only way . . ."

I stare at him.

"What?"

"I mean, yes. Exactly that."

"But you wouldn't *actually* get married though? I mean, you're only nineteen, and . . ."

"Yes. I would *actually* have to get married. The authorities over there . . . they check everything. It's helpful that our friends are a good family. Well respected. Anna's father, he's an excellent doctor, and Anna, well, she is a lovely, kind girl, but she isn't you. The last thing I want is to marry someone, anyone, other than you, Hetty."

"*Married?*" Weakness spreads through my body.

"I mean, it's a lot to ask of her, too, of course. I've no idea if she . . . has someone else. It's so good of her to help me out."

Good of her to help you out. What would I not give, to be in her position?

My brain has numbed. I cannot conjure any words.

Walter stumbles on, as if trying to fill the silence. "She's the sort of girl my parents would want me to marry, I know, even if all this . . ."

I spring away from him, anger surging, sudden and unexpected, through my body.

"Don't imagine for a single second this is easy," Walter says fiercely, grabbing both my hands. "In addition to leaving you, and having to marry someone I have no interest in marrying, I have to leave my parents behind, and to what sort of future? This is tearing me apart. I told them I wouldn't go. That I'd stay and see things through here, but my parents won't hear of it. The fact I have a chance of a new life is all that is keeping them going." Tears flow freely now, down both of his cheeks. It's the first time I've ever seen a man cry.

I nod, a lump forms in my throat, and I close my hands around his. We've always been doomed, us two.

"I love you, Hetty. I always will. But it seems *we* could never be. Not properly. Not here."

"I've had these stupid daydreams, that one day, somehow, some way, we can be together. Live in another country, far from here where nobody cares who or what we are. But now . . ."

"I know."

My nose begins to run and he hands me his handkerchief. I wipe my eyes and nose and put it into my pocket. Something of his to keep.

"How soon?"

"Nothing is fixed. I have no visa yet from the British, nor any permission to leave here because we have to pay the damned exit tax, and we don't have any money, so honestly, I don't know. It could be as soon as a few weeks. Let's try and see each other as often as we can until then."

I stare at him through the wash of my tears, trying to absorb all he has said.

"But everything's changed now." The enormity of it finally hits. "You're getting married to *another girl*."

"She will never know about us."

Something collapses, folds in. A silent scream.

He pulls me toward him. "I am so very sorry. If it could be any other way, you know I would change it."

"But we can't let *this* continue, can we?" I push him away, slap his chest. I want to yell at him. Hit him. Make him feel my pain. "It's better we stop it now."

I stand in a rush and back away.

"Is that really what you want?"

He comes toward me, tries to take me in his arms, but I fight to be free.

"No, Walter, of course not. None of it is. But it has to be, doesn't it?" I'm trying to hold the pieces of myself together. "I have to go. Good luck with your new life in England. And good luck with Anna."

"Hetty—this isn't fair!"

I walk away.

"So this is it? Just like that?" He runs after me. "Hetty—"

"It's for the best. For me, I can't . . . Please, Walter. Just let me go."

I feel him watching as I walk. Silently. In shock.

I don't look back as I leave the park and pass quickly beneath the looming university buildings, casting a deep shadow across my path. I should go home, but I can't bear to. I keep walking until I can no longer see Walter, nor him me. Then I collapse against a wall and sob. Deep, racking cries, as though I've been told my life is to end. My life might as well be over.

No longer caring if I'm late, I wander the streets for a long time. It's one thing to accept Walter may have to live somewhere else, one day. But this. *This.* Walter to marry a girl called Anna.

How can I ever come to terms with that?

SOMETHING IS WRONG.

A sense in the air that makes the hairs on my arms stand up as I step through the front door. Ingrid appears, her face pinched; she has a tense look in her eyes.

"Oh, Miss Herta. At last. You must go straight to the afternoon sitting room. Your parents are waiting for you." She hovers while I take off my outside shoes. Her words, her tone, aren't unkind. Her usual sneer, absent.

I hurry in to find Vati standing near the window, silhouetted against the light. Mutti is on the sofa. She looks up at me, her face tearstained. Her eyes are red and swollen.

"Oh, Hetty—" She slaps a hand over her mouth as she begins to sob, deep, heart-wrenching sobs.

"I'm sorry I'm so late. I didn't mean to frighten you." I peer at the clock on the mantelpiece. I must have lost all track of time.

Vati shakes his head. "It doesn't matter now." He comes over to me, his face the color of ash.

Mutti lets out another sob. Could she have found out about

Hilda Müller and the girl-child? Did Oma die? Have they found out about Walter?

"It's Karl . . ." He can't finish the sentence and stares at me with stricken eyes.

"*Karl?*"

"There's been an accident." He holds a telegram limply at his side. "He's . . . dead."

Through the thin brown paper of the telegram, I can make out the outline of the mighty Luftwaffe eagle, uneven letters stamped into words beneath. News. Plain, simple news.

The telegram blurs and a buzz as loud as a swarm of bees fills my ears.

"It can't be true." I exhale. "Mutti?"

People don't die when they are nineteen years old. They don't die when they are brimming with life and energy. They *can't* die when they are beautiful and strong and Karl and my brother.

The words are wrong. They must be.

But Mutti continues sobbing, her hand over her mouth, her whole body heaving and shaking. Vati goes to her and wraps his arm tightly around her shoulders. I can't bear to look at his slack face and hollow eyes.

"Please," I try again.

"It's true," Mutti gasps through her tears. "Karl's dead."

"Your brother—" Vati begins, but then shuts his mouth and shakes his head.

A numbness engulfs me.

I'm sitting on the sofa, staring at Vati. Willing him to say something. Something that will make it all better.

When I was little, Vati was the biggest, strongest person I

knew. He was in command, and I was safe and secure. In my world, he had the power of God. But now, his big frame is crumpled. In the face of death, he is as helpless as the next man.

"What happened?" I'm numb, trembling.

Vati slides his arm from Mutti's shoulders, collapsing forward as if he no longer has the strength to hold himself upright, and rests his forearms on his legs.

"Not Karl," Mutti sobs, mopping her eyes with a sodden handkerchief. "Not my boy. Anyone but Karl . . ."

"What the hell happened?" I'm suddenly angry. "Why won't you tell me what happened?"

Someone slips a cup and saucer into my hands.

"Have a drink, it'll help with the shock." Bertha's voice, soft and gentle. "Come now."

I do as I'm told but my hand is shaking so much I can barely lift the cup to my lips.

"I spoke with Hauptmann Winkler, just a few minutes ago," Vati says; his voice is tremulous. Like an old man's.

He takes a slug of whisky, or brandy, or whatever is in the glass Bertha hands him. He nods to Mutti to do the same. She gulps hers and coughs.

"He'd been on a routine training exercise, preparing for a test on aerobatic maneuvers," Vati says, his features dropping as though pulled down by a great weight. "He had to learn how to handle an aircraft at high speeds. It was good and clear this morning. A little gusty, but Karl had flown in more difficult conditions before. It was all going very well, but ten minutes into the flight, Winkler said, Karl misjudged the speed of a steep descent and was unable to pull out of it in time. He crashed the aircraft into the ground." Vati takes a deep breath. "He had multiple injuries, most seriously to his head. He arrived at the hospital in a coma. But the doctors were unable to save his life."

"He crashed . . ." I say, processing Vati's words. My ears still buzz. There's a growing pressure in my chest.

"Why was he in the aircraft on his own?" Mutti asks, her voice rising. "I mean, he was inexperienced! What on earth were they thinking!"

"Shh, my dear, don't upset yourself even more." Vati rubs his pawlike hand on her thin knee. "He'd been flying for over a year. It was a single-seat plane. A Heinkel He 51. According to Winkler, he'd flown one many times before and had impressed his superiors. A bright future cut tragically short, he said. The only consolation is, had he lived, his head injuries were so horrific it would have meant very severe disablement, so in the end, it was probably for the best."

"For the best?" Mutti's eyes are wild. She turns to Vati and begins to shout at him. "Who the hell does he think he is, saying what was best for our son? It was that major's fault our Karl is dead and he thinks he knows what's best? He probably told the doctors to stop trying to save him. He probably ordered them to kill him—"

"Hélène!" Vati says sharply. "You are overwrought. Hauptmann Winkler was devastated. I could hear it in his voice. You think he wanted to lose one of his most promising pilots in a stupid, senseless accident? Of course not."

"Oh, Franz . . . how can I . . . ?" Her eyes brim with tears again. "Not Karl . . ."

Vati stands slowly. He looks sapped of all strength.

"I'm going to call the doctor to bring you a sedative," he says as he shuffles toward the door. "Look after her, Herta."

I move to sit next to Mutti and slip her hand into mine. It's limp and delicate, like the foot of a bird. I squeeze it, but she barely responds. She stares into space, tears sliding one after the other down her cheeks.

"I'll take care of you, Mutti," I tell her, trying not to think of Karl lying somewhere on a slab in an icy morgue.

The crushing pressure in my chest intensifies, threatening to squeeze all the air from my lungs and strangle my heart until it stops beating altogether.

KARL AND I are in the treehouse. I can smell his cologne, clean and crisp, mingled with his own warm, oaty scent. He smiles and the corners of his mouth fold up, revealing the white of his teeth. His deep brown eyes wrinkle, just a little, at the edges and his skin is sun-kissed and glowing. He turns slightly and I see the soft fuzz of baby-fine hair at the back of his neck.

"Let's play Roman soldiers," he says, handing me a wooden sword. "Whoever wins can be the emperor and the other has to obey their orders for the rest of the day."

"That's not fair," I say, sulking.

"Why not?" He smiles at me, knowing exactly why, but he wants me to say it anyway.

"Because you *always* win. You're bigger than me."

"Then fight harder, and cleverer. It's the cleverest who win," he says, leaping up and tapping me with his sword.

I try to hit him back, but I can't reach him because Karl is at the controls of his bomber. I'm sitting behind him, but he doesn't seem to know I'm here. I try to shout his name. To warn him, but no sound comes from my mouth. The plane is shaking violently and he is sweating, fighting to regain control. It lurches and rolls, dropping fast. The engines roar. I scream, silently. There is a stench of oil, gasoline, and hot metal. And something else: sweat and impending death. The ground rushes and then the dreadful crash and a screeching sound of metal being crushed.

I jolt awake. Stare into the darkness, sweating and breathing fast.

I switch on my bedside lamp and peer at the clock. Three-fifteen in the morning.

Karl is dead. The last conversation we had was that awful one, full of distrust and accusation. Karl was the center of my universe when we were children. Where did it all go wrong? How can I live with that dreadful exchange being our parting words?

Tears slide from the corners of my eyes, dripping onto the pillow. The room is so still and quiet it's as if time has stopped and the world is no longer turning.

But the clock still ticks on my mantelpiece.

I turn toward Hitler's portrait hanging above it. He looks smugly down at me, over his bristly mustache.

You did this. How could you let this happen to my beautiful, dear brother?

He stares back, his eyes stony black, arrogant and taunting.

This is your punishment, Jew lover. It's all your fault, for consorting with the enemy. You chose the wrong path. You chose evil, and this is your reward.

But Karl was your perfect child. He gave you everything he had. His love, now his life. Not like me. Why didn't you kill me instead?

We all know what happens to those who make a pact with the devil . . . A wry smile plays on Hitler's lips.

A rush of heat and I cannot bear the sight of him any longer. I've made my choice. No matter that Walter is leaving and will soon be married to this Anna girl. No matter that I shan't ever see him again. He has taught me things I never understood before, but I do now. You have lied, Herr Hitler. And Karl is dead. You *bastard.*

I run across the room, ripping the portrait from the wall, pulling out the nail and a chunk of plaster. I throw the picture to the floor and I stamp on the Führer, cracking the frame and pounding his head, grinding my heels over his eyes.

I hate you. I hate you. I hate you.

Now I'm certain. It wasn't God who sent him. It was the devil himself.

I shove the broken picture behind the wardrobe.

Thirty

October 8, 1938

The next morning, Vati locks himself in his study to make the necessary phone calls. Mutti sleeps late after taking the sedative prescribed by the doctor. I sit in my window seat, Kuschi tucked next to me, pressing his shaggy black body against my thighs, comforting and steady.

Life inexplicably continues on the street below. Cars trundle past. A boy on a bicycle. A couple walk arm in arm along the pavement; the woman's shoulder-length hair is curled at the bottom, a shade lighter than Erna's.

Erna.

Erna. My stomach drops. I must tell Erna what has happened.

A soft knock at the door. Ingrid. Her face is drawn and pale.

"Can I get you anything, fräulein?" she asks. "You've had no breakfast . . ."

"I'm not hungry."

"I understand. It's . . . it's such a dreadful shock."

She stands close and for a moment I think she's going to reach out and touch me, but she grips her own hands tightly instead, the whites of her knuckles showing.

"It's the worst thing that could ever have happened," I tell her.

"I . . . I know. I'm so very sorry. I mean, Bertha and me, we're awfully upset too."

I look at her properly. Straight into her pale gray eyes, trying to see into her soul. But she's as impenetrable as steel. Anger flares. Who does she think she is, with her snide comments and stealthy manner? Her smirks and her flirtation with Karl. Was she the one who told him about Walter? How dare she presume to understand what it feels like to lose my brother. "Why should you care?"

She takes a step backward.

"I'm sorry. I never meant to offend . . ." She's blushing.

"You haven't answered my question," I press her coldly. "Why should *you* care so much?"

"Karl was always kind to me," she stammers. "I mean, he is . . . was . . . so handsome, and kind. But the best thing about him, he listened. Took time to talk and get to know me, like he cared—"

"Just how well *did* he know you?"

"I don't understand what you mean," she says, shaking her head and looking miserable. "What are you implying?" She flushes deep red.

I stand, square up to her.

"Nothing. I'm not implying anything."

We stare at each other.

"I don't want any food," I tell her, turning away. "I just want to be alone."

"I only wanted to help," Ingrid says, her tone clipped. "That's all."

I hear the door click shut behind her and return to stroking Kuschi. I should speak to Vati and get her fired for spying on me. But if she knows what I've been doing, what then? What would Vati do if she were to tell him?

Wissen ist macht. There is nothing I can do about her.

I lean my head against the shutter. Drained and exhausted, I shut my eyes.

I have lost my brother. Life will never be the same again.

THE LATE AFTERNOON air has a chill to it as I make my way to Erna's flat. Autumn has arrived without me noticing. Or perhaps the cold is coming from inside. Hunger gnaws at my belly. I haven't eaten a single thing all day.

Erna greets me with a welcoming smile at her front door.

"Oh, Erna." I grab her hands to stop mine from trembling. "I have some terrible news."

"What? What's happened?"

Erna's arms are around my shoulders. Her warm green eyes search mine and I begin to cry. The pressure in my chest spreads, until my whole body is gripped and wrenched cell from cell by the realization Karl will never again come home.

"Come inside," she says, guiding me up the four flights of stairs to her flat.

Before she opens the door, I turn to her. I imagine her parents still don't know about her relationship.

"It's Karl." I choke out the words. "There was an accident."

She freezes and in the gloom of the hallway, the whites of her eyes grow.

"He died yesterday morning."

"Dear God, no," she whispers. "It can't be . . ." Her disbelief mirrors my own.

We step inside Erna's comfortable flat and climb the narrow stairs up to her attic room.

"Tell me," she says, her eyes filled with tears, "exactly what happened."

I don't have much detail. The last twenty-four hours have been a blur, but I tell her what Hauptmann Winkler told us.

Erna sinks onto the bed, her eyes moist, twisting a handkerchief between her fingers, listening while I talk.

"Oh, Hetty . . ." She holds her arms out, and we hug each other for comfort.

"I'm sorry for you, too, Erna. I know how much you meant to each other."

We lie next to each other on Erna's bed, my head rested on her shoulder, her auburn hair fanned around us both.

"It makes no sense," she says after a long silence. "It just makes no sense at all."

"Mutti blames Hauptmann Winkler. Vati blames the Jews. He vows revenge."

Erna shifts. "How can he blame the Jews?"

"It's because of them that we have to build our armed forces. Not altogether rational," I say with a sigh, "but he has to direct his anger against somebody."

I don't tell her that his ranting is making me sick. That Mutti's flopping about like a wringing rag makes me want to scream and shake her. And I don't tell Erna that I honestly cannot see how we are all to live anymore.

Thirty-One

October 12, 1938

The more people who arrive here, the lonelier I be-come. The more family who gather, the more obvi-ous is Karl's absence. He was the beating heart of every party. He breathed life into the dullest room. Everyone creeps around, talking in hushed tones as though speaking loudly or smiling will somehow offend the dead. It makes me mad. I remember how it used to be, long ago, when we were children. When all three of us—Walter, Karl, and I—could play and laugh together without a care. Before we knew about death and anguish and forbidden love. If only we could go back to that time.

I snap my journal shut and hide it in its usual spot. It's mid-afternoon and Mutti and Vati are napping. The last few days have been a blur of unwanted visitors and funeral prepara-tions and we are all exhausted. The house is full of extended family. Like Christmas, but without the cheer. This week is the autumn holidays, but I've been excused from school for next week, too.

I leave my room and pad through the hushed house to the kitchen where Bertha is stuffing a chicken for the evening meal.

"Dear Fräulein Hetty," she says when I come in, "I've barely seen you these last two days. How are you bearing it all?"

"Not great."

"Come, have a seat. I made cookies and an apfelkuchen. You must eat. Keep up your strength." She clicks her tongue. "What a dreadful business."

She washes her hands and puts the big cake on the table, cutting us both a slice. She sits down heavily and sighs.

"I'm not complaining, but goodness, with all these extra people in the house . . . Ingrid and I are rushed off our feet."

"They'll all be gone after the funeral," I say, picking a few crumbs from my slice. The cake is both sweet and tangy. "Then the house will be deathly quiet again."

"Such a terrible *waste* of a young life." Bertha shakes her head. "And there'll be plenty more casualties like him. Should've learned our lesson in the last war. And here we are, sending our young men off to Spain, and goodness knows where else." She clucks again.

"Did you lose anyone close in the war, Bertha?"

"Did I just." She gives a snort. "I lost my two brothers *and* my intended."

"Oh, I'm so sorry. I didn't know."

"That's all right. Why would you? I suppose I'm telling you because I know how you must be feeling."

"Your intended?"

"Yes. I wasn't much older than you in 1915 when we got

engaged. Twenty-one—farmer's son. He was kind and had a wicked twinkle in his eye. I know you might find it hard to believe, but I was pretty enough back then." She smiles at the memory. "He never came back. Missing, lost in action, they said. I kept hoping, thinking one day he'd just walk through my door. Wouldn't have cared if he was deaf or blind or missing his limbs. Or all three. Just so long as he came back."

I reach across the table and squeeze her fingers. She smiles sadly at me.

"Oh, it's a long time ago now. Anyways, he never came back, of course, and nor did my brothers."

"Did you not meet anyone else?"

"No." She shakes her head and sighs again. "There weren't enough men to go around all the girls in my village after the war. So many young men lost. I wasn't much interested anyway, I was that heartbroken. So, when my parents suggested I go into service, I snapped up the chance. I went to Halle first, but then the family I worked for moved to Leipzig, so I moved with them."

"Where was that?" I ask out of politeness.

I take another small forkful of cake, but it sits in my stomach like a stone.

"Here," Bertha says, matter-of-factly. "With the family who lived in this house, before you."

"The Druckers?" I look at her in surprise. "You worked for the Jewish family who lived here?"

Bertha nods her gray head and drops her eyes from mine.

"I never knew that, either."

"No," she says quietly. "I don't suppose you would."

"But . . . I mean, how . . . What I'm trying to say is"—I turn to check no one else is in the room and then—"what were they like?"

"Years and years, I was with them." She hesitates.

We stare at each other, trying to work out how much to reveal.

"Look," I say at last, "I've heard the rumors. About how my father came by this house. But I know nothing of the people. How can I judge what is right or wrong—"

"It was a terrible business," Bertha whispers. "They were good people, but I don't get involved in politics. I keep my nose out of it all. It's safest that way. That's what I try to tell Ingrid, but she's a tricky one. She doesn't want to listen to an old crank like me. She's full of this new Germany and thinks that the youth rule. She's certain she has 'right,' whatever that is, on her side. She likes to gossip and get herself in the good books of . . . certain people." She looks at me. "You're an unusual one, Fräulein Hetty. You keep your allegiances with people who matter to you. Since you were young—always stood up for the underdog. Even if they are . . . not who you should be mixing with, if you follow my meaning. I suppose that makes you brave, not like the rest of us. But it's a dangerous thing."

"What on earth do you mean, Bertha? Has Ingrid said something about me?" My heart beats in double time.

Bertha sniffs and wipes her nose and mouth with her hankie. Her plate is clean.

"She says she knows you have a young man. She *thinks* it's serious. But she won't say *how*, or *what* she knows. Says she once saw *proof* of something . . . sensational. I've more than an inkling who the young man is, and I'm certain she does too. So far, I think she's only talked to Karl and me, but it wouldn't be hard for her to make trouble for you. I've warned her, but she's not interested in authority, not from the likes of me. Just be careful, fräulein, that's all."

She saw us together, that time in Salamander's. Her word against mine. It has to be more than that. Proof? Of what? My mind jumps about wildly. The notes we pass between us via Lena. Tomas. Places Ingrid could have seen us. And what about the broken picture of the Führer? She's bound to have noticed it missing from my wall. Perhaps she even found the pieces shoved behind the wardrobe. I'll tell Vati it fell down and broke. Ask him for another. My heart swoops. *The diary.* What if she found that? The thought of her fingers turning the pages, her eyes hungrily reading my innermost secrets, makes me want to scream.

"But . . ." I put my fork down and give up the pretense of trying to eat. "How did *you* know?"

Bertha fingers the tea towel. "I saw the two of you together, some weeks back at the tram stop. Recognized him straightaway. Don't forget, this was once his second home. I always had a soft spot for him. I recognized how it was between you, that look, of being, well, lost in each other. Reminded me how I felt once, a very long time ago."

I look at her properly for the first time. Bertha, who has always been here, like the furniture. I've never once given her more than a passing thought. And yet here she sits, soft and round and simple and kind. She knows so much and yet has never spoken a single word of it. In her eyes, I see worry and weariness. As though the weight of what she knows is too much. A sudden wave of fondness washes over me.

"Thank you, Bertha. He saved my life once, you know. A long time ago. Did you know?"

Bertha shakes her head.

"Anyway, there is nothing more to worry about as he's leaving Germany. For all I know, he could have left already . . ."

Bertha nods slowly. This time, she puts her hand on top of mine.

"Just be careful, Fräulein Herta. Given who your father is, and keeping that sort of company . . ." She hesitates. "Things could be very bad, especially for him."

"As I said, it's nothing to worry about. He isn't part of my life anymore." But with these words comes a deep, physical pain. "I'm going to take Kuschi for a walk," I say, pushing back my chair.

I attach his leash and give Bertha a quick wave as I head out the back door. Still sitting at the table, she lifts her hand in reply.

It's good to be out in the blustery wind, buffeting my body, chilling my face and hands. Perhaps it will help to clear the jumbled chaos of thoughts and ease the agony of grief that stubbornly sits, a permanent, unwelcome visitor, deep within my soul.

Thirty-Two

October 23, 1938

After the funeral, Mutti flees to stay with her sister, Adèle, in Weimar.

"She needs to be cared for," Vati tells me firmly. "She's in no fit state to look after anyone else. Time away from prying eyes and gossipers will help her heal."

"But I could take care of her. I could go with her to Weimar."

"No, you must stay in Leipzig. Oma Annamaria is coming this afternoon from Berlin to keep an eye on you, and the household. Tomorrow you return to school. Life must get back to normal."

"But it isn't normal anymore." My heart sinks at the thought of Vati's strict mother—a true Prussian, with her sucked-in cheeks and ramrod straight back, dressed as always from head to toe in black—in place of Mutti's soft, perfumed presence.

"A new normal. We must be strong, Herta. Strong for your mother and strong for the Fatherland." Vati stares into space, as if seeing visions of all he must achieve. "I have to work. It's the best way to cope." He heads toward the study. "I may have to be away a good deal, so don't give your oma any trouble."

How very convenient. Send Mutti away and go to your mistress for comfort.

I follow Vati into the hall, wondering what to do with myself, when there is a knock at the front door. Another visitor.

Tomas is on the doorstep holding a bunch of yellow roses. I usher him inside and put the flowers in a vase; they are cheerful. Full of hope, like spring.

We sit opposite each other in the morning room. He looks awkward and uneasy in the armchair. His hair is neatly slicked back, glasses cleaned. His best jacket on.

"Thank you for coming to see me. It's kind of you."

"I've wanted to come for ages. Soon as I heard. But it's hard. Long shifts, you know. Besides, I wasn't sure if you wanted me to . . ."

He uses the same soft, low voice as everyone else. It's unbearable. Suffocating, like air turned to water, it's hard to breathe.

"Such a fuckin' awful thing to happen. What a shitty waste." He speaks harshly, through gritted teeth. The change of tone, the swear words make me smile.

"Would you like coffee?"

"Please."

I ring the bell and ask Ingrid to bring us a fresh pot. She looks from Tomas to me and back again. Is that a hint of surprise in her eyes? Perhaps I should get Tomas to visit more often.

"You look worn out. And thin," he says, studying me.

"It's hard to sleep. And eat."

"Of course. How's your mother?"

"Inconsolable. She's gone to stay with her sister in Weimar for a while. I've got the pleasure of my oma, Vati's mother, coming to look after me. She's awfully strict."

"I'm so sorry, Hetty. Truly. If, you know, there's anything I can do. Just ask, yeah?"

So everyone says. But really, what can they do?

"It's very nice to see you, Tomas," I say, meaning it.

AFTER OMA HAS arrived and settled down for her afternoon nap, I change into my BDM uniform. My palms are clammy and I fumble at my buttons with clumsy fingers. I know I shouldn't go, but the desperate need is too strong. Karl's voice sounds loud and clear in my brain. *Stay away from him, Little Mouse. Stay away.*

"It's fine, Karl," I say out loud to the empty room. "He's as good as gone anyway. This will be the last time I see him. I promise."

I head toward Walter's uncle's warehouse. The Brühl is packed with people heading back to work after lunch. Grand stone buildings run the length of the street. The heart of the Jewish business quarter. Or at least, it had been. Many of the department stores, fur businesses, and law offices have changed hands now. The street is becoming Aryanized. Walter's uncle's firm, Keller & Co., Furriers, est. 1878, stands at number 24, and is one of the few still run by its Jewish owners.

I stand on the opposite side of the street and watch people walking back and forth in front of the double doors to the building. I recognize no one. I cross the street and try turning the iron handle. It's locked. Peering through the glass, I see a tiled passageway running straight toward the back of the building. I can just make out the shape of the iron cage of an elevator at the end. There are no lights on. All looks deserted.

I walk to the end of the building and find the entrance to a covered alley running back from the street. A little way along the alley, set back into the wall of the Keller & Co. building, is a door. Surely this must be the warehouse. I take a deep breath and try the handle. The door opens smoothly, the room beyond, dimly lit.

"Hello," I call cautiously, hovering on the doorstep. "Hello?"

The door swings wide open and there he is, standing in front of me.

"Hetty!" His face is drawn and pale.

"I came to say sorry. I was ghastly to you and—"

"You've nothing to apologize for. It was my fault . . ." He looks over my shoulder into the gloom of the alleyway.

"Can I come in?"

"Quickly." He raises an arm and I duck underneath. He shuts the door behind me, looking uncomfortable. "I'm down here on my own, doing a stock inventory," he says. "But it isn't safe, coming here."

My eyes are slow to adjust to the darkness of the vast warehouse. On one side, I make out bales of something piled to the ceiling; on the other are lines of dark, inert shapes hanging down. There is a strange, cloying odor. The atmosphere is so still, it's as if the air inside the warehouse is frozen.

"I had to see you."

"Oh, Hetty . . . It's been so hard to stay away from you. Every little thing that happens, you're the first person I want to tell. Every idea, every feeling, every doubt. I want to share it with you."

"I know—"

"I came looking for you."

"You did?"

"The other day, outside school, but I didn't see you. Then I walked past your house. But there seemed to be a lot of people coming and going."

"I thought you might already have gone to England."

"If only it were that easy." He sighs.

"I wasn't there. At school, I mean. Walter, the most dreadful thing has happened. I've been desperate to see you for days, hoping against hope you were still here."

"Come with me. Tell me . . ." He places a hand between my shoulder blades and guides me toward a brightly lit office at the back of the warehouse.

"Rabbit skins," Walter explains as we walk, pointing at the bales, "for making hats."

He points at the shapes dangling from hooks in the ceiling. Through the gloom, I can see they have heads and tails. Even the little feet are still attached.

"These are raw skins. Silver fox and mink. Once they've been treated, they'll be sold to be made into coats and jackets."

The smell in the warehouse is overwhelming. It makes my head spin and stings my throat.

"Whatever is that stink?" I ask, covering my mouth and nose with my hands.

He chuckles, looking more relaxed. "Naphthalene," he explains, "to kill the moths. They would destroy the skins otherwise."

"How can you stand it?"

"You get used to the smell. I don't even notice anymore." He turns to the rows of dead creatures. "Aren't these beautiful?" He runs his hand along the silvery white fur of the fox skins. "I wish I could dress you, head to toe, in a coat made of these."

I stare at the dead creature hanging directly in front of me, trying to imagine it draped over my body. Its four little paws hang down forlornly. The inside of the skin is stained red where the flesh has been peeled away and the eyes are a dull, milky white.

I shudder.

Walter grabs my hands, pulling me close. "Tell me, what happened?" His face is serious. "Hetty, you look exhausted. Whatever is it?"

"Karl . . ." The tears begin to flow, and Walter's face swims and dissolves before me.

We hold hands across the table in the little glass office, surrounded by this warehouse of the dead. My head aches from breathing in the chemical stink and from the effort of retelling the story of what happened to Karl. Even though he is holding my hand, Walter feels a long way away. A table between us, when I want to be in his arms.

"I'm sorry," he says at last. "What a terrible shock for you all."

He seems distant. There is something stony about the set

of his mouth, the look in his eyes. It isn't the reaction I'd expected. Perhaps he's come to terms with the thought of marrying Anna. Perhaps he's even looking forward to it. Or maybe he's secretly happy Karl is dead. I pull my hands from his.

"This is my *brother*. I don't know how to exist without him." How can I make him understand? "While you and I were together that morning, talking about your plans for England with your new *wife*"—I spit the word at him—"Karl was being rushed to hospital fighting for *his* life, and losing it. You don't give a jot whether he's alive or dead, do you?" There is heat in my neck. It rushes to the top of my head like a boiling wave, erupting from my mouth. "You stupid, unfeeling *bastard*! I was an idiot to come here, to think you would even understand."

"I *do* care, Hetty. I care that you are so upset."

He tries to take my hand, but I fold my arms across my chest.

"You don't care he's dead, though, do you?" I shout.

"Shh! Someone will hear." Now he stands, leans on the table, body bent toward me. "Karl rejected me and treated me like a piece of dirt." His lips are thin, drawn back; his face taut, like skin stretched over a drum. "He could have been like you and valued *me* as a human being. So, in all honesty, yes. I've been angry and hurt. More than you could ever know. But I didn't wish him dead. And I'm sorry for your loss. That's the truth. What more do you want me to say?"

"You really don't understand what it's like for us, do you?" I want to shake him. Make him see. Make him *feel* as I do. "Karl didn't have a *choice*. He *had* to reject you. What people secretly think, it doesn't matter anymore, don't you see? We have to be this way. Why do you imagine it's easier for us than it is for you?"

Walter straightens and turns away. "Then you are blind, Hetty Heinrich. People see what they want to. We all have a choice. Each and every one of us. We *choose* how we treat each other. You chose, didn't you? Karl simply chose differently." His face is hard, eyes angry, words acid.

"I *hate* you, Walter Keller," I sob. "I *hate* you."

I should walk out now, leave. Slam the door. Never see him again, but I can't make my feet move. I just sit, sobbing, my shoulders heaving, my wretched heart aching like it has never ached before.

"You don't mean that," Walter says at last. "I know you don't."

There is a pause, a teetering on the edge of something, and then, somehow, I'm standing and he's holding me. I'm crying from the inside out, and he is whispering "Shhh," softly in my ear, rubbing my back, and I am saying, "Sorry, I'm sorry," over and over, because I mean it more than anything.

"I'm sorry, too. You know I would never do anything to hurt you. I love you, Hetty Heinrich."

We collapse into the chair, together, and slowly everything calms. We don't speak; there is no need for words. He kisses my hair, my cheek, my neck. Then he kisses my mouth and a hunger grows inside.

Suddenly, from somewhere upstairs, there is a loud banging of doors. We stare at each other and a few seconds later, more bangs. The muffled sound of footsteps.

"I think it's a raid." Walter's whisper is barely audible.

"Why?"

"About the taxes. It's just an excuse. Hurry, they might come down."

He grabs my hand and leads me toward the back of the warehouse.

"Why don't we leave?"

"There'll be Gestapo crawling around outside. Quickly."

He pulls me into a dark corner. Bales are piled high but behind them, between the mountain of rabbit skins and the wall, is a narrow gap. We can just squeeze in sideways.

We hear the outer door crash open. Shouts. Clipped footsteps. We freeze in horror. Walter nudges me to keep going and we edge inch by inch along the gap, between the bales and the wall, right to the end in the pitch blackness. With luck, torchlight won't penetrate far enough in to see us.

"What if they find us . . ." I hiss to Walter.

"Shh. Don't think . . . just be silent."

The gap is so narrow. The wall is hard against my back and the weight of the bales press in front and above me, Walter to the side. Boots pound across the floor. The bark of an order. The darkness is impenetrable. My eyes strain against it, trying to make out pinpricks of light, but there are none. Someone shouts, nearer now. I'm suffocating. Terror overwhelms me. Walter fumbles for my hand.

"It's okay. Stay calm."

There's a rasp of metal on concrete. Footsteps. Close. Very close. My ears strain. I try to stop shaking, stop the sound of my heart crashing in my ears, still my breathing.

The men are in the office, slamming open drawers and doors. One or two, it's hard to tell. Another door bangs open, this time the inner, not the street door. Clipped footsteps and voices. Walter stiffens.

"Vati and my uncle Josef," he whispers.

I press myself hard against the wall, trying to increase space between my face and the rabbit bales; its surface is rough against my back. I wish it would absorb us, envelop us in the brickwork.

"Leave my son out of this." I hear Walter's father's voice clearly. "He has nothing to do with anything. If you must take someone, take me. But he is not responsible. He's just a lad—"

"How old?" barks a voice.

"Nineteen," Walter's father replies.

"Old enough to know right from wrong. We'll arrest all three of you."

"For what?" a plaintive voice now. "Come on. There is no need for this . . ." That must be Josef.

There is a shuffle, a heaving sound, then a cry.

"On your knees, you *Jewish filth*."

"I don't understand . . . we've paid all your exorbitant taxes—" Josef's voice again.

"Shut up!" The Gestapo man's voice is low with threat. "Where is your son? We will confiscate this stock . . ."

"No!" Walter's father shouts. "It's all we have! Check the papers—look. It's all in there, please!" I imagine him pointing at the little glass office.

"How dare you." The Gestapo man's voice trembles. Just

listening, I can pick up every nuance, every emotion in the words they are saying. "Are you calling me a liar?" the Gestapo man continues, his voice loaded with threat.

"I didn't—"

Thwack. A crack, like gunfire, but not. The sound of something solid, metal perhaps, connecting with flesh. A cry and Josef, "You bastards! You didn't need—"

"Shut up. *Pig.*" A thump, a yell.

Suddenly Walter lurches. "They're killing him," he hisses. "I have to do something!"

"No! Walter, stop. What good can you do?" I whisper, desperately pulling his arm. "They'll only kill us, too!"

There is a groan.

"He's alive! Walter . . ."

Walter hesitates; he's tensed, ready. I hang on to his arm tightly, both hands. I can't let him go.

"Where is the boy?" Another voice.

"Probably at home. Where he should be." Josef's voice, firm but trying to placate.

More groaning, low down. Walter's father must be on the ground.

"You have us. Why would you need him, too?"

"For questioning on another matter. There has been a serious accusation."

Walter and I grip hands tighter. Ingrid must have tipped off the Gestapo. What else could they want Walter for?

"Search the place," someone barks. "You, go to the home address."

I feel Walter shudder, tense against me.

Oh dear God, I know I have sinned and been bad in so many ways, but please, please, if you are listening, I will change. I will go to church, I won't forget you again. Just don't let them find us. Please God. Don't let them find us.

I have not prayed to God since I was small. But I do it now, over and over. What else is there to do? My legs are so weak and shaky that if I wasn't propped between the wall and the bales, they wouldn't hold me up.

The men crash about the warehouse. Their boots click, their voices harsh and ringing. There are thuds and bangs. Torch-light flashes. The boots come closer, but somehow, miraculously, *thank you, God, if you really are there, I won't forget this*, they don't find the gap between the mountain of rabbit skins and the wall.

They leave as suddenly as they arrived. The lights are switched off and a key turns in the lock. A deep blanket of silence descends. Shakily, we inch our way out.

Walter begins to sob. I put my arms around his shoulders. "Let's get out of here."

"But what shall I do?" he asks quietly. "They're after me."

He cannot go home, that's clear. He must disappear for a while.

And I know just the place I can hide him.

THE DARKNESS IS thick, like treacle, as I stand, ears strain-ing, on the landing. The evening passed at an agonizing pace as time stretched over dinner and coffee and silent pauses between the few words passed between Vati, Oma, and me earlier in the evening. Around me, the house heaves and creaks. Breathes and watches. I'm still for a long time, listening, checking for light beneath doors. All is quiet.

Working in slow and silent motion, I gather blankets and supplies from the kitchen. I close the back door behind me and take it all to the treehouse.

"Walter?" I call softly from the base of the tree.

"Up here."

My heart swoops with relief.

The treehouse is in surprisingly good shape after all these years. Watertight and solid, if rather dusty and neglected. A nest, hidden from the predators prowling below. Walter sits with his knees to his chest while I spread the bedding on the floor to make him comfortable. He shivers now and then and says nothing. He refuses food, but it will keep for tomorrow.

"Come," I say at last. "You need to get some sleep."

"How can I sleep? I have no idea what's happening to my father or uncle, nor my poor mother. She'll be wild with fear. Besides, what if they should find me, Hetty?"

"They would *never* think of looking here. It's the safest place to lie low for a couple of days, trust me."

"I do. But"—through the darkness, he reaches for my hand—"I can't stay here long." He squeezes my fingers. "Do you think you should go back to the house?"

"Not yet. I intend to make the most of every moment I have with you. I'll go back before it's light. I don't want to leave you here on your own. Not yet."

He says no more and we lie together on a soft eiderdown, beneath the blankets. Slowly, his trembling lessens and finally ceases altogether. We press together for warmth and comfort.

The wind tosses the branches of the giant tree, twigs scratching and scraping at the wooden sides of the treehouse, as if trying to enter and tear us apart.

It feels safe here, in the warm cocoon of soft down and blankets, high up in the ancient oak tree. Far above the madness playing out in this city, in this troubled country of ours. I screw my eyes tight shut and bury my head in the crook of Walter's neck. His scent is overwhelming. They can't take him away from me. I won't let them. If only I could save him from whatever the future holds.

We lie face-to-face. He shifts and our lips connect. His kisses are filled with sadness. Desolation. Then slowly I sense a change to yearning and desire. His feelings seem to mirror mine. Is this what love is? To know how the other feels, without ever having to explain? His fingers begin to wander, to explore beneath my clothes.

"Shall I stop?" he asks, several times, his voice low, his breath soft in my ear. "We shouldn't . . ."

Stop. Now. Before it's too late.

"No, we shouldn't." I'm on a precipice, teetering on the edge of cataclysm. I know I should pull back, but it's impossible to fight. I don't want to fight it. "Don't stop," I murmur at last. "I don't ever want you to stop."

Whenever I imagined this moment, which was often, late at night, alone in my room, I didn't picture it here, in a dark, drafty shack, perched halfway up a tree in my garden. It was always in a canopied bed, where I would lie on my back with my hair spread out on the pillow, like a movie star dressed in silk. He would take control, instruct me, and I would comply, but I would be afraid of doing it wrong or that he might not like me without my clothes. Afterward, we would lie in each other's arms, my head on his chest, and we would both be smiling with love and happiness.

But this, this real-life enactment of my fantasy, couldn't be more different. A piece of me steps out, watches in amazement as I transform into someone else. This someone who doesn't freeze with the shame of her own nakedness. Whose body seems to know better than her what it is to do. Who is not afraid to explore a man's body not just with her hands but with every inch of hers; and who surrenders the most intimate parts of herself to him. Because unlike the act that took place in my imagination, this is not merely a mechanical transaction of intertwined body parts. It is so much higher and greater than the awkward tangle of limbs—the wet, the smell, the blood, the pain, the pleasure. It's the joining together of our spirits, finally playing out our love, our desperate desire for each other that has simmered to boiling after all these months of wanting.

WE LIE, NOT speaking, but closer than we have ever been before. His heart beats, quick and strong next to my ear, and he runs his fingers along the line of my naked back; a feather touch, soft, tingling. I don't want to move, to destroy this moment. I drift in and out of sleep for what seems like hours.

"I must go," I whisper at last in Walter's ear.

"I don't want you to leave." He clutches me tight.

"I must . . ."

It's still long before daybreak. Reluctantly I peel myself away from his warmth and creep quietly back to my room. My legs are sticky. They'll smell it on me. The sex. They'll know.

Alone in my bed, I try to sleep, but it's impossible. Events replay and replay in my mind. An energy fizzes inside, keeping me on high alert, so much so that I fear I may never be able to sleep again. What on earth have I done?

I pull out my journal and begin to write, to pass the time, as the night ticks relentlessly toward morning. Writing my feelings down risks discovery, but it's the only way to calm the turmoil in my brain. I will find a place for it where Ingrid *cannot* think to look.

> *What do you think of me now? After what we did? According to the law, we have sinned. The worst of all sins. I think of our bodies, our sweat, our blood, mingled now, forever. It can't be undone. I'm ruined and damned. But how could something that felt so natural, so perfect, be a sin? Indeed, it is not. It cannot be. Walter is the best, the most kind, the most gentle. In his arms, I am safer than safe. It is they who are wrong, not us.*

Thirty-Three

November 3, 1938

"Come to the BDM fund raiser this afternoon, Hetty," Erna urges at the end of school. "You need a change of scene," she adds, looking carefully into my eyes. "A . . . break. Besides, I miss him, too, you know. I haven't seen you, properly, since . . ."

"I know. But Mutti is home. I must take care of her. Soon, I promise."

She gives me a sad smile and I hurry home.

Mutti returned yesterday. Impossibly thin and angular, she looks like she could be snapped in two. More streaks of gray are visible in her glossy, dark chignon. Like her dress, her eyes are dull. She smiles and hugs me. Tells me it's good to be home. She's here, but she isn't here. The mutti she used to be is buried alongside Karl in the graveyard.

After lunch Mutti and I walk arm in arm to the florist's on the corner of Hallische Strasse, Kuschi padding quietly at our side.

Mutti looks and looks at the selection of colorful blooms but is unable to decide.

"How about these?" I point to some blue cornflowers. Her favorite color. Her favorite flowers.

"Too cheerful." She shakes her head.

I look over the selection. Is there such a thing as a flower without cheer?

"Can I help you, dear ladies?" The shop owner sidles toward Mutti, a dazzling smile beneath his stiff-looking mustache.

Mutti gives him a withering glance.

"I'm looking for something suitable for my son's grave," she says.

I wince at her words.

The man extinguishes his smile and adopts a suitably respectful demeanor, head bowed, face downcast.

"I'm so very sorry," he says. "Let me help you. Please."

He swiftly gathers blooms from various buckets: tiny gypsophila; cream roses; white willow sprays; and pale lilies, lightly brushed with pink. He bundles them together with brown paper and presents them to Mutti.

"Yes," she comments. "Just right."

We walk arm in arm again to the graveyard and place them on Karl's grave.

"There," she says, looking down at the perfect pale flowers against the fresh, dark earth.

Such a waste that they should lie here to wither and die.

We sit on the bench beneath the spreading branches of a big fir tree and look out over the graveyard toward the church.

Faint strains of organ music reach us, but mostly it's just the wind sighing in the trees.

"I miss Karl, too," I say.

She grips my hand tightly and sobs, her whole body trembling with the loss she has suffered.

"Mutti," I say at last, when her tears are all spent. "I'm due at a fund-raising meeting at the BDM this afternoon."

She looks at me vaguely. "Yes, yes, you must go. I'll stay just a little longer."

"Are you sure?"

"Yes. I'll be fine. Go. I'll see you at supper." She gives me a thin smile, then turns back to watch over Karl's grave.

I walk softly away.

Once I leave the graveyard, I quicken my pace and make for the woods near the river. I can hardly breathe. Is he safe? Will he be there, like he promised? My legs feel jellylike as I push them to go faster. Or could there be a trap when I get there? A vision of the woods crawling with Gestapo, ready to arrest me for my sullied, filthy blood, flashes in my mind. I grasp the iron railing beside the pavement, which swoops and rolls, then rights itself.

A woman passes and gives me a strange look. I release the railing and continue on my way, slower now, less steady on my feet. Can she know that I've been with a Jew? Not just once, but three nights in a row. I glance over my shoulder, but the woman is walking swiftly away, head bowed against the wind.

In my pocket is the note Walter left for me with Lena at the café after his stay in the treehouse a week ago. I clasp it as though my life depends on it.

My darling,

How I have missed you! Not a second passes without a thought of you, and our three nights together. I feel tremendous guilt that in among all the anguish, I should have shared such bliss with you. I'm desperate to tell you what has happened. It isn't safe for us to meet in the open. The woods are best. I'll wait for you at 3:30 p.m., tomorrow, just off the path by our favorite picnic spot. I hope you remember.

W xxx

He's already sheltering beneath the trees, hat pulled low, when I reach the curve in the river where we once sat beneath the hot summer sun. It might have been another lifetime.

"Thank God you're here." He steps forward to greet me.

"And you. I was so scared they would arrest you when you got home."

"Not yet," he says. "I'm doing everything I possibly can to avoid it."

He takes my hand and leads me deeper into the woods. The undergrowth is tangled and it's difficult to pick our way through. He stamps on brambles and holds back branches to stop them whipping my face.

A light drizzle is falling, but that's a good thing. Fewer people will be out for an afternoon stroll.

We stop in a small clearing. At last I'm able to look into his pale, tired face.

"Please tell me—what's happened to your father and your uncle?"

"The Gestapo let them go. They kept them for two days—"

"But that's wonderful!"

Walter shakes his head. "Of course it's good they're home. But at an enormous price. Hetty, it's awful. They were beaten and interrogated nonstop for two days and nights. They were starved and weren't allowed to sleep. They broke them. In the end they were so weak they agreed to sign papers to transfer the business to the National Socialist Party in order to be released. They also have a hefty fine to pay and only have until the end of the year to pay it."

"Oh God no. I'm so sorry." His news is sickening. Shame, unbidden, floods me. To think I'm part of it. "On what basis can they do this?"

"Tax fraud! Utter lies. They invented the worth of the business, which is in reality almost bankrupt, and taxed us on fictitious profits. Then they accused us of not paying tax bills, worth more than the stock and net worth put together. It's preposterous. Josef and my father can't fight it anymore. The bastards have got what they want. Perhaps now they'll leave us alone. My father still writes letters hopelessly, all over Europe for a place to go, but since the conference at Evian in the summer, no country will take any more refugees. Even Palestine. He fears the Nazis will soon take my grandmother's house, too, and then the whole family will be homeless."

I see a change in his face. A collapse. An acceptance that the worst is to happen.

The lump is back in my throat.

"And what about you? Did they come for you?" My voice drops to a whisper. Something about the way he shifts his body and drops his gaze stirs the fear in my belly. He sidles a little closer to me and reaches for my hand.

"It was a good job you hid me." I can tell he's struggling to keep his voice light. "They did come looking. But, well, for now at least, they're having to leave me alone."

"But why? Looking for you for what?" I grip his hand tight and press my body against his.

"It's very bad, Hetty." He hesitates. "There's been an allegation of Rassenschande—"

"No!"

"So it seems someone really *is* watching us."

"It's Ingrid, it must be. Bertha warned me—"

"What do you mean?"

"She . . . She told me that Ingrid suspected I had a young man, and that she had seen proof of something *sensational.*"

"I know you thought she saw us together that time, but you said she wouldn't remember who I was . . ."

"I don't know if she did, and just seeing us in the shop, in itself, isn't a crime. So I think it must have been something more . . . Oh, Walter, I think she found my diary."

"Hetty, don't tell me you wrote any of this down . . ." He looks at me. "Did you actually mention my name?"

"Yes," I whisper.

Walter sinks his head into his hands and groans.

"I'm so sorry."

"Of all the stupid—"

"I'll destroy it. As soon as I get home. I promise."

"So she doesn't have it?"

"No! I used to keep it under my mattress. But I found a much better hiding place. She couldn't possibly have found it there—"

"She can't have; that's why they couldn't arrest me." Walter chews his nail while he thinks. "They've no proof. The person who made the allegation has so far refused to name you. To bring me to trial for *Racial Defilement*, the other party—you—cannot be prosecuted, because you would have to give evidence of the defilement, thereby implicating yourself. And you can't give evidence against yourself. I think that's why this *person*, whoever they are, has withdrawn the accusation, for now. They've no evidence to back up their claim. Perhaps they hope to catch us together. Or maybe they're afraid of the consequences of dragging your family name into the whole thing. But, if they had hold of your *diary*, and it confirmed everything . . ." Walter stares at me, his eyes stretched wide. "Hetty, you *must* burn that thing. They could prosecute you, too, you know that? Please promise me!"

"I promise . . ."

Fighting the grip of panic, I peer through the trees at the water-blackened branches and sodden leaves, whose earthy hint of decay rises, musty and sweet. Like some menacing omen, the threat closes in, slipping silently between the trees, ever closer to Walter.

I cling to him.

"Walter, you must go *now*. Leave for England, please."

He nods, holding me tight. "Anna's father has gotten me a visa at last, by providing financial guarantees and assurances about my ability to support myself and my future wife." The word makes me flinch. "He's really been very good to me. He's even arranged the wedding date, as firm proof of the intention, for March next year."

"March next year," I echo, for a moment allowing my mind to project further ahead than the next few days. What future has this Germany in store for *me*, without Walter, without Karl? It stretches ahead, like this forest: bleak, empty, desolate. It has to happen, I know, but the cold reality is a bitter poison on my tongue. "I want you to be safe, Walter, I do. But I can't bear the thought of you and her—"

"I know. I can hardly bear it either. But I don't see how I have any choice. I'm so sorry. Shit," he says, letting go of me and burying his face in his hands. "Words are just so inadequate . . ." He raises his head, eyes watering, and pulls me by the shoulders to face him. His jaw is fixed, teeth clenched. "I feel like a traitor, leaving you and my parents behind. I'd give anything to take you with me. As for my parents, as soon as I'm in London, I'm going to work like hell to get them to England. I'll do everything I can, work twenty-four hours a day if I must, to make it happen. Besides, if I don't think of it as a rescue mission, none of it is bearable."

I float my head onto his chest.

"I've already made some progress," he says. "I've been in touch with contacts of Josef's. We've registered a company, Keller & Co, London. The British are keen on new business—jobs, prosperity for them, too. If I can get things started quickly, and convince them it's vital to have Vati and Uncle Josef to grow the business, it just might work out." Even as he says it, I can tell he fears it's futile.

I think of Ingrid and the Gestapo.

"How soon can you go?"

"I don't know. We still have the exit tax to pay, that's the hitch. My grandmother is trying to negotiate a gift of all her artwork, and the most valuable furniture, to try to keep the house. The rent on letting the upper rooms is our only income. Without it, our family will be destitute."

We sit in silence, both of us lost in our own thoughts.

"How I wish I could come with you," I whisper, turning to him. "Walter? Could I? How can I stay here, without you? How can I be part of this"—I search for the right words—"Nazi *thing* when I don't believe in it anymore? When I can *see* how the reality is so terrible, so *wrong* . . ."

Walter looks at me then, his eyes full of sorrow.

"Even if you could get a visa, which would be impossible as a start, you realize that you and I couldn't be together? I can only *go* to England and *stay* in England as Anna's husband. I have to register as an alien. I'm permitted to stay only for one year. I have to justify my presence annually for my visa to be renewed. Without Anna's father sponsoring me, I will be sent straight back here, to Germany. And it's the only hope I have to save the rest of my family. Our friend is hardly going to put everything on the line if you follow me to England, is he? Besides which, *you* wouldn't be safe. The Gestapo will find you and punish you. They are keen to make an example of those who are anti-German, anti-Nazi. You of all people should know that."

The grim trees press in; the clouds drop down and gloom

pervades this deserted spot. He tries to kiss me, but I turn my head away.

"Hetty . . . look at me, please."

The lump in my throat is huge and hard. "I'm going to miss you more than I can bear," I mumble at last.

"One day, I hope, this madness will end. With luck, England, America, the Western world will fight for freedom. Hitler won't stop here, that's for sure. And then, who knows? We must have hope. For now, you must bite your tongue and pretend to go along with things, just as you always have. Nobody can know what you really think. Stay safe, and true to yourself." He gently wipes my tears away with his fingertips. "I will love you always and forever. Every day for the rest of my life; if the worst happens and you never hear from me again, you must know this." His voice breaks then, and there is no more to be said.

LATER, DURING SUPPER, Mutti barely eats a thing while Vati eats with gusto. I stir the greasy pork around my plate; its full, fatty flavor turns my stomach.

Ingrid brings assorted pastries and a small glass of sweet pudding wine. I gulp half a glass, swill it around my mouth to cleanse it of the sickly taste of pork. I stare at her, try to work her out. Is it her?

She carefully avoids my eyes.

Vati clears his throat and looks at me.

"Your mother and I have been talking." His water-pale eyes are serious. Red rimmed. He exudes exhaustion. Like a shroud, the shadow of Karl's death smothers us all.

"School will be over for you soon and we have decided what your next step should be."

"I want to go to university. You know I do. I want to become a doctor . . ."

"Herta," Vati snaps, "we've been through this. It's impossible."

"I could go abroad."

He snorts with contempt. "University is out of the question. You will go to Hausfrau school."

"What!" I shriek. "I don't want to go to Hausfrau school! I would only learn needlework, or to speak politely at a cocktail party, or plan a dinner for twelve. I have no intention of getting married, so—"

"Don't talk to your father like that," Mutti scolds. "You are being unspeakably rude."

They both glare at me, and I close my mouth. Heat flares.

"You've been allowed too much free rein. Freedom has infected your mind. May I remind you"—Vati's voice is low with warning—"that selfish desires, if allowed to perpetuate, spell the death of civilization. Duty comes first, above all and everything. Of course," he continues, "you want to get married. Early marriage is good for the young. Curbs their natural inclination to be flighty and out of control."

"I'm not . . . What do you mean, free rein? What am I supposed to have done wrong?"

Neither answers me. "I know my duty. I don't understand—"

"Your *duty* is to marry and produce as many children as you can for our Führer, for the future of this country. That is all." Vati is angry, red in the face. "Your brother did his duty.

He was prepared to give his *life* to do his bit for the Reich. While you? You cavort around, more intent on entertainment and enjoyment, cultivating wild plans for . . . for . . . travel, and university and jobs and other *ridiculous* notions." He thumps his fist on the table. Mutti and I both jump.

"Your mother has lost control of you," he continues. "It's not that I blame you, Hélène, given what has happened, but it isn't right for a girl of your age, Herta, to be granted such freedoms. Always out and about doing heaven knows what, with heaven knows whom, and no brother to keep an eye on you."

I look around for Ingrid, ready to throw daggers at her, but she's left the room. Blood pulses in my temples. They cannot stop me going out. How I wish I could point out how Vati carries on.

"Franz, I'm sorry, she shouldn't . . ."

Ingrid returns to clear away the dessert.

"Coffee?" she asks, her voice bright and cheerful as though she has been listening gleefully outside the door.

"In the sitting room, if you please, Ingrid."

She leaves the room again, without bothering to shut the door.

Vati wipes his mouth on his napkin. "Your cousin Eva has just finished at a very good school in Halle. Or perhaps you could go to Dresden, or Berlin."

Hausfrau school!

"Vati, I would like to take my Abitur." I try to keep my voice steady. "Please. I'm a good student—I should get an excellent mark."

"The Abitur is a waste of time, especially for girls. You can study teaching at Hausfrau school, if you are so set on a job. That would be acceptable to your mother and I."

He places his hand over hers where it lies, limp and pale on the table. He smiles at her, then at me. His anger has evaporated. He has that look on his face that says, *I'm being so very indulgent. I'm kindhearted but I don't give in to hysteria or weak-minded women.*

I look from one to the other. Mutti is closed off and I'm all alone. If Karl were here, he would know just what to say. He would make them see reason.

I collapse back in my chair. Words are useless. They won't listen. Mutti and Vati move on, talk of something else. The air around me is leaden, pressing me down. Squeezing and suffocating. More than ever before, I'm aware of the confines of the walls of this house, solid and impenetrable as a prison.

I will not go to Hausfrau school, Vati. I simply will not go.

Back in my room I shove the linen aside in my cupboard and, with shaking hands, pull up the loose floorboard. Reaching into the void, my fingers brush the journal. *Thank you, God. Thank you, thank you.* I pull it out and stare at the patchwork of colors on its cover. I remember, as though it were yesterday, when Karl sat on my bed, anxiously awaiting my reaction when he gave it to me. And how the light dazzled in his eyes when he knew the pleasure it gave me.

I imagine burning it. Watching the pages curl and blacken in the heat. Would the cover turn to ash, or would traces of it be left in the grate for Ingrid to find in the morning?

I smooth my hand back and forth over its cover, as if it were a precious pet. One day I'll be old and my memories will be all I have. When they fade, what will there be to remind me? What if I should forget altogether?

Carefully, I fold the journal in a pillowcase, place it in the void, and drop the floorboard back into place. If Ingrid hasn't found it yet, she is hardly likely to before Walter leaves this country for good. And I'm going to make damned sure of that.

Thirty-Four

November 7, 1938

The concierge calls up to Erna's flat. I wait outside in the dank air. Woodsmoke hangs, mingling with the scent of molding leaves.

"I'm so happy to see you." Erna smiles, as her flame-gold head appears in the doorway.

"I need your help," I begin, once she joins me on the pavement. If I wait, I might lose courage.

She loops her arm through mine as we walk.

"Ask away," she says cheerfully.

"It will shock you. You probably won't like me anymore."

"Gosh, how intriguing. Can't wait to hear . . ."

"No! It's serious, Erna. Really. You can't repeat this to *anyone*. Do you hear?"

"Okay, okay! No need to be quite so fierce. I won't, I promise."

"Really promise?"

"Yes, I really promise! For heaven's sake, what is it, Hett?"

I take a deep breath.

"I . . . I've fallen in love with someone. I mean, really, properly, fallen in love."

Exhale. My breath, a foggy stream, mingles with the winter air and evaporates.

"Wow . . . well, that's wonderful." She smiles, then frowns. "It's a bit sudden, though, I mean with Karl and everything." She looks uncomfortable, then rushes on. "I didn't mean you shouldn't. It's a good thing, to take your mind off—"

"It isn't sudden. It's been going on for over a year."

"What? A *year*!" She stops walking. "Why didn't you tell me?"

I keep walking and she jogs to catch up.

"I know what you must think after I was so ghastly to you and Karl. I've been a terrible friend, and trust me, I feel utterly wretched about it. But there were good reasons I couldn't tell." I can't look at her. Head down, I keep my eyes fixed on the wet pavement, stepping between piles of soggy leaves.

"Yes. You've been a terrible friend. The worst kind." She pokes me in the ribs and laughs. "But seriously, who is he? Tell me, and I'll forgive you everything."

We walk a few more steps. *Do it now.*

Deep breath. "He's a Jew, Erna. I've fallen in love with a Jew."

"You've . . . oh, ha ha, Hetty. What a hoot."

"No, it's the truth. His name is Walter Keller. Perhaps you remember, that day at school when he and Freda . . ." Erna has stopped smiling. She nods. "A long time ago, he was a friend of Karl's. That's how I knew him. I bumped into him during the summer, last year, when I was walking Kuschi. I tried to stay away from him, but I couldn't. You see, there is no one like him. No one I've ever met. I couldn't help but fall for him, and him for me. It *feels* like we're meant for each other, even though we aren't."

"For heaven's sake . . ."

We reach Nordplatz. The wide green square and tall handsome church are ahead of us. Like a river, I can't stop the flow, now I've started.

"I tried to stop seeing him so many times. He tried. But we just couldn't. I know that if we get caught—we almost have a few times—it will be disaster for us both. My crime will be equal to his. But I love him so much, Erna."

I can feel Erna's fierce gaze at my profile. "So why are you telling me this, now?"

"Someone has reported us. It could have been our maid, who might have seen me with him. She watches me, Erna, and I have to be so careful. Anyway, the Gestapo want him for *Rassenschande*. He has a visa to go to England, but only if he marries a girl there . . ."

"Jesus."

"But," I rush on, "he can't leave Germany without a passport and his exit tax paid. I need to help him. And I need an ally."

"This is . . . a lot to take in."

We stop by the church. Near the spot where I declared myself to Walter so long ago.

At last I dare to take a look at Erna's face. Her eyes are wide. Her skin pale with shock.

"Well, what do you think of me now?" I ask, looking into those deep green pools, where her soul, pure and clean, meets, perhaps in her eyes, my filthy, tarnished one.

For a few ticks, she says nothing. "I can hardly believe it," she says at last.

"You promised you wouldn't tell . . ."

"No! Hetty, never!" She grabs both of my hands. "I love you, you silly old thing. I love you *more* for this. More than ever . . ."

An exhaustion engulfs me. I feel so tired, my limbs leaden. As if letting out this secret has finally released me to feel the weight of it.

"You see, Hett . . ." Erna drops her gaze. "I have a confession of my own."

"What?"

"I should have confessed before. My father is no blithering old fool. He can be, of course, but he's much more than that. He's a vehement, secret anti-Nazi. He loathes Hitler and all he stands for. We all do." She looks around the nearly empty square, dropping her voice to a whisper. "There is a small network of us in Leipzig. Just a handful. Not enough to make any difference. Everyone is too afraid."

I shake my head, trying to clear it. Keep it thinking straight, the implications of all this.

"It's why my father wanted me in the BDM. Encouraged me to do well, to avoid suspicion. He's convinced the Gestapo are watching."

"But what about Karl? Why did you walk out with him?"

"Yes. That's the other part of my confession. I liked Karl, of course. He was hard *not* to like, so handsome and sweet. But I didn't *love* him, not the way he loved me. He was so good to me. I feel ashamed. But I was worried about my father, he can be . . . indiscreet. I was afraid for him, and I thought, if I was with Karl, it might protect him. Keep suspicion away . . ."

The ground shifts; the world twists and turns.

Is there anyone who is truly as they appear?

"Being close to Karl and your family has helped," Erna goes on, but her words spin around my head unheard. She has used us. Both of us. Karl and me, for her own ends. I don't mean any more to her than that, never have. I always found it hard to understand why anyone as charming, sophisticated, *accomplished* as her, would want to be my friend.

Well, now it's clear.

"And don't go thinking I only became friends with you because my father wanted me to." She seems to be able to read my mind. "That simply isn't true. I was friends with you long before I understood any of these things. That's the truth."

Is it? I glance up at the tall tower of the church, climbing up into a thin spire, dark against the low, slate-gray sky. Once, I believed in God. I felt blessed by him and could see my place in his universe. But I was guided away from church and God. Mutti and Vati frown on religion. So I grew an unwavering faith in Hitler, and the absolute, indisputable righteousness of our glorious new Reich. But first Walter and now Erna have shaken the ground beneath my feet. Karl is gone. There is no perfect German. Where is my faith now? I'm stripped bare. Rootless.

"We'll be late for school," I say at last. Unable to process my jumbled feelings, I don't know what else to say.

"Hett." Erna grabs my hand and squeezes it. "I'm telling you this to show you that your secret is safe with me. I'd do anything to help you. I don't judge you, and I hope you won't judge me, either. Karl and I never did 'it.' He said he would wait. That I wasn't '*that* sort of girl' and he hoped one day we could even be married. He said there were plenty of *those* sorts around, and he would rather spend time with me, just enjoying my company. So I did nothing to hurt him, and he never knew I felt differently than he did. He didn't suffer. Not one little bit."

Perhaps that's true.

Perhaps Karl was getting his kicks with Ingrid instead.

I bite my lip and we both hurry into school.

Oh, Erna, I hope I have not made a terrible mistake opening my heart to you. Can it really be true that you've always hated the Nazis? I can picture you, at every BDM meeting; at school; with Karl and me. You always sang the loudest, saluted with the most vigor. You led the younger girls in the way only a perfect German could. How could you be so convincing if you didn't believe in it? Or are you the best actor in the world? If it's the former, then how can I trust that you will not inform on Walter and me? And if the latter, I'm relieved, but can I truly trust that you are my friend? Either way, you've lied all along. Time alone will prove which of these is the truth.

Thirty-Five

November 8, 1938

There's a wild storm raging. Driving rain splashes against the windows, and rivulets track their way down the panes. The bare branches of the cherry tree bend at an alarming angle and thrash against the iron railings in violent gusts. Doors rattle and slam in the wind. The house groans and creaks.

Mutti is in the sitting room, drinking coffee and listening to the wireless over the din.

"I'm off to school," I announce from the doorway as I button up my coat.

"What a day," she says, watching the trees sway in the wind. "And I don't just mean the weather . . . That terrible trouble in Paris."

"What trouble? What's happened?"

"Didn't you listen to the news this morning? Franz told me it may not be safe to go out. At least for a little while."

"Why?" I ask, coming into the room, putting my bag down. "Don't I have to go to school?"

"He had to attend an emergency SS meeting," Mutti continues, ignoring my question. "No good will come of it."

"No good will come of what? You're speaking in riddles, Mutti!"

She nods her head at the paper lying on the coffee table. "Read it yourself," she says, turning her back to the window and the wrath of nature outside.

I sink onto the sofa and spread the paper across the table, turning to the cover page.

8 November 1938

From our correspondent in Paris.

HEROIC GERMAN DIPLOMAT IN
PARIS FIGHTS FOR HIS LIFE!

Ernst vom Rath desperately clings to life, following the assassination attempt yesterday by a Polish Jew. He lies in hospital, awaiting the arrival of the Führer's best doctors, already on their way to Paris, who will try to save him. The talented young diplomat was shot five times at close range by Herschel Grynszpan, who lied his way into the German Embassy. Grynszpan was arrested at the scene and immediately confessed his crime. It is thought that the scoundrel intended to kill the ambassador, Count Johannes von Welczeck.

Vom Rath is a promising young lawyer. An embassy spokesman has described him as hardworking and honest, a talented advocate with a bright future ahead of him. A young man of whom his family, and his country, is rightfully proud. It is said that Grynszpan harbored evil intentions and acted out of spite and vindictiveness. This terrible crime reminds us of the chilling realization that no German, wherever he or she is in the world, is truly safe. Safe from the ever-present threat of the Jew, waiting for the opportunity to do him harm.

The story sounds sensationalized. I remember Vati's words about news and stories and the truth.

"Do you think it's true?"

"Of course it is. Why wouldn't it be?"

"A friend of mine says you shouldn't always believe everything you read in the papers."

"Well, you had better tell that friend to get ahold of their senses. How dare someone make that suggestion." She has the look of someone who has been personally insulted. "Why would you question Vati's good judgment as to what to print because of the ignorant remarks of a so-called friend?"

Mutti would defend Vati to the ends of the earth. He doesn't deserve her devotion. A knot of anger forms in my belly.

I change the subject. "Do I have to go to school?"

"I don't see why not," she says in a thin voice. "Vati didn't say you shouldn't." She leans toward me, narrowing her eyes and lowering her voice. "This is the beginning. The conspiracy. The Jews." Her eyes are wild. The pupils, huge black pits. There's a madness in them. Her hands tremble as she pulls a cigarette from the pack on the table and places it carefully between her lips. "They've been scheming and planning this for years." She pauses to light the cigarette, shaking out the flame on the match and tossing it into an ashtray.

"Planning what?"

"The revolution! This is the start of their push for world domination."

"You cannot seriously believe . . . Mutti, come on. This isn't true."

"Oh, I'm deadly serious." Her voice is shaky with emotion. She takes a long drag on her cigarette and it seems to calm her. She stares a little past my left ear into the middle distance.

"Mutti?"

Her eyes refocus. She takes another drag and blows a plume of smoke from the corner of her pursed lips. Her cheekbones protrude too high now; her skin is sinking in, giving her a gaunt, haggard look.

"If I'm to go to school, I had better go. I'm already late," I say, picking up my bag from where I'd dropped it on the floor. I need to get away from her hateful words.

She nods and refills her coffee cup, slopping some into the saucer as she pours.

"Yes, yes. But come straight home. Vati will know more after his meetings. I can tell you this much: The Jews have it coming to them. They will be sorry they were ever born."

FRAU SCHMIDT TALKS of literature, usually my favorite subject. But I cannot focus. I can only think of Mutti and our strange conversation this morning. My brain jumps from one vision to the next. An innocent German man, shot, blood spurting from his chest as he stands, stunned and defenseless, on the steps of a building in Paris. Countless Jews descending like vermin over our city, smothering, foul and evil; Walter looking on, smiling because I fell for his charms. Me, duped and ruined forever. Or all these vile lies, and Walter, the boy I love, innocent of everything, dragged from his home by the Gestapo, thrown into jail, and left there to rot.

My palms sweat. My heart beats. I watch the teacher's face; her mouth moves but I hear nothing. She writes on the blackboard, but I can't make sense of the words.

At the end of the lesson, Frau Schmidt asks for our homework to be handed in. Less than half the class have completed it.

"Sorry, Frau Schmidt, I've been too busy with my BDM activities; I've not done any homework," I tell her when she holds her hand out for mine.

She starts with surprise.

"That isn't like you, Herta," she says, with a disapproving tone.

"It can't be helped." I look her straight in the eye. "BDM is more important than schoolwork."

She won't risk arguing with that. We stare at each other for a moment. She gives a quick nod and purses her lips. Moves on to the next girl.

I push my way through the chattering crowd at the doorway, spilling into the corridor, searching for a red-gold sweep of hair. I'm carried along with the tide of girls to the gymnastics hall where they splinter into groups, sheltering from the rain outside.

She's waiting for me. We ignore the rain and run down the steps into the deserted playground. Huddling against the building to stave off the worst of the drizzle, I find I can't meet her eyes.

"About yesterday . . . what I said about Karl." Erna pauses. "I'm sorry if it came as a shock."

"It did, rather."

"And what you told me, about Walter. That was rather a shock, too. I barely slept last night."

"Me neither."

"Hett—"

"Thing is, Erna"—I summon the courage to look into her flecked green eyes—"once you find out someone isn't what you think they are . . . it's hard to trust. Hard to go on, as we were."

"*Exactly!*" Erna's face becomes animated. "Hetty, I trust you to the ends of the earth. You could have informed on my father. You heard what he said, but you didn't. Now I know how you feel about Walter, and the treatment of people who aren't racially pure, well, that just brings us closer together. Perhaps you can help the fight against—"

"Oh, Erna. I want to help. I wish I could. But . . . I'm not sure what I can do. Vati is traveling up the Party ranks and Mutti supports everything he does. At least, she did. She's so broken now, after Karl . . . I'm not sure how she'll ever recover. Besides, Walter says I should keep my head down. Stay safe, because with luck, all this will one day be over and then we can be together. Oh, I don't know. What on earth can we two girls, with no money or influence, actually *do*?"

"But don't you see what you've done *already*? It's incredible. You've dared to think differently."

"It's not incredible, Erna. I've only fallen in love, that's all. If it hadn't been for Walter, I'd . . ." What would I be? I'd still be as fervent a follower as I was. I'd never dare to think differently. I'd still believe I was destined for greatness as Hitler's child. Wouldn't I? There's a pounding in my temples. "I don't know what I'd be," I say quietly.

"It doesn't matter what you would or wouldn't be. What matters is now. You can help us. The resistance. As things get worse, more and more will join. You'll see." Erna lays a hand on my arm. "Your father must have information. Surely you must hear things, see things?"

"You're asking me to *spy* on my father?"

She looks at me hard. "Do you want to help Walter, his family, and thousands like him? Without trial, more and more Jews and political opponents are being herded into camps. The Nazis are expanding the network, building more. They want to force Jewish people, all of them, out of their homes, into ghettos. And that's not all. The Nazis' promise of peace and prosperity—it's a lie. They are pushing us toward war. Hitler wants his empire. If we don't do something, where will it end? It's *our* future, Hett. We're the young. *We* should be fighting it."

I nod dumbly. I think of Bertha, Lena, and the countless others who don't share Hitler's vision of the future but are too scared to say anything, do anything. I've been so blind, buried my head so deep and believed in all the promises. I *wanted* to believe.

Erna's staring at me. Waiting for me to speak.

"I'll . . . do what I can. I'll try." I think of Mutti and the strange conversation we had this morning. "What do you think of this story about vom Rath?"

"My father said Grynszpan did it out of frustration at the expulsion of the Polish Jews from Germany. A couple thousand of them had to leave Leipzig alone. Apparently, they were hauled from their beds, shoved onto trains in the early hours of the morning, and sent back to Poland. But Poland won't let them back in and so now they're stranded on the border with nowhere to go. His parents are among them. That's why he did it. I'm not saying it was the right thing to do, but I guess that's why he was so angry."

"How does your father know these things?"

"He has his sources," Erna says and winks at me. "It's probably just a big fuss over nothing," she continues. "It will fizzle out over the next couple of days, or until the newspapers are filled with some other scandal."

I remember Vati's warning about things not being safe.

"I'm not so sure about that. I think something big is brewing. I'll try and find out what."

"Thank you, Hetty. You are a true friend, you know that?"

We exchange a weak smile and make our way back into the school building.

FOR THE FIRST time since I've been at the gymnasium, Mutti meets me at the school gates. It reminds me of when I was small and she'd be there, every day, outside the gates of the volksschule, waiting for Karl and me.

She hooks her arm through mine and steers me along the pavement toward the old town.

"I felt restless at home," she explains. "I thought we could go to the Fürstenhof Hotel for lunch. It'll be a nice change of scene. Oh, and Tomas telephoned for you. Asked if you would like to go for a walk on Sunday afternoon. Does he have designs on you, Herta?"

"No, Mutti. He's just a friend. That's all."

As we walk, I can see nothing about the day that seems different than usual. In the Fürstenhof, waiters, aloof and unsmiling in black, with pristine white aprons tied around their waists, serve us cold meat and salad followed by delicate cakes and dainty cups of strong coffee. A pianist plays soft Bach melodies; the clientele relax at neat little tables arranged at discreet distances around tall ferns in the glass-domed café.

Mutti eats well and even manages some strudel for dessert. She is calmer than she was this morning.

"Did Vati tell you anything after his meetings?" I ask.

She leans across the table, eyes widening. "He has spoken *directly* with Herr Himmler today. Your father really is moving in the highest circles now."

"Circles?"

"Well, you know. I'm no politician, but surely if he has the ear of such people of *importance*, who trust and rely on him, then . . ." She glances around and whispers, ". . . promotion may soon be on the way. We could move to Munich, or Berlin." She leans back. "You know, Herta. I think perhaps that is what I need. A change of scene. Somewhere new. This city, our house. There are just too many memories of Karl. It's so hard . . ." Her voice trembles. "Hard to move on."

"And me? What about me?"

"Well," she says brightly, "soon you will leave school, go to Hausfrau school. Get married, perhaps even have a job for a while. I mean, you said yourself you wanted to travel. There is nothing to hold us here, is there?"

"I suppose not," I mumble, wondering fleetingly if Fräulein Müller and the child will move with us. Then I think about Erna and the resistance she spoke of. I *do* want to help. I want to do more. With Vati's promotion, perhaps I'll have access to information that might be of use to Herr Bäcker, but I shall need to take care. Be vigilant. How on earth can I do any of this if we move away? But that's all in the future. I've spent too long living in a dream of what my future may hold; if I'm to make any difference at all, I shall need to act *now*. I swill the last of my coffee around the cup.

We leave the Fürstenhof and weave our way through busy streets, full of shoppers, hawkers, and workers heading home for their evening meal. The story from this morning's papers is everywhere. Hastily pasted to billboards. Screaming from headlines on newspaper racks.

VOM RATH FIGHTS ON!
GERMAN HERO REFUSES TO GIVE UP!
COLD-HEARTED JEW, SPLATTERED IN THE
BLOOD OF OUR BRAVE COUNTRYMAN,
BRAZENLY TRUMPETS HIS GUILT!

"And what of this story?" I ask Mutti. "What did Vati say about that?"

"He said nothing more on the telephone. But he can't be expected to tell us all about important matters of state."

It's an isolated incident, in another country. The papers are making a big issue of it to improve their sales. But I can't shake a feeling of unease.

"I'M GOING TO rest," Mutti says when we arrive home. "I still don't sleep well, and I feel so tired now." She smiles thinly.

I sit on the bench in the hallway, listening to her soft tread on the stairs. There is a distant click as Mutti closes her door, then silence settles, cloaklike, over the house.

And then a rustling. I creep toward it and see the door of Vati's study is ajar. Peeping through the gap, I spy him sitting at the desk, head bent over a stack of papers.

He puts the papers down and stares for a moment into the middle distance. Then he clears his throat and picks up the phone.

"Operator, yes, put me through to Obergruppenführer Heydrich, please. His private line." A pause. "Yes, he is expecting my call. Tell him Obersturmbannführer Heinrich is on the line. It's important."

There is another, longer pause.

"Ah." He sits up straighter, his voice loud. "Obergruppenführer, thank you for taking my call. Heil Hitler." His tone is deferential, not one I've heard Vati use before. "Yes. I'm reporting in, as requested. All local units are ready to go. We have briefed the police, the mayor, the fire service. We await your orders."

He is quiet again. His eyes dart about. Can he see me in the crack of the door? Slowly, I pull back and move to the side, breathing shallow and fast. I pin my ear to the door.

"Of course," he is saying. "No, it blatantly hasn't worked . . . absolutely, a change of strategy is needed . . . it is indeed the perfect catalyst . . . the German people are ready, as you say. We are more than ready, believe me, the men are itching for it . . . those Jews need to realize the full force of feeling against them . . . Certainly, just as soon as I have your word to go . . ."

This sounds like more than a fuss about nothing.

Fingers of fear crawl up my back.

Walter. I must go to him. Warn him something terrible is about to happen.

Thirty-Six

November 9, 1938

At school, during break, I tell Erna all I heard of Vati's conversation yesterday.

"I need to find a way to warn Walter."

"But what does your father mean?" she asks. "The German people are ready . . . Ready for what?" She looks at me, eyes full of fear. "I should tell my father."

"I don't know. I'll try and find out more. I need to go to the café and get a message to Walter, but Mutti will want me home this afternoon."

"Tell her you're having supper this evening with me. You can go and find Walter instead."

"Are you sure?"

"I'll cover for you, if for any reason she should check. What else are friends for?" Erna smiles.

Later, when Mutti is taking her usual afternoon nap, I send Ingrid on an errand to buy some fabric and strong thread for a school needlework project. Bertha decides to take a break in her room. The house is quiet. A gem of an opportunity.

I stand alone in Vati's study, straining my ears. The silence crackles as, dry-mouthed, I press my back against the closed door. I tiptoe my way across the room to the desk. Ever since we moved into the house, this has been a hallowed place. Vati's sanctum. Forbidden to all but him. The back of my neck prickles.

The room is gloomy in the late afternoon. I click on the lamp, casting a soft yellow circle of light over Vati's desk. It's perfectly neat. The big square of leather-bound blotting paper lies in front of his chair, the pot of ink at the top end. A marble ashtray and his fountain pen are on one side of the blotting paper, next to some wooden trays neatly stacked with papers.

I carefully pull out the top drawer of the old oak desk. It creaks and I freeze. No footsteps sound in the hallway. The door does not fly open.

Exhale. Inhale. Carry on.

Inside the drawer I find an assortment of personal letters. On one I recognize Oma's beautiful cursive with the Berlin postmark. Underneath the pile are a stack of small folded envelopes, written in a female hand. Hilda Müller's, surely. My fingers itch to open the little envelopes and read the disgusting secrets held inside. But at the same time, I'm repelled by them and would rather not know. I close the drawer quietly. They are a distraction. They're not what I'm looking for, and Walter needs me to be focused.

I move to the next drawer. A spare blotting pad, writing paper, and envelopes. The bottom drawer is empty. I sigh and lift my gaze. On the wall opposite the desk, deep in shadow, are the various framed accolades to Vati. His Nazi Party membership certificate. Number three thousand, two hundred and thirty-five. Above them, Hitler's portrait, in pride of place in the room. We stare at each other, eyeball to eyeball.

I loved you once.

His eyes are piercing black. His voice resounds in my head, clear and deep. *You have sinned in the worst way imaginable. You will pay a price. Your punishment will be of the worst kind . . .*

Shut up, SHUT UP! I cover my ears and screw my eyes shut.

I sink into Vati's big chair, slowly open my eyes, and concentrate on the papers in the trays. The top two sheets are memoranda to newspaper staff about timekeeping and behavior codes for journalists. Then an invoice for a repair to the car. The rest is a mixture of business correspondence and other invoices.

I move to the second tray. Right at the top is a letter marked, "To All Regional and Local SS Commanders: TOP SECRET. WITH UTMOST URGENCY." It bears today's date, 9 November 1938, and is signed by Herr Fischer, head of the Leipzig branch of the Gestapo, following direct orders from Heinrich Himmler, Reichsführer-SS. I snatch it up.

Operations against the Jews, in particular against their synagogues, will commence very soon. There must be no interference. Preparations must be made for the arrest of between 20,000 and 30,000 Jews across Germany. In particular, affluent Jews are to be selected. If any Jew is found in possession of weapons during the operations, the most severe measures must be taken. Further directives will be forthcoming during the course of the night. SS may be called upon for the overall operations. As soon as events permit, as many Jews from all districts, especially the rich, as can be accommodated in existing prisons are to be arrested. For the time being, only healthy males are to be detained. The appropriate concentration camps are to be contacted immediately for prompt accommodation of the Jews arrested.

The room spins. What sort of orders are these? I place the papers and trays carefully back in the right order with shaking hands.

Twenty to thirty *thousand*! It sounds like the size of an army. Is this an army of Jews about to attack Leipzig? But something about the wording doesn't seem right. I retrieve the order and read it again. *Operations . . . against their synagogues . . . in particular affluent Jews are to be selected . . . if any Jew is found in possession of weapons . . . the most severe measures must be taken.*

None of it makes sense. My brain feels foggy and slow. *Operations against their synagogues?* That's no order against a *threat.* I wonder again about the concentration camps. These shadowy places that shape-shift in my mind as misery-filled, medieval-style prisons; or a Roman model, with work gangs of slaves tied together with ropes and whipped if they don't work hard enough. Such tales of atrocious conditions in these places that leak in from foreign press reports are denied as vicious propaganda. Radio coverage, just the other day, said that Germany is merely following this camp invention of the British, who maltreated women and children in the Boer War by incarcerating them. At least in our version of the camps, we only hold men. Which tale is true?

I must go straight to Erna, then find Walter. I am reaching out to slip the paper back into the tray, when the study door swings wide open.

"Franz?" Mutti's voice is slurred with sleep. "Oh! *Herta?*"

"Mutti!" I quickly replace the letter and jump to my feet.

"What are you doing in here? I saw the light beneath the door . . ."

"I was looking for"—my mind races—"Oma's address. I thought I would write to her. I've been very lax."

"You can't expect me to believe that," she replies, sounding more awake. "You could have asked me for Oma's address. Why are you snooping around Vati's study?"

"Okay, okay. I'm sorry. I was just trying to find out what was going to happen. You said something big was going to take place. I just wanted to know. I shouldn't have. Please don't tell Vati."

Mutti takes a few steps into the room.

"You're right. You shouldn't be in here. Vati would be very angry. There are important, confidential papers in here. I would never dream of looking through them. It's very wrong of you, Hetty. How could you?"

"I'm sorry. I won't do it again, I promise." I snap off the light and move away from the desk toward her. "Please forgive me for being foolish and nosy."

"I can't ignore this." She stands, stiff and straight, un-yielding.

"I just want to know what's going on. Please, Mutti—"

"Go to your room. Stay there until your father gets home." She ushers me out.

"Mutti, please. I'm sixteen! I'm not a child anymore. And I'm supposed to be at Erna's this evening, for supper."

"Don't answer back! You're going nowhere. Your father will deal with you when he gets home. And don't for one second consider defying me on this." She is quivering with rage, with sucked-in cheeks, and a thin, hard line to her mouth.

My cheeks burn hot as I thunder up the stairs and slam my bedroom door behind me. How dare she treat me like a child. How dare she keep me a prisoner in my own home.

Breathing hard, I stare out my window over the top of the bare limbs of the cherry tree, toward the corner of Fritz-schestrasse. A ghost of Walter walks down the pavement to-ward our house, hands in his short-trouser pockets, satchel slung over his shoulder, on his way to walk to school with Karl. *Preparations for arrest . . . Jews from all districts . . .* How did it come to this? I can't just sit here and let this happen. I must go to him.

Throwing open the window, I maneuver myself onto the sill. From here I can easily reach out and touch the tips of the branches of the tree. But they bow easily under the lightest pressure. There is no way they will take my weight. I cry out and slam the window shut in frustration. Pacing the room, I rub away my useless tears with balled fists.

"Fräulein Herta?" Bertha's voice outside the door, accompanied by a soft knock. "What is it?" She opens the door a crack. "May I—"

"Oh, Bertha!" I fly to the door and pull Bertha inside. "It's the most terrible thing . . ." I whisper, embracing her as though she were my mother. She freezes in shock, arms locked at her sides. Then slowly, gently she layers her arms around my back, patting between my shoulders as she might a small child.

"There, there," she says soothingly. She is warm, her body solid against my own. I let myself melt into the comfort of her.

After a few moments, she gently takes my shoulders and holds me away. "Whatever has happened?" she asks, studying my face.

Watching the door and speaking in a hoarse whisper I quickly tell her that Mutti caught me in Vati's study. I give her the briefest outline of what I read in that shocking command from Herr Himmler, and tell her I'm desperate to leave the house and warn Walter and his family of what is going to happen.

Bertha shakes her head and bites her lip. "You can't do anything, fräulein," she says after a pause. "This is too dangerous to involve yourself in. You must obey your parents, Herta. There are some things that are too big, too *much* to take on alone."

She's right. It is too big. But if I can do this one *minuscule* thing that might help, at least Walter's family, then I must do it. He would do it for me, I know it.

My tears have dried and I'm calm.

"I've a plan, Bertha," I say slowly, looking deep into her troubled eyes. "I just need two tiny favors. Please, will you help me?"

I scribble a note.

My dear Erna,

That matter we spoke of yesterday is much, much bigger than we thought. People must be warned that terrible things are going to happen tonight. They must not fight back. I hope your father can do something. It's all I can say for the moment. I hope you understand.

Yours,

Herta

Bertha promises to have it delivered and reluctantly agrees to my second request.

When Vati comes home, I'm allowed downstairs, to learn my punishment. Sitting in his study, he pours himself a whisky and drinks it down in a few gulps. I watch as he pours another.

"I truly don't know what's happened to you, Herta. Upsetting your mother. Defying me. I'm giving you one chance. What is going on?"

"Nothing is going on, Vati." I meet his pale eyes. He moves his gaze. He's agitated, nervy. He walks around the room. "I'm sorry I looked at your papers. It was wrong of me, but Mutti told me something big was going to happen. Nobody ever tells me anything *properly*. I decided to find out for myself."

He swings around to face me, red-faced and angry.

"What you did is unforgivable. There are state secrets in this room."

I think of the little stack of letters, neatly tied together with a ribbon. Personal secrets, too.

"I've heard something," he says, "a rumor, which troubles me. I refused to believe it. But if it's true—"

The telephone on his desk jangles.

"What things? What have you heard?" I brace myself for the accusation.

Vati stares at the ringing phone, snatches up the receiver, listens intently, and grunts, "I'm leaving immediately. I'll be there in fifteen minutes."

"I've no time for you now," he says, replacing the receiver. "Events are moving too fast. We'll discuss it in the morning. In the meantime, I forbid you to come in here again, and I forbid you to leave this house until we've spoken, and that's the end of it." His face is serious and unsmiling. "Vom Rath has lost his fight for life. Our nation has been attacked and we must act now to ensure worse will not follow."

My guts squeeze thinking of Walter.

I follow him out to the hall where Mutti hovers.

"Take care, Franz. Please be careful tonight," she says, her voice tremulous.

"I've been handpicked to do the Führer's work," he tells Mutti as he shrugs his coat on. "If Herr Himmler trusts me, you must too. Don't wait up," he adds, striding from the house, leaving behind him a faint aroma of liquor.

Mutti and I stand staring at each other.

"It's all ready, Frau Heinrich," Bertha says, hovering in the dining room doorway. "Shall I go ahead and serve the soup?"

AFTER A DINNER where Kuschi lay across my feet as if trying to protect me, Mutti and I go to the afternoon sitting room in silence. She knits ferociously, her lips pursed, brow furrowed. I hold a book in my hand but cannot focus on the words. Bertha won't let me down, I'm sure. But with each minute that passes, whatever is happening outside on the streets of Leipzig puts Walter in danger.

Unable to sit still, I go to the window and gaze out at the dark, empty street as if in some vain hope he might be standing out there, beneath the cherry tree, leaning nonchalantly against its trunk, his hat pulled low. He isn't there, of course, and I return to the edge of the sofa. The empty space in the house grows. Room after room filled with priceless objects and the ghostly shadows of long-departed inhabitants. Mutti's needles click, click, click together, louder and louder until I want to scream at her to shut them up.

Bertha comes in with the coffee and gives me a long look. She carries a crease in her forehead. I meet her eyes and I know she won't let me down, even though every fiber in her body is against my idea.

She places the coffee cups carefully on the table.

"I've told Ingrid to get off home to her parents," she tells

Mutti. "She's no good to me, getting under my feet, stressing and worrying. You know how she is."

"That's fine, Bertha." Mutti sighs, not looking up.

"So I was thinking," Bertha continues, throwing me a look, "as we're getting so close to St Nicholas's and Ruprecht's Day, perhaps Hetty could help me make the gingerbread house?"

Mutti finally looks up from her knitting.

"Yes," she says finally. "Domestic chores will do her good. Herta, be so good as to put something on the gramophone before you go to the kitchen. Some Wagner, I think. It feels appropriate for tonight."

"Yes, Mutti," I say, picking out a record and placing the needle into the groove with shaking fingers. She settles back into her chair and waves me away with a dismissive hand.

I follow Bertha to the kitchen. She bangs the door shut behind me.

"God, help me, I don't know why I'm doing this . . ." she begins in a low voice, beads of sweat appearing on her brow. "Go warn that boy. I'll collect the coffee cups in an hour or so and tell her you're knee deep in flour. That'll buy you a little longer. After that, though, she'll be wanting to go to bed and she'll come in here, so you'd better be back. It's my neck you'll be risking, too, you realize," she adds briskly.

"Are you sure about this, Bertha?"

"Damn well get out of here before I change my mind. And by God, you'd better be back in an hour, two at most, or I'll skin you." She wipes the palms of her hands on her apron, and breathing heavily, she pulls the big mixing bowl, flour, and butter from the cupboard.

I don't wait to see any more. I'm bolting out the back door, wondering where I should look for Walter first.

I START WITH the café. Lena is taking an order at one of the tables. She glances up as I rush in. Her eyes widen when she sees me.

"Come with me," she says, passing close with a tray. No need for any pretense. She leads the way behind the counter and through a small kitchen where an elderly lady, probably her mother, is working. A wireless sits in one corner from which the voice of Zarah Leander is singing "*Eine Frau Wird erst schön durch die Liebe*." I follow Lena into a tiny sitting room at the back. A dark-haired boy of eleven or twelve is doing his homework at a table, books spread around him. This must be her son, who has delivered messages between Walter and me.

"He isn't here . . ." she begins.

"Do you know if he would be at home? I need to find him, quickly. He . . . could be in danger . . ." My voice is shaky and Lena nods quickly.

"My boy will fetch Walter for you," she says, leaning over him, gently rubbing his shoulder and speaking softly into his ear. He nods eagerly, dropping his pencil, and tears out the back door. "It is best. Nobody will notice a child. It's safer than you going yourself." Lena shakes her head and sniffs. "Sorry, but I must get back to the café. You can stay in here."

"Thank you," I whisper and perch on the edge of a narrow green sofa pushed against the back wall of the room. A threadbare rug covers the floor in front of the blackened fireplace.

A draft floats in from the open back door. There is a clattering of pots and pans in the kitchen and the warbling voice of the singer crackles from the wireless. Presumably Lena has a husband, too. Where is he? She looks too young to be married, or even to have a child. Until now, she'd just been a girl. A person to pass messages. But like so many other ordinary folk, she must be full of fear for her son, for her mother toiling away in the kitchen. Perhaps I should tell Lena what I know? I owe her at least that for sending her son out onto the streets for me. Will he be in danger too? I chastise myself for my own paranoia. How ridiculous. Nobody would want to hurt a child, would they?

A news bulletin comes on after the song. I can't make out the words above the sizzling and clanking. The voice drones. I study a broken nail on my thumb; cross and recross my legs.

There is a rush of cold air and the boy is back, breathing heavily as though he has been running. I stand up, expecting Walter, but the boy shakes his head.

The old lady appears in the doorway, a wooden spoon in her hand, strands of gray hair drifting loose from her bun. The boy whispers into her ear. She nods and places a hand on his shoulder.

"He says Walter wasn't home. He went into town earlier this evening with his uncle and father. There has been some trouble. Jewish shops targeted by youths. They went to help friends defend their property." She shakes her head and purses her lips.

"I think worse might be to come. Take care, all of you. Perhaps its best you go home soon." It's the most I dare to say.

MY STOMACH SOMERSAULTS as I take a tram toward the city center. The clock is ticking. I must have wasted twenty minutes. The dark pavements outside the brightly lit tram seem strangely quiet.

Please, God. If you are there, let me find him, unharmed and safe.

The tram winds its way around the outskirts of the old town. There are more people here. Shouts and cries in the distance. Has it already started? Four workmen jump on and stand near my seat. They talk in low, gruff voices.

"What's goin' on then, Wilhelm? What d'ya hear?"

"Riots." The man sniffs and shrugs.

Another man says something I don't hear, but the others laugh. I catch the word *Jew*, and my skin contracts. The tram screeches around a bend and I can't hear any more. It stops at the top of the Brühl. Should I get off here? He could be anywhere in the city. I decide to wait. The workmen leave and the tram moves off toward Dittrichring.

I jump off at the next stop. The street is busy and I turn to cross the road to head toward Thomaskirche. A crowd of young men pass me, heading in the opposite direction, down Gottschedstrasse. On a whim, I follow them. The air becomes heavy. My throat stings and my lungs heave.

Smoke.

I reach the corner of Gottschedstrasse and Zentralstrasse

and stop. I'm facing the building Walter took me to that first time we came into the city together. I remember how I stood outside the synagogue, feeling such shame and anger as I waited for him. I see his face as it was then, proud and excited, filled with love, as he presented me with the Kafka from beneath his jacket. I let out an involuntary sob. People turn and stare at me.

Heat is intense on my bare skin and I gape at the flames engulfing the synagogue, licking skyward, roaring and crackling. The fire is consuming the whole building, curling from the windows and underneath the roof. A crowd is assembled, watching the spectacle from a safe distance away. A fire engine stands in front of the building, the firemen leaning idly on their vehicle, watching the inferno.

"Why do they do nothing?" I ask the man standing next to me.

"They won't save the synagogue," he answers, "but they stand by in case the fire should spread to German property."

"But . . . what if there are people in there?" I say, my chest tightening. What about the rabbi? "Shouldn't we do something?"

The man shrugs his shoulders. "Be my guest," he says with a sniff.

And what of the Kafka? The prospect of the book Walter so lovingly presented, and I later rejected, being consumed by the flames is more than I can bear.

I slip around the back of the gawkers. To one side of the burning building lies a pile of books and papers. Two men have set fire to that, too. A desolate little group stand silently watching. The only one to speak is a little boy who asks, "Why do they burn our things? Those are our things!"

Nobody answers.

Turning, I run through the center of old Leipzig. Here, nothing is changed. It could be any ordinary evening. People out for a stroll, visiting the bars and restaurants. How can they, the thoughtless swine? I run faster until my chest is fit to explode.

At the top of the Brühl, I slow to a walk, drawing the air in great, heaving gasps. There are clusters of men. Strange sounds. Shouting.

I hug the walls of the buildings as I enter the street but soon abandon this. The safest place to walk is in the middle of the road. The air is filled with acrid smoke. Mobs of boys and men smash the windows of shops, battering in doors, yelling as they loot the contents. They don't even notice what they grab—anything, great armfuls of it. They whoop in delight. The pavements shimmer with shattered glass. Policemen stand around making no attempt to stop the madness.

Two men emerge from a covered passageway next to a tailor's shop just in front of me. The windows, like so many others, have been broken and some boys, no older than fourteen, are grabbing piles of cloth from inside. The two men cry out and jostle past me as they rush forward to save their possessions. I huddle, frozen in fear, against the wall as other men push past. A crowd rolls in, surrounding the men, hiding them from view.

These men, no longer fathers, brothers, sons, are wild creatures, smelling blood and power and chaos. The veneer of civilization is shattering, revealing the true nature of man. Wild and dangerous. Beast.

I watch, my feet stuck like glue to the road. I had half expected some sort of army of Jews out on the streets, locking arms with the National Socialist defenders. Not this. This is just thugs, running amok, belligerently smashing up shops.

I should leave. It isn't safe. Surely Walter isn't here.

I turn to retrace my steps, but see up ahead, on the right, the sign for KELLER & CO. It's stupid and unlikely that he's there, but I don't know where else to go. I make my way slowly down the crowded, narrow street. Another window is smashed. Shrieks of victory. The smoke-filled air is choking and hot.

What the hell am I doing here?

And hell-like it is. All these men, high on violence and destruction. My bowels shift. I should just turn back, go home. Poor Bertha, risking all she has for me. Even if I find Walter, what could I possibly do?

A movement catches my eye. A youth. Something familiar about his shape, the way he lunges forward. I look again.

Tomas.

Tomas, but not in uniform as he should be when on HJ business. Tomas, full of fury wielding a pickax. He's with a group about his age, some younger. It's his schar, but why in civilian clothes? He shouts something and the mob attacks the window of a department store. He turns, as though he senses me watching. He shouts to me, but I don't hear. I stay rooted, and he drops his ax and runs to me.

"Hetty! What the hell are you doing? You must go home, it's not safe out here."

I nod dumbly.

"Does your father know you're out?"

"No! I mean, yes. I-I-I was with friends, but I heard all this commotion and came to see . . ."

"C'mon, I'll take you home." Tomas wraps his arm around my shoulders and begins walking me up the street. I let him guide me, suddenly weak, limp, like I can't hold my own weight.

"Why are you here, Tomas? What's happening? Why aren't you in uniform?"

"Orders." He taps his nose as though it's all subject to secrecy. "Destroy or be destroyed, that's the choice, Hetty. I should get back there, but I'll see you safely home, or at least onto a tram first . . ."

Our feet crunch on broken glass. My throat is raw; my eyes sting. Shouts to the left. Two men, roughly dressed, drag an elderly man in a suit from his shop door, out into the street, right in front of us.

"Fuck you! Fuck you all!" yells the old man, resisting. He pulls an arm free and with lightning speed throws a fist into the face of one of his captors.

"Stupid bastard!" shouts the punched man, and they start to beat the older man. Blow after blow. The man is screaming, high pitched, desperate. A raw animal sound that penetrates me, deep inside. The man is down, twisting and turning on the pavement. They kick him, vicious and hard.

"Look away," Tomas's voice says in my ear, but I can't.

His yells are reduced to whimpers.

They are battering the life from his body.

"Stop," I say, "STOP! Do something!" I turn to Tomas, but he stands, like me, and does nothing. "Jesus Christ, they're killing him," I yell. Everything goes black around me, except a red-tinged vision of the old man, and the two men kicking him, in the center, as if I'm seeing it through a camera lens. I lurch toward them.

Strong arms hold me back. I struggle against them, crying out. The men don't stop, they continue beating him until he whimpers no more.

"Leave it, Hetty, come away," Tomas is saying in my ear, gripping my arms so hard it hurts.

The men stop. Chests heaving, they look at me.

"Get her out of here," they tell Tomas. "She's a liability. This is no place for a girl." And they walk away, leaving an inert body, twisted and bloody, in the dirt, the glass, the shit on the road.

Tomas drags me firmly by the shoulders, maneuvering me past the dead man, propelling me away from hell.

We wait at the tram stop. Everything looks the same. The wooden shelter. The single streetlamp throwing out its paltry glow. Away from the horror unfolding in the Brühl, it's eerily quiet. I wish I could forget what I just witnessed, but I know with absolute certainty that I never will. The brutal violence. The way those men *wanted* to kill another human being. His desperate cries for help as he writhed in agony in the dirt.

It replays and replays, blinding me to my surroundings.

I did nothing. I stood and watched the life drain from him. I didn't even offer comfort in his death throes. What sort of person does that make me? Complicit?

And Walter? What if it's Walter's body kicked and battered, lying in a gutter somewhere? A noise escapes from deep within. I've not found Walter.

Tomas peers down at me. "Are you going to be okay?"

"I'm fine," I lie, clenching my teeth to stop them chattering.

I've lost track of time and check my watch. I'm surprised only an hour has gone by. I can still get home and Bertha will be happy.

A tram turns the corner, its light piercing the gloom as it trundles toward us.

"Thanks for looking after me, Tomas. I'm fine now. Really."

"I need to get back." He looks toward the Brühl. "But I should make sure you get home safe." He looks down at me.

"Seriously." I try to laugh. "I'll be home in five minutes. I'm fine."

The tram passes slowly, then, metal screeching on the line, it comes to a stop.

"Tomas." I muster all my strength to look straight at his eyes without wavering. "Thank you for taking care of me. I will be perfectly safe. Go back to your duties." I force my face into a smile, jump on the tram, and wave.

"Go!" I say lightly. "I'll see you soon, I promise."

I watch him standing there as the tram pulls away, legs slightly apart, torn between his duty and my safekeeping. He raises a hand finally and then turns to go.

Nausea and a wave of dizziness overwhelm me. I sink onto a wooden bench, my head falling to my knees.

Walter. Please just be alive.

I CAN'T STOP shaking. That contorted body, splattered blood. The head, crushed, facedown in the road. Maybe he had a wife. Children. Grandchildren. People who loved him, called him nicknames, laughed with him. Not anymore.

The image of his face morphs into Walter's. I begin to retch. I can't stop it. I get off the tram halfway up Hindenburg- strasse and vomit at the side of the road. My stomach heaves and heaves. But I don't feel any better when I've finished. Still shaking, I walk up the main road toward where Walter told me his grandmother's house lies. Perhaps he is safely home now.

It's quieter than the city center, but a smell of burning per- vades the air, even here. It's as if war has broken out, in the center of our most civilized city. I feel as though I'm walking through a hideous dream I can't wake from.

There's another fire ahead. It's hard to know, but it could be Walter's house. A fire engine is parked in the street. Again, the firemen stand idly by, watching.

I stare up at the elegant façade, flames taking hold, roar- ing from within. The rock in my stomach grows. From what Walter's told me of it, I'm certain this *is* his house.

I push my way to the front of the gawping crowd.

"What happened to the occupants?" I ask a woman, staring up at the flames with her two young sons.

"They fled squealing like rats from a burning barn," she replies, curling her mouth downward, her face as sour as her words. "That idiot, Schloss"—she waves a hand at the green- grocer's shop across the road—"took the women in. Gestapo arrested the men."

"The men," I echo. "What men? Where have they taken them?"

Am I too late? I swallow the sour bile in my mouth.

"Shipped them off to god-knows-where for the night. 'Bout time too," she adds, sniffing hard. "Been complaining about them for months. Having Jews in our midst like that. Heaven knows what they might have done to our kids. Been living in fear, you know, it's awful. I *told* Schloss, not that he listens to me, I *told* him he's making trouble . . ."

I push my way roughly back through the crowd and run across the road to the greengrocer's. "Hateful, rotten *cow*," I say out loud. Please let that horrible woman be wrong. Please don't let them have Walter.

Herr Schloss stands in a narrow doorway, to the side of the shop, talking to a bunch of angry youths.

"You're as bad as they are, if you hide the buggers in with you," one is saying.

"Send 'em out," adds another.

"These are women and children, frightened to death. I'm not sending them out to face you lot," Schloss tells them firmly.

"Then we'll have to smash your windows in and fetch 'em out ourselves," says the first youth, raising a wooden bat.

"Now, now." Herr Schloss raises his hands. "Be reasonable. You've no argument with these poor souls. Look, I've no wish to have 'em in my place, I can tell you. But their house is burning down, and they've nowhere to go tonight." He points at the burning building. "I'll send them on their way first thing. You've no argument with me, lads."

The boys exchange glances.

"They'll be gone first thing in the morning, I give you my word," Herr Schloss repeats firmly.

"They'd better be," growls one of the youths. "We'll be back early, Schloss, and if they're not, expect the worst . . ." He turns and walks away, the others following him.

Herr Schloss steps back to close the door, and I rush forward. "Please!" I shove my foot in the doorway. "Please! I want to help."

He grabs my arm and pulls me through the door, slamming it shut behind me. He stares at me, raising his eyebrows high.

"I'm a friend of Walter Keller," I explain. "Is he here? Is Walter here?"

A woman appears at the top of the stairs. Walter's mother. I recognize her instantly. But she's thinner, older, and more haggard than I remember. She walks slowly down the stairs, her clothes smudged and dirty. Tears leak from her eyes and make a pathway through the soot on her cheeks. Another, plumper woman follows her down with three children. Walter's cousins and aunt?

"It's okay, Herr Schloss," Walter's mother says in a soft voice. "Who are you?" She peers at me.

"I'm Herta Heinrich."

She instantly recoils.

"Walter was once great friends with my brother," I rush on. "We bumped into each other a few months back—"

"I know," she says, her tone hostile now. "He told me. And I remember just how upset—"

"Frau Keller, I'm not making any excuses for my family. But the important thing is Walter. Is he safe?"

She shakes her head. "They have them all." Her cheeks are pinched and her lips drawn back, reminding me of a cornered, snarling dog. "My husband, my son, and my husband's brother. Taken into custody by the SS, only this time they said they will be transferring all of them to Buchenwald Concentration Camp in the morning."

The night blackens. I've failed him. The world tilts sideways and I grab the banister to steady myself.

"I tried going to the Gestapo headquarters, but I was turned away. They've not even done anything wrong," she cries, raising her hands to her anguished face. "And my Walter! He's supposed to go to England. To start a new life. To marry and have a chance to be happy. What now? How am I to get them out of that place?" she demands.

I sink down and sit on the bottom stair. "I don't know." I have no more strength. I should have come earlier. Found a way as soon as I read that dreadful order. I let my head sink into my hands. Behind my eyelids, Walter's face, his smile, his eyes. I can almost catch his smell, feel his hands, gentle and warm.

"The children are terrified," Frau Keller is saying. I look up at her. "We've nowhere to go, except to the Jewish house in the morning. We have nothing left but the clothes we stand up in. Even if he were free, we now have no way to pay Walter's exit tax, so he cannot leave. Everything we ever had is gone." Her voice quivers and the children begin to cry.

They stand there, staring at me with desperate, wild eyes.

"I'm so sorry," I mumble. I've never felt so powerless.

I look at my watch. It takes a moment for the clock hands to make sense. I've been gone well over two hours. It'll be nearer three by the time I get home.

"I have to go."

Nobody says anything as I pass Herr Schloss. He opens the front door for me.

"I'm not like my father," I tell them as I step outside. "Not one little bit."

I PUSH OPEN the back door, as quietly as I can. The passageway is in darkness and for a moment I think that, with luck, they've gone to bed. But a silhouette appears at the head of the passage and Mutti's voice, shrill and loud, cuts through the silence.

"Where the HELL have you been?"

She runs and grabs my shoulders with long, thin fingers, shaking me with surprising strength and yelling into my face.

"You stupid, stupid girl! You were *forbidden* to go out. I telephoned everyone I could think of, but no one knew where you were," she rages, barely taking a breath. "I left a phone message with Vati, and I was just about to call the police . . ."

We move into the hall and that's when I see Bertha, her face tearstained and stricken, her hands trembling. Shame washes over me.

"I'm sorry . . ." I croak.

My mouth is like sandpaper. I collapse onto the bench. Walter is gone, and I've ruined everything for Bertha. A stab of fear for her, and for me, when Vati finds out.

"Look at the state of you! You're covered in soot, and muck . . . Is that blood? Hetty, you stink of . . . of *smoke*! Where on earth were you?"

She slaps me. A sudden, stinging blow across my cheek. I hold my face where she struck it.

"Hetty?" Concern, now, added to the anger in Mutti's voice.

"I need some water."

"Bertha—please." Mutti's hands are on my knees. She crouches down and tries to look into my face, but I can't meet her eyes. "I don't understand," she says. "Why do you punish me like this? I've lost one child, I can't lose you, too." She grips me tight.

Bertha hands me a glass of water. I drink it in gulps. It's cool and refreshing, a salve to the bitter burning in my throat. Then she hands me a warm, damp cloth to wipe the dirt off my face.

"You may go," Mutti tells Bertha coldly. "I'll deal with you in the morning. I can't face it tonight."

"Yes, Frau Heinrich." Bertha sniffs and heads for the stairs.

"What did she tell you?" I ask when she's out of earshot.

"That she sent you out to borrow some ginger from Frau Weber across the street because we'd run low, and you didn't come back. She was frantic with worry, but she should never have sent you out. Just because Ingrid wasn't here . . . how dare she use you as a maid—"

"It isn't true," I say quickly. "She's trying to protect me. I lied to her. I pretended we'd run out. I begged her to go; she didn't want me to, but I needed an excuse to leave the house. It's not her fault, Mutti. It's entirely mine."

"Why?" She rocks back on her heels in shock. "Vati's right, you *have* become a wild thing. What with Karl . . . I should have paid more attention—"

"No, Mutti. It's not you." I twist the cloth in my hands. "I hate being cooped up in this house. I want to join in the fight for Germany. It isn't fair that the boys have all the fun."

Mutti regards me with a look of disgust.

"That's it? That's why you ran off? Getting Bertha into trouble because you want to fight like some stupid boy? Vati forbade you to leave the house. You went *directly* against his orders, Herta. What on earth has got into you?" Her eyes are full of anger again. "Go and get properly cleaned up and then go to bed. When Vati returns, he will decide what to do about you and Bertha."

I shut myself in the bathroom and scrub at the filth until my skin hurts. Once alone, the enormity of the evening's events hits me like the full force of a wave. The death of that man and the violence and destruction around Leipzig. I've done nothing whatsoever to help Walter. In fact, I've probably made his situation worse. The desperation on the face of his mother and his young cousins. What if Vati finds out where I've been? As for poor Bertha, what is to become of her? Whatever it is, it will be my fault. Whatever I touch turns sour. I laugh out loud. I used to think I was chosen for great things. That I was somehow better. How foolish. People, *good* people, like Bertha and Walter, have risked so much for me, and in return, with blundering foolishness, I let them down when they needed me most.

Later, much later, I creep up to the top floor. A slice of light shines beneath Bertha's door. I knock quietly. There's a pause. The door opens a fraction and her face appears in the crack.

"I'm so dreadfully sorry," I whisper.

"Yes," she replies crisply.

"They've taken him to a concentration camp."

"Then I'm sorry, too."

We stare at each other through the crack.

"Go to bed, Fräulein Herta."

I'm not sure I shall ever be able to sleep again. I'm haunted by what I saw tonight. How can men do such things to other human beings? Nature is harsh, but such brutality—this is the domain of humankind alone. Whatever our religion, race, where we are from. Whatever our hair or eye color, our nose shape or the size of our feet, we're all just people. People who feel pain, joy, love, anguish. Who have hopes and dreams; families, friends, and loved ones. How can one lot of people be so utterly blind to this and treat another lot of people as if they are no more than inert objects beneath their feet? And what of you, Walter? Whenever I close my eyes, all I see is you, being beaten to death and left, broken and rotting, on the hard, cold earth. Please, please, be alive.

Thirty-Seven

November 10, 1938

I drift fitfully in and out of sleep. Every little sound jolts me awake, sending my heart thumping in case it's Vati coming home. But as dawn emerges, it hits me. He isn't coming home. I think back to that hateful letter on his desk. *Operations against the Jews . . . Preparations for arrest . . . concentration camps.* Of course, he's been out on the streets all night, ensuring his orders are carried out—that Jewish males are locked up in jails, or, for those who resist arrest, are shot or, worse, kicked and battered to death and left in mangled heaps on the street.

I shudder and turn over, screwing my eyes shut, putting my hands over my ears to block out the world. But my brain keeps whirring.

If he isn't home, where might he be?

I sit up properly, wide awake, my brain suddenly clear, despite the lack of sleep.

DURING BREAKFAST, A flustered Ingrid hurries into the room, tying her apron behind her back.

"So sorry I'm late this morning, Frau Heinrich," she begins breathily. "The bus was delayed and there were all sorts of holdups trying to get across town. Didn't even have time for breakfast." She smiles, her cheeks flushed and her hair wispily disheveled. "Glad I don't have to make that journey every day. So much easier to live in . . ."

Mutti invites her to have breakfast with us, as she sometimes does when Vati is away.

"Oh, thank you very much, don't mind if I do!" She piles a plate with the food Bertha has laid out on the sideboard and sits down. Bertha herself is nowhere to be seen. Ingrid's cheeks still have a high color and her eyes dart about. She is practically panting with excitement.

"Have you heard what went on last night?" she asks. She doesn't wait for a reply. "Everyone was talking about it on the bus. They rounded up all the Jewish men, women, and children in Gohlis and brought them right down here, close to the zoo, then chased them down the steps into the water of the Parthe! Imagine that, at night, in November!"

She takes a breath and then a bite of buttered bread, her jaws sawing, lips pressed closed.

"They drove them, like a herd of sheep, right into the river itself, and kept them there several hours!"

"Goodness," Mutti says and pours herself another coffee. She stubs out the remains of her cigarette into the ashtray and lights another.

"Some say freezing in a dirty river is what they deserve. For all the evil *they* do in the world." She takes another bite of her bread, her eyes lingering on mine.

"And what happened to them then?" Mutti asks.

"They were shivering like mad, of course, so after a few hours of keeping them in the water, they let the women and children go home. The men are being taken to a camp, they said. Just imagine it, though. Herding up people and sticking them in the river! Who would've thought that up, eh?"

"Indeed," Mutti murmurs. She gets up and switches on the wireless set. It crackles to life.

"I also heard"—Ingrid leans toward me in a conspirational manner—"that anyone caught . . . *fraternizing* . . . as it were, or helping one of them, would end up in the camp too! Fancy that, Fräulein Herta, eh?"

"I . . ."

But mercifully, the voice on the radio drowns out all other noise in the room.

"*. . . The patience of the German people has been exhausted. The events of last night were neither organized nor prepared. In cities all across Germany they broke out spontaneously. The Jews were the instigators of this wave of violence. The long-suffering German people were merely responding in an outbreak of fury. The Jews have made a tremendous mistake. A very costly mistake. They must pay for the damage they provoked. One billion marks will be levied from them. It will cost the insurance industry six billion marks for the destruction of shops, synagogues, and homes, but not a penny of it will reach their criminal pockets. Twenty thousand of them remain incarcerated while they reflect on their misdeeds.*"

I've heard enough.

"I'm going to school," I announce.

"You are to come *straight* home, Hetty, do you understand?"

"Yes, Mutti, I promise."

I grab my satchel, put on my coat, and hurry out of the house.

AT SEVEN FIFTY-FIVE, from my vantage point across the street, I watch the receptionist, bundled in a fur coat, unlock the double doors to the offices of the *Leipziger Tageszeitung.* The lights flicker on inside the building on the ground floor. After a few minutes, other members of staff begin to arrive, greeting each other and pushing their way through the doors.

Five minutes later, I enter the building myself. The young, blond receptionist fixes me with big blue eyes. She is still setting herself up at the desk facing the big front doors.

"Good morning," I say brightly.

"Can I help you?"

"Yes, I'm looking for my father."

She smiles indulgently at me.

"And who might your father be?"

"Herr Heinrich."

"Oh!" Her expression changes. "I'm sorry, Fräulein Heinrich, but I don't believe he is here yet." She is flustered as she telephones through to Vati's office.

"I'm sorry," she says again after a few moments, "it's as I thought. He isn't here."

"Are you sure?"

"I just spoke with his secretary." The receptionist replaces the receiver and gives me a nervous smile. "He's left a message saying he won't be here until lunchtime." She hesitates. "Forgive me, but have you not just come from home?"

"Yes, but . . ." I look around me, then lean forward and whisper, "He's been out on SS matters. Please could I speak directly with my father's secretary?" I add, "It is an emergency."

"Of course." The girl snatches up the phone again.

If I'm right, Vati must have someone to cover for him. His secretary fields his calls.

Vati's middle-aged, bespectacled secretary appears. We shuffle to the side of the entrance hall, away from the ears of the receptionist.

"I need to find my father," I begin. "Something bad has happened."

"I don't know where he is right now. I can organize a car to take you home, Fräulein Heinrich, if that would help?" Her voice is gentle, kindly.

"Look," I say quietly. Urgently. "I know about Vati's mistress. I don't care about all that," I lie. "I just need to find him, as soon as possible. It's very important. Just give me the address of the fräulein. Please."

The woman freezes and stares at me.

"I won't say it's you who gave me the address. You won't get into trouble," I urge. "I just need to see Vati. It's very important."

Still she stares at me, and suddenly I'm gripped by panic. *Have* I got it dreadfully wrong? Her lips are a thin, straight line.

"She lives at flat 3, number 17, Schmiedestrasse. It's just the other side of König Albert Park, toward Plagwitz."

Exhale.

The first hurdle is overcome, but the bigger one must now be faced. Stay strong.

You can do this. For Walter.

I ARRIVE OUTSIDE the entrance of a newly built apartment block in a road filled with similar nondescript buildings. There is no doorman, but one of those new intercom devices is fitted outside the front door. I take a slow, deep breath then press the bell for flat 3. There is a buzz and after a pause, a voice sounds through the intercom. "Yes? Hello?"

Her voice.

"Good morning, Fräulein Müller. I'm Herta Heinrich. I'm here to speak with my father."

There is a long pause.

"It's an emergency," I add, into the crackling silence.

"He isn't here"—her words are clipped—"I don't know why you would think . . ."

"But he's due here, isn't he? Please may I wait for him?"

Another pause. I lean against the door, palms spread. There's a buzz and the door clicks open.

Thank you.

"First floor," she says, through the intercom.

Hilda Müller is waiting for me outside her front door. She's just as I remember her. The same light brown hair, tightly plaited and folded up around her head. Little pink ears. Fat lips. She is young. Very young, at least, compared to Vati. Midtwenties at a guess. Certainly closer to my age than his. We stare at each other for a few moments, then she beckons me inside.

"Your father . . . he's been out all night. But he's on his way," she says.

The flat is larger than I expected. Bright, tidy, and furnished in a modern, simple style. Nothing like the fussy antiques filling our house. I follow Fräulein Müller's square and solid figure into the sitting room. What can Vati see in this woman? Apart from her youth, she is nothing compared to elegant Mutti.

I sit on the edge of a patterned sofa while the woman hovers, not meeting my eyes. Awkwardness crouches between us like a nervous dog.

"May I have a glass of water please, Fräulein Müller?" I ask at last.

"Of course, I should have offered. And it's Hilda, please." She hurries off to the kitchen.

Her nervousness has the opposite effect on me. I'm suddenly calm and in control. After all, it's Hilda who is in the wrong, not me. It's as if I'm the adult and she the naughty child.

Hilda returns with a glass of water. I drain it.

"You were thirsty," she says with a half smile. "Would you like another?"

Before I can answer, a little girl appears wearing a loose pink nightdress. Her fine, blond curly hair is a creamy cloud around her face. She rubs her eyes as though she has just woken. She is bigger than I remember from that day at the station. She must be, what, three or four years old now? Given the ugliness of the mother, she is remarkably pretty.

The girl stops and regards me with suspicion in her saucer-size eyes.

"Who is this, Mutti?" she asks, not taking her eyes off me.

Hilda sits and lifts the little girl onto her lap.

"This is Herta," she tells her, gently stroking the hair back from her face. "She has come to visit. I said she could wait with us until"—she throws me a glance—"until Herr Heinrich arrives."

The little girl gasps. "Is Vati coming here now? In the morning?"

An electric shock.

She called him "Vati."

The girl twists around to look at her mother's face. Hilda nods and stares down at the carpet. She squirms beneath my glare. She couldn't know that I saw the three of them at the station that time.

"Yippee!" the child exclaims, then she turns to me and says, "Hello, I'm Sophie. Can you play cat's cradle? I love cat's cradle, but I'm not very good. I just learned it. Will you play with me? It's fun." She wriggles off her mother's lap and runs to fetch some string. She returns, smiling broadly.

I shake my head. "Sorry. I don't know how to play."

"I can show you," she cries brightly.

She stands right in front of me, waving the string in the air.

"I really don't want to play," I say firmly.

"Don't bother Herta, Sophie," Hilda says. "Not everyone wants to play games in the early morning. I'll go and make some coffee," she adds, disappearing into the kitchen.

Sophie begins to dance from foot to foot in front of me, waving the string like a flag.

"Shall we play something else if you don't want to play cat's cradle?" she asks.

"I don't want to play anything, Sophie. Sorry."

She frowns then skips to the other side of the room and puts the string on a bookshelf.

I watch her. This child, who has been a specter, an evil, mocking spirit in my head. Now the real thing is here, in the same room, talking with me, smiling, wanting to play a game. She has a name. Sophie. In any other circumstance, I might think her sweet. Charming even.

She's your sister!

I don't want a sister.

I need to plan exactly what to say to Vati when he arrives. But this is all too much, and I can't think properly. Sophie is prattling away to herself. She holds a doll in one hand and a toy dog in the other, facilitating an imaginary conversation between them. I try to see hints of me or Karl in her. Perhaps there is a resemblance, about the eyes. I look for signs of evil in her. But I can't see the spirit that haunted me in this flesh-and-blood girl-child. That was an invention of my imagination.

I suppose the child in front of me is as innocent of the faults of her parents as I am.

"No, no, you naughty doggy," Sophie is saying, "if you run off again, I shall have to punish you and you shan't be allowed to play with your friends in the park . . ."

She looks up and sees me watching her.

"Do you like doggies, Herta?" She smiles.

"I—"

The intercom buzzes loudly and we both jump at the noise. Hilda appears and looks at me with nervous eyes.

"Vati!" Sophie shouts with glee, tossing the doll and the dog to one side and running to the front door.

Hilda and I stand together, frozen, as Vati's bulk fills the doorway. He stares at us wordlessly with wide eyes, while Sophie reaches up to him.

"Vati!" Sophie tugs at his hand. "This is Herta. She is very nice and I want to teach her to play cat's cradle."

I search Vati's face for horror or rage or shame.

But there is nothing. His face is as blank as a sheet of paper. He simply looks tired. And old.

HILDA PUTS ON her hat and picks up her basket.

"Come along, Sophie. Let's visit the baker's. We can stop and feed the ducks on the way back, if we're quick," she tells a now neatly dressed Sophie.

Vati exchanges a look with Hilda as she passes. A private, intimate look. A chill runs down my spine. How they understand each other, these two. I never see Vati look at Mutti that way.

We are finally alone.

"How did you find me, Herta?" Vati asks as soon as the front door is shut. "How did you know?" He sinks onto the sofa and presses two fingers between his eyes. "Is this what you were looking for in my study?"

I remain standing, fighting the urge to physically hurt him. To assuage the rage creeping through my veins at the thought of how this happy little domestic setup with Hilda and Sophie would hurt poor Mutti if she were here now.

"I've known about this for a long time," I tell him. "It was ages ago. I saw you once with Fräulein Müller and the little girl, Sophie. I saw . . . Well, I just knew."

"Poor Herta." He peers up at me. "That wasn't the best way to find out. I always intended to tell you, and Karl, of course, eventually. When the time was right. I want you to have a relationship with your half sister. And Hilda is expecting again. Nothing will replace Karl, but it will be good for you to have more siblings."

Karl is dead and Hilda is expecting again. *You think that is good for me?*

I fold my arms across my chest. Keep my distance. Keep the fire inside in check.

"Come," he says, his voice weary. "Sit down." He pats the cushion next to him.

I stay where I am.

"I need you to do something, Vati. For me." My voice is tight. "Many arrests were made last night. Of Jewish people."

"What of it?"

"Some friends of mine were arrested," I say with a pounding heart. "I want you to help them. Walter Keller. Karl's friend from . . . before, and his father and uncle are being transferred to Buchenwald. I want you to get them out."

Vati stares at me.

"How on earth do you know . . ." His voice tails off. I can almost see his brain computing behind his eyes. "And just why would you want me to do that?" he asks, his tone acid.

"Because he used to be Karl's friend. But mostly because he saved me, that time, from drowning. One good deed deserves another." Finally, I smile at him.

Vati sits up straighter. Shuffles around to face me. He opens his mouth, closes it. Shakes his head. He seems to be struggling to put thoughts into words.

"I tolerated that boy hanging around our house far too long . . . Hélène was too soft . . ." He looks at me. His face changes, a shadow of something. "What does that boy mean to you?" His voice is low with warning. "Karl tried to warn me. Now I understand." He seems to drift off. Shifts his gaze toward the window. He snaps it back to me. "Ingrid. She told me she'd made an allegation to the Gestapo. But then she withdrew it the next day. Said she was too afraid . . . Was that about you, and that boy?"

You sly snake, *Ingrid*.

"There was *nothing* between us," I say firmly. "Karl, Ingrid, they got it wrong. But I bumped into him a few times, yes. And I went to tell him about Karl—"

"Why the hell would you do that?"

"Because they'd once been best friends. Because I thought he would want to know."

"Of all the goddamn stupid, ignorant, *dangerous* things to do! You foolish girl!" All softness is gone. Vati jumps up, rigid with fury.

"I'm sorry . . ."

"You damn well will be, girl! Can you *imagine* if this gets out?" He begins to pace the room. "My daughter, fraternizing with a *Jew*? This is *my* reputation at stake!" He jabs his finger into his chest. "How could you be so stupid?" He quickens his pace. "Pig-shit Jews. That boy has turned your head. I knew you had too much freedom. This was *exactly* what I was worried about. Let those vermin out?" He is clammy and gray. His face scrunches up. "No chance. That boy can rot in hell."

I force myself to breathe slowly, make sure I don't say the words screaming inside my head. *You're wrong! You are the vermin, not them! How can you talk about human beings like this!* I remember Walter's warning. I must not reveal my true thoughts.

"He has a visa for England. If you let him free and arrange to take care of the exit tax, he'll go. That family have nothing left. Their house burned down—"

Vati is pacing, shaking with anger. "Over my dead body."

Everything is going wrong, slipping out of my control.

He stops near the window. Looks out at the block of flats on the other side of the road.

"You know that Ingrid's leaving us soon," he tells me, his tone suddenly calm and quiet.

"What?"

"Yes. She's going after Christmas. With my blessing. She wants to do her bit for the Reich."

"Why are we talking about Ingrid?"

"She's going to a Lebensborn home. Do you know what that is?"

I shake my head. I have no wish to talk about the sow, Ingrid, although I'll be glad to see the back of her.

"It's a state-sponsored program for providing the Führer with Aryan children. The children will be raised with one sole intention. To fight Hitler's war against the Jews.

"Ingrid has passed all the medical and family history tests to ensure she is pure of blood and has no inheritable diseases. She has proved herself to be of good character. She will be matched to an equally good specimen of an SS officer. Together they will make a baby and when he is born, she will hand him over to be raised as a child of the Führer, along with many others like him. She is doing a marvelous thing. Selfless, and for the good of our country. When she has finished, she of course will be welcome to come back and work for us again or get married. The choice is hers."

My insides curdle. "Why are you telling me this?"

Vati takes a few steps toward me.

"Perhaps, Herta, we should consider enrolling you in the same program. Sadly, you don't have the ideal hair color or stature, but perhaps they would make an exception for a daughter of mine."

I swallow the bile that has risen into my mouth. "I'm too young. You can't *make* me do this."

He smiles at me. A thin smile, which doesn't reach his eyes.

"Are you trying to *frighten* me, Vati?"

He doesn't reply and I turn away. His words roll over in my mind, infuriating me.

His *reputation*.

"Why do you have Hilda and Sophie? Is Mutti not good enough? Am *I* not good enough?"

"Don't be stupid, Herta. None of this is about you or Mutti. I love your mother very, very much, and she can never, ever know about Hilda. Her nerves couldn't take it, especially after Karl . . . But sometimes a man needs more. You are a young woman. You couldn't possibly understand. But we men, we have . . . needs. Needs women just don't have."

You have no idea about my needs, you brute. *Nor any other woman's, seeing as you aren't one.*

"And Germany needs children," he continues. "Lots of them. It's a man's duty to produce as many as possible with good bloodlines. It's too late for Mutti, but Hilda is young. Hopefully she will have many more children. Lots of sons. I know it's a shock for you, but one day, perhaps, you will understand."

I hold Vati's gaze. "You're right, Vati. Mutti would be devastated, *destroyed*, if she ever found out. But your secret is safe with me."

He manages a weak smile.

"I promise you, I will not tell a soul about your mistress and other daughter if you arrange for Walter and his father and uncle to be released."

"I've already said. That is out of the question."

"Besides, if others were to find out, how would that look, against your Moral Crusade in the *Leipziger*? It would look especially bad, wouldn't it, if it were to come to light that your own *daughter* had sullied her blood with a Jew? Those false rumors could be stoked . . ."

Vati's eyes drill into mine. Small and ice blue. Pale and wet. I won't be bowed by them.

"You're *blackmailing* me," he says at last, his face reddening. "My own daughter. That Jew boy *is* something to you!"

How I long to tell him the truth, ache to see the shock and horror on his face.

"No." I speak carefully, using every ounce of strength to keep my voice steady. I cannot give away the turmoil inside.

"He is engaged to be married to a girl in England. But it doesn't matter what I say, does it? If you plan to punish me and send me to this . . . this Lebensborn place, then what choice do you leave me? I have to protect *myself.* They won't want someone with sullied blood. And if that means telling Mutti, and the world, about you, as well as lying about myself, then I will."

"You know what they would do to you, Herta, hmm? If they think you have had *relations* with this boy? They will shave your head and parade you through town. They will lock you up, throw away the key. Is that what you want?"

"Of course not." I grit my teeth and ball my fists. "But it wouldn't do *you* much good either, would it, Vati? Especially when Mutti is so hopeful you will get a promotion. I'm asking just a small thing. Release them and arrange for the family to leave Germany. Then all this will be forgotten."

Vati walks across the room, his eyes locking on mine. Beyond the pale gray of his irises, behind the pinprick black pupils, is that uncertainty? Fear? It's definitely something. A weakness. Capitulation. I take a step closer.

"I will do nothing for the father and the uncle," he says at last. "Without a visa, there can be no reason to release them. If I find a way to get the boy out . . ." His face creases in disgust. "*If* I find a way, then you will keep your bloody mouth shut and never say a word about this, or Hilda or Sophie, to anyone, *ever.* Do you understand me?" he says viciously.

I unclench my fists. "You have my word, Vati."

"And if I do get him out, you stay away from that Jew boy. Should you disobey me this time, Herta, I will not protect you; I will not support you. I will have nothing to do with you ever again. Besides"—he fixes me with a look of pure malice—"we will get them in the end, you know. We will get them *all*, in the end."

I walk slowly and shakily down the stairs. As I leave the building, Hilda and Sophie are returning, holding hands as Sophie skips along beside her mother.

As I pass them, a sudden anger toward Hilda hits. "How can you bear it?" I say to her. The words tumble out before I can think about them. "How can you put up with sharing a man who belongs to another?"

She regards me with sad eyes. "I do not expect you to understand, or to forgive," she says quietly. "But we love each other very much."

And with that, she clutches more firmly to the little girl's hand and walks up the steps to her apartment block with her head held high.

Thirty-Eight

November 17, 1938

I know I should destroy this journal. But I just cannot bring myself to do it. Perhaps one day it will be the death of me, but for now, somehow, it makes me feel closer to Karl and to you, dearest Walter. I've barely seen Vati in days. When I do, he makes his anger with me very much felt, refusing even to be in the same room, as though he is disgusted by the very sight of me. And it's agony not knowing if he is going to help. I try so hard not to ask. If I do, it will only antagonize him. Mutti asked once if we had argued. I told her it was just a disagreement over Hausfrau school and she said no more. She is so preoccupied with her own grief that she is oblivious to the tense atmosphere between us. On Sunday morning, Erna, Tomas, and I went to watch the news at the cinema. At least Vati doesn't prevent me from doing that, yet. Tomas is kind and attentive, making sure I am all right after what I witnessed that night. But I'm disgusted and sickened. I don't see how *a nation that calls itself civilized can behave so brutally and thuggishly. I don't see how our great German state's leaders, who talk of honesty and truth and peace and morality, can lie so blatantly to its people. But it feels as though I'm almost alone in seeing the truth.*

After days of waiting, Vati finally calls me to his study. I stand in front of his desk like a pupil called in front of the headmaster to learn her fate. Vati doesn't meet my eyes and the evening meal curdles in my stomach.

"It's been arranged," he says flatly.

"Is . . . Do you mean Walter is being released?" I ask, leaning on the desk for support.

Vati is smoking a cigar. He breathes out a long stream of sweet, cloying smoke.

"I've had to pull strings." His voice is bitter. "But it turns out there are too many of them clogging up the camps, anyway, which is helpful to you, I suppose. Those that have exit visas must leave now. So that means your filthy Jew can go, but as I said before, the father and uncle cannot."

We stare at each other across the desk. There is no love. He controls it well, but I sense the rage rippling beneath his skin.

"He must leave before the end of the month," he continues. "That's where my friend Judge Fuchs has been useful. We've furnished him with the requisite papers, the passport, and affidavit confirming tax has been paid." He taps some ash into the ashtray and takes a drink from his whisky glass. "Fortunately for you, Fuchs owed me a favor. I kept his name out of the papers not so long ago. An unfortunate incident with a young boy. It would gravely have damaged his career. But we all make mistakes, right?"

He takes another few puffs on his cigar, without taking his eyes from mine.

"Vati, thank you, I won't—"

"Sit."

My hands are shaking as I grasp the arm of the chair and sink into it.

"Did you know, Herta, that the only Germans being punished for what they did during the riots are SA men who raped Jewish women?"

I shake my head. He leans forward in his chair, his face reddening.

"Because," he continues, "their crime is worse than murder. Do you know why?"

I stare at him. Shake my head again.

"No? Well, I will tell you. It's because they broke the inviolable law against sexual intercourse between Aryans and Jews. They jeopardized the single most sacred thing we have. Our racial purity. And there is nothing more precious, more important than the cleanliness, the *purity*, of our blood. It's what we are here for. What we strive for each and every day. It's our most precious asset and they have dared to threaten its sanctity . . . Those men have all been expelled from the National Socialist Party. And that is only the beginning of their punishment, the treacherous, idiotic *fools*." He grinds the stub of the cigar into the ashtray.

"What will happen to the murderers?"

"They have all been released. Of course, *they* were only following orders."

I wait for him to say more, but he is quiet. He takes a slug from his glass.

"Why are you telling me this?"

"Oh, I think you know why. We understand each other, yes?" He smiles then. A smile of victory. He thinks he has the measure of me. It's a warning, and he thinks he is safe to assume I won't ignore it.

For a moment, Karl floats between Vati and me. *Take care, Little Mouse. I can't protect you any longer.*

My cheeks burn hot.

"Yes, Vati," I say. "We understand each other."

"It's done," I tell Erna later, now that I'm, once again, allowed to attend BDM meetings. There's no fear that I'll be sneaking off to visit any more Jews. Erna, at least in Mutti's and Vati's eyes, has an untarnished reputation. She's still considered an acceptable influence. If only they knew the truth.

"Oh, thank the lord for that," Erna says, giving my hand a squeeze. "I can't believe you pulled this off."

We're waiting in Fräulein Ackermann's sitting room for everyone to arrive. Tonight's meeting is to plan a pre-Christmas concert. There is to be music from our schar's band and from the local HJ troop's too. There is always an extra flutter of excitement when we combine with the boys' groups. Any opportunity to meet the opposite sex is greeted with enthusiasm. A low hum of chatter, with the outbreak of occasional giggles, fills the room. Erna and I stand by the window, away from the others.

"I'm walking on a tightrope from now on, though," I tell Erna. "Vati will never trust me again."

She nods. "When is Walter coming out?"

"In a couple of days. I'm forbidden to see him."

"Of course."

"I will, though."

"Naturally." Erna smiles. "Happy to provide cover."

A lump forms in my throat. "Thank you."

Fräulein Ackermann enters the room with a tray of sandwiches and jugs of juice. "I think we'll make a start. Most of us are here." She casts her eyes over the group. "Come and sit over here, you two." She waves at us. "There's room down here on the rug."

We obediently take our places with the other girls.

"Let's begin with a song," she says, once we are all seated. She flicks through the pages of *Wir Mädel Singen!* "We'll start with '*Volk ans Gewehr.*'" There is a shuffling of pages and clearing of throats.

> *Do you see the eastern morning glow?*
> *It's a sign of freedom, toward the sun.*
> *We keep together, whether living or dead, whatever may come.*
> *Why do you still doubt?*
> *Stop the wrangling; in us still flows German blood in our veins:*
> *Our people to arms!*
> *Our people to arms!*

I cannot bear to form the words. I stop singing, my mouth tight shut until Erna nudges me, hard, in the side. She frowns and shakes her head imperceptibly. Reluctantly, I join in for the final verse:

Young and old—man for man embraces the swastika banner.
Whether citizen, whether burgher, whether farmer, whether
*   working man,*
they swing the sword and the hammer for Hitler, for freedom,
*   for work and bread.*
Germany awake, end the suffering!
Our people to arms!

Later, as we walk home together, I tell her the vow I made to myself in that room, mouthing those words to the songs.

"Once Walter's left, I want to help your father with the resistance. Please, tell me what I can do."

She hooks her arm through mine.

"It's too dangerous for you, given what's happened."

"I don't care about myself. Not really, not anymore."

"I don't have much to tell, anyway. It's not like there is an organization, as such, to join. To have anything more than a few loose connections is pretty much impossible now. The Gestapo have ears everywhere. The second there is a whiff of anything so much as an antigovernment whisper, they'll make arrests. People are too afraid."

"So what is it your father does?"

"He just has a few contacts. There's an underground web. No one person knows everyone in it, for safety. Thus, if anyone is arrested, they can't give the whole network away. From what

I understand, they pass information. Try to help people leave Germany. Give them shelter, let them know where it's safe to go. Especially children."

"I want to help. In any way I can."

And we walk the rest of the way home, in quiet contemplation.

Thirty-Nine

November 22, 1938

I'm becoming fond of this drafty little sitting room at the back of the café, with its threadbare rug and worn-out, faded green sofa. A place of safety. A haven where I can meet Walter before he leaves Germany tomorrow. Strange how I should feel sheltered and safe here, among strangers, but exposed and vulnerable in my own home.

I peer out the door into the little backyard behind the café with its coal store, toilet, and bins. I listen to the gentle clattering in the kitchen and the low hum of voices in the café beyond. My heart beats hard and strong.

I'm staring into the bare fireplace when Felix, Lena's son, returns and slinks silently into the kitchen. A stranger has followed him. A pang of fear as I wonder who this is. There is nothing familiar about the gaunt, bald-headed figure who stands in front of me. His cheekbones stand proud, too proud, out of his face; his eyes are sunken, and deep purple bruises and scabs cover his hairless head. One hand is thickly bandaged. His shoulders sag. A homeless beggar, perhaps. He is instantly repelling, and I take a step backward.

Then I look into his eyes.

What have they done to you?

"I never thought I'd see you again," the stranger says.

I step forward. Raise my hands to his face, his cheeks wet beneath my fingertips. I trace his gray skin upward and feel the fuzz of new hair growth on his head. His beautiful blond curls, hacked off. Gone.

"No," I whisper. "No, no no . . ."

We sit on the sofa. Lena, her mother, and Felix are in the room. Lena's hand is over her mouth and she stifles a cry at the sight of Walter. Her mother hands us tumblers of some sort of strong liquor. I take a gulp and shudder as the fiery liquid slides down my throat.

"Get him some food," she instructs Lena. "Can't you see he needs food?"

"No," he croaks, "no food," and his hand trembles as he raises the tumbler to his mouth and drinks the whole lot down. "More of this. Please."

"Fetch the cooking brandy, Lena. Felix, come with me, the café needs our attention." She shoos them from the room, and we are alone.

"Walter. What's happened to you?" I whisper. I long to touch him, but he looks as if he might just break if I do.

He shakes his head. His eyes are wet but he doesn't seem to notice.

"It isn't fair," he says finally. "It isn't fair that I'm out here, and they are still in that . . . that . . . hell."

"Tell me." Gingerly I place my fingers on his arm.

He glances at me, wipes a heavily shaking hand across his mouth. "I can't. I–I don't have the words."

"I'm so sorry I ever doubted what you told me was the truth. Walter, I'm so sorry." I reach for his unbandaged hand and give it a gentle squeeze. How could I once have been so blind? I look at him, struggling to process what I'm seeing. He's a shadow of what he was thirteen days before. My throat closes as a wash of emotion takes hold. *How could they do this?*

"I tried," I begin, "I tried to get them out, your father and uncle." It sounds so lame. So useless.

"I know. I know it was you who saved me. Friends in high places, they said, before they let me go. Thank you. It didn't stop them giving me a final beating, though." He lifts his shirt and shows me his bruised and battered body. "Twenty-five lashes for the road."

"Dear Jesus." I bite my fist.

Lena returns with the bottle of cooking brandy. She fills his tumbler, three-quarters full. She quickly leaves again, her cheeks pinched, eyes full of horror.

"What happened to your hand?"

He doesn't answer. He just swigs great gulps of brandy. Beads of sweat appear on his forehead. Slowly, slowly the brandy seems to calm him. His breathing eases and the trembling subsides.

Tears brim in my eyes and Walter's image swims. They wash down my cheeks, a flood of shame and pity.

"The camp . . ." He shakes his head.

"Tell me. Please."

He looks down at the fat bandage covering his left hand. He takes another mouthful of brandy, then he begins to speak in a flat, low voice I barely recognize.

"The day I arrived, the eleventh of November, we were taken to the front of the camp on trucks. We were made to jump out and run through two lines of SS thugs to get to the gates. They were armed with clubs and iron bars to beat us with as we passed. There was a holdup at the gate, so many were trying to get through, to get away from the SS. I momentarily rested my hand on the wall, to keep steady as people were shoving to get past. A brute hit my hand, full strength, with an iron bar. He broke three of my fingers. Crushed them. The tip of the smallest was pulverized to not much more than pulp. The pain was . . . excruciating. I think I passed out, because I was on the ground, but they beat me until I got up again." His voice is that of an old man.

"But why? They're out of control. Surely once their superiors . . ." Even as I say it, I think of the order I saw on Vati's desk, the beating to death I witnessed in the street, and I swallow my words of incredulity.

"Their superiors. The commander *ordered* them to do it. They beat us constantly." He swallows hard. Looking down at the threadbare rug, his voice is scarcely above a whisper. "That first day . . . when we arrived. One man, his ear was beaten off his head. Another, blinded by an iron bar to his eye . . . then, when we got in there, the camp couldn't cope. I've learned since, ten *thousand* of us were taken to that . . . that *place* . . . in just a couple of days. There was nowhere to put us all, so we were made to stand, all the rest of that day, then all night and all the next day, too. They gave us no food or water until the second evening. People were getting sick. My father, my uncle—I don't know what happened to them. We got separated before we even arrived, put on different trucks. We weren't allowed to move from our muster group. If we tried to speak, or escape, we were beaten, or worse."

He stops and swallows more brandy. I rub his arms, his legs, gently, careful to avoid his bruises, his dreadfully injured hand.

"The third day, some of us were rounded into a barracks, if you could call it that." His voice is becoming slurred from the drink. "It was a cattle shed—no windows, no light or heat, no floor, just freezing, stinking mud. We were covered in it. There were lines of wooden bunks, well, planks, four layers high, for us to lie in, one on top of the other. There were no latrines nearby. It was so cold, Hetty. Bitter like I've never known before. If we weren't in the sheds, we were lined up outside. They rounded us up, in at night, out in the day, like cattle. Worse than cattle. We were made to stand, for hour upon hour, while they barraged us twenty-four hours a day through the Tannoy system . . . messages about us Jewish pigs, how we cheated the Aryans. How we'll be made to pay."

He stops to take another drink, swaying slightly as he sits. It's a miracle he's even alive. A tableau of images flows through my mind. Articles from the *Leipziger*; Herr Metzger preaching the sins of the Jews; passages from *Mein Kampf*; Mutti's warnings against the evil race, *Hetty, stay away from them, stick only with good people, like us*; the violence of the night of the riots. Hitler, spreading his words of hate.

All of it leading to this.

Guilt-ridden vomit rises in my throat.

"Shh," I say. I don't know why. Perhaps because there are no words. No words of comfort I can possibly summon for him. "Shh."

"They humiliated us, utterly," he continues. "The SS Scharführer in charge of our section thought it would be amusing to make several of us share our cabbage soup from one tin bowl with no spoons. We were made to stand for hours, then sit for hours, on the damp muster ground all day from morning until night and were refused permission even to relieve ourselves. We had to sit, walk, eat, sleep in our own piss, shit, and filth . . . My father won't survive this. He isn't strong. I was there only ten days, Hetty, and I know the person I was, the person I used to be, died in that camp. This person, this shell you see now"—he pats his chest—"I don't know who this is anymore."

Anger flares inside me. White-hot fury.

I take his face in my hands and look deep into his eyes. "I know you," I tell him, fiercely. "I know you are good and kind. You are the most wonderful of humans. You will go to England and carry on being that person. You will do good in the world, I know it. Because you can't let them beat you. You mustn't let them . . ."

I'm not sure he believes me. But I'm certain that deep inside he is still there, my Walter. Injured, frightened, traumatized. But still there. I need no more convincing of who is right in our debate. Something is going deeply, crazily wrong in our country. I saw it that night of November 9. I see the result of it now, in Walter. Ordinary men and women, carried along by something huge and ugly—each other or some overwhelming hatred or fear. It makes them do unthinkable, unspeakable things.

"I'm so scared," he says, "of what will happen to my family. My poor mother, my little cousins, my dearest old grandmother. I don't even know if my father and uncle are alive. There were deaths in there, you know." He stares at me with wild eyes. "In the camp. Two dead men in my shed, just left there, right next to the living, beginning to rot."

"Oh, Walter . . ."

"You have to help them," he says, becoming agitated. "You have to do anything you can to get them out of there. Out of that camp, and you must help all of them leave. You have to, Hetty."

"Yes, yes, Walter. I'll help." The words spill from me with ease. I can't bear to see him suffer. To know of the suffering without doing anything. "I'll find a way to get them out. Shh, shh, don't upset yourself. It'll be okay. I promise you. This will calm down, sense will prevail, and it'll be okay." I try to reassure him, but I know that I'm utterly, sickeningly powerless in the face of something so vast.

"It won't, Hetty," he says, shaking his head violently. "It won't be okay. It'll never be okay. You didn't see it. You didn't see what I saw."

"No, no, I didn't. But I've seen enough. I will do whatever I can to help your people. You have to believe me. I promise you, Walter. I promise."

My words seem to calm him. He falls silent and his hand

still shaking, he drains his tumbler. I watch him, still not believing that this gaunt creature is all that's left of my Walter.

"Thank you," he says, turning to me again. "I believe you will. I leave for England tomorrow. I've booked a train ticket. It will kill me to leave them here. But at least once I'm there I can try to help them. It's their only chance."

Will it kill you to leave me, too? How I wish I could go with Walter. Away from this place. Away from Vati and his mistress and his scheming. Away from my disintegrating life. *I only want to be with you. To heal you, darling Walter.*

"I'll help in any way I can," I repeat, choking on my tears.

"I know."

"I'm not brave, you know. I'm terrified of the future." I swallow hard. "I don't even know if I'll see you again. That's what scares me the most. Walter, I couldn't bear it if—"

Finally, he draws me in, holds me gently in his arms. I cling to him as though my life depends on it.

"We don't know what the future holds," Walter whispers into my ear. "But know this, as long as you are alive, as long as I am alive, somewhere in this world, that is a *good* thing. One day you will find happiness, I'm certain of it. That is enough for me. I will always hold a place in my heart for you. Always. You saved my life, Hetty Heinrich, and I shall never forget that."

And you have saved me, Walter Keller, then and now.

You have opened my eyes and made me see.

Forty

November 23, 1938

I bury my head at the base of his neck and feel for the last time the softness of his skin against my cheek. He is so thin, I can feel his ribs through his clothes. I breathe in his scent. Try to commit it to memory. His arms are wrapped around me and we stay like this a long time, eyes closed, immersed in each other.

"I must go," Walter says, pulling away from me. "My mother and grandmother are waiting on the platform. I can only disappear to the toilet for so long." He smiles.

I nod, hardly bearing to release him. We huddle out of sight in our prearranged spot behind the station, away from the hurrying crowds. I couldn't let him leave without saying good-bye.

"Take care of yourself," he whispers, studying my face.

I swallow the lump in my throat. "Take care of yourself, too," I reply, holding tight to his good hand. "You'd better go."

"Yes," he says, slipping his hand from my grasp and picking up his case. "I'll write, I promise. Just once, to let you know I'm safely there."

"To Erna's address."

"Yes. And don't worry. I'll be fine."

"Make sure you get treatment for your hand."

"I'm going to the right place for it."

He takes a deep breath and walks away, turning just once, to blow me a kiss.

"I love you, Walter Keller," I call recklessly after him as he rounds the pillar.

I follow at a safe distance onto the platform where the train waits, steam hissing.

I watch Walter embrace his mother and grandmother. He climbs onto the train, slams the door, and leans through the open window, his baldness covered by his hat. He waves to the two forlorn figures, clinging to each other on the platform as the whistle blows, loud and shrill. The engine puffs hard and the train inches forward along the track. Walter's eyes begin to search the crowd. I will him to see me, to look at me one last time. I daren't wave. At last, as the train, pulls away, his eyes find mine, and in them is my everything.

At least he will be safe now, my beautiful Walter, with his gentle eyes and kind heart. His body will heal, his hair will grow back, and hopefully his fingers will recover. But the loss of him, as he puffs farther and farther away, is overwhelming. It's as if hope itself sits beside Walter, leaving me bereft. It will accompany him to Munich, across the border to Zurich, and stay with him as he begins his new life in England.

With Anna.

I have not allowed myself to think of it before. All that mattered, until now, was that Walter was safe. But standing on this deserted platform, I can picture it. Him running toward her. I watch them smile into each other's eyes. Hold hands. Share a joke. Share a bed. I see his hands on her body, doing the things he did with me. I see them, laughing in the rain (because it always rains in London); heads together, they whisper to each other as they window-shop for their wedding.

And I suddenly loathe this Anna. This faceless girl who has stolen my future.

I turn my back on the empty platform and walk all the way home. It's a raw, damp morning. I think of those still incarcerated at Buchenwald on that freezing, lonely hill in Ettersberg, prob-ably at this moment numb to their bones in their lines, or sitting in the mud and filth. My hands are toasty warm in the fur-lined pockets of my coat and a rash of guilt engulfs me. Walter was in a horrific state after less than two weeks. What must it be like for those still there? What can I do? The *authorities*—the govern-ment, the police, the law—they are all on the side of the jailers. My mind searches through wild solutions—sending anonymous letters to foreign governments, begging for help; pleading with Vati or his cronies; marching to the Party headquarters to protest. But nothing I can think of would make a jot of a difference. I'd only end up joining them in that camp. I am wretchedly useless.

When I get home, I tell Mutti I've been taken unwell and cannot cope with school today. Schoolwork has no value for me anymore. She pats me on the head and suggests I lie down. I take my diary from its hiding place, plump the cushions in my window seat, and, with Kuschi beside me, I begin to write.

I made you a promise before you left. I shan't forget it, but I know now that I won't be able to keep it. I promised I would do everything in my power to help your family. You've only been gone a few hours, but I'm confessing already that I will let you down. I cannot help them. Vati loathes the sight of me. I've disgraced myself in his eyes by making him help you. I suppose he is at least glad you're out of my life. But he won't do anything else, and if I threaten him again, he will simply pack me off to a Lebensborn home to make children for the Führer. So what can one helpless girl, with no influence, do? I've heard that some men are now being released from the camps; with luck your father and uncle will be among them. As for the women and children in your family, other than beg Herr Bäcker for help, I have no clue what I can do. When I think back to the early days of the Reich, all the hope and excitement that such good things were to come, I wonder how, in just a few short years we went from that, to this. A monster was unleashed that nobody fully understood. It was allowed to grow until, now, it's an uncontrollable force, and we are powerless to stop it. The fact is, I'm not the person you thought I was. I'm not the person I thought I was. It turns out I'm nobody special at all. It turns out I was never destined for great things. I'm just me, and I'm infinitely smaller than I ever thought possible.

Part III

Forty-One

December 20, 1938

I t's a crisp afternoon and Erna has come to see me.

"How are you?" she asks, watching me warily.

"You know," I reply, shrugging.

She smiles. "I have something for you."

My heartbeat quickens as she takes the envelope from her pocket.

"Is it?"

"Yes."

She hands it to me.

"Thank you," I whisper, putting it quickly into my skirt pocket.

"Visit me soon," she says, buttoning her coat. "You need to get out more."

I fetch Kuschi from the kitchen, pull on my warm coat, and, fingering the letter in my pocket all the way, walk down to the river near the allotments. It seems like a fitting place to read it. I sit on the still frost-covered bank and pull out the envelope, smoothing the creases with my fingers. Erna's address, written in Walter's neat script. My heart dips and twists, as though it were the real person here, in my hands. I look at it for a long time before I allow myself to tear it open.

My darling Hetty,

Well, here I am. I've arrived. I'm safe, which I suppose is a good thing. But I'm also numb and empty. Of course, I miss my parents horribly, but there is also a massive, Hetty-shaped hole inside me, which I doubt can ever be filled.

It is strange to be here, to put it mildly. As you know, my English consists of only a few words. It is a baptism of fire, and I shall have to learn quickly. Anna and her family speak only English now, even to each other at home. They are so keen to be English that German is forbidden. But they have been kind and welcoming. The very first thing her father did was to attend to my fingers. I needed surgery, which I have now had. They had to amputate my badly injured finger. The other two are saved, although misshapen. So my hand is still bandaged up. I suppose I will learn to manage with four fingers on that hand. It could have been much worse.

So I can hear you ask, what is life like? Well, we live in a small town south of London. The people dress a little oddly—there is a certain frivolity and carefree abandon in their clothing that I hadn't expected of the English. Their manners are somewhat strange. I must remember not to click my heels and be too upright. The English are more tactile than us. There is much clapping of backs and handshakes as well as a good deal of nodding and smiling, but I'm sure I will get used to it soon enough. They are friendly, on the whole, a little suspicious perhaps, but being unable to speak their language is rather a barrier, I suppose. I am determined to learn fast. Truthfully, though, everything is utterly confusing, strange and new. I try my best, but some days I feel like I'm a small child, wading through molasses. I try to be brave. Thinking of you makes me more so.

I have met a most helpful man, Herr Gunther, who is a big name in the fur trade here. He is helping me to correspond with the British authorities regarding my own business, and my plan to get the rest of my family here. He has even gone so far as to offer financial help and has given assurances as to our family's good reputation. But there are so many needy cases. Thousands and thousands apply every week. So far, the British government has said they cannot take any more refugees.

But I've heard rumors that the British are offering sanctuary to Jewish children, until they can rejoin their parents at a later date, in Palestine or Germany. My grandmother, mother, aunt, and her three children are living in the Jewish house now on Humboldstrasse. They share one room. I wonder if the children might qualify to come here. They are fifteen, twelve, and eight. I believe the upper age limit for this kindertransport to England is fourteen. Perhaps just the younger two might come? How hateful it is to split our family up in this way. I wonder, darling Hetty, whether you might make any inquiries on your end?

I suppose you are wondering how it is with Anna. I can only be honest with you, my darling. It is awkward: painfully uncomfortable. When we are alone, I really have no idea what to say to her. She keeps saying it is because I have been through so much, and it is fine. But really, it isn't. How can I tell her that I've given my heart to you? I can't, of course, so I say nothing instead. She is gentle and sweet natured and I cannot be unkind. In fact, I feel guilty, because I don't know that I can be the husband she deserves. I feel like an actor in a bizarre play that will never end. I try to always keep busy because the worst time is when I'm alone, at night, and my mind wanders freely. That is when the pain is at its most unbearable and I'm not sure I can keep on living.

I didn't know whether to tell you, but I don't want to keep secrets, my darling. So, with heavy heart, I must tell you that the date for the wedding is set for the fifteenth of March. I know how much this will pain you, but please do try to be happy, my love. I do so want for you to be happy. You've done so much for me, completely unselfishly. You should seek happiness with another. And for this reason, I wonder if it would be for the best for you, and least dangerous, that, as we discussed, we don't stay in contact?

Tell me what you think, my love. I long to hear your news. I must ask you to write to the post office address I enclose here. Anna doesn't yet know about you. I will tell her, but not yet. It hurts too much for now. Use the post office address, also, if there is ever an emergency. Hopefully there won't be a need for it, but in case you hear any news of my family you need to relay, then do use it.

It will get easier, for us both soon, I hope.

All my love and gratitude,
Walter

The letter is a stab to the heart. I am his past. Anna is his future.

He is never coming back. He won't be in contact again.

I read his words over and over. I touch the paper he touched. I try smelling it, to see if there is any hint of him on the page. But there is none. Just a taste of his new life. And once his family is gone, no trace of him will be left here, in this city of his birth.

"You've missed coffee and cake!" Bertha exclaims when I eventually push open the back door and return with Kuschi, still fingering the letter in my pocket.

"I'm not really hungry anyway," I tell her, releasing Kuschi from his leash. He noisily laps water from his bowl on the floor.

Bertha picks up a cloth and begins to dry the crockery she has recently washed.

"Everything all right, Fräulein Herta?" Bertha asks, tilting her head slightly, concern in her hooded gray eyes.

I swallow the lump in my throat.

"Sit down," she instructs. "I'll make you some hot chocolate."

I sink down onto the bench at the big oak table.

"Thank you, Bertha," I mumble. I watch her pour the milk into a pan, fetch the cocoa, and spoon it into a waiting pot. She adds the sugar and leans against the stove as she stirs the milk. It seems that she, at least, is forgiven by my parents.

"You're missing him, I suppose," she says.

"Is it so obvious? He sent me a letter. Seems to be settling into London life."

"That's good, isn't it? Not much of a life here for him, was it?"

"I know. He deserves a good life, after everything . . ."

She flashes me a look.

"And so do you, Fräulein Herta. So do you."

"Even after I risked all that trouble for you?"

"All's forgiven, Fräulein. Forgotten about." She takes the pan off the heat and pours steaming milk into the pot, stirring.

"He's getting married, you know. He had to, to get the visa."

Bertha places the pot, a sugar bowl, and a cup and saucer on a tray.

"I don't know much about most things, it's true," she says slowly. "But I know a little about love affairs. And I know this: You can't hold on to Walter forever. He's gone now. Safe, but gone. It's time you moved on and found someone new."

"But you never did."

She places the tray in front of me and looks me squarely in the face.

"Which is exactly why I know what *you* must do. It's over. Blessedly no harm's come to either of you, and that's to be thankful for. You're young. You have plenty of time." She places a hand on my shoulder, gives it a squeeze, and walks back to the draining board to continue her work.

I pour the steaming chocolate from the pot and cradle the cup in my hands. I watch Bertha with a grateful heart.

Forget him. Move on. Live a normal life once more.

I'll try, dearest Bertha. I'll try.

LATER, WHEN EVERYONE is asleep, I sit up in bed and switch on my reading lamp. Propped against my pillows, I pen a reply to Walter. I will pass it to Erna to send on. I can't risk Ingrid, the snake, or anyone else reporting back to Vati that I've been spotted in the post office, sending letters to England.

> *My darling,*
>
> *I'm so very relieved you have arrived safely, and that, although different and strange to start with, you have received a good welcome in England. I very much hope that you are able to live the life you deserve to live, and that England stays free of the Nazi ideology.*
>
> *I cannot begin to tell you how alone I am now that you have gone. It's as though my heart has been ripped*

from my chest. It made me smile when you mentioned the Hetty-shaped hole in your life. You should know that I am living with a Walter-shaped hole in mine. It is, of course, larger, given our relative sizes. I can hear you laughing at that.

Kuschi has been my main comfort, in all honesty, but Erna is also being a stalwart at propping me up, and now that you are gone, I'm finally allowed more freedom again. So a return to the interminable BDM meetings and school. I can barely stand the BDM anymore, but I have no choice but to go. So instead, I will throw myself into schoolwork and hope that I can gain a good enough result in the Abitur to allow me to study abroad one day. I should still so much like to become a doctor.

I will speak with Erna's family to see what, if anything, can be done to help your cousins make it to England. I must be careful to not raise suspicion because Vati hasn't forgiven me.

If only there could have been a way that we could have left Germany together. But there wasn't, and for this reason, even though it pains me so much to even write it, I know it will be best for you that I don't stay in contact. I do not want to make trouble for you and your soon-to-be-wife. I think of Vati and his secret lover and it's quite unbearable what this would do to Mutti if she knew. I know you are honorable and good, and you would not want to mistreat your wife. You must start a new life with your Anna properly. I will never be "the other woman."

I am not entirely sure that I will ever completely recover from all this, but I will try.

Please know that I shall never stop thinking of you, ever.

All my love, now and forever,
Hetty

Forty-Two

December 31, 1938

Champagne flutes clink; quiet conversation purrs. Soft laughter. Background music on the gramophone—Bruckner, I think. Nothing inappropriate for a family still grieving their firstborn and gathered together to see in the New Year. Close family and friends only, comforting with the intimacy of their presence.

I watch them from my position next to the fireplace, my back pleasantly warmed by the lively fire burning in the grate. Oma, dressed in black, is seated in the center of the room in Vati's armchair, sipping sherry and resting her swollen ankles on the ottoman. Mutti, her sweep of hair midnight dark against the claret red of her dress, a thin smile painted on her pale face, moves among her guests. My bubbly aunt Adèle, her rather dour daughter, Eva, and Eva's fiancé, a fair-haired SS officer, stand close to her, smiling and attentive, as I suppose one would, in that position. Lord Mayor Otto Schultz, his wife, and three grown-up children stand together with Judge Fuchs and two other men. I recognize the editor, Josef, from the newspaper; Vati's secretary and a few of Mutti's closest friends and their husbands are also here. I was permitted two guests, and I chose Erna and Tomas, who stand together with Eva, her intended, and Adèle.

I have no wish to talk with anyone in the room at all. A glass of champagne hangs in my hand in readiness to usher in the New Year. I've not yet touched a drop.

Vati, resplendent in his velvet dinner jacket, rushes into the room.

"Friends, guests, look at the time! We must listen to Herr Goebbels make his New Year address." He turns on the radio and someone lifts the arm to silence the gramophone. It has already begun.

. . . 1938, a year of miracles. With the Anschluss of Austria, eighty million Germans have been united in one great Reich, with the return of ten million in just one miraculous year. It would be easy to forget the magnitude of what we have achieved in such a short space of time. It would be easy to forget the impossibility such achievements would have seemed before they happened, which appear almost easy, now that they have. The doubters among us, of which a few remain, scoff and point to the inevitable small and trivial problems that crop up from time to time. These doubters, this minority, with their money and education, trust more in their cold reason than in the warm, idealistic hearts of the masses. They dwell in the past, hardly in the present and not at all in the future, lacking the imagination to see the greatness of our national German future. For these weak and quivering doubters, problems are there to be surrendered to, not mastered and surpassed. We will not win these complainers over. But the masses want nothing to do

with them. At the close of this momentous year, the people can be delighted with what has been achieved, and we can look forward with confidence and courage to 1939 . . .

Tomas is suddenly at my elbow. He smiles down at me, then leans in and says into my ear, "I have some . . . particular . . . hopes for 1939."

"Oh . . ." I veer my head away.

He slurps champagne from his glass in a way that makes me think he hasn't drunk any before. I smile at him, and he rocks back on his heels, his face a poster of optimism.

The speech is over, and Vati claps his hands to say a few words.

"As you all well know, it has been a difficult year, particularly for my dear wife, Hélène. But, with your support, dearest of friends and family, I believe we are through the worst. Let us hope that 1939 brings us personal peace, and we go forward to this new year with courage, steadfastness, and resolve in our hearts to continue this great mission of ours, now we are part of a family of *eighty million* great German hearts, beating as one, toward our common destiny. To the Fatherland, Heil Hitler!"

Applause breaks out around the room and everyone drinks to the future.

Erna and I lock eyes and she knows I am thinking of Walter at this moment. How can I toast the Fatherland that has driven an ocean of despair between us? She dispatches Tomas to find Ingrid to top up her glass.

"Hetty," she says, once he's out of earshot. "You're pale as a ghost. What is it?"

I don't tell her of the niggling worry I've had the last few days. Something that should have come, but hasn't. We move to a quiet corner of the room where we cannot be overheard.

"Two days ago," I tell her instead, "I went back to Lena's café and met with Walter's mother. I'd made him a promise . . ."

"What promise?" Erna brings her head close to mine, so no one else can hear.

"I said I'd help. I promised Walter I'd try to get Walter's father and uncle out of the camp."

"But, Hetty, you can't—"

"It was so pathetic, Erna. *She* was so pathetic. She begged me, cried and cried and begged and begged as though I were her last and only hope. If they've not been released by now . . . Honestly, I wonder if they're even alive."

"There is nothing you can do, Hetty. Nothing! What did she expect—"

"Here we are!" Tomas lurches into us, shoving a full champagne flute into Erna's hand. Some of the contents fizz over the side of the glass. "Prost! Down the hatch!" He smiles and tips his own glass into his mouth.

"Sip it, Tomas, slowly, please," Erna says with a sharpness in her tone. "It isn't beer. Actually, could you give Hetty and me a few moments? Please?"

He looks from Erna to me and winks.

"Fine. But I'll be back." A shudder runs down my back.

He sways off toward Eva's officer. I wince at his ungainly frame, his loud laugh.

"I shouldn't have invited him."

"He's okay." Erna smiles and waves a dismissive hand. "You were saying?"

"I remember her, Walter's mother. Years ago, long before we moved into this house. Mutti, Karl, and I must have been invited there for tea. I was probably only six or seven. But I do remember her. She seemed so elegant. Not like Mutti's elegance, but something different. She had a sort of carefree confidence. Mutti has always been *vulnerable*, I suppose. Reliant on Vati for everything. But this lady, so petite and delicate, yet vibrant and full of energy. The person in the café, Erna, was totally different. She was this miserable, feeble, reduced person. Unwashed and poor and desperate. It made me realize: if a person is treated like a stray dog, they become one."

"That's awful, Hetty, truly. But *you* can't do anything. It's too big a problem for you alone."

"No. I realize that now. But there may be a way we can help the children. Walter mentioned in his letter about this *kinder-transport*. Special trains are taking children to families in England, until their parents can find somewhere safe to go. Do you think your father might know how this can be arranged?"

"I don't know. I'll ask him. But promise me, you mustn't do or say anything in the meantime. It could jeopardize everything. If your father should get an inkling of what you're up to—"

"But I promised Walter. How can I not even try? All the men of importance are here in this room. They talk of great achievements and victories, but there's another side to it, isn't there? I should use this opportunity. To *speak out*. If I don't, who will? I'll never be able to go back to that café with my head held high. I can't sit and look at that woman and tell her I can't do anything."

Erna's eyes widen.

"Hetty, you're not thinking straight. You managed to help Walter, and that has nearly cost you dear. If you say anything *at all* against Hitler or the government, you are finished and so, very likely, will be our little resistance movement. You'd be signing *my* family's death certificates too."

Tomas returns again and we stop talking.

I look around at the guests, at Mutti and Vati, and wonder how it came to be that I feel like a stranger in the room.

IT'S THREE THIRTY in the morning and Vati says his good-byes to the last guests to leave the party, Otto and his family. The front door bangs shut and the two of us are left, face-to-face in the entrance hall, silence settling around us. Mutti has long since gone to bed. Ingrid and Vera, the girl who will shortly replace her, are finishing the clearing up in the drawing room.

"Well," he says stiffly. "Time for bed."

He moves past me and I catch his arm.

"Vati . . ."

He starts as though a vile creature has landed on his arm.

"What?"

Erna's and Bertha's advice reverberates through my mind. *Keep quiet. Forget Walter. Move on.* But visions of damaged, broken Walter plague me. The thought of what's happening to those remaining in that camp, and what *could* happen to his dear mother, won't let me rest.

"What?" Vati barks again, his face hard and impatient.

"I'm . . . I'm sorry for everything. I hope you can forgive me."

It's meant as a preamble, but even to my ears they sound like the words of a coward.

"Yes. Well, that will depend on you, and how you conduct yourself from now on."

"I'll do my best, Vati."

He straightens his shoulders and looks at me, eye to eye.

"We will put it behind us, but I shan't forget. There is to be no more wandering around this city without your mother knowing your whereabouts. There is to be no more . . . mixing . . . with undesirables. You will be the daughter I deserve. Nothing less."

"Yes, Vati," I whisper.

"Go to bed, Herta."

I swallow the words I promised myself I'd say this evening and watch him walk heavily upstairs. Instead of begging words, a different plan is replacing them. I will not be bowed by Vati and his threats. I can be a better person than that.

Forty-Three

It's happening again. That tight ball in my stomach. I will it to relax. But there is too much saliva. I can't swallow. I jump up and run down the corridor to the bathroom, retching bright yellow bile into the clear water of the toilet bowl. Shaking, I flush it away, then splash icy water over my face.

In the gloomy early morning light, my reflection in the mirror is ghostly pale. Eyes, dull and lifeless. Beads of sweat shine on my forehead, despite the chill. If the past few days are anything to go by, the vomiting will only provide temporary relief. The nausea will soon return and stay for the rest of the day.

Back in my room, I swing open the shutters and stare through the gray misty dawn at the empty street. The frigid branches of the cherry tree are bare. It looks dead. But deep inside its broad trunk, life slumbers, waiting for the warmth of spring to pulse sap to the very ends of each and every twig. Then the blossoms will come.

Nineteen thirty-nine. A new year. New hope. New life.

Still the relief of bloodied underwear evades me.
Please God. Please do not let me be pregnant.

"Where's Bertha?"

Mutti is in the kitchen, alone, stirring something in a pan on the stove.

"Gone."

"Gone?"

"She had to. After what she did, that night . . ."

"*What*? Please tell me you haven't fired Bertha?"

Mutti doesn't look at me. The rolling nausea in my belly intensifies.

"Vati and I discussed it. One has to trust one's staff. Once that trust is broken, there's no going back . . ."

"But why? It wasn't Bertha's fault . . . I told you! It was mine. Why didn't you tell me? I didn't even get the chance to say good-bye."

"We'd have done it sooner, but it was hellishly difficult to replace Bertha just before Christmas. We agreed with her she could stay until we found another decent cook," Mutti says, spooning egg from the pan into a serving dish. "Someone new will start next Monday. We shall just have to manage ourselves until then. I used to cook myself," she adds, almost with surprise. "I'm sure I can remember what to do." She picks up the dish and leaves the room. "Breakfast is served."

How dare Vati get rid of her like that. It was my fault, and I've had no chance to say . . . what? Why didn't she say anything to me, if she knew? It never occurred to me there might be a time Bertha wasn't here. She's a part of this house. A part of my life. Until this moment, I had no idea how precious she is. Will whoever comes next chat to Kuschi and throw him kitchen scraps? Will she be there, square and comforting, with cake, coffee, and a listening ear? It's only now that I understand the void of quiet affection, gentle kindness, and understanding she has left. I am wretched with guilt.

"Where has she gone?" I follow Mutti into the dining room. "The least you can do is tell me. I want to apologize. Say good-bye."

"I believe she's found a position in the kitchen of a guest-house. We gave her a good set of references and a month's salary. We were most generous, given the circumstances. Oh, I almost forgot." Mutti pulls an envelope from her pocket. My heart double flips, but the handwriting is unfamiliar.

"What is it?"

"It's from Tomas," she throws over her shoulder as she heads back to the kitchen.

Fräulein Hetty,

I tried to find the courage to ask you before, but found I lacked it. I thought a letter would be the right thing for someone like you. I should very much like it if you would come for a walk with me Sunday afternoon (tomorrow) at three p.m. for one hour. I know how you like to walk your dog. So maybe you could walk me, too?

I would also be most honored if you would come to the dance put on by my HJ schar in four weeks, Saturday. There will be girls from the BDM there you'll know.

Erna is invited too. But I would really like it if you would
come as my personal guest.

With sincere best wishes,
Tomas Köhler

Oh, Tomas, what am I to say? I need you as a friend but nothing more. Is it possible to say that to a boy without offending him?

I think about Walter's fierce instruction to find another love. And Bertha's kindly advice. It seems impossible at this moment, but perhaps I should try. Not Tomas, of course, but maybe there will be a kindred soul at this dance. I shan't know if I don't go with an open mind.

All right, Tomas, I'll walk with you tomorrow, and go to your dance.

As your friend, mind. Just as your friend.

"I'VE BEEN CALLED to a meeting on Wednesday in Munich," Vati tells us after dinner that evening. "This is it, Hélène." He exudes an energy I've not seen in him since before Karl died. "They are going to promote me to Oberführer."

"How can you be sure?" Mutti breathes.

"I've been informed, you know, on the quiet."

"Oh, Franz, this is wonderful news!"

"The Schutzstaffel is expanding so fast, those who have proved their leadership must be promoted to ensure discipline and absolute authority at all times." He relaxes back in his chair. Takes a swill of coffee. "I've been reliable and dedicated.

Especially during the riots in November. Our men behaved in an exemplary fashion . . ."

I dig my fingernails hard into the skin on my arms beneath the table until it hurts.

"Will we have to move?" Mutti asks.

"For now, no. Indeed, I've been tipped off that if the next six months go well, I shall be moved swiftly up the ranks to SS-Gruppenführer. There are plans that those with such rank or above may head up not only their SS district, but also that of the police. I know they have me in mind. This way we can oversee everything in the region, within the SS, the police, the intelligence, and the administration. Brilliant of Himmler to streamline so the SS retains complete authority over all the agencies. That way there can be no competing or infighting among them that will distract us from our ultimate, and most important, goals."

"Such wonderful news, Franz. Although I had been looking forward to a new start somewhere else . . ."

"I will have to give up the newspaper," Vati continues with a frown. "My SS duties are too great to keep it on. I'll promote Josef Heiden to run the paper for me. He already does so much of the day-to-day work; I trust him completely. And, my dear"—he leans over and pats Mutti's hand—"I was thinking that perhaps we should take a place in the country? To escape to for the odd weekend. We can bring friends and entertain there. What do you say? To make up for staying on here."

I see a pretty country house, smoke curling from the chimneys, a big garden, perhaps some chickens and a horse or two.

Will he take Hilda Müller and his other children there? His two families, alternating weekends.

My stomach contracts and vomit rises, stinging my throat, but I force it down.

"Vera? Is that you?" Mutti calls as footsteps sound in the hall.

"Yes, Frau Heinrich?" Vera appears in the doorway in her coat. "I forgot to pick up the washing earlier . . ."

"Ah good, I have some letters for you to post," Mutti says, leaving the room to fetch them.

"So, what do you think, Herta, eh? Your father, climbing to the very top of the ladder?"

"Perhaps," I say before I have time to really think through what I'm saying, "in such a position you will think hard about some of the policies against the Jews—"

His chair creaks as he leans toward me, eyes as frozen and hard as glass.

"Don't you *ever* say such a thing again," he says, his voice gritty. "I will never forget what you have done, girl. How you blackmailed me. The more I think about it . . ." He presses his lips together, fists clenched. "Were it ever to get out, it would jeopardize everything. The stakes are higher than ever." He opens his mouth to say more, but Mutti is back in the room. He shuts it and sits back. He doesn't look at me again.

And all I feel is the quickening thud, thud, thud of my heart.

THE FOLLOWING AFTERNOON, at three p.m. exactly, Tomas knocks for me. Ingrid smirks as Kuschi and I leave the house. She doesn't need to say a word; the look on her face is clear enough. In only a few days she leaves for her Lebensborn home, to become impregnated with the seed of a perfect SS officer specimen. Ergo, she is superior in every way to me. I cannot wait for her, and all that she knows of me, to be gone. I pray that she chooses never to come back.

Rosental park is deserted as Tomas and I walk side by side, Kuschi sniffing along eagerly out in front. A brief flurry of snow falls but fails to settle on the sodden ground.

"Damned cold," Tomas comments, screwing up his face, digging his chin deeper into his turned-up collar. His breath momentarily steams up his glasses. "Sorry."

"It's January, Tomas, what did you expect?"

He shrugs. "Just not very pleasant, that's all."

"I don't mind."

He looks at me and his face brightens.

"Did you like my letter? Thought writing *might* get your attention. I know you like that stuff."

"Yes, but Tomas, you don't have to write . . ."

"And you'll come to the dance?"

"Yes, but—"

"See, Hetty, I was so nervous. Actually, writing was easier."

"You don't need to be nervous, Tomas, we've known each other forever."

"But not in *that* way, and, see, the person I used to be, you know, when I was a kid, well, I'm not like that anymore, and I'm worried that's how you see me, still, like that useless little kid . . ." He picks up his walking pace, in time with his speech, which gets faster and faster.

"But I never thought you were a useless little kid—"

"Oh, but I was. I was pathetic. I got beaten up all the time. But now, *I'm* the one doing the beating. I'm strong, see, and when this stupid apprenticeship comes to an end this year, I'm joining the Heer and then you'll see, Hetty, you'll see what I am. What I'm capable of. I've got ambition, and I can't wait to join the fight."

"Tomas, stop, please. You've nothing to prove to me . . . especially after, well, you know, that awful business with Walter."

He's striding out in front now, and I'm not sure he's heard. I'd been carefully planning what to say, so he isn't under any false hope, but he's hardly even looking at me, let alone listening.

"I know I'm not the right sort, not yet. But I promise you, I will be. I never dreamed . . . But you know, miracles can happen, right? I mean, there's plenty of examples, aren't there? And I *know* I'm better than the shit-brained idiots I have to put up with at the factory. I'm so much better than them all put together! Seriously, you'd be shocked, Hetty, at their conversations. The jokes—they tell the most dreadful jokes of poor taste and some are about the Führer. They don't do it in front of me anymore, not since I shopped that pig, Bruno, to the authorities for his loose talk, but I know they do it. The dumb idiots."

He stops to take a breath, his chest heaving.

"Tomas, it's okay, I know you aren't like them . . . you've nothing to prove to me."

He shakes his head.

"You're kind to say that, but you're a sweet thing. I have to *show* you."

"You don't need to prove anything because we're *friends*, Tomas," I say quickly. "I mean, you don't feel like that with Erna or other people, so you shouldn't with me either . . ."

Finally, he stops and looks at me, properly, through those grubby glasses. His breathing calms and he nods, arms clamped to his sides, his body stiff.

"Yes, Hetty. Yes, I see. Sent from above," he murmurs. "Not that I believe in that stuff, but . . . How's your mother?"

"Um, she's fine."

Did he even get the message?

"Good. Good, that's good." He checks his watch. "I know they don't want you out too long; shall we turn around?"

We have reached the far end of the wide expanse of grass. The dark woods are ahead of us, and dusk hovers. I shudder involuntarily.

"Yes, perhaps you'll come in for a hot drink?"

He nods, looking pleased.

"Kuschi, we're leaving," I call.

There is no response, so we stand and wait, peering between the slim, naked trunks.

"Kuschi!" I call again, louder this time.

Finally, his black shaggy shape appears hurtling through the trees, ears flattened, tail streaming out behind, as though he is being pursued by the devil.

It doesn't get any easier, my love, you not being here, and I wonder if it ever will. That day, March fifteenth, the day you are to marry, approaches ever closer. I wish you had never told me when it is to be. I read your letter over and over, I know it by heart! Sometimes my resolve weakens and I pick up pen and paper to write to you. But if I start, I'll never stop. I must stay strong, so this journal is my outlet. I know you have been in touch with Erna. She told me you're worried about me and how you think of me all the time. That you just want to know I'm okay. I've urged her to tell you I'm fine, just getting on with life, but I suspect you won't believe it. Erna's father met with an English volunteer who came here but they were inundated with requests from desperate parents. He didn't manage to secure passage this time. I feel so useless and tired. How I would love to turn back time and be in your arms. I picture us walking by the river, you and me, with Kuschi happily bounding beside us. I imagine what you would say to me. You'd say: Hetty, together we can do anything. But it isn't like that, is it? You exist only in my mind, a hazy memory.

Forty-Four

February 4, 1939

The party is in full swing when Tomas and I arrive. Two large Hitler Jugend boys on the door check our names off the list and let us in.

We push our way through the smoke-filled room toward the bar. The smell of cigarette smoke is almost unbearable and I feel a rush of nausea. I spot Erna standing with a gaggle of BDM girls. She waves and we weave toward her. Tomas buys us a sherry each. I take a large gulp, hoping its sweet, medicinal taste will help bury the sickness. All around us, heads turn to look. Their eyes flicker over me and, as usual, come to rest on Erna—the beautiful objet d'art.

No wonder Karl fell so heavily for her. Poor, darling Karl.

Erna is impervious to the staring eyes. We stand and watch the dancers, careful to move correctly. No daring American moves under the critical eyes of several Gestapo officers who hover around. I drain my glass and am left with a warm and slightly fuzzy feeling. I feel a little better. Tomas smiles at me from where he stands, a little distance away, talking to a boy in the field-gray uniform of the Heer, cap at a rakish angle.

Would you like another? he mouths.

Yes please, I mouth back.

Tomas and the boy come over with the drinks and join Erna and me. The band strikes up a new tune. The dance floor is filling up.

"Dance with me," Tomas says and holds out a hand.

He slips his arm around my waist and leads me around the dance floor, weaving in and out of the other couples. Our step is out of time and I keep bumping against him. Different from Walter whose body and step fitted so neatly with mine. I glimpse Erna over Tomas's shoulder, her mouth close to the ear of the good-looking Heer boy, capless now, his blond hair tousled. I sense Tomas looking down at me, willing me to look into his face, but I can't. I won't.

I begin to feel dizzy. The drink, the smoky atmosphere, all these sweaty bodies pressing in. The band, the chatter and laughter. Suddenly it's all too loud.

"I need some air," I whisper to Tomas, leaning against him, fearing I might faint.

"Of course. Let's go outside." He grips me around the waist, drawing my arm around him, and leads me to the door. The fresh air hits me in the face, instantly reviving. We move away from canoodling couples clustered around the entrance and rest our backs against the wall. I take several deep breaths and my head begins to clear.

"Thank you." I smile at Tomas.

"C'mon," he says, "let's find somewhere quieter still. You'd like that, wouldn't you?" He looks at me intensely.

I nod, glad to be in the clear air. Glad not to be feeling ill. He leads me by the hand into a little park across the road from the bar. We sit on a bench between two trees. It's peaceful and dark, away from the streetlamps and the noise of the bar.

In one swift movement, Tomas swings around and pushes me against the arm of the bench. He dives onto me, and his tongue, rough and probing, forces its way deep into my mouth. He stinks of beer and cigarettes. His body is heavy and solid on top of me, the arm of the bench digging hard into my back. I'm paralyzed with shock. This is nothing like Walter's soft, light touch. Tomas is brittle and unyielding. I can feel a hard bulge swell in his trousers and he begins to grind his crotch against my thigh.

I want him off me. I'm suffocating and struggle against him for air, but he resists and presses harder. He slips his hand inside my dress and grasps my breast, pushing my legs apart with his. Panic rises and I try to push his tongue from my mouth, twist my face away. My arms are pinned down. He's hurting my breast and I try to resist the weight of him parting my legs, but he's too strong. He pushes up my dress and claws a hand up my thigh. *No, no, no. Please don't do this.* I struggle harder, against the solid roughness of him. He's tugging on my underwear, fumbling, pulling at it, scratching in his desperation to get it down.

I wrestle now with all my strength, wild with panic, screaming into his mouth. For a few more seconds he resists, pressing harder, then suddenly he releases me. Pulls away, sits up. Chest heaving, breathing hard.

We stare at each other. I curl up. Knees to chest. Arms wrapped around. A small, tight ball.

"What the hell. Shit." Tomas slides away from me along the bench.

"Why didn't you stop? You hurt me," I say, sobbing.

I run backward in my mind. What did I say, what did I do to lead him on? What made him think . . . ?

He puts his elbows on his knees. Head in his hands. He's shaking. "I'm sorry, Hetty, I got carried away. I never meant to . . . hurt you."

I wipe a trembling hand across my mouth.

Was it me?

"Shit. Shit. Shit. I've had too much to drink. Forgive me, please. Can you forgive me?"

"It's . . . it's okay, Tomas."

"Damn it. I just really like you. I mean. If you knew how much I like you. Love you. For so long. I shouldn't have come on so strong."

I'm trembling uncontrollably. I hug myself tighter. It wasn't my fault.

"Don't ever do that to me again."

"Thing is, Hetty, I've thought about this for ages. Realized I've approached it all wrong. So, I thought, it's now or never, see?"

"Now or never for what?" I straighten my dress. My back hurts where the arm of the bench dug in. My breast is sore. I wish I could stop trembling. Wish we could go back to the bar. Wish I could go home.

I thought I knew you, Tomas. But it seems I got you wrong, too.

"I've been too much of a coward. Never been able to pluck up the courage."

"What on earth do you mean? I thought we were friends. *Only* friends."

"I thought about it and realized, I'd not been forward enough. I needed to *show* you how much I want you, see, and I thought that's the sort of thing you wanted. You know, after I saw you with that . . . *dirty bastard.*" His fists are clenched and the muscles in his jaw contract. "It still haunts me, Hetty."

Anger rises like bile in my throat.

"What *did* you think I wanted, Tomas? Exactly what kind of girl do you think I am? How dare you assume . . ."

I have to get away from him. He's mad, unstable. I jump up and stumble away from the bench.

He rushes after me, catches hold of my arm.

"Wait! Look. I'm sorry, okay. I got it wrong. Badly wrong. I always seem to when it comes to girls. I can't help being jealous—you're all I've ever wanted. You're better than every other girl. But you were always out of my reach. Living in that great big house. I mean, you were *untouchable*. Like some sort of angel. Even when we were kids you were different. When everyone else picked on me, you didn't care. You ignored them all and stuck by me. But you did it from a great height. Like I was someone to pity. I mean, the bullying only stopped because of you. You saved me, and I could never match up. I'd've done anything to impress you. I *did* everything to impress you. But I knew I never had a hope in hell. A girl like you would never want to be with someone like me." He takes a breath and jabs the toe of his boot into the ground.

My head whirls and I begin to feel sick again.

"That's not true, Tomas." I sigh, suddenly overcome with weariness. "I always liked you, as a friend. I never pitied you."

"But then . . . that awful morning. When I saw you with *him*." Tomas's face twists in disgust. "It ate away at me. I kept seeing it. Couldn't understand, couldn't *bear* it. Then I realized—you aren't so perfect. You're tainted, like the rest of us. So that meant I *did* have a chance. The Jew brainwashed you, I know that—it meant I could forgive you, because it wasn't your fault. But I didn't tell anyone what I saw. Kept my mouth *shut*. And I've been bloody patient . . . So I deserve *something* in return for all that, don't I?"

I stare at him. There is a sourness on my tongue.

I won't be anyone's reward.

"I still want to beat the hell out of him," Tomas says, shuffling his feet, pushing his glasses up his nose.

"Well, you can't. He's left the country, so you've no need to worry about him anymore," I tell him coolly.

"Thank God for that." Tomas exhales heavily. Then he grabs my hand and looks earnestly at me, his words a little slurred. "I'm sorry about earlier, honest. Won't make that mistake again, but Hetty, *please* be my sweetheart. I shall go mad if I don't have you."

Vati is entertaining when Tomas delivers me back to my front door.

"Herta, is that you?" I hear him call from the sitting room.

I long for nothing more than to climb the stairs, sink into my bed, and disappear into the black oblivion of sleep.

"Yes, Vati, I'm back from the dance."

Whatever happens, always be true to yourself. Walter's words. I hang on to them, a lifeline to pull me from the waters of despair.

In the sitting room is a man I recognize from pictures in the newspapers. Theo Gratz, head of the Leipzig division of the Gestapo. Lord Mayor Schultz is also here, but I don't know who the other two men are.

"Come on in, Herta, my darling. Don't just stand there, come here, so I can show you off to these lovely gentlemen!"

Vati, rosy cheeked from an evening of red wine and good food, beckons me over, arms wide and welcoming. The men all stand and nod to me as I make my way over. Vati wraps an arm around my shoulders.

"My delightful daughter," he announces. "Seventeen, and ripening nicely." The men all chuckle. "Isn't she pretty?" he asks, looking around at them.

I want to run far, far away, but I stand exposed in the middle of them all, like a brood mare, while they look me up and down.

Vati laughs and pats my hair. "A bit fiery, this one, but a spell at Hausfrau school should do the trick. Calm her down. She'll make someone a good wife one day."

The men nod and smile at me.

"Where's Mutti?" I ask in a whisper.

"Gone to bed." Vati mimics my whisper in reply. "And left us men to it," he adds in a normal voice.

"Yes, I should get home myself," says Gratz, looking at his watch. "I must send my report on all this to Dresden before nine tomorrow morning. Can we finish?"

"Of course." Vati becomes serious. "Off you go, my dear. Get your beauty sleep."

"Good night, Vati. Good night," I say to the men.

In the hall, I collapse onto the bench to remove my shoes. I ache all over and wonder if I have the strength to do it. I sit for a long time staring at my feet, back resting against the wall, listening to the men talk through the open door.

". . . estimated to be around fifteen hundred in the Leipziger Meuten alone. We've clearly not done enough. The resistance has spread to towns all over Saxony. Dresden knows only too well . . ." It's the voice of Theo Gratz, I think. I listen harder.

"And you know where these pockets are operating from?" Vati now.

"The working-class areas primarily—Plagwitz and environs. Some are Communists. Some just troublemakers. But enough to be a worry. Most concerning is they are predominantly *young*. They pick fights with the HJ, calling them prigs and snobs. Actively seeking them out for attack."

Silence for a moment. My heart beats wildly. Could this be what Herr Bäcker is involved in? He's neither young nor working class, but it's possible. Or is it another resistance group? Perhaps there are many, springing up everywhere. A glimmer of hope. A sign that everything may not be lost.

"Recommend to Dresden that we take swift and decisive action." Vati's voice again. "We cannot allow this dissent to continue. We should use the Marxist rhetoric as an excuse for prosecution, and fight this with full brutality. Stamp it out, fast. We should make an example . . . discourage others . . ."

Murmurs of agreement.

Someone clears his throat. "I must be away, Franz. Thank you for your kind hospitality . . ."

I'm spurred to action, quickly kicking off my shoes. I tiptoe to the stairs and dissolve into the darkness of the upper floors of the house.

Forty-Five

February 5, 1939

The conversation I overheard last night about the Leipziger Meuten replays through my mind. In the crisp morning light, I wonder what I should do.

I wander through the downstairs rooms, Kuschi at my heels. I should pass the information to Herr Bäcker. Would he know the leaders of the Meuten? They need to be warned. Unease grows. This is beginning to feel horribly like it did before Kristallnacht last year.

In the garden room, my eyes fall on a two-day-old copy of the *Leipziger*, which lies on the coffee table. Hitler's recent speech to the Reichstag is printed in full. It takes up more than a double-page spread. I sink into a chair to read it.

> ... when the outside world insists Germany is threatening other peoples by military extortion, it is on the grounds of grossly distorted facts. Germany has realized the right to the self-determination of ten million German people without the mobilization of any

forces, contrary to the fictitious reports by the foreign press. In this area, neither the English nor other Western nations have any business meddling. The Reich does not pose a threat to anyone, it has merely defended itself against the attempts at intervention by third parties . . . We will not stand for Western states meddling in our affairs . . .

. . . What is the reason for our economic woes? Simply the overpopulation of our lands! The German people survives with 135 inhabitants per square kilometer, and yet the rest of the world has looted Germany throughout the past one and a half decades. The German people are not enemies of England, America, or France and desires to live calmly and peacefully, while Jewish and non-Jewish agitators persist in rousing the animosity of these peoples against the German people . . . Germany will not be swayed from its reckoning with Jewry. It is a shaming display when we see the entire democratic world filled with tears of pity at the plight of the poor, tortured Jewish people while at the same time crying that they "cannot possibly admit the Jews!" And these world powers have no more than ten persons per square kilometer! Small matter that Germany has been good enough to provide for these elements for centuries, with their infectious political and sanitary diseases. What we do today is no more than to set right the wrongs these people committed.

. . . Europe cannot find peace until it has dealt properly with the Jewish question. In the time of my struggle for power, it was primarily the Jewish people who mocked my prophecy that, one day, I would assume leadership of this Germany and would press for resolution of the Jewish question. The resounding laughter of the Jews then may well be stuck in their throats today, I suspect.

Once again I will be a prophet: Should the international Jewry succeed in plunging mankind into yet another world war, then the result will not be a Bolshevization of the earth and the victory of Jewry, but the annihilation of the Jewish race in Europe.

I put the paper down. What if there is another war? What if it reaches England and Walter is no longer safe there, either? What if this *thing* spreads all across the world? I think of the Leipziger Meuten and I know for sure: if we don't fight this here, now, then it will gather force and sweep over Europe and beyond. It's time I put aside my own problems, my own safety, and live up to my promise to Walter.

Dressed for school, I first make for the café. I've not seen Lena since that awful day in December when I met with Frau Keller for the first time. The door jangles as I enter and she looks up in surprise.

"Hetty!" She comes to the door to greet me. The café is semifull of workers, either having finished a shift or about to go on one. There is a strong odor of sweat, tobacco, and grime. "Come through, to the back."

Her mother is working in the kitchen. She looks older than I recall. More stooped and gray. Her dress hangs loosely from her shoulders. Lena also looks thin, her cheeks drawn in. There are lines on her forehead and around the corners of her mouth I'd never noticed before.

"How are you?" I ask. The two exchange a look. Lena's mother turns her attention to the stove and places potato and bacon into a pan with a sliver of butter.

"Oh, you know," Lena says, wiping a hand across her forehead. "We're getting by."

I nod. There's an awkward pause.

"I was hoping you would be able to get a message to Frau Keller. And"—I hesitate—"it might be of interest to you, too. For your boy."

She nods quickly. "Yes?"

"The British are organizing for children to travel to England, to be looked after by foster parents, until it is . . . safe for them to be reunited with their parents. Someone I know is trying to find places on one of the trains. It's very difficult—there are more requests than spaces. But he will keep trying, for the Keller children, and for your boy, if you would wish it?"

She nods again. "I heard talk of this. And also, that a politician in America is trying to organize a similar program. If he's successful, they will be able to double the numbers . . ." Her face crumples. "What has it come to, that we must send our precious children to the care of strangers in foreign countries?"

On a sudden whim I grab her hands. "Don't give up hope, Lena. We must all . . . fight this, however we can."

Lena's eyes fill with tears, and she looks away, embarrassed.

"I must go, I have school. But I'll try to come back soon. Hopefully with good news," I add.

I leave the café feeling better than I have in weeks. I'll find an opportunity at school to tell Erna what I heard about the Leipziger Meuten. Herr Bäcker will know what to do about it. At last I feel useful. It may not be much, but it might make a difference.

Wissen ist macht, after all.

And I smile to myself as I hurry to the tram stop.

Forty-Six

March 1, 1939

The nausea has gone. Nothing more to worry about. Sudden shock and grief can stop bleeding. I heard that somewhere, and it's a relief to be without the dreaded monthly cramps.

As I'm gathering my books for school, Kuschi barks loudly from the hall, heralding the arrival of the postman. I find Mutti in her bedroom. Unusually, since Karl's death, she is dressed to go out at this time of morning. She's sitting at her dressing table, arranging her hair into its usual neat chignon.

"Good morning, Mutti," I say, unable to mask the surprise in my voice. "Do you have an appointment?"

She smiles at me in the mirror.

"It's time I pick myself up and get back to my charity work. The need for the children's home becomes more urgent every day," she says. "Truthfully, Hetty, I don't have the heart for it, but the doctor says I must, otherwise my malaise may never leave me. And I'm not sure I can bear to live with it forever," she adds with a quiver in her voice.

I place my hand on her shoulder and give it a gentle squeeze.

"He's probably right," I say softly. "Nothing will bring Karl back. He would want you to be happy, Mutti."

She nods and taps my hand with her own.

There is a knock at the door.

"Come in," Mutti calls, sliding a final pin into the back of her hair and patting it.

Vera appears. "I have a letter for Fräulein Herta," she says, handing me an envelope. I recognize Tomas's handwriting.

Dear Hetty,

I've not seen or heard from you since the night of the dance, but I've thought about you all the time. Day and night. I'd hoped you might write and soothe my nerves and let me know that I'm forgiven entirely for my mistake. I hoped you would come to see it as a compliment, because it demonstrates my passion toward you and the strength of my feelings, which are undented by your silence.

I went too quick for you and I shan't make that mistake again. There is something wholesome and good and old-fashioned about waiting and I'll wait, so you needn't worry. So please say you will come for a walk with me on Sunday. You will be perfectly safe. Perhaps we could see a film together another day soon as well?

Yours devotedly,
Tomas

I fold the letter slowly and put it back in the envelope. I try to picture myself with Tomas, holding hands or kissing him, and my skin crawls.

"Who is it from?" Mutti asks, fixing her hat in place with a pearl-topped hatpin.

"Tomas."

"What does he want?"

"To walk with me on Sunday. To take me to the cinema. Ultimately to become my sweetheart, which I don't want."

"So write to him and say no. Surely he knows you're too good for him?"

I look at Mutti as she stares at herself in the mirror, hair perfectly arranged beneath her hat, her dress neat, an amber pendant hanging from a delicate chain around her slender neck, and in that moment, I realize fully the helplessness of us women. She, at the mercy of Vati, the sun in her universe, and yet he loves and fathers children with another; I, forced to walk out with a boy because he has a hold over me through what he knows. *Wissen ist macht.* I shall never get away from it.

"But Vati was *your* inferior, Mutti, and you married him."

"Don't be silly; look what he has achieved in life!"

"He was just a poor farmworker's son with no prospects."

"Not when I met him. He was already apprenticed at the newspaper."

"Still . . ."

"Well, it seems I chose well, in the end, doesn't it?" She bristles.

"So shouldn't I give Tomas a chance? He's an apprentice

with ambitions. He's going to join the Heer in September. Perhaps he will be more acceptable then."

"Herta—"

"I shall tell him we are simply friends, Mutti. Don't worry. I'll make myself clear. Will it be all right for me to go?"

"If you make your position absolutely clear, then yes. It can't do any harm. You've known each other for a very long time." She stands and picks up her handbag.

"Thank you." I sigh. It's going to be harder to extricate myself from Tomas than I've made out. But I'll find a way. It might just take a little time, that's all.

I peck her proffered cheek as I leave her.

A brisk wind numbs my face as I walk toward Erna's flat. Tomas's letter is unsettling. He isn't going to leave me alone. Despite defending him to Mutti, the thought of being with him again, after his rough and desperate groping outside the dance, repulses me. Even though he stopped short of *it*, what he did still feels like a violation, and every cell in my body is telling me to stay away from him. But if I reject him, he still might talk about Walter and me. I cannot risk the accusation of Rassenschande, with Ingrid and whatever she knows lurking in the background. This threat will always hang over me. Shall I ever be rid of it?

"I'm worried about you, Hett," Erna says, peering sideways at me as we push against the wind toward school. "You don't seem yourself," she adds. "You look so pale."

"Vati still hasn't forgiven me. Whenever he's home, unless he's in the company of others, he's so *frosty* with me. I honestly think if he never set eyes on me again, he wouldn't give a damn."

"Oh, I'm sure that's not true. He's just busy with his new role. In time he'll forget it all."

"And, in two weeks, Walter will be getting married. It'll be unbearable to think . . ." I swallow the lump in my throat.

"Ah, so that's it."

We cross the grassy slope of Nordplatz and into the full force of the wind. Erna hooks her arm through mine, and we bow our heads.

"You need cheering up." Her voice is raised against the gusts. "Let's get you out and find you a new love interest. I met this absolute *dish* last week at that BDM and HJ Celebration of Youth march. Shame you missed it. He would absolutely have loved you. Too short and intellectual for me, but for *you* . . ."

I dig her in the ribs and laugh for the first time in days.

"I don't need anyone new, Erna, truly."

"Oh yes you do. It's the best way to get over an old love. Trust me, I've experience of these things." She winks and smiles. "Besides, it's the perfect cover. What better way to convince your father you are back on track? Come to the Heer dance on Saturday evening. Please, Hetty."

"I don't want to go."

"Why not?" She stops before we get within earshot of the pupils gathered around the front of the school. "I don't understand."

"I'm sort of . . . walking out with Tomas," I admit at last.

"What? You are joking . . ."

"No."

"*Tomas*! I know he's always had a crush on you, but I didn't think . . . I mean, I like Tomas and everything, but, Hett, you could have *anyone*."

"He's been . . . persuasive. He writes to me. We walk sometimes on Sunday afternoons with Kuschi. He wants to take me to the cinema."

"Don't tell me you've *done* anything with him?"

"No, I haven't. He tried to once, but I made it clear it isn't going to happen. He's said he'll be the perfect gentleman from now on."

"But, Hetty, if you don't feel the same way, you have to tell him."

"Yes, I know. When I find the right way, and the right time."

"Don't leave it too long. It'll only get harder."

I should tell her what's holding me back, the power he has over me, but I don't. She'd tell me I'm wrong, or that I could reason with him. But where Tomas and I are concerned, reason doesn't seem to come into it. He'd take it as an affront that I would do with a Jew what I wouldn't do with him. It would infuriate him beyond measure, and he would be sure to want revenge. There would be no way of silencing him then.

I decide to change the subject.

"What of the *kindertransport*? Is there any news?"

Erna brightens. "Now, on that subject there is something positive. The English government is raising the age from fourteen to sixteen, so possibly within a few weeks, all Walter's cousins could go together." Her face falls. "On the downside, there is a long waiting list. Besides, America has voted down its plan for a similar program. President Roosevelt's own *cousin* and wife of the immigration commissioner said that twenty thousand charming children would soon grow into twenty thousand ugly adults."

"What a horrible thing to say."

"Yes. Look, Hetty, we can only do what we can do. Try not to get too . . . involved."

"What do you mean? You're involved."

"Yes, but only in the smallest of ways. Look, the Meuten have been brutally treated, broken up. The ringleaders were sent to prison. It's getting harder and more dangerous, all the time."

All my inner strength drains as I recall Vati's discussions about the Leipziger Meuten. We are powerless. "I know. You're right."

She gives me a pat on the arm, and I follow her into school.

Forty-Seven

March 15, 1939

Today is the day. I don't know what time. I suppose it doesn't matter. If only I could block it from my mind, think of something else. I told Mutti I was feverish and didn't want to go to school. She doesn't care whether I go or not. School has little meaning anymore, and Mutti is so absorbed in herself that nothing really touches her these days. The midday light is strong, and patches of sunlight splash color onto the rug by my bed. I roll onto my back and stare at the ceiling. But it isn't possible to think of anything else.

Today, the love of my life is getting married, only not to me.

My hand strays to my belly. I leave it there, resting on the soft curve of it. Under my fingers, the faintest of flutters. Butterfly wings. I quickly turn onto my side and they're gone. Slowly, I roll back, gingerly placing my fingertips once more on the low part of my belly. My heart stops. There it is again. A tiny pulse beneath my skin. Like some ghastly insect has gotten trapped in there and is tap, tap, tapping to find a way out.

Something Walter left behind.

I'm frozen, hand on stomach, a buzz in my ears. Hundreds,

or is it thousands, of kilometers away, Walter is about to get married, and I am carrying his baby in my belly.

I can't deny my swelling breasts and the soft rounding of my body anymore. I must be four and a half months gone.

With trembling fingers, I take Walter's letter from where it is folded and hidden inside the pages of my journal. The paper has softened and thinned with so much handling. I stare again at the post office address at the bottom of the letter. He says to write in an emergency.

I doubt if this is the type of emergency he envisioned.

I picture him on this day. Twenty years old, at the start of everything. Excited? Nervous? Sad his family members aren't there? Will he spare a thought for me? And then there is Anna. This faceless girl I know nothing about, who will begin a future with this most perfect of humans. She will be wearing a beautiful dress. Her hair curled and styled. Radiant and happy beyond words. Her belly flat and empty. But for how long? And when she feels this fluttering of new life, she will be excited, and he will be there for her.

I pulse with hate. And fear.

I haul myself out of bed and dress slowly. I have no enthusiasm. I'm bone-achingly weary. I dress carefully. The skirt a little looser in style than one I'd have chosen before. The pleats cover my thickening belly.

What on earth am I going to do?

"WHY DIDN'T YOU come to school today?"

Erna is at the front door. Her cheeks are pinched, her lips pressed closed. Her usual smile is absent.

"I'm not feeling great, that's all."

"You didn't tell anyone, but it's okay, I covered for you."

"They don't care whether I'm there or not."

"Probably not. But anyway . . . can I come in, Hett, or do we have to talk on the doorstep?"

I pull the door open wide and we climb the stairs to my room.

As soon as the door shuts, I burst into tears. Floods and floods of self-pity.

"What is it? Hetty, whatever is wrong?"

Erna's arms are around me, and she hugs me tight. I'm crying so hard, I can't say anything, I just shake my head.

"Please, whatever is the matter?" Erna pleads.

"It's—"

But how can I possibly tell her? The shame, the horror, of the Jewish fetus in my belly. The absolute proof that I have committed a crime worse than murder. That I've sullied the purity of my blood.

"Shh, shh. Come on, whatever it is, it can't be *this* bad." She tries to laugh, guides me to the window seat. Strokes my hair.

Slowly, my body stops heaving and the tears dry. I'm so exhausted I can hardly form words.

"He got married today," I tell her.

"Oh, Hett . . ."

"And I need to get rid of Tomas. He's supposed to be coming again on Sunday . . . I can't face him. But I'm scared, Erna, scared if I reject him, he'll tell people he once saw me kissing Walter. I never told you, but he has this hold over me . . ."

"Is that why you've been walking out with him? Because you're afraid he'll expose you? Oh, Hetty, he won't talk. He wouldn't dare. Besides, Walter's out of the country and it'd be his word against yours." Erna half laughs. "Come on, it's really not that bad. Which of you would they pay more attention to? Look, I know you're upset about Walter, but it's done now, and you have to move on. You've lost Karl, too, and with Tomas breathing down your neck . . . it's just all too much."

She straightens.

"That's it!" she says firmly. "That's how we get rid of Tomas, for a while at least. And once he joins the Heer, well, then he'll be properly off your back."

"How?" I wipe my eyes and blow my nose. My head throbs.

"You leave Tomas to me. I'll tell him you're still grieving for Karl and he needs to give you space for a few weeks—no, months. To leave you alone and not bother you. That will let him down gently. How does that sound?"

I nod slowly. It would give me space and time to think of how I can deal with *this* mess. Perhaps it will just go away. It happens, doesn't it? Miscarriage. You hear about them all the time. Perhaps that will happen to me and then everything will be okay. Much better that I don't see Tomas, because the way he looks at me, he's sure to notice soon enough.

And he, of all people, will be able to work out who the father is.

"Thank you, Erna. You're a true friend."

"It's nothing." She squeezes my hand. "I just want to see you smiling again, dearest Hetty."

AFTER ERNA HAS gone, I settle back in my window seat with my journal. The soft cushions mold in familiarity to my back and around my legs. Kuschi jumps up and curls himself against me, thumping his tail on the cushions. I stroke his silky coat a few times, then begin to write.

I know you are married now, but I shan't ever stop thinking about you, dearest Walter. It would be impossible because you are part of my very being. I cannot see that this will ever change, however much time passes by. Today has been torture. I don't need to say why. But now that it's done, I feel some kind of weird, inevitable calm. As though as your new life starts, mine is somehow over. I hope you are happy though, I really do, and I'm glad beyond anything you're safe. That's why I've made up my mind. I am not going to tell you. I'm keeping what's happened a secret, because it will be better for YOU that way. And that's what matters to me the most. My love for you is completely unselfish. As for me, I shall pray every day that this problem will solve itself. Because if it doesn't, I know that I am doomed. I cannot even bear to think . . . Perhaps that night Tomas got carried away, perhaps it would have been better if he'd gone through with it. Then this would have been easier to explain. But it's too late now. Much too late. Nobody can help me. So please, God, if you are there, make this easy for me. Make this thing go away.

Forty-Eight

March 16, 1939

I need to complete a science project for Herr Metzger," I tell the librarian during lesson break. She nods and leads me through the deserted library to the science section.

"On what subject, precisely?" she asks.

"Hereditary disease, and abortion," I say casually.

She pulls a few books from the shelves and carries them to the big table in the center of the room.

"That should be sufficient. If not, there are a couple more that may help you."

"Thank you." I smile at her, holding my belly in as tightly as I can.

She returns to her desk, facing me, and continues cataloging a big pile of books.

I flick through the science manuals. There is not much of any help. It's easy to get an abortion, it seems, if the mother is a carrier of a hereditary disease, or if she is racially of poor stock. If not, it is almost impossible. I stare at the gruesome pictures of the procedures. Metal wires, catheters, poison. Bleeding to death is a common complication. I find my hand on my belly as I look in horror at the illustrations.

I glance up and see the librarian is watching me.

"Found what you are looking for?"

"Yes," I reply. "Thank you so much. Very helpful." I snap the books shut.

Back in class, Frau Schmidt's voice drones, but I don't hear a single word. I'm nauseated after looking at those pictures; and from the sudden realization that far from wanting to end this life growing inside me, my instinct is to protect it.

"COME ON, HETTY, faster!" Erna yells, holding her hand out for the baton, and jogging on the spot.

I will myself to speed up. Normally I have no problem passing Gerda or Eva, but today my legs are like lead and I can't outpace them. We round the bend of the athletics track and I'm last, mouth open gasping for breath. I can't seem to take in enough air. I stumble forward and thrust the baton at Erna. She snatches it and is away, sprinting on her long legs toward the finish line, closing the gap with the leaders.

My head becomes thick and dizzy. A buzz fills my ears and my vision dims, swirls, and then blackness folds in . . .

"Herta? Herta? Get the nurse, will you?"

Someone is holding my head, rolling me onto my side.

Instinctively I curl into a ball. My head bangs with pain and I groan.

Someone touches my shoulder, pulls at it.

"Get off," I say weakly. "Leave me alone," and I bat the hand away. Roll up tighter. Hide my midriff.

"Hett, are you okay? Hetty, can you hear me?" Erna's voice, far away.

"She's fainted!"

"Is she all right?"

"She's never done that before!"

Voices, clamoring and loud.

"Move aside, give her space," says a loud commanding voice. "Herta Heinrich? Can you hear me?"

I flicker my eyes open. The school nurse's face looms in front of me. I close them again. *Please no. She's going to find out.*

"Yes," I hear myself say. "I'm quite all right."

I summon all my strength and sit up. My head pounds and I'm trembling uncontrollably.

"Please don't fuss," I tell the crowd around me. "I don't know what happened, I just felt a bit . . ."

"Head between your knees," the nurse commands me.

I do as she says, clutching my knees and hiding my stomach from the gawping onlookers. I can feel the nurse's eyes boring into me.

"Time of the month, is it?" The nurse's voice is brisk and businesslike.

"Yes, yes that must be it." I nod, my heart thumping. The dizziness recedes and slowly I raise my head.

Someone hands me some water and a sweet biscuit. I didn't realize my mouth was so dry.

"I feel much better," I say after a drink, which is almost true.

"Common affliction in young girls," says the nurse with authority. "Go home and rest. Don't come back until you are well."

"I'll make sure she gets home," Erna says, helping me to stand. "I'm sorry I yelled at you to run faster, I had no idea . . ."

"Don't be silly, of course you didn't."

She's looking at my stomach. I realize I'm clasping my hand over it. I drop it guiltily to my side.

"Do you have cramps?" she whispers.

I nod. Press my lips together. Resist the urge to cry.

"It's a sign of good fertility, you know. Cramps," says the nurse.

"Come on, let's go home." Erna takes my arm.

The other girls begin to lose interest and drift away.

I lean against Erna as we walk slowly back toward the school building.

A narrow escape. But how much longer before someone makes a correct diagnosis? The weight of impending disaster presses down on me. Like being buried alive, however hard I scrabble, whichever way I turn, I can't see a way out.

Forty-Nine

April 11, 1939

Dear Hetty,

I know you don't want me to call on you. Erna told me you need space and time. Well, I've tried to do that, for a whole month. And in that time I've decided sitting at home and being sad all the time won't do you any good. The best way to get over your brother's death is to do things that will make you happy. Be in good company. So I'll call for you this Sunday. I've been saving up and I shall take you out for lunch. I shan't take no for an answer. I can make you happy, Hetty, I know I can. And I will.

With devotion,
Tomas

I scrunch the letter into a ball and put it in my pocket as I climb the stairs to my room. Slamming my bedroom door closed behind me, I fumble desperately for the fastenings at the back of my skirt. My fingers slip and the clips stay firmly closed. Breathe in. Slow down. I release the hooks one by one. I sewed them on myself a couple of weeks ago, when the buttons would no longer reach the buttonholes.

There is exquisite relief when it's done. I let the skirt drop to the floor, unbutton my blouse, and allow my belly to bulge out. It aches from being constricted and sucked in all day at school. I look down at my distended abdomen. Deep red indentations mark my belly where the waistband dug in for so long. Five and a half months gone. I feel it all the time now. No longer flutterings, these are proper, strong kicks of two little feet. I'm not going to be able to hide it much longer.

Tears work themselves loose from my eyes. I've shed so many, but they don't solve a thing. I clench my fists and rub them away, knuckles hurting my cheeks, but I don't care. I deserve it.

I walk bare-legged to my window seat, resting my back against a cushion and stretching my legs gratefully out in front of me. The cherry tree is in full blossom once again. It's so full this year with pink-tipped flowers that some of the delicate ends of the branches appear to bow under their weight. I wish I could be that tree. It doesn't suffer human anguish. It lives in blissful oblivion of mine, and of the German boots marching their way across eastern Europe. Vati says war is inevitable now. A war to annihilate the Jews.

My bowels shift. This threat to the life that scrabbles and squirms inside me. A mischling child, whose Jewish blood is considered to be so abhorrent that it would surely be in the greatest danger if it were to be born. And whose existence may also be the end of mine. I think of Hilda Müller. How I despised her for her poor morals and husband stealing. Now I am just like her. Only worse. Because there is no Vati in the background giving me a flat and money and love. Even if she does have to share him with Mutti, at least she has a part of him.

I wish Walter was here. I screw my eyes closed and conjure his spirit with every pore of my being. I can see his face, his hair, his smile. I feel the touch of his hand, the smell of his skin. I'm drifting in his arms. There is water swirling, but I'm safe; after all this lonely time, I'm safe.

I barely register the sound of the door. I open my eyes, turn my head. Mutti is in the room. She is speaking, walking toward me. It all happens in slow motion.

"I've called you three times, why aren't you answering?" She stops. She is staring at me. Staring at my round, exposed belly.

My brain clicks. Everything speeds up. I tuck my knees in, wrap my arms around them to hide the bump. But it's too late. Mutti is standing statue still, her mouth half open as if to speak, but no words come out. Her eyes are wide; she doesn't blink.

The air is static. Time stops.

"Herta?" Mutti's voice is a hoarse whisper. "Is that . . . Are you . . . *in trouble?*"

The clock ticks again and something releases. Like water through a loosened plug, all my suffering flows out. Freely, copiously, the tears come.

"Yes, yes, yes . . . I'm in trouble. Terrible trouble."

At last. Someone knows, and the relief is infinite.

I SIT WITH my legs folded beneath me, enveloped between the cushions of the big armchair in the afternoon sitting room. I'm wrapped in my dressing gown and my fingers are curled around a warm, milky cup of cocoa.

Vera and Margot, our new cook, have been told I'm unwell. They both paint a look of concern on their faces, but really, they don't give a damn. Not like Bertha. Oh, how I miss Bertha.

Mutti paces the room. Her eyes flicker about nervously. Some strands of her usually neatly groomed hair fall free and trail softly over her ears. Her waist beneath her slim-fitting dress looks impossibly narrow. The beautifully cut fabric of the skirt swings as she walks, caressing her long, slender thighs. I cannot imagine how Mutti could ever have been pregnant. Twice.

She grabs the packet of cigarettes and matches lying on the coffee table as she passes. Her movements are jagged, clipped. She walks the room, one arm up, holding the cigarette between her fingers, wrist cocked; the other arm is hugged across her waist. She hasn't been this agitated since that doomed day last October that shattered our lives forever.

She stops in front of me and perches on the edge of the sofa.

"For heaven's sake, Herta. *Why?* I mean, after all we've been through. How could you *do* this to us?"

"I'm sorry . . ."

"Stupid girl. *Stupid, stupid* girl." She thumps the arm of

the sofa with her fist. "I just don't believe . . . How could you . . . I didn't bring you up to behave . . ."

"Mutti, I'm sorry," I sob. "I really am . . ."

"You will be." Her tone is harsh. "He's going to have to marry you, you know. He does know that, doesn't he?"

"Who?" I whisper.

"The goddamn father," she says. "Who else? What a damned shame. You could have done so much better for yourself. Tomas—I take it, it's him—is . . . not exactly what your father and I had in mind for you. Vati will be so *disappointed*. But it's too late now. You can forget any dream of having a job. Taking your Abitur. You do realize that, don't you?" Her hand trembles as she moves it to her mouth. She sucks hard on the cigarette, narrowing her eyes.

"I don't know who the father is," I say softly.

"What?" She sits up, staring at me as if I've gone mad. "Jesus. How can you *not know*! I just thought Tomas . . . How many other boys have you been with? You dirty little slut!" Her voice is high pitched, on the edge of hysteria.

"I don't mean that. I mean I do know. I just don't want to say."

"Good God, what is this?"

"Oh, Mutti. I wish I could—"

"Well! You had better write and tell whoever-it-is. And fast. He will get a hell of a shock. But then"—she laughs a hollow laugh—"he should have thought about the consequences before he did it to you. Shouldn't he? Stupid men. They never do, though, do they? Hmm? Think. Or at least, they think only of *one* thing." She shakes her head and jiggles one leg up and down on her tiptoes.

I bury my head in my hands.

"Herta. You have to tell me who the father is."

"I can't."

"Don't be ridiculous, Hetty. This is *serious*. Don't you realize? Are you so stupid . . . You have to tell me, and you *have to marry him!*"

"You don't understand. I can't, I just can't."

Mutti's leg stops jiggling.

"Who the hell *is the father?*" she screams, leaning toward me, red in the face. "Do you have any idea what Vati is going to say when he finds out?"

She's going to strike me. I lean away. I've never seen her so angry. We stare at each other, then she howls in frustration and jumps up, paces the room again.

I stare at the floor. The geometric patterns on the rug beneath the coffee table swim and merge. Rust red. Olive green. Burnt orange. Camel.

"Please, Hetty. I can't help you if you won't tell me. Come on . . ." Her mood changes; her tone becomes cajoling, pleading.

"I can't."

"At least tell me the reason *why* you can't name him."

I glance up at her. Her eyes have grown large. I shake my head, tears welling once again. A look of horror falls like a shadow over her face.

"Oh, Herta," she says, "he isn't married, is he?"

"No, Mutti . . ."

But he is.

Blood curdles in my veins. Vati, who is in Dresden until the weekend, could, at this very moment, be with his mistress and their newborn son, instead of being on the official SS business Mutti thinks he's on.

Lie upon lie upon lie. The falsehoods gather and pile up, one on top of the other like a castle formed from layers of packed, wet sand, until one day the sand will dry, and the castle shall crumble and come tumbling down.

Fifty

April 16, 1939

Their voices travel from the dining room, unnaturally heightened, when I arrive home, midmorning, from Kuschi's Sunday walk. The door is ajar, and I listen from behind it.

"Really, Franz, I have no idea who the culprit is. I'm shocked by her behavior, truly. But I can't imagine why she won't name him. She's protecting him. I suppose he's married . . ." There's a pause. "It's my fault. I should have been more careful with her. But I was so distracted with losing Karl . . ." Mutti's voice breaks.

"No, Hélène. It's not your fault. I've a damned good idea why she won't name him." Vati's voice is acid, and my stomach turns over.

"You know who it is?"

"Oh yes, and it's worse than you imagine."

"Franz, tell me! What can be worse than a married man?"

Vati grunts. I close my eyes. I'm in free fall. I prop myself against the wall, breathless with terror. Walter comes to me, behind my eyelids. His presence is calming. Strength returns to my limbs.

"For heaven's sake, *tell me!*" Mutti pleads.

"It's that Jew." Vati's voice is dangerously low. "That bastard who used to come here all the time. We showed him kindness and tolerance, back then, *and this is how he repays us!*" Mutti gasps and the vision of Walter is lost. I snap my eyes open. "Karl warned me . . . Herta swore it was nothing . . . I even helped the evil swine leave the country. If he were here, I'd murder him with my own hands. I can't bear to think of him violating her. It's . . . it's . . ."

I draw a deep, deep breath and swing the door open.

They stare at me. Both of them. Rag-doll Mutti with her eyes popping out. And Vati.

Oh, Vati, with your lies and your deceit. You might not recognize it, but we are the same, you and me.

I hold my head up high and meet his eyes, full of hate.

His fury hits me with the force of a hurricane.

"You disgusting, filthy . . . How could you do such a thing? You are vile . . . make me sick . . . ruined us . . . downfall!" He yells incomprehensible words at me. He lunges and I step back, too slow, as he hits my face so hard I stagger sideways, lose balance. The corner of the dining table smacks the side of my head hard as I fall. I land awkwardly on all fours and roll into a ball to protect my belly.

Blotchy faced, he towers over me; his eyes are tiny blue-black holes in the furrows of his shaking flesh. Mutti is grabbing his arm and shouting, "Stop, stop, please, Franz . . ."

"It wasn't Walter," I scream. "He never touched me, I swear!"

"I don't believe you, you lying little bitch." He shakes Mutti's arm off. "You've turned into one of them! Manipulating, scheming, and plotting. Blackmailing your own father! Look at you . . . nothing but a filthy *whore* . . ."

He aims a boot at me, but I roll away and he misses.

He will go for my belly, kick the baby from my body.

"What do you mean, blackmailing? Franz! Have you lost your mind?" Mutti grabs him again, both arms this time. "Get up, Hetty, get out of this room, NOW."

Vati is trying to shake her off, but she is gripping him as though her life depends on it. I pull myself up holding the table. My head throbs. I stumble for the door. Someone is there. Standing in the doorway. Vera? Another nosy little cow. She'll gossip with all her stupid maid friends and by tomorrow the entire neighborhood will know the shameful truth.

But it isn't Vera. This person is too tall. A man's silhouette. The door swings wider, and Tomas's lanky frame comes toward me.

Could this get any worse? I wish I was dead.

So now he knows the truth, too, and he can confirm Vati's suspicions. He gives me a long look, then turns to Mutti and Vati.

"Herr, Frau Heinrich. Heil Hitler." He salutes, wearing his Sunday-best suit. "I'm very sorry to intrude. The front door was open. Nobody came when I rang the bell. I wanted to surprise Hetty, collect her early, and take her for lunch."

He stares at me. I must look a disheveled mess, my clothes twisted around, my hair loose, and blood running down behind my ear. "Can I help, Hetty? Are you quite well?"

Vati deflates. He sinks to the sofa, head in his hands. "I'm done for," he mutters.

Mutti turns to Tomas. "I'm sorry. This is not a good time. Herta has gotten herself into trouble . . . and . . ." Her voice fades.

Tomas's eyes flicker over my stomach. He looks into my eyes. His expression is unreadable. What does it matter now, anyway?

"She refuses to reveal the father, you see, so . . ." Mutti stammers, rubbing her hands together and glancing at Vati as if for permission to say these things. He is mute, his head still buried.

There's a moment of quiet and I tenderly touch the sticky lump that has formed on my temple. Tomas steps toward me and takes my arm.

"But, darling," he says steadily, "why wouldn't you tell them? The baby's mine, see?" He speaks firmly, smiling broadly at us all.

Vati's head shoots up. The three of us gape at him.

The sunlight in the room intensifies. The air stills. Mutti and Vati are silent. I cannot breathe.

I stare at Tomas, willing him to meet my eyes again, but he is looking at Vati now. His cheeks are pink and his smudged glasses sit halfway down his nose. He pushes them up, just as he did in the classroom all those years ago. He swallows and his Adam's apple rises and falls in his throat. Tiny white pimples dot his cheeks. An unlikely hero, but right now, this is the sweetest, dearest face imaginable.

"I'm sorry you had to learn it this way, Herr Heinrich,"

Tomas says. "It wasn't how I planned it. We'll marry as soon as possible, of course, won't we, Hetty? I can prove my Aryan ancestry. I've got all the paperwork. Not a drop of Jewish blood runs in my veins, so we shan't be denied permission on that test." He turns to look at me. "I'd been planning to ask you over lunch, my dearest."

Vati and Mutti are still mute. They glance at each other.

Mutti laughs nervously.

"But, Herta, I don't understand. Why did you deny it was Tomas? Why the secrecy?"

Everything is moving too fast. I can't think properly.

Tomas answers for me.

"It was my fault," he says. "I told her not to tell. It came as a shock. Never expected to be a father at seventeen! I was ashamed but I've got my head around it all now, and I couldn't be happier. I love your daughter with all my heart, Herr Heinrich."

That part, at least, seems to be true.

Vati, who had been lost in thought watching Tomas, suddenly seems to snap awake. He looks once more at Mutti, then steps forward and shakes Tomas by the hand. He begins to smile. Mutti too.

"Well!" Vati exclaims. "This is indeed wonderful news. Herta had me worried for a few minutes, but never mind that now. I'm sure I can speed up the permission process. A doctor will need to examine you, Herta, but with Tomas guaranteed as the father, that won't prove a problem. This calls for a celebration. My daughter married and the first of many children on the way. A drink! It isn't too early for a drink at eleven forty-five, is it? Tomas, what will you be having?"

I have to sit down; I'm shaking all over. Mutti sits beside me and rubs my back, fusses over my head. She rings the bell and asks Vera for ice, cloths, and iodine to wipe the wound.

Vati and Tomas smoke cigars and toast each other with champagne.

The soon-to-be father- and son-in-law.

An unexpected life begins to float in my mind like a weird, surreal dream. A little flat with Tomas. Me a wife. A baby. Walter's baby. I shall always have a piece of Walter with me. I place a hand on my belly and for the first time, I can begin to imagine a future where this new being inside me will be okay. Hetty and Tomas. Tomas and Hetty. It sounds all wrong.

Can he really want me this much?

The thought makes me shudder.

But he is giving Walter's baby and me a chance. I cling to that thought with all my might, to stop myself from drowning.

MUTTI INSISTS WE stay for lunch instead of going out as planned. Vati's mood, fortified by champagne and plenty of wine, is jolly.

"Listen, young man, I had humble beginnings. There is nothing wrong with that," he tells Tomas. "You have proved yourself to be a good, upright German, despite the . . . difficulties caused by your father. That shows determination. Moral courage. I've no doubt you will do well in the Wehrmacht. We need many more young men like you. I'm fortunate I have all this." He gestures to the grandness of the room. "I'll help with the rent on your first flat. Until you can stand on your own two feet. With a wife and child to support, you'll need it." He looks at me. "And Mutti will be close by to help with the baby—it will be good for her to have something to distract her from, you know. Something positive . . ."

After lunch, Tomas and I walk together in Rosental. I'm nervous to be alone with him. It's so strange. To passersby we must look like a nice young couple, strolling hand in hand. In love, baby on the way. A perfect little German family.

If only they knew the truth.

"It's warmer than I thought," I comment as we walk. "I should have worn my shawl, not my coat." Tomas doesn't reply.

"The trees are in full leaf already," I try. "Do you think it will be hot this summer?"

I prattle on, banalities, barely knowing what I say, to fill the void.

We sit down on a bench facing the lake. The matter has hovered, unspoken, since we left the house.

Filth. Slut. Ruined. Destroyed the purity of your blood. A long-silenced voice awakens.

Tomas is deep in thought and picks up a pebble from the pathway in front of the bench. He turns it over and over in his hands, smoothing his fingers over its flat, gleaming surface.

"I know how much I've hurt you, Tomas," I say, breaking the silence, "and I'm sorry for it. I will try to be the best wife I possibly can. I will be so good to you, as you have been to me. But I want to understand. Why are you doing this?"

He exhales long and forcefully, clutching the pebble tightly in his hand. "Because I must save you. You are a fallen angel.

This *thing* that has happened. It doesn't change that. In fact, you need saving more than ever." He lifts his gaze to the sky, as if he can see angels circling gracefully above him.

"Tomas, come on. This angel thing . . . you don't really believe . . ."

He looks down at the stone in his hand, stroking it with his fingertips. "I tried so hard *not* to love you. I really did. But it's impossible. And I realized, a greater force is pushing me to do this. To save you."

"Save me from what?"

"The Jew. He forced you. He must have. It cannot have been your fault. That way, I can bear it. And I won't let anything bad happen to you again. I will protect you." He raises his arm and flings the pebble out across the lake. It arcs over the water and lands with a deep splash.

My heart begins to pump faster. Harder.

Tomas rubs his hands over his face. He repositions his glasses.

"I don't want thanks," he says, his voice smooth, level. "It is out of love that I do this. But I want you to understand one thing. I'm sure you know it anyway." My throat tightens. "The baby has to go. I *won't have that mischling child*. It might be hard at first. But you'll be grateful in the end." He drops his eyes to my stomach and a look of revulsion clouds his face.

I'm hit by a wave of nausea.

"What do you mean, you won't keep the baby . . . what are you expecting me to do?"

"You don't seriously expect me to raise a bastard Jewish

mongrel? Every time I saw it, it would remind me. It's inconceivable, Hetty."

"But you said! You told Vati and Mutti the baby was yours.
That you would marry me because of it. Why would you do
that? I don't understand." A dark shadow descends.

"Yes, but I said that to protect *you*, not the brat. Besides,
why would you want to keep it? I mean, surely you would want
to put all that . . . trouble . . . behind you. So you can give
yourself fully and completely to me. We will have babies of our
own. Lots of them."

He grabs my hand and squeezes it, but I can't breathe as my
throat twists and shuts.

The ground somersaults and darkness closes in.

"Hetty?"

The lake swirls back into focus.

"Are you okay?" Tomas's thin face and smeared glasses are
in front of me, his eyes full of concern. "Shh," he says. "Don't
try to speak. Take deep breaths."

I do as he says.

Breathing becomes easier, and my heartbeat slows.

"And what exactly would you have me do with it?" I say at
last, keeping my voice even. Restraining the hysteria. "I mean,
how am I to dispose of it when it's born? This is a *baby* we are
talking about. Would you have me tie it in a sack and drown it
in the river like a litter of kittens?"

You are no savior. You're a sick bastard, like the rest of them.

"No, of course not." He laughs. "But seriously, I don't know
or care—it has to go. I mean, there are orphanages, aren't
there? For unwanted brats."

"But what would we tell people? They will know I'm expecting. How will we explain the disappearance of a baby?"

"I don't care." His voice is harsh suddenly. "Tell them it died. Babies do. With any luck it will, then that will solve the problem, won't it?"

"How can you say that?" I splutter. "How can you say that about an innocent baby? Besides, it wasn't like that. Walter is a good person. We loved each other, and what we did—I *wanted* to do it." My throat has closed. I can no longer speak. I stare at him in horror. Will him to say something more. To turn to me and say it was just some awful, cruel joke. Surely even Tomas cannot be this cold-blooded.

But he says nothing, refusing to look at me, his mouth turned down, his glasses sliding down his nose. I can no longer stand the sight of him.

Everything has a price.

This baby is the price of loving Walter.

Losing it is the price Tomas demands.

What choice do I have? I'm doomed if I pay it, and doomed if I don't.

But the thought of being married to Tomas, sharing his life and his bed, fills me with utter dread.

I stare out over the lake and remember how Walter pulled me from its depths.

How I wish he had let me go.

Fifty-One

April 19, 1939

W hy are you avoiding me?" The hurt in Erna's voice
echoes down the telephone wire.

"I'm not . . ."

"I don't understand, Hett. Please tell me what I've done. If I
said something to upset you—"

"You haven't upset me."

"That makes it worse. Pretending it's nothing . . ."

"It's the truth. You haven't done anything, Erna—"

"Then why have you avoided me for the last three weeks,
Hetty? You've not been at school. I've called at the house, I've
phoned. It's as if you've got the plague or something."

"It's the spring holidays, Erna!"

"I know, but we always see each other during the holidays."

I feed the telephone cord through my fingers.

"Come over," I say after a pause. "This afternoon, while
Mutti is paying her monthly visit to the soldiers' home. Come
at four."

I replace the receiver. She is going to find out soon enough anyway. Mutti has written to the school to tell them I shan't be returning after the holidays.

Better that Erna hears it from me.

VERA LETS ERNA into the house. I hear her pound up the staircase, then her quick tread along the corridor. I force myself to face the door as she comes in, the shame of my bump clearly exposed beneath my clothes. I hold my breath and wait for her disgust.

"Hetty?"

She walks toward me, looking at my face. Instinctively, my hands drop to my belly and only then does she lower her eyes.

"Christ Almighty!"

"Yes."

"*That's* why you've been avoiding me?"

"It might as well be the plague . . ."

"Oh, Hetty . . . How . . . Who's the father?"

"Do you really have to ask?"

"Walter?"

I nod and begin to cry. Big, fat tears. They never seem to end.

She's beside me, her arms around me, and I sob into her shoulder.

"*Why didn't you tell me?*"

"I couldn't. I was so ashamed. I hoped it would just . . . go away."

"But . . . but . . . how far are you?"

"I'm five and a half months."

"For the devil's sake, Hett, how did you keep it hidden?"

"Desperation."

She sinks onto the bed and stares at me. "You should have told me," she murmurs. "I could've helped."

"How? What could you have done? I'm doomed. That's all there is to it."

"What d'you mean, doomed?"

My nose is running, and I search for a clean handkerchief in my top drawer. Finding it, I blow my nose and sit next to Erna on the bed.

"When Vati found out, I thought he was going to kill me. I really did. He hit me so hard . . . ."

"Oh no, that's awful . . ."

I show her the scab and the remaining lump on the side of my head. "If Tomas hadn't walked in at that moment, I really think Vati would have."

"Tomas? I thought he was staying away."

"He wrote and said he'd had enough of that, and he wanted to take me out for lunch. Anyway, he turned up in the middle of this almighty row and announced the baby was his."

"What? *Why?*"

"Exactly. He's . . . not right in the head. He thinks I'm some kind of fallen angel who needs saving. He told Vati he'll marry me. At first, I was relieved. I don't *want* to marry Tomas, but I thought if it means Walter's baby will be safe, and if we can live together as a family, well, I could make that work." I gulp. Take a breath. "But he told me I have to give the baby up. Put it in an orphanage . . . He said he couldn't bear to raise a mischling child. He's forcing me to give it away . . ." I begin to cry again. "How can I bear to do that? I hate him, I loathe the sight of him, and now I have to marry him!"

"No, you don't. You don't have to marry anyone, Hetty, not if you don't want to," Erna says, putting her arm around me again.

"But I do. If I marry Tomas, I'll save myself, but sacrifice my baby. If I try to go it alone, what then? Vati will disown me. I'll have no money. No way of supporting us. Besides, without proof the father is of pure German blood . . ." I don't bother to finish the sentence.

Erna squeezes me tight. She lets go and walks to the window, staring out at the falling spring rain. I lie back against the pillow, resting my head on the headboard. My belly, firm and round as a small melon, protrudes beneath my dress.

She turns to me. "You have to tell Walter. If you'd told him earlier, before—"

"Before he got married? How would that have helped? It just would have ruined his life as well as mine. I'm not doing that to him, Erna. He's no good to me here, and if he can't stay in England because of this, I would be no good to him, either. I've made up my mind. I'm not going to destroy his chance of a good life."

"Christ, Hetty, that's all very noble, but he has a right to know. It's his child too."

"I can't tell him. It would ruin *everything*."

"Shouldn't you let him decide? Perhaps it wouldn't be as bad as you think. Perhaps you would be able to go to England too."

"Oh what, then the three of us could live together in perfect harmony? Walter and his two wives? He is living with her family and is totally reliant on their support to remain in England. You're being ridiculous."

"But he's *there*. Maybe the English will let his child join him, and as the mother of his child, you would be able to go, too, maybe not right away but—"

"Stop it, Erna. It's never going to work. I can't go to England, even if he wanted me to, what would I do there? All I *can* do is try to find a way to save this baby. From whatever fate Tomas has in store. I've only got a few months to find a solution. Please help me to think."

"What about Walter's mother? His aunt? Couldn't they take it in?"

"I thought of that, too, but how could I dump a baby on them? They have nothing and they've been forced to live in that Jewish house on Humboldstrasse. I couldn't send my baby to live in such a terrible place. The men remain in Buchenwald, assuming they're even still alive. I would be consigning it, to what fate? Besides, why would they ever want to help *me*?"

"And what about *you*?"

"I will just have to marry Tomas. I don't see I have a choice. Perhaps if he has me, he will change his mind about the baby."

The look on her face confirms what I already know.

That this baby, with the blood of a Jew coursing through its veins, is condemned before it has even been born.

Fifty-Two

Time crawls when there is too much of it. Without school, with no BDM commitments. With few visitors, the minutes, the hours, the days stretch longer and longer into one interminable wait. I hide away in my room and watch the world from my window, my shame unseen and unknown. Only four people in all the world know in advance that my baby will not survive after its birth. Vati is no fool. He soon worked out who the real father is. But it suits him to keep it quiet and out of the news, so he, Mutti, and Tomas plot its demise together.

I'm taking care of the arrangements," Mutti informs me briskly one afternoon. "For the baby. Vati wants nothing to do with it, for understandable reasons. Besides, he cannot risk any connection."

"What arrangements?"

"The orphanage. It's . . . my area of expertise. Given my work with the children's home."

"Will it go to *your* home?" I could visit every day. Nobody need know. Hope soars in my chest.

"Of course not," Mutti says, giving me a firm look. "My home is for racially pure children. Your child will be a . . . It will not qualify."

"Then where . . ." The words stick as my throat closes.

"There's a Jewish orphanage in Berlin. I have been in touch, *anonymously*. They will take the child in return for a large donation." Her jaw contracts. "They will do anything for money," she says through pursed lips. "But in this case, that is useful for us. You will go into a mothers' home before the birth, in Berlin. I've organized this, too. We cannot risk you being seen by too many people around here, and I don't want any local midwives to attend the birth."

"But, Mutti, please. You *can't* make me do this. This is my *baby*."

"*Jewish* baby."

"There's no difference! It's a baby. Please—"

There is a knock at the sitting room door and Mutti, with a warning look, puts up her hand to silence me. I say no more as Vera pokes her head into the room.

"Tomas is here to see Fräulein Herta," she announces.

I exhale pent-up tension. "Tell him I'll be right down, Vera," I manage to say. "Thank you."

Mutti is talking to Vera, but I don't hear any of it. I think of my baby and the Jewish orphanage and try not to cry. I sit for a little longer, gathering the energy to hold myself together, before making my way downstairs.

Tomas's face lights up when he sees me.

"What would you like to do today, darling? A walk? You spend too much time inside, you need some sunshine on your skin. You'll end up frail, like one of those . . . pallid, floppy girls. I need you fit and strong, like you used to be."

"Okay," I say and put on my outdoor shoes. I keep my voice calm and measured, but inside I'm seething. Never before have I felt such animosity toward another person.

"I guess it's that thing." He lowers his voice. "That parasite in your belly, sapping all your strength."

"Stop it." Something snaps. "My health is fine, Tomas. But my mother has just told me what is going to happen when my baby is born. How it's been sold, effectively, to a Jewish orphanage in Berlin—"

"Shh, you don't want the maid to hear." He puts a finger to my lips. I slap it away and march out onto the street in front of him.

"I've always admired your fiery spirit." He laughs as he catches up with me.

Firmly, he hooks his arm through mine and marches me down Fritzschestrasse.

"I've some good news for you."

"Oh yes?" My pulse quickens. I look up at him. Perhaps he's had a change of heart?

"The wedding date! The racial permissions have been granted. We can marry immediately. Your father would like it sooner rather than later, and a quiet affair, for obvious reasons. There can't be any sniff of a scandal. So how about the Saturday after next?"

You bastard. There is no change of plan. No reprieve. No redeeming quality in the man I'm being forced to marry.

"You really want to marry me, like this?" He will want to take me to bed on our wedding night.

His mouth twists up into a laugh. "Of course, I would prefer to marry you *not* in that state, but we must, for your father's sake. Besides"—he gives me an intense look—"I cannot wait to have you all to myself."

"But . . . where will we live? We haven't sorted anything—"

"Ah. That. Well, it's what I want to talk to you about."

We turn down Berggartenstrasse. It's a beautiful day. The sun is high in the sky, the scent of jasmine in the air. I inhale deeply. That snap I felt earlier—like a match lit, it's taken hold. A small fire burns inside. It's time for me to take back control.

"Your parents have kindly suggested I move in," Tomas is saying, "until we can find a suitable place of our own. There's plenty of space in your house. We can look for a flat in August, after . . . Anyway, in plenty of time before I join the Heer in September."

"And in between?" I ask him. "It seems to have all been decided *without* me having any say. I am to go to some home in Berlin, give birth, and then hand the baby over to strangers. Then I'm supposed to come back here and play the happy wife, with you. I can't do it, Tomas. I won't."

My change of tone makes Tomas jolt.

"You hardly have a choice, Hetty. Do you? You've risked your father's reputation and career. You risk being thrown into a concentration camp yourself. This is all your— Well, it's that vile Jew's fault, not mine. I'm your *savior* here. I'm doing this out of the goodness of my heart. Helping out a dear old friend. And, once you've sufficiently recovered, we will put all this behind us and start our married life together. Properly."

The heat is spreading. I'm burning up inside, boiling with a rage I've suppressed for weeks. "You're *my savior? Doing this from the goodness of your heart?* Don't kid yourself, Tomas. This suits you just fine. Get rid of the problem and be left with just the part you want. Me. But what if I don't go along with your plan? What if I say no?" I stand still in the middle of the street, every cell in my body screaming. "I am not like you, Tomas. It wasn't *that vile Jew's* fault I'm pregnant. He never forced me to do anything. We *loved* each other. I did it willingly with him because I wanted to. Because he is a wonderful, kind human being. Jews are no different from anybody else. It's all lies. All of it. There is no evil conspiracy to take over the world, unless you're Hitler, of course—"

"Shut up!"

"No, I *won't* shut up. For once, I'm going to speak the truth—"

Tomas grabs hold of both of my wrists, squeezes them hard. Shakes me. But I won't stop now.

"Yes! That's the truth. Hitler's the evil one who's wrong, who lies. There is no master race, no inherent superiority. Everyone is the same, Jew or non-Jew, African or Aryan. We're all *humans*—"

"Shut *the fuck* up!" Tomas shouts, shaking me harder. "How dare you—"

"I'm going to keep this baby!" I yell. *"Over my dead body will I let anyone take it away!"*

Tomas jerks my wrists so hard I cry out in pain.

"Enough," he commands, without relinquishing his grasp.

I'm gasping for breath, my cheeks wet with tears.

"Have you finished with the dramatic little outburst?"

My energy is spent and he loosens his grip, dropping my wrists. We stare at each other, eye to eye. And then, his mouth twitches. A snigger at first, then full-on laughter. He stops laughing and lunges forward, grabbing me around the waist, bringing his face right down close to mine.

"Hetty," he says, in a high voice, "we will never mention this conversation again. But you remember just who you are, and what you have done. You *have* no choices. I'm your only hope. And don't worry, I shan't lay a hand on you until that *thing* is out of your belly. The idea is repellent. I shall wait. I've grown used to waiting. And when you are ready, I will cleanse you, mind and body, and you will belong to me, completely."

He pulls me toward him and kisses me on the mouth, full and hard.

I choke, try to push him away, but he's too strong.

My mind clears. *Oh, Tomas, you think you have the better of me. But as long as I live and breathe, I will* never *love you, because my love belongs to another.*

And know this, too: my mind will always be free.

FIVE MINUTES AFTER Tomas leaves me at home, I walk fast to Erna's flat. Thankfully she is there. I'm shaking so much it takes me time, and a long drink of water, before I'm calm enough to talk.

"I can't go through with this, Erna! I can't let them take my baby. They've planned it all!" My voice rises as panic seizes me. There's a viselike grip around my throat, and I can't breathe. Black stars dance in front of my eyes. "They're throwing it in an orphanage . . . a Jewish orphanage . . . and then what?"

"But you always knew—"

"I hoped, prayed, that Tomas would change his mind. It's all he has to do. Let me keep my child. It solves everything, doesn't it? I'm happy because I have my baby, and it is safe because people will think it's Tomas's. He's happy because he has me. Vati is happy because nobody can ever know the truth and his reputation is saved. Mutti is happy because she has a grandchild to love and care for . . ."

The speech exhausts me. I collapse into a chair, heaving air through my narrowed throat.

"But . . . Hetty, right from the beginning, Tomas never said he would let you keep it." Her tone is gentle, but her words, the harsh truth, stab all the same. "To him, this child is abhorrent. It would be like . . . welcoming the enemy, the *devil* into his own home—"

"You're defending him!" I choke out the words. "How can you say such—"

"No! I'm not defending him, never! But you have to be realistic. From his perspective, there is no benefit to him keeping this baby. It's far better for him to have it out of the way. He's never going to let you keep it, Hetty."

"You're right." I watch Erna pace the room, deep in thought.

"Of course you are. I've been so stupid—so soft and pathetic. I've made it all too easy." I sit up straight. "I'll refuse to marry Tomas *unless* he lets me keep the baby. I'll threaten to go to the press. Expose Vati and his affair and his worthless daughter who went with a Jew . . ."

Erna looks appalled. "You can't do that. You know what would happen to you then."

"What?" I challenge, but I don't need to ask. We both know I'd end up in a camp. Vati, for his part in the cover-up, would likely be stripped of his position, his house, his beloved newspaper.

"Your child wouldn't survive, Hetty," Erna says, her face grim. "Truth is, they would take it to a room and smother it. What you're proposing, it isn't an option."

"What has this nation come to? That they would take babies and smother them . . ." My anger has dissolved, replaced by an overwhelming weakness, the feeling of hopelessness.

Erna is nodding, tears in her eyes. "They would, Hetty. I'm so sorry, but they would." She comes to me then, looks into my eyes, and says, "You've no choice but to go along with their plan, for now. I'll . . . I'll try to think of something. I promise."

Fifty-Three

May 20, 1939

My wedding day. The dress, pale yellow, is laid out on the chair next to my bed. It's all folds and layers. Mutti cleverly designed it to distract the eye from my bump. It doesn't feel real, somehow, this day, this marriage. How do I feel? I hear you ask. Well, my darling, I suppose I'm resigned to it. It's not the day I imagined. That fairy tale of white sequins and handsome prince with the happy-ever-after is not for me. I think about you and wonder, should I not be jealous, or angry, that you've gotten away from all this? No. Not a scrap of it. I'm glad you have escaped. That I helped to save your life. Somehow, that thought makes this day bearable. And now I just have to do the same for our baby. So for the present, I go along with this grotesque plan and hope for a miracle.

The room in the Hotel Sachsenhof, on Johannisplatz, is decorated with violets and sprigs of white gypsophila, making it look jolly and bright. Several rows of wooden chairs with cream seats are set out so the few guests can watch our civil ceremony take place. A long table is set at the back of the room for refreshments later in the proceedings.

Tomas, smarter than I've ever seen him, wears a new, light brown suit and patterned tie. His hair is neat, and like the boy who won first prize, he wears a swagger alongside his broad smile.

"You look . . ." He pauses and takes my hands as his eyes flicker over my face, down to my chest, and back to my face. "Radiant," he says. He raises my hand to his lips and winks at me. My guts curdle.

"Now, you remember my mother, Hetty," he says, guiding me toward her. She is a tall woman, strongly built, with cropped graying hair. A dark blue dress hangs awkwardly over her frame, as though neither the dress, nor she, are truly comfortable with the arrangement. In her face is the hard grit that has helped her, and her seven fatherless children, survive.

"So lovely to see you again." I try to smile, but her expression is like a blast of icy air. I glance up at Tomas. He has never once invited me to meet with her. Clearly this was a mistake. Perhaps I should have insisted, before today, but I'd been so wrapped up in myself, it hadn't occurred to me.

"Well, here we are." She looks me up and down. "It's a serious thing, marriage, you know," she says. "Children. A responsibility."

"Yes, and we're prepared for that, aren't we, Tomas?" I grip his hand tightly.

"Of course," he agrees smoothly. "I've told you, Mutti,

Hetty is going to make me a perfect wife and mother. She's a natural."

She makes a noise. Something between a snort and a cough. "It'll be a different life to what you've been used to," she says, narrowing her eyes. "When you've not got maids and cooks and nursemaids to do the daily grind. When you're up all hours of the night with a crying baby and an ailing child and you still have to get breakfast on the table in the morning, scrub all the floors, make the beds, launder the clothes, buy the food . . . Without much money if you've a husband with a taste for beer." She stops to take a breath. "Well, then. The romance tends to go out of it."

I shrink from the bitterness of her words and Tomas puts a protective arm around my shoulders.

"I shan't let Hetty have a life like that. She knows I've got ambition. She knows *that* life is a thing of the past in our new German Reich."

"Huh, that's what you all think, you fools. The young always believe they're going to change the world." She gives a bitter laugh. "But they never do. And you lot won't be any different. False promises, and you've bought them all."

Tomas's jaw is set. "Just remember who you speak with."

"Oh, I do, Tomas." She stares back at him. "Do you think I could ever forget? The ones who stole my husband and sent him to his death—"

"Be quiet! I warned you . . . I should never have let you come." He pokes his finger toward her face, making her take a backward step. "Say another word and you'll be following in his footsteps faster than you know it."

He jerks me hard by the arm and pulls me away from his mother.

"Sorry. I've tried to protect you from her bitter, stupid tongue. Silly cow—"

"Tomas! You shouldn't talk of your mother like that. It's understandable that she feels that way . . ."

"No. She has no right to feel anything except gratitude. My father was nothing but a filthy traitor, and she should disown the bastard. But she won't do it. She won't. She has no vision. Anyway . . . I won't talk about this anymore." His face is red, and his teeth are clenched. "How dare she try to ruin this day for us."

"She hasn't ruined it—"

He looks at me, and his face relaxes.

"No. You're right. She hasn't. She can't. This is going to be one of the best days of my life. And once, well, you know, once we are free to be together properly, well, then I shall be the happiest man on earth."

The room pitches.

"I should like to sit down for a few moments, Tomas."

I sink onto one of the chairs. Tomas goes to speak with Vati, who stands, big and awkward, in the corner of the room, looking as if he would prefer to be anywhere else in the world but here. Tomas's mother has turned her back, shoulders hunched, and is whispering something in the ear of the tallest of Tomas's brothers.

The door opens and Erna, the only person outside the family I've managed to convince them to trust and allow to come, slips inside. Like ice cream on a hot day, she is the most welcome sight. Her eyes dart around the room and she smiles when she sees me sitting alone. She comes to me, her hair neatly braided, her nose freckled from the sun.

"Are you doing okay?" She sits next to me and studies my face.

I swallow. "I don't want to talk about me. Quickly, while there's a chance. Have you thought of anything? Could there be another option?"

"I have . . . contacted a trusted friend." She stops. Her face closes. "It's complicated, Hetty . . . but we're working on things."

"Who is? What things?"

"I can't say more at the moment. I hope to have news soon."

"But I don't have time, Erna!" Invisible hands claw at my throat. "I'm to go to Berlin in just two weeks. Everyone is being told I'm spending a few weeks at Hausfrau school, until closer to the time the baby is due. Vati wants me away as soon as possible. He cannot bear the sight of me."

"Okay, okay." Erna holds her hands up. "We're doing our best."

"I'm sorry."

"Please don't cry, Hetty. Not today. Look, I'll come and visit you soon. Trust me, we'll find a way."

"Herta," Mutti calls, "it's time." She hurries over to me, fiddles with my dress, tidies my hair.

The small wedding party take their seats. Tomas guides me to the front where the official waits for us, solemn faced. The chattering dies and silence descends over the room.

The ceremony begins.

Fifty-Four

May 23, 1939

Mutti and I are in the garden room a few days later when Erna pays a visit in the early afternoon. Mutti is knitting booties; I, a little hat. Rather odd, considering I'm to give this baby away, but we don't speak of this.

"Erna, how good of you to come by," Mutti says, looking up when Vera shows her in.

She has news. I can tell it when our eyes meet for a fraction of a second. But I don't know if it's good or bad. I desperately want Mutti to leave, but she carries on knitting, asking Erna politely about school exams and her parents and her future plans.

Suddenly, I can't bear it any longer.

"Mutti, would you mind if Erna and I take Kuschi for a stroll?"

It stops her midflow.

"We've agreed," she says, "that Vera will take the dog out from now on. And until you get back from your . . . break."

"Yes, but it can't do any harm, can it, Mutti? Just a short walk, with Erna."

She sighs. "I suppose not. Don't go too far, and stay on the quiet roads, yes?"

What she means is, don't go places people we know might see me. The fewer who know, the less explaining we will have to do later.

"No, Mutti. Don't worry, I know the rules."

OUT OF THE house, I can breathe again. Just to feel fresh air on my cheeks and escape the oppressive walls of home is uplifting. With Tomas living in the house, too, the claustrophobia grows. He's moved into Karl's old room. It was Vati's idea. Mutti had visibly stiffened when he suggested it. There are plenty of other spare rooms he could inhabit, so why Karl's? It's right next door to mine, which seemed appropriate, Vati had said. Nobody suggested he should join me, in mine.

In the end Mutti accepted it, but she doesn't like it, and nor do I. The rank factory smell follows Tomas into the house when he returns at the end of a shift. Sometimes beer and cigarettes. It's not for long, he assures me. A few more weeks and he'll be done there forever. Then I shall have to get used to being the wife of an army recruit.

"Thank heavens she let you leave the house," Erna says, as soon as we are out of the gate. "Come to my flat. My father is there, and he'll tell you what can be done."

"You have a plan?"

Erna slips an envelope from her pocket.

"This is for you. From Walter."

My hand trembles as I take it from her. To see his writing on the envelope. My name formed by his fingers.

"Erna—you didn't tell him?"

"Just . . . read it."

I wait until we reach Erna's flat before I open it. Erna goes to be with her father, leaving me and Kuschi alone together in her room.

May 1939

My darling Hetty,

The first thing I must say is do not be angry with your dear friend Erna. I know that you did not want me to know, for the sake of my happiness, what has happened. But she has told me, and she was right to do so. I cannot imagine how you have borne this on your own all these months.

I also cannot write here all the emotions I've felt since I had news of your pregnancy. I am just so sorry, and so full of self-hate that I let this happen, and that I've abandoned you when you need me most. You know that I would desperately love to be with you forever, and to raise our little family together. It would make me happier than you could ever know. But there is little point in dwelling on this, because it is impossible.

Erna has given me the basic facts of your awful situation. That the pregnancy is a secret and once the child is born, your mother has arranged for it to be taken to a Jewish orphanage. Hetty, I do believe the full facts of what is truly planned for us Jews are being suppressed in Germany. Suffice to say here that I worry our baby is in grave danger. For this reason, I believe there is only one solution to give him or her the chance of a decent life.

I have told Anna all about you—about us—and now about this baby. I needn't go into detail, but after many tears and frank discussions, Anna has agreed that, if you are also in agreement, the baby should come to live with us. She will raise it as her own, love and nurture it, as, of course, will I. Anna is afraid that if one day you were ever to come for him or her, you may try to steal me away, too. I have done my best to reassure her, but in my heart of hearts, how can I make such an emphatic promise, when, should you turn up one day at our door, I do not know that I could stay. A large piece of me will always belong to you, and I suppose she can sense that. It is not an easy way to start our married life.

To be writing these words, to think of you reading them, is torture. I want you to know that, whatever we can do to help you, I will move heaven and earth to do it. I cannot bear to think of our child in an orphanage. The priority must be to get him/her out of Germany as soon as possible. It is almost unconscionable to think that anyone would do any harm to a baby, but after what I experienced in that camp, I do not doubt it. In these last six months, I have seen the worst, and also the best, of what humankind is capable of.

Herr Bäcker is working hard to get passage for our baby, as well as for Josef's three children, Lena's boy, and several others, on one of the kindertransports leaving Berlin. We will be fostering all the cousins and Lena's boy. It will be a strange and difficult transition for Anna and me, to go from just the two of us to suddenly being a family of seven! I have no idea how we shall manage, but with the help of Anna's parents, we will somehow make it work. It's quite an extraordinary program, Hetty. English families from all walks of life are stepping forward to offer these complete strangers, these poor traumatized mites, temporary homes, until such time as they can be reunited with their families in a safe place.

I'm writing this in haste to ask if you can agree to this plan? Please think about it and reply soon.

With all my love, now and forever,
Walter

I reach the end of the letter in a flood of tears. I wonder, if I were in Anna's place, would I be so generous? Anna: You have my man, and soon you will have my child. I should hate you even more.

But instead, I feel only love and gratitude.

A soft knock at the door. Erna comes in with a pot of tea and apfelkuchen on a tray. She places it on the bedside table and sits on the edge of the bed, smiling.

"Well?" she asks softly. "What do you think?"

"Oh, Erna . . . Yes, of course yes. A thousand times yes."
I try not to think of the moment I will have to part with this
baby who kicks and squirms inside me. I place a hand on my
belly as though to reassure it. My heart squeezes tight. I focus, instead, on the moment when we can be reunited. When
somehow all this madness is resolved. When I can see Walter
again, even if he is married to another. For the first time, I see
things from Anna's side.

"You must tell Walter I'm married too. It would be better
for his new wife to know that . . . She might find it easier with
the baby if she knows there is no threat. Tell him I'm happy.
Please."

After a pause, Erna nods and squeezes my hand. "Good. My
father is pretty certain, given there is a sponsor for the children
in England, that he can get them a place on the *kindertrans-*
port. The problem is the timing, with your baby not yet born,
and the other children ready to go anytime. But with all the
demand there is a backlog, so the timing could just work out."

"But how are we going to arrange it? I'm to leave for Berlin
soon. I'll be a prisoner in a maternity home . . ."

"Ah, we thought about that, too, and my mother and father
have said you must come and stay here, with us. We know a
Jewish doctor who might be able to help with the birth. We'd
keep it all quiet, of course. All you have to do is convince your
mother—"

"You would do that? For *me*? Surely this could put you all
in danger?"

She laughs at my expression. "I hope you finally understand
how much you mean to me, Hett," she says. "Besides, we *want*

to do something. It feels good to be helping. There is nothing worse than sitting back and being helpless when faced with something so . . . huge . . . you can't fight it. What's happening is so against everything we hold dear. Even if we do something small, help just *one* person, well, that's defiance, isn't it? And that's worth it. Just in itself."

I look at my dear friend in awe. She has been so kind, so brave, and so forgiving. She could easily have turned her back. "Oh, Erna, how can I ever thank you?"

"There's no need."

I bite my fingernails. "I don't know how to get out of going to Berlin."

Erna fixes me with her bright green eyes.

"You have to get your mother on your side. You'll work it out. But right now, we need to send a telegram to Walter and let him know your decision."

Fifty-Five

May 31, 1939

In the quiet of the early morning, I pull out the letter Erna handed over to me yesterday. I reread the words, over and over.

My dearest Hetty,

It is once again in a turmoil of emotion that I find my-self writing. I'm relieved, terrified, devastated, and filled with overwhelming love at your decision to send our baby to England. I dare to hope that one day, you will be able to follow and that this will somehow turn out to be for the best, and we will all be reunited.

Erna also tells me that you are married to Tomas. In all honesty, I have struggled to come to terms with this. My reaction was utter disbelief, but she swore this was what you wanted, and that Tomas has been very good to you. If this is true, then I will try my best to be happy for you. But this cannot be the truth. I find it strange, to say the least, that Tomas should take a wife already expecting another man's child. I also believe I know you well enough to know this can't be what you really want. I suspect that you, like me, have been swept along by events over which you have no control. I suppose we are neither of us in this situation out of our own choosing.

I also want you to know that Anna is a good, forgiving person and I know without any hesitation that she will treat our baby with love and tenderness. Were things different, I feel certain the two of you would easily become the best of friends. Know only this, my dearest love, I will never stop loving you, from this day until my very last.

Yours,
Walter

Tomas and Vati are eating breakfast and reading the morning papers when I come into the dining room. Mutti has not yet appeared. It still gives me a jolt to see Tomas sitting in Karl's chair at the table.

Vati glances at me as I come in. He folds his paper and slurps the dregs from his coffee cup.

"I must be off," he says, pushing back his chair. "Busy day."

Don't worry, Vati, just a few more days and I won't be here to pollute the atmosphere and offend you any longer.

"Morning, darling," Tomas says, watching me help myself to juice and slices of bread.

He reaches for my hand as I sit across the table from him,

drawing his fingers across my skin. I pull my hand away and begin buttering the bread. "I shall hunt for a place for us to live, while you are away," he continues. "It'll take my mind off your absence. Just seven more weeks at that *arschloch* factory. I can't wait to get out of there. I begin my training mid-September, so we shall have some time together before that. Then I will be close by for twelve weeks. After that, who knows? There are rumors, you know."

"What rumors?"

"That Germany will take Poland."

"What do you mean?"

"We need more space. And the Poles . . ." The skin on his face contracts. "I *hate* them."

Mutti hurries into the room.

"Goodness, I overslept this morning! I haven't done that since . . ." She doesn't finish the sentence. She pats her neat hair, smooths her dress.

Tomas folds the paper and taps the front of it. "See that?"

I look at the images of smiling war veterans proudly raising gold medals for the photographs. "5,000 German Soldiers Return from Spain Triumphant!" the headline proclaims. "Göring Awards Medals for Valor."

"One day," Tomas says, "I plan to make *you* proud by winning a medal of my own." Mutti has her back turned, helping herself to coffee from the sideboard. Her shoulders hunch, and I frown at his thoughtless words. "But for now"—he sighs, as he gets up—"I'll have to make do with dreaming about it." He kisses my forehead as he leaves.

At last, I have Mutti alone. I wait until she has drunk her

first cup of coffee, smoked her first cigarette, and is relaxed in her chair with the newspaper.

"Mutti," I say, before she becomes engrossed, "I need to talk to you about something."

She looks at me expectantly. My mind goes blank. I need the right words. Exactly the right words.

"Well?"

"The plan," I begin, "for me to travel to Berlin on Saturday . . ."

"We've been over this, Hetty, lots of times."

"I know. But . . . please let me say something. Hear me out before you reply—"

"Nothing is going to change, whatever you say. I thought this might happen. The closer it got to the end." Mutti's body is upright and stiff. Unyielding.

"Please. Just . . . listen."

She shrugs her shoulders and lights another cigarette. I gag slightly; the smell of smoke still induces nausea.

"I know you all see me as a problem to solve. And I know how you feel about . . . the baby. But I'm speaking to you now as a mother. A mother who gave birth to two babies. Who must know how it feels to carry a new life around inside her for nine months. To grow attached to that life, more than you ever thought possible, even though you've never met that person . . ." Mutti has her lips pursed and is shaking her head.

My mouth is dry, and I take a gulp of fruit juice.

"I'm not suggesting a change to the ultimate outcome. I know I can't keep this baby, because of who its father is. But I can't let it go to that orphanage. Through . . . a friend . . . we've found an alternative. To send the baby to its father, in England, where it will be well looked after and safe. I just want it to be loved and have a chance—"

"No! Absolutely not, Herta. I've spent a lot of time making these arrangements. You cannot expect me to change—"

"Mutti, please—"

"You are infuriating! It's out of the question. What if this were to get out? You realize Vati would be ruined? His good reputation is vital to his career, to *everything* we have. He has worked so hard to get to where he is. I cannot jeopardize that, even if I wanted to. No, what's been arranged keeps everything tight. Very few people know anything, and I'm paying a fortune to those Jewish pigs, a fortune to keep their mouths *shut* . . ." Her eyes widen. "Who have you been speaking to? You were warned to tell *no one.*"

"Mutti, it's fine. Don't worry, the secret is safe. I promise you—"

"What does it take to make you learn, Herta? Time and time again you do this . . ."

She's getting angry. She begins to jiggle her leg.

"Mutti—"

"You know I would *never* go against your father's wishes. I would never be disloyal to him. This is an *utterly* pointless discussion."

"There's a thing or two you should know about Vati's loyalty," I cry out in anger and desperation. It's time she learned the truth about her precious husband. I've kept his dirty secret for long enough and I couldn't care less about sparing her feelings anymore. "Things I've found out. Things Vati wouldn't want others, *especially* you—"

She holds up a hand. "Stop right there," she says, her voice hard. "Don't say a word more."

I meet her eyes. And then I see it.

"For Christ's sake." I exhale. "You know, don't you?"

"Of course I know. Do you think I'm stupid?" Her leg is jiggling again. Up and down, like a piston.

"Why? Why do you put up with it?"

"What choice, exactly, do you think I have, hmm? I put up with it, *because I have to*. And I love him." Her eyes fill with tears. "Without him, I am nothing. So I fill my time with other things, I close my mind to it, and we carry on. He pretends it's not happening, and I pretend the same. That's how it is. We all have our shadows, Hetty. The demons that keep us awake at night. Don't think your life will be any different, because it won't be."

"Oh, Mutti . . ."

She dries her eyes and pours herself another coffee.

"As long as he thinks I *don't* know, everything will carry on. Everything will be okay."

There is desperation in her voice, as though she is telling herself this because she doesn't quite believe it, and she hangs on to it. Like a lifeline. But none of this is helpful. My brain whirs.

"Then you understand, Mutti, even better than I thought, what it is to lose both the love of your life and your child."

"Yes," she says, looking at me. "Yes, I suppose I do."

"Then *help me*. You don't wish the same fate for me, do you? This can be *our* secret. Vati must never know. You deserve to keep something from him. This is your *grandchild*, Mutti.

Your grandchild fathered by the boy who saved your daughter from drowning all those years ago. Together, we can do this, Mutti. Do it for me, and do it for *you*."

She looks at me in silence for a long time.

At last, she opens her mouth to speak.

"What, exactly, is it you need me to do?" she says.

Fifty-Six

July 24, 1939

Perhaps Mutti does really love me, after all. Perhaps having lost her own dear son, in some strange way she is the only one who truly understands. And so here I am, as far as Vati and Tomas know, holed up in Berlin, awaiting the imminent arrival of the bastard brat. But instead, I'm just a few streets away, grateful beyond words to Erna and her parents for all they are doing for me. I have the small attic room next door to Erna's room. It has just a single bed, a wardrobe, and a chest of drawers. It's comfortable enough, and through the little window under the eaves, I have wonderful views of Leipzig.

A knock at the door.

"Yes?" I say, instinctively closing the book and shoving it behind me.

Frau Bäcker's head appears around the door.

"I'm just checking you are all right," she says, assessing me with a look of concern.

"I'm fine," I tell her with a smile.

"Are you sure? Have the pains gone away?"

"No, but they aren't bad. Not yet. Truly," I reassure her.

She nods. "Well. Let me know if there's anything you need. Or if you want me to call the doctor." Her forehead creases. "Perhaps I should do that, anyway, before it gets too late in the evening?"

"Really. I'm fine. I promise I'll let you know."

She smiles and backs out of the room, closing the door quietly behind her. Once I'm certain she's gone back downstairs, I continue.

> The pains have been coming, on and off, for a few days. Discomfort, rather than pain. It's hard to know what to do with myself. I'm so big now, my abdomen tight and swollen. The Jewish doctor, Dr. Kaufman, who retired from doctoring years ago, partly because he's old but mostly because he isn't allowed to treat Germans, and who has been engaged by Frau Bäcker to care for me, is a kindly man, with a gray beard and sad, watery eyes. He knows of Walter's family and has been acting as liaison between me and them, as well as helping the Bäckers communicate with the families they are trying to help in the Jewish house.

I put down my pen. This is more than discomfort now. I pace up and down the little attic room. My back aches and I rub it as I walk. I control my breathing, like I've been told to. In, out. In, out. The pain grips and bites, growls around my underbelly. In my pocket is the handkerchief Walter gave me the day he told me he was getting married and leaving for England. I finger it as I pace and it comforts me. The pain eases, and I sit on the bed again. I want to finish the diary entry. There's so much I want to say, but I have just one last page to fill, and then this book will be complete.

> *Walter said to me once that he thinks all people—Germans, Jews; Nordic or Africans; Slavs or Americans—we all have the same capacity for good or evil. That no one race is different from any other. He said that although some individuals are worse than others, everyone is a mixture of both. But I know this is wrong. Perhaps he's right about most of us, but not all. Some people really are better. They sacrifice so much for the good of others. Their own safety, their own lives. These are the real heroes among us. The ones who possess so much strength of mind and fortitude, not to take the easy route, no matter what personal cost is to be paid.*
>
> *The Bäckers are such people. Others may think they are like them. But few would match up. They are as rare as the Lady's Slipper orchid, and more precious. One day I truly hope I will find a way to thank them.*

I drop my pen, gripped by a wave of pain so fierce I cry out. In the few moments that it eases, I scrabble for the pen on the floor and place it, with the journal, back inside the bedside drawer, on top of the small pile of letters Tomas has written, delivered surreptitiously by Mutti to a box at the post office.

Another wave of pain, stronger than the last. I break out in a sweat. My breathing becomes ragged. I reach for the door.

"Frau Bäcker?"

She appears at the base of the narrow stairs to the attic.

"It's getting worse," I tell her, my voice breaking as the pain grips again. I bend double on the landing.

"It's all right," she soothes. "I've already called Dr. Kaufman. Hermann?" she calls to her husband. "Boil water and fetch fresh towels from the linen cupboard. Quickly now. Erna, come with me."

The pain is all consuming. I'm enslaved to it; I walk, sit, lie, sway, bend to its demands.

Why does love end in pain?

I try to remember the fun Walter and I had together. The endless walks by the river. His kisses, tender and sweet. The light in his eyes when he met mine. His words, his hands, the warmth of his body against me. His dear, beautiful face.

Oh, Walter, how I miss you.

And the pain overwhelms me once again.

DR. KAUFMAN IS trying to get me, freshly shaved and the enema having done its trick, to lie on the bed. But I don't want to lie on the bed. It feels all wrong, lying on my back with the great weight of the baby pressing down. So I'm on all fours, making a slow crawling circuit around the room, bathed in sweat, groaning with each building mountain of pain. As the light outside fades, the louder I groan. In some weird way, this eases the suffering.

"I wasn't able to get ahold of any sedative," Dr. Kaufman says apologetically. "It's very difficult for me to get any supplies."

"Just do whatever you can to help her," Frau Bäcker says, wringing her hands. "We've tried our best to sterilize the room. I've boiled all the towels and bed linen . . ."

I'm tossed over and over on great waves of agony. Time rolls by until I've lost all track of it. Minutes pass, or hours. I've no idea. I'm inside myself. Deep inside. Conversation between Dr. Kaufman, Erna, and her mother goes on above me. I swirl in and out of it. I rock back and forth, possessed and controlled by some animal instinct. I've lost all other care for anything.

Why in hell's name do people have babies?

"I need to listen to the baby's heartbeat," Dr. Kaufman tells me gently. "I need you to get onto the bed so that I can check it is okay."

"No," I tell him. "I'm not getting on the bed."

"I need to examine you. Down there"—he points between my legs—"I have to see how close to the birth you are . . ."

"No way," I shout. "I'm not getting on the bed and you're not looking at me!"

I begin to sob and resume my crawling.

"It's been hours now," I hear Dr. Kaufman tell Erna and Frau Bäcker. "I'm worried the baby has become stuck. I really need to perform an examination, but she won't allow me. She's getting more and more tired. She will need the energy to push, when the time comes. Assuming everything is okay."

"What do you mean?" Erna's voice is anxious. "Why would it be stuck?"

"Any number of reasons," Dr. Kaufman replies. "The cord might be caught around the baby's neck. The position might be wrong. The head might be too big. She's young. It's a first baby. Sometimes it's complicated. You know, it is only me and there are limited things I can do. I have forceps but . . ."

"All right," I snap. "I'll get on the bed."

I try to stand, but my head swirls with pain.

"I can't," I cry. "I just can't." I sink back to the floor.

I'm swept up under the armpits and the three of them haul me onto the bed. As they pull me upright, a rush of fluid floods down my legs.

"I'm sorry . . ."

"It's okay, just the waters breaking. This is a good sign," Dr. Kaufman says.

I'm vaguely aware that Erna is clearing up the mess.

From the bed, I can see out the window. The gray light tells me dawn is breaking. I hadn't even noticed it got dark.

Dr. Kaufman's head is bent over my belly, listening with his stethoscope. His face scrunches. He meets my eyes.

"What," I gasp.

"It's . . . it's all right. But the baby's heart rate is very fast. Too fast. It can be a bad sign. Perhaps the cord . . . We need to get this baby out quickly. I have to see how dilated you are."

He pulls my knees apart and I wince at the discomfort.

"Herta," he says, his voice gravelly and low. "I must get this baby born as fast as possible. You must be brave now and still."

I groan. I'm so exhausted I just want to sleep, but suddenly the urge to push is too strong. I'm going to split in two.

Dr. Kaufman is listening with his stethoscope again, but he is shaking his head and clicking his tongue. He has Erna and her mother running to and fro, gathering towels and water, and he's splashing Lysol solution between my legs. My brain is working too slow to understand what is about to happen as he pulls long, tapered scissors from his bag. Erna and Frau Bäcker are each holding firm to one of my legs and I scream with the burning flare of pain as he slices the scissors through my flesh. I'm screaming and screaming and writhing and they fight to hold me still. He has another instrument in his hand, bigger than the last, but the pain is so intense that I'm swept under a carpet of darkness.

Consciousness returns as Dr. Kaufman inserts the big instrument inside me and begins to haul and twist and pull the baby from my body. Erna and Frau Bäcker still have hold of my legs, which they have pushed hard against each side of me.

"Push," yells Dr. Kaufman, "push as hard as you can!"

I push and push, and Dr. Kaufman pulls, and suddenly, in a bloody gush, the baby slithers out.

For a beat, the room is still. The baby lies on the bed between my legs, a thick, twisted purple cord joining us together. Dr. Kaufman cuts the cord.

"It's a boy," someone says.

Then silence.

Dr. Kaufman is slapping the baby on his back. He's a red-purple color, like raw steak.

Time ticks.

He turns the baby over, wipes his nose and mouth.

"Come on, come on," he says to him.

We all stare.

The silence is more than I can bear.

He coughs. A tiny movement. Then a bigger one. At last, a small cry, then a full-on howl. The tension in the room breaks and suddenly everyone is smiling, laughing, crying. They wrap him in a towel and Dr. Kaufman hands him to me to hold.

"Thank you," I whisper, "thank you, thank you."

He delivers the placenta and cleans me up, stitching the cuts to my flesh. I barely notice though, because for the first time, I'm staring into the face of my baby boy.

And suddenly I know love, like I have never known it before.

Fifty-Seven

August 1, 1939

His head is covered in downy hair, so fair it is almost transparent. He smells of warm milk and biscuits. He has deep blue eyes, and already he focuses them so meaningfully on mine. We are one, he and I. It's as though he can read my mind and I, his. He wants to know me. His eyes trace every contour and line of my face with such avid attention that his little mouth forms an "o" shape as he pants with excitement and his arms and legs thrash about.

I examine every inch of his body, over and over. I never imagined I was capable of producing anything so perfect. His hand wraps itself firmly around my finger and he grips with surprising strength, but he doesn't yet know how to let go. When I lift him, his legs scrunch up and his back curls over as though he doesn't realize he has all the space in the world to stretch out. And when I feed him, his fingers reach and grab at my skin, just as a tiny kitten would knead its mother as it suckles.

He is a thing of extraordinary wonder.

And more precious to me than anything in the universe.

I can hardly bear to sleep, because when I do, I'm not conscious of his presence. Time moves too fast, and each night that falls and each day that dawns brings the dreaded parting closer. I kiss his forehead and gently wipe away my tears that land on the soft down of his head.

Under the sloping eaves I imagine this is a safe and cozy nest. That the steady marching boots that tramp outside through the streets of Leipzig, Berlin, and all the other towns and cities of Germany cannot get to us. If only we could hide up here forever.

We need to come up with a name for this tiny human. Time is running out to register his birth before the inevitable day of our separation.

George. Henry. William. Edward. The names of English kings. You can't get more English than that.

No. I want something simple. A name so he will fit. That other English children might have. I need to get this right as I shall play no other part in his life, for how long, who knows? All I can give him is a name, so it had better be a good one.

A distant memory of being with Mutti and Vati in Berlin a long, long time ago emerges. I must have been around seven or eight years old. It was a hot day and I was dangling my hands under a refreshing stream of water falling from the mouth of a strange mythical stone creature at the top of a fountain. Nearby was a street café with tables and chairs outside on the pavement. A little boy, younger than me, kept climbing down from his seat and running toward the fountain, his mother in pursuit. Vati tut-tutted at the lack of discipline the English have over their children. *Stanley*, the mother had called after him repeatedly. *Stanley.* The lady spoke fast and firmly to the little boy, but I could only pick out a few words as it was all in English. I understood "sit" and "father" and "now," but the rest was lost on me. To my amazement, the little boy ignored his mother and laughed. That's why I remember, because in my young life, I had never witnessed any child so openly disobeying. He ran around and around that fountain and laughed and laughed as if everything in his life were pure, sweet joy.

I stare down at the little boy nestled in my arms. I lay him, sleeping peacefully now, in the empty drawer lined with soft blankets and padding. I could leave him awhile and join Erna and her parents in the sitting room. But I don't want him to be all alone.

Instead I take out Walter's letter, the one he sent the moment he heard of the birth, and read it for the thousandth time.

> *My darling,*
>
> *I'm scribbling this note in dreadful haste. I received the telegram this morning from Erna with the news of our son's birth. I'm in such torment. I am of course relieved and overjoyed to know you are both well. But thinking of you bearing this alone and soon having to part with this baby, I know how this must be killing you. I have walked the streets of London all morning with tears pouring down my cheeks, thinking of you.*
>
> *It's not been easy at home. I suppose I have been rather difficult to live with. Anna knows how I think of you. If she is jealous, she never says, and she is handling this*

situation with fortitude and bravery. I admire her more than ever. And I can tell you, she will shower our baby and my poor cousins with such love. We will do our very best to make them feel at home here. I know that is little consolation. But in my heart of hearts, I'm sure that one day it will be possible for you to be a proper mother to our son. I hope and pray to God that that day will come sooner than we all think.

Stay strong, my darling Hetty. Things will get better, and please know that I love you more than ever before. This will never change.

You are in my heart, now and always,
Walter

"Hetty?" Erna pokes her head around the door. "Are you okay?"

"He's asleep," I say, folding the letter and putting it away. "I didn't want to leave him."

She sits next to me and smiles at the baby asleep in his nest of blankets. His two little fists are clenched and stick straight up above his head.

"Oh, Hetty," she says, "isn't he just perfect?"

I look at my friend in wonder. She's seen me at my lowest. She has watched me give birth. She has cleaned up my blood. She is risking her own life for me. How can I ever repay such a person?

"I've thought of a name," I tell her. "He is going to be called Stanley."

Fifty-Eight

August 18, 1939

For three weeks and two days, the sun rises and sets. Very early in the morning of the twenty-fourth day since Stanley was born, I am wide awake and stand at the little dormer window in Erna's attic room.

I watch him sleeping, cuddled in close to my chest. His eyes flicker beneath the pale lids, dark lashes delicately curled. His chest rises and falls, calm and gentle. He breathes through partly opened lips. Every now and then his little brow furrows, as if he knows what is to become of him. As if he is struggling to understand it all.

But why are you sending me away?

Because I love you too much to keep you.

Erna and her mother will be here soon, to take him from me. We've all agreed it's better that I stay behind. They will travel with him, together with Josef's children, Lena's boy, and five others—ten in all—to Berlin, where the children alone will board a train to Hamburg. Then on to Rotterdam and to Harwich. They will be in the company of hundreds of other lost and confused Jewish children, sent away by desperate parents, bound for the safety of England. Walter will meet them at Harwich and take the five children to their new home.

If only I could go with them, and never come back.

But the doors to the rest of the world have been slammed shut, and only a trickle of children are allowed to dash through the last tiny crack before England's door closes too. Stanley must go now, and I will have to take my chances here.

I've written his name and his father's name on the label to go around his neck, like a parcel to be sent in the post. His papers are prepared, stamped, and waiting with his little case of clothes, diapers, tins of evaporated milk and bottles, and a cardigan of mine that will smell of me. It might help calm him if he becomes agitated. I wonder how Stanley's fifteen-year-old cousin, who has never met him, but will care for him on the journey, will cope.

I must have faith that all will go well.

Because faith is all I have left.

There is one more thing that must go into the case. I open the drawer and take out my journal, filled to the very last page with my neat handwriting. I place it carefully beneath the clothes. If the worst should happen, and I am never reunited with my son, this is his story. Everything is here, the best and the worst of me. It will be up to Walter and Anna if they ever decide to share it with him.

There is a knock at the door.

"Come in," I say, not taking my eyes off Stanley.

"Hello." Erna comes to stand next to me. "It's time," she says quietly.

I nod, but don't move.

"My father is waiting outside. We must meet the other children at the station in half an hour, if we're to make the first train to Berlin," she adds. "I'm sorry, Hetty, but we really don't have much time."

"Yes. I know," I say. "Just give me one minute. I'll bring him down."

She nods and closes the door behind her.

"Well. This is it," I tell Stanley. "I want you to have a good life. And I want you to know that I love you, and always will. I hope somehow, this awful prospect of war will go away, and that, very soon, I shall find a way to come for you. And I will come for you, my darling boy. I promise you that. I will come for you."

Cuddling him close, I plant a kiss on his forehead and drag my eyes away to look out the window. It is a glorious view. Higher than most of the surrounding buildings, I look eastward out over rooftops, trees, and squares. The sun has not yet appeared over the horizon and the clouds, drifting away from the pool of yellow light, are lit red, then pink, fading to deep purple and charcoal where the rays have not yet reached.

The light in the sky grows quickly, becoming ever more intense and changing the color of the clouds as I watch. They become paler, pink and fluffy, then white where the light is strongest. Suddenly, the top of the sun appears, a brilliant curve of shimmering gold, its rays finally penetrating the very edges of darkness in the sky. It grows above the horizon with incredible speed until the whole sky is lit for a moment, like a pool of yellow fire.

The birth of a new day.

Epilogue

June 1994

My dear Walter,

I realize that this letter will come quite out of the blue, so I hope you are sitting down. It has taken me almost five years of work to trace your whereabouts. Well, two years of thinking about it, and not really knowing where to start, if I'm completely honest. It's been a long story of false starts and dead ends, but I'm persistent if nothing else, and with the aid of, can you believe it, a Jewish charity in America, I've found you at last.

I thought long and hard whether to send this. Whether to risk trying to find out what happened to you, my first love, and, of course, to my son, who I knew only for the first three weeks of his life. Suffice to say, not an hour of any day in the last fifty-five years has gone by without thought of him. I have lived the bulk of my life with a piece of my heart severed and, I have hoped, living a happy life in England. After the war, life under the Soviets was indescribably hard. Each day was a battle for survival. I *wanted to try to find you, but as time went on it became impossible, and I also came to believe it would be for the best, for you and for Stanley, if I stayed out of your lives. But I am getting older every day, and I do not want to go to my grave not knowing what happened to my son, and of course to you, dear Walter. And so, here I am.*

There is no quick or easy way to sum up the last fifty-plus years. For the most part, I suppose, one just gets on with the day-to-day business of living and working. I try not to think of the war years, full as they were of terror and hardships and the communication restrictions. I try not to think of the horrific years that followed, and the trauma rendered by our Russian occupiers. This may be a conversation for another time. But once that passed, and life became tolerable again, I did, you shall be pleased to know, go back to finish my education. Unlike the Hitler years, the Communists did allow us women some modicum of equality of opportunity, even though it was more a question of necessity than a true vision or openness of spirit.

But it did mean that after some years, I was able to realize that dream of becoming a doctor. Not quite the type I once envisaged. No, but one rather desperately required. I became a doctor of psychotherapy, now retired. I worked all my life with children, trying to put back together the pieces of broken minds, and in so doing, I suppose I went some way to nursing my own. And one other thing I achieved, of lesser importance but no less meaningful. I overcame my fear of water! I used to swim every day during the summer. Each time I did, I thought of you, and how you would have been proud. It made me smile to think of it.

I never had any more children of my own. My marriage to Tomas was short-lived and not a happy one. He was sent to the front before the end of our first year together and did not see his twentieth birthday. I had no interest in remarrying then. I focused first on survival, and second on my work. But, much later in life, long after I'd given up on ever again finding personal happiness, I met Max, an older, uncomplicated man, with the gentlest of hearts. We married and we were happy. He died twelve years ago.

And what of the others? Vati committed suicide when Berlin fell. Mutti never stopped believing in the Nazi dream nor in the greatness of her husband. Eventually, she died, too, of a broken heart. I'm so grateful that Karl never saw the horrors that were to come. I never knew what became of Hilda and little Sophie. After the war, I moved away to a small town far from Leipzig.

And your family, Walter? I think of them often. I know they were all, in the end, sent to Buchenwald and from there, I suspect, on to Auschwitz or Theresienstadt. I cannot imagine the pain and suffering they must have gone through. It haunts me to this day.

But most of all I remember Erna and her parents, without whom I would not be sitting here today. All three of them, beacons of goodness, perished in a camp. One day in the autumn of 1942 I went to their flat, and they were gone. The flat was turned upside down. There was no warning, and not a day goes by when I don't think of my wonderful friend Erna, and her halo of auburn hair, destined to be forever young in my memory.

Nor shall I ever forget the day I had to send Stanley away. I think of the thousands of other mothers who did the same, feeling their pain as they sent their own precious children into the unknown, desperately entrusting them to strangers. And I think of the countless parents who were unable to save their children's lives.

And never for one day will I forget what I once was, when I was one of the believers. It was you, dear Walter, who first turned my head and made me see that people are people, regardless of anything else. It was you who made me understand that we all have immense capacity for both good and evil. That we must stand up and speak out against those who preach hate. Every day that I live I wish the Nazis had never come to power, that the camps had never existed. Every day I live with the shame and guilt of the part I once played and will do so until my dying day.

Walter, I hope this letter hasn't come as too much of a shock. I should dearly love to know my son, just a little. If it is only to know he is alive and well. I realize that it might be too much to ask of him, and you and your family, but I dream that one day I can meet him in person. You may never, of course, have told him anything of his *past, and if you would prefer for me to stay away, then of course I shall honor your wishes.*

At present, I could not possibly afford a trip to England, so for now, I would be incredibly happy just to hear from you.

With love and best wishes,
Herta Roth (Heinrich)

London
Summer 1995

For the third time I check the address on the crumpled piece of paper in my hand, then look again at the number over the door of the café. This is definitely the right place.

I take a deep breath and push open the door. A little bell jangles somewhere out the back as I enter the warm, coffee-scented room. A couple sit holding hands in the corner next to the window. The only other customer is an elderly man reading a newspaper, its pages spread all over the wooden table in front of him. I read *The Sunday Times* in large letters on the discarded front cover. I should have done that. Brought a newspaper. It would have been something to do. Something to make me look less conspicuously alone. And good practice for my English.

I'm forty minutes early. But better this way than to be late. I'd been so afraid of getting lost, or something going wrong, I barely slept last night.

A young girl appears behind the counter. She looks at me expectantly.

"Can I help you?" she asks.

"A black coffee, if you please." I speak carefully, trying hard with my pronunciation.

"Sure. Anything else?" she asks.

There is a huge array of cakes and pastries arranged on display behind the glass counter. My mouth begins to salivate at the sight of them.

"And I'll take one of those, too." I smile at the waitress and point to a twisted pastry with blanched almonds on the top and something that looks deliciously sweet and creamy oozing from the middle. "And how much is the cost?" I hope I'm using the correct English grammar.

"Don't worry. Take a seat and I'll bring it all over. You can pay at the end, when you've finished." She nods toward the tables.

It seems very self-indulgent to eat such a thing so soon after breakfast. Even though all the years of deprivation are long gone, there is an overwhelming urge to treat myself. Just in case it is all taken away again.

Besides. It will help to pass the time.

"Thank you. You are most kind," I say.

The waitress gives me a warm smile. The other customers don't even look up. No one seems bothered by my German accent.

But that's silly of me. Why on earth would they be? The war was half a century ago. The couple by the window are too young to know anything of it. Perhaps the man did, though. I stare at his profile as he reads, engrossed in something. I certainly still flinch if I hear a Russian accent. Try as I might, it isn't possible to block all they subjected us to from my memory. People might wonder why I let those soldiers do what they did to me. Why I never bothered to put up a fight. But it was survival. You did whatever you had to for a piece of bread.

London is like a different planet. Foreign, full of wonder, and terrifying all at the same time. I've been locked behind the Iron Curtain for over forty years. Once the worst years were past, we settled into a day-to-day life that was pleasant enough. As long as we had food, and a roof over our heads, that was enough. It lacked luxury, but it was certain, cohesive, and everyone was the same. Here, life feels precarious and chaotic. I can imagine all this speed and freedom is exciting for the young, but for my generation, the crumbling socialist blocks are safe and familiar, like comfortable old shoes. Yesterday, I walked for miles around London, staring up at the shiny towers of metal and glass, the smart houses and shops full of *stuff*. So many big, expensive cars. So much noise and bustle. It's frenetic. Bewildering.

While I wait, I sip my coffee and will myself to eat the sweet pastry and its almond filling slowly. I take tiny bites to make it last longer, savoring each mouthful. I watch my own hands tremble at the thought of what is to come.

I open my handbag and there, tucked between my purse and the folded, off-white square of Walter's handkerchief, which, after all these years I still carry with me as though it is a lucky charm, is the envelope containing the response to that first letter I sent to England over a year ago. I needn't take it out. I've memorized its contents. I leave the letter where it is and instead find my lipstick and mirror. I reapply the pink sheen to my lips, snap the mirror shut, and place both back in the bag.

The café door swings open and the room fills with new-comers. An elderly woman with gray hair tightly wound into a bun on the top of her head comes in first. She is slight, with bright brown eyes and a long, narrow face, and instantly I know it's her. Anna.

Tucked beneath her arm is a book, the colors of its textured cover in faded, geometric patterns. It's as much as I can do not to cry out at the sight of it. I swallow down the lump in my throat.

Behind her is a slightly built, middle-aged man. His face is open and pleasant, and his light brown hair is flecked with gray at the temples and cut short. He glances around and I catch the light blue eyes and high cheekbones. My heart skips.

My son.

I might have passed him on the street and not known he was mine. All those missed years. My throat tightens and my eyes well up. Will I ever know him now? Properly know him? Will he ever call me Mutti and come to me when he has a problem? Unlikely. A lifetime of memories have been stolen from me, but he is alive, and he looks well and happy. That is all a mother could ultimately want for her child.

He meets my eyes and we gaze at each other. I can't read his expression, and no doubt he cannot read mine, either. We are strangers, my Stanley and me. Everyone here, the café, the clink of china cup against saucer, the smell of freshly ground coffee, the background chatter—it all fades away. It is just us. I have dreamed of the moment I would be reunited with my son for fifty-six years. That it is happening, right here, now, is too vast to take in. I'm numb, almost, with the shock of it. We are really here, in the same country, standing in the same room. This man, searching my eyes, just a few short feet away. What can he think of me, a daughter of the Reich, who abandoned him as a baby. I'm shaking with fear and emotion. But then he dips his chin into a nod and smiles, warm and unjudging, and I feel a rush of gratitude. We will be okay, Stanley and me. It may take some time, but we will be okay.

He stands to one side to enable a boy of around fifteen to come through the door. Long-legged and already taller than his father, awkward in his own body and hiding behind a curtain of dark hair.

My grandson?

Now a girl, presumably the boy's older sister. She glances around the café and her enormous blue eyes meet my gaze. My breath catches in my throat. The resemblance is extraordinary. She wears a big floppy sweater over ripped jeans and her long, dark curls bounce over her shoulders. It is as though I am looking at my seventeen-year-old self. Strange to think that at her age, I had already given birth to Stanley.

I wish there was one more figure to come through that door. But there are no more. I think of the letter, written in an unfamiliar hand in my handbag, the contents of which are imprinted in my mind.

My dear Hetty,

I am writing this hasty response to catch the next post, so you do not have to wait a moment longer for a reply to your wonderful letter. I shall send you another, longer and more detailed, in the next day or so. I send this with mixed emotions—firstly of joy to find you are indeed alive. Walter never gave up hope of trying to find you, after the war. He spent years making fruitless in-quiries, and only found dead ends. But then communi-cation with East Germany became almost impossible for an outsider. We feared you had not survived the war. To find out you are alive and well is indescribably won-derful. And so now for the bad news. I am so sorry to have to tell you; Walter passed away three years ago, very suddenly, of a heart attack. Walter, as well you know, was the best of men. During the war, he played his part in fighting the Nazis. Suffice to say here that he was extremely brave. He ran a successful hat busi-ness until his dying day. He diversified away from furs as the world rather turned away from such material, into the couture world of ladies' hats! He was always charming and the ladies, of course, loved him. But he was a good husband and we—Stanley, the cousins, and our own children (we have three)—remain devas-tated to have lost a wonderful husband, father, and uncle, and I hate to have to tell you such sad news by letter. But, Stanley, your remarkable son, is alive and well. He is a successful lawyer, married, and has two *children of his own—teenagers now, one boy, one girl. I have been lucky to have been part of his life—he is a joy. It is inconceivable that you should not visit. We will make arrangements. Stanley has done well in life and we shall pay for your trip over. You are welcome to stay for as long as you like. I will write again soon.*

Yours,
Anna

Anna approaches my table and I stand. For a moment we stare at each other, blue eyes searching brown. There is no hint of hatred, only sadness. Understanding, perhaps. But there is something else, too. A glimmer I can read because it is this which has kept me going through the darkest of times.

Hope.

And Anna, the woman I have never met until now, who has haunted my dreams for half a lifetime, comes forward and enfolds me in the warmest of embraces.

Acknowledgments

I owe so many people, so much, for the existence of this book. Expressing my appreciation here seems a small and paltry return for the time, generosity, and support I have received from so many. In time, I hope that I may somehow repay you all. This book is as much yours as it is mine.

First, enormous thanks to my wonderful agent, Caroline Hardman, and all at Hardman & Swainson, for believing in this book and in me as an author. You have made all my dreams come true. To Liz Stein and the team at William Morrow, and to Hannah Smith and the team at Head of Zeus, for your enthusiasm and insightful expertise, and for helping to shape this book into its better self. It has been an absolute pleasure to work with all of you.

To Dr. Hubert Lang, Dr. Andrea Lorz, and Dr. Thomas Töpfer at the Schulmuseum, Leipzig, my heartfelt thanks for your patience and careful answering of my many and varied questions. Your generosity of time and knowledge was invaluable. Also, to the late Peter Held, who, as a true gentleman in his nineties, welcomed me, a total stranger, with open arms and entertained my sister and me at a memorable and wonderful lunch. You so kindly dug into painful memories from a very long time ago. I am sad that you never got to see this project of mine come to fruition.

To Russell Schechter, David Savill, and Scott Bradfield, my MA tutors who helped me to write so much better and taught me the value of tough critiquing. Huge thanks also to my wonderful MA and writing group friends: Lara Dearman, Andy Howden, Jennifer Small, Magdalena Duke, and Gwen Emmerson, for your insightful commentary, the camaraderie, friendship, and ongoing support. You are all brilliant, and I'm not sure what I would have done without you. To the generous, supportive, and talented bunch that are the Savvy Writers' Snug; what a wonderful group of colleagues and friends you are.

Thanks to my early readers: Suzanne Miller, Karen Kelly, Brenda Fein, Julian Pike, Millie Pike, Josh Pike, Diane Pike, Jane Elliot, Shauna Bartlett, and Shannon Monroe Ashton. Your comments and support have been invaluable. To the truly fabulous Stephanie Roundsmith of Cornerstones, who rescued me when I was ready to throw this manuscript in the bin. Without you, this book would not have seen the light of day. You helped so much, in so many ways; I owe you one enormous drink!

Finally, and most importantly, to my family. My wonderful mother and my late father, for igniting my love of reading, for gifting me self belief and an insatiable thirst for knowledge. You have honestly been the best parents any child could wish for. Special thanks, however, must go to my mother, who was widowed when I was just seventeen. Your constancy, love of life and learning, and incredible kindness and humanity have made you the best of role models.

To my sister Kathleen, for your invaluable help with my research, your company, and your encouragement. Our journey together has been a wonderful thing in itself. I have gained so, so much from having you at my side. To my other sister, Sarah, for being an ear, and for always being there for me. To my mother-in-law, Di, for the chats, the meals, the sewing, the housework, the kindness; thank you! To my dog, Bonnie, for the company, every day, as you lay at my feet while I tapped away, and for the walks that helped solve plot hitches.

And, most of all, thank you to my darling husband, Julian, and my three wonderful children: Millie, Josh, and Lottie. Each of you are my inspiration every day. You make me utterly proud, and I love you all so much it hurts. Thank you for your steady and unshakable belief in me, for encouraging me to "go for it." You are all my everything.

About the author

About the book

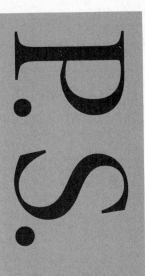

Insights,
Interviews
& More...

Meet Louise Fein

Jed Leicester

LOUISE FEIN was born and raised near London. After earning a law degree at Southampton University, she worked in Hong Kong and Australia and enjoyed traveling the world before returning to London to settle down to a career in law and banking. She holds a master's degree in creative writing from St. Mary's University, London. Louise lives in the beautiful Surrey countryside with her husband, three children, and small dog. *Daughter of the Reich* is her debut novel. ◠

A Note from the Author

My father's family were Ashkenazi
Jews, originally from Brody, which is
now in the Ukraine but was formerly
in Galicia, a province in the northeast
of the Austrian empire. During the
nineteenth century, the Fein family
business, in common with many other
Jews at the time, traded hides and skins.
They traveled back and forth from
Brody to Leipzig, an important center
of European fur trading for the fairs
that had operated there since the
Middle Ages.

Changes to the laws in Saxony in
the late 1830s paved the way for the
establishment of Jewish settlements,
and in March 1870, the Fein family
officially became Saxon citizens, settling
in Leipzig. The Feins fully integrated
into German life. Well educated and
ambitious, they built up a successful
fur trading business (established in
1904) in the Brühl, at the heart of the
Jewish fur trading quarter, and owned
property. All of this was ultimately to
be stolen by the Nazis.

My father became a doctor of law in
1931 and established his legal practice in
the summer of 1932. On June 30, 1933,
my father was banned from practicing
law in Germany because he was a Jew.
He applied for positions all over Europe,
but to no avail. Anti-Semitism was on
the rise all across the continent. Having
read *Mein Kampf* a few years earlier,
my father was only too aware what ▶

3

A Note from the Author (*continued*)

danger a newly elected Hitler posed. Toward the end of 1933, he left Germany (his young wife, who was expecting their first child, followed a few weeks later) on a temporary visa to England, a status that remained until he was finally granted citizenship in 1946. Until then, he had to apply annually to the Home Office to remain in the country. He was permitted to do so—without ever being interned—on the basis of providing evidence of the success of his business, and therefore his ability to support himself and his family financially.

Unqualified to practice English law, he set up the London branch of the family business, which dealt mainly in rabbit skins for hat making. Once in England, at home and beyond, he and his family spoke only English and adopted all things British. In 1943, he was given permission to serve in the Home Guard; was elected onto the Executive Committee of the Export Group in London, working closely with the Board of Trade, an honor for a refugee from enemy Germany; and even made a wartime broadcast on BBC radio on the varied uses of rabbit skins. My father embraced English life absolutely and completely, grateful to the country that had given him shelter and enabled him to create a successful business and home for his family. From him I learned to value liberty and freedom as the most precious of ideals, and to appreciate the paragon of democracy that was England.

During the remainder of the 1930s, other members of the Fein family left Germany and went to either London or New York, where another branch of the family business was established. Some left as late as 1938, following Kristallnacht and after their arrests and short stays in the Buchenwald concentration camp. One of my father's uncles was so badly damaged by his three weeks of incarceration there that he died just a few years later. Other members of the family waited too long to leave and were eventually murdered at Auschwitz and Theresienstadt.

My father, who was sixty-one when I was born and died when I was seventeen, never talked about his life in Germany or the experience of living under Nazi rule. He refused to buy German goods and never spoke German. As a child, by some sort of osmosis, I assumed a sense that my father's Jewish background should be kept a secret, fearing that if someone found out, we would be in danger. Occasionally, I would lie awake at night and imagine being taken away and put in a camp. I planned escape routes and how we could save one another. I never admitted to anyone my father's Jewish roots until only a few years ago.

I cannot remember exactly when the idea of a novel inspired by my father's past first came to me, but it fermented over a long period of time. I knew so little of his life in Leipzig that I felt instinctively it should be a work of fiction. Ideas mulled, characters came to me, and I began to read and research in earnest. The book, though inspired by what I learned about my father, is not about him. In writing this story, I hoped to show parallels between the early 1930s Germany in which he lived, and the Western world since the crash of 2008. Economic hardship of the 1920s led to the rise of nationalism and its extremist views and actions. New forms of mass media (radio and film) enabled the delivering of messages directly into homes and cinemas. All media, old and new, were used in highly effective propaganda across the nation. By these means, and by silencing voices of discontent, an entire population could be controlled and manipulated. Today, we potentially face a similar trajectory with the resurgence of nationalism; the fast-developing far right and far left sentiments; and extremism in many awful forms. Populist leaders stunning the world by winning elections. Brexit. Calls for closing borders and increasing racist sentiment. Anti-Semitism rearing its ugly head once more, including in once-centralist political parties. Ludicrous rumors of a Jewish conspiracy again circulating. People learning their news increasingly through the false bubbles of their social media networks.

With all this happening around me, writing a book of fiction seemed, often at times, a ridiculous, self-indulgent game when there were so many more important things going on *out there* in the real world. But stories—fiction—have a power. A good book can reach out and pull a reader into a world they know nothing about. It can emotionally engage in a way that facts—news— often cannot. Characters from a great book can live on in the minds of the reader.

My original plan had been to write the book from the Jewish ▶

5

experience. But the more I learned, the more I wanted to understand the mind-set of the Nazis. How could a people of a deeply civilized, democratic nation become so unbelievably cruel, dehumanize one another, and commit atrocities on such an unimaginable scale? The more I read, the more I realized that what I wanted to say could perhaps be more powerfully told if I were to climb inside the head of a Nazi. To tell the tale of someone young, who was fed a twisted ideology and taught hatred from day one. Someone who knew no other way. What could possibly change their outlook when it went so against everything their family and the society around them believed?

To research for the book, I read widely, including a large variety of texts—both nonfiction and fiction—accounts of those who lived through those times, and contemporaneous letters and diaries; listened to recordings of testimonials; and had the benefit of access to PhD theses and family papers. I also read *Mein Kampf* and visited Leipzig. In all of this, I had a good deal of help from my sister Kathleen with both research and translation. In Leipzig, I was able to interview some incredibly helpful people, including Dr. Thomas Töpfer, the then-director of the Schools Museum; Dr. Andrea Lorz, a German historian specializing in the history of the Jews in Leipzig; and Dr. Hubert Lang, a retired lawyer with a special interest in Jewish legal history in Leipzig and the author of books on this subject. I explored the town extensively, including the area of Gohlis (which is featured in the book), where my father and his family lived. I was put in touch with a gentleman in London, Peter Held, who had traveled to England as a teenager on the *kindertransport*, and who had lived on the same street as my father's cousins in Leipzig. He remembered my father's family well. He was ninety-four when I met with him in the summer of 2016. Sadly, he passed away only a few weeks later.

Certain aspects of historical detail have been altered for the sake of the story. For example, certain people, speeches, locations, and events are the product of my imagination or the amalgamation or alteration of facts. One particular invention is the "Hausfrau school." There actually were various Reich Bride Schools in existence at the time, offering courses in household management. In fact, there were some courses designed for the more working-class wives-to-be and others for the more middle-class women—or the "elite"—who were marrying members of the SS. The "Hausfrau school" Hetty is threatened with is, in my imagination, more of a residential finishing-school-type institution, hence I have differentiated it from what really existed by giving it a different name.

Writing this book has been a journey on so many levels. I hope that, if I have done my job well, readers will experience a sense of this tumultuous period in history through the eyes of Hetty and Walter. I hope that readers will also mull over the precariousness of the freedoms and rights we take so much for granted in our own times. And above all, I want to show that the lessons of the past must never be forgotten. ☙

Q&A with Louise Fein

Q: What was your toughest challenge and greatest pleasure while writing this book?

A: I suppose the toughest challenge in writing this book, yet also the greatest pleasure, was the research. It was an enormous task, partly because there is so much information available on this period, and partly in making sure I didn't just dump information into the book. In common with many other historical novels, only a tiny fraction of the research I did actually made it into the book, because a novel should feel like a work of fiction and not a history lesson. That said, most of the research is revealed in a visceral sense, in the background: the sights, the scents, the smells, the conversations and actions of the characters. Ideally, it pulls the reader into that world, so that the book is not just hard facts but rather a multisensory experience of the time. I suppose the challenge, and the pleasure, is achieving that authenticity. One of my biggest concerns has been to get the facts correct. Sometimes this is harder than it sounds because there can be conflicting information, or hard-to-find, obscure points. For instance, the road names in the book caused me some stress. They often changed names several times during the period in which the story takes place, or half a road was called something different. I spent about three days just checking and rechecking road names! There are some inaccuracies in the book, sometimes out of necessity for the flow of the story. For instance, I have put a fictional Jewish graveyard in a location where there wasn't one. Being only an amateur historian, I have learned so much from studying the background for this book. One specific thing I found extremely difficult was reading *Mein Kampf.* I had to really steel myself to do that, and it was almost seven hundred pages long, so it took some time to wade through it. I concluded that Hitler truly was a narcissistic madman, and how people bought into his often conflicting, ridiculous rants is still beyond all understanding.

Q: What was your writing process like? How much did the story change from your first draft to today?

A: I wrote a terrible first draft of the book before beginning my master's degree, just trying to get the basic bones of the story down but knowing it needed a lot of work and improvement. I originally told the story in the third person from both Hetty's and Walter's perspectives, written in past tense with some elements from the present day. I ditched that draft and started again, telling the story from only Hetty's perspective, and then experimented by switching to a first-person, present-tense narrative. Finally, I was on my way. "Being" Hetty rather than observing her made all the difference, and suddenly she became the full-fledged character she is in the final book. I would say that while the story itself has varied very little from the first draft to today, the manner of telling it is completely different. With each draft, I also added layers and minor story lines which increased the depth and nuance of the story. I've lost count of how many drafts I went through before the final version you see today!

Q: You did an extensive amount of research into World War II–era Germany to write this novel. Was there anything you learned that was particularly surprising?

A: I think one of the most surprising things was that despite all that the Nazis were saying or doing, and the warning signs, most Germans did very little to try to stop them. There was a sense of inevitability and headshaking and concern, but an overwhelming feeling of "Well, what can we do?" Most people just continued on with their daily lives and hoped it would all go away. In the letters and diary entries I read, people expressed discomfort and despair, but also a sense that ordinary people were powerless to change anything. There's a certain parallel to some of today's issues, such as the rise of nationalism, ▶

Q&A with Louise Fein *(continued)*

hate-filled rhetoric, and climate change. People comment on social media and discuss the issues with friends, but there is also a belief that altering the course of world events is outside our control. We, too, have a tendency to cross our fingers and hope it will all be okay in the end.

Q: As a child raised in a Nazi family, Hetty spends a good portion of her youth—and the book—sharing many of their beliefs. Was it difficult to write a character who expressed these sentiments yet still remained likable?

A: Actually, Hetty's character was relatively easy to write. She came to me as a fully formed person, and there was never much doubt as to how she would react in any given situation. I think it was easier to be sympathetic to her because she was taught her reprehensible beliefs as a young child and it is hard to judge someone in that situation. Hitler knew that it was vital to get to the youth because they are the easiest to brainwash. Indeed, that whole generation of Hitler's children had to be de-Nazified. I found Vati more difficult to write. It was hard not to make him a stereotypical heel-clicking, black-booted Nazi. However hateful, Nazis were also human, and I had to make him a rounded person who was a husband and father as well as someone who thought and did despicable things. The same went for Tomas. Tomas had a troubled childhood and took his troubles into adulthood. He became twisted and warped, just like the world around him.

Q: We first meet many of the characters as children, and then get to follow them through the years over the course of the book. What was the experience like of writing the same characters at different ages? In particular, how did your approach to writing from Hetty's perspective change as she grew up and became more mature?

A: It was quite a challenge to write the characters as children in an adult book. In fact, the early part of the book probably changed the most as it was hard to get it right—to make the characters sound age-appropriate without the tone feeling juvenile. That said, it was incredibly useful to explore how the characters' childhood experiences made them the adults they became. In lots of ways, it was rewarding to follow their journeys into adulthood. It would have been interesting to see what sort of person Karl would have turned out to be, but sadly, like many boys of his time, he didn't make it far into adulthood. With respect to Hetty, she went on a huge journey of character development. Her inner conflict was so interesting to explore, especially once, with Walter's influence, she began to question the prevalent attitudes around her. It was satisfying from a character development perspective to write Hetty's journey from Hitler worshipper to vehement anti-Nazi.

Q: What would you like readers to take away from Daughter of the Reich?

A: The main thing is a sense of how easy it is to brainwash a nation. I would like readers to think about what they might realistically do if they were placed in such a situation. We all like to think we would be heroes and resist the forces of evil, but it's different when it is your own loved ones who may suffer the consequences. I believe we all need to think about the messages and actions of governments today. Many may seem small and insignificant but added together they could potentially become more sinister. Our institutions of democracy and freedom are fragile and need protecting. Above all, I hope the book engenders discussion and discourse. ᗢ

Reading Group Guide

1. As a child, Hetty becomes an enthusiastic follower of Nazi beliefs. With the benefit of hindsight as a teenager, she may appear naïve in her unquestioning adherence to these morally reprehensible views. How does one acquire a moral compass, and who are the most important influencers—parents, school, friends? How challenging is it to think differently from those around you, particularly as a child or young person?

2. Hetty continues to tolerate Tomas as a friend, even though she has moved up the social and economic ladder, leaving him behind as his family's status deteriorates. Why do you think she keeps hold of his friendship, even as she sometimes appears ashamed of Tomas? How does the dynamic of their relationship change over the course of the novel?

3. Unlike Hetty, Karl's attitude toward the Nazis is not brought into question in the book. He appears to be a devoted follower of Hitler, but do you think he ever questions his own allegiance? What evidence is there for your opinion?

4. Mutti, as a French woman rather than a German, is an ardent Nazi and steadfast admirer of her husband. Even after the war, and knowing of her husband's infidelity, she does not lose faith in either. What drives her to behave and feel the way she does?

5. Hetty credits Walter for changing her way of thinking. Do you think she would have continued her unquestioning support of the regime as the truth of what was happening to Jews and other minorities emerged, even if it weren't for Walter? On what do you base your opinion?

6. Although there were fractured pockets of resistance in some German towns and cities as the 1930s progressed and the hold of the Nazis became increasingly extreme, there was no grand-scale resistance in Germany as there later was in

France. Why do you think this was? How does the way German society is portrayed in *Daughter of the Reich* influence your opinion?

7. Walter and Hetty took huge risks as their relationship evolved, particularly in their clandestine meetings. Erna's family took enormous personal risks to help Hetty, but also to help total strangers. Why do some people act in ways to save others, even if it jeopardizes their own safety? Which characters in the book would you consider heroic, and why? Which character(s) do you associate with?

8. One of the recurring themes in the book is that of female relationships: between Hetty and Erna, between Mutti and Hetty, and between Hetty and Anna. Discuss the complexities of each of these relationships. Do you see a common thread?

9. After Walter has left for London, Hetty says, "What can one helpless girl, with no influence, do?" Even though she had promised Walter she would do anything in her power to help his family, she quickly realizes how utterly helpless she is. Consider her position as the teenage daughter of a Nazi officer. What do you think she was realistically capable of doing? In what ways are her intentions to help doomed from the start? How does Hetty's inability to make a difference represent the reality of so many Germans caught in the cross fire of the Nazi regime?

10. Hetty becomes involved in the *kindertransport*, a program through which thousands of desperate mothers sent their children away for their own safety. While some children were lucky enough to have relatives to go to, most were sent to strangers who agreed to take these refugee children into their own homes for indefinite periods of time. What do you think persuaded people to offer to take such children in? Do you think such a program would or could be implemented today? ↶

A Select List of Sources

United States Holocaust Memorial Museum
Calvin University, German Propaganda Archive
(English translations of speeches by Nazi leaders),
Professor Randall Bytwerk
Schulmuseum, Stadt Leipzig
Buchenwald Memorial, Weimar
The Weiner Holocaust Library, London
JSTOR—"Before Auschwitz: The Formation of the
Nazi Concentration Camps, 1933–9"
oldimprints.com—old maps, brochures, and invitations to
Leipzig Fairs

NONFICTION

A Hitler Youth: Growing Up in Germany in the 1930s,
Henry Metelmann
Ein Volk, Ein Reich: Nine Lives Under the Nazis, Louis Hagen
Nazi Women, Cate Haste
*What We Knew: Terror, Mass Murder and Everyday Life in Nazi
Germany: An Oral History*, Eric A. Johnson and Karl-Heinz
Reuband
Jüdische Spuren in Leipzig, Bernd-Lutz Lange and Andrea Lorz
The Diary of a Young Girl, Anne Frank
Hitler's Empire: Nazi Rule in Occupied Europe, Mark Mazower
Six from Leipzig, Gertrude Dubrovsky
Hitler Youth: Growing Up in Hitler's Shadow, Susan Campbell
Bartoletti
Growing Up Female in Nazi Germany, Dagmar Reece
The Rise of Adolph Hitler and *The Triumph of Hitler*,
Philip Gavin, The History Place
The Rise and Fall of the Third Reich, William L. Shirer
Sylvia's Story: A Memoir, Sylvia Wildmann
"'Aryanization' in Leipzig. Driven Out. Robbed. Murdered,"
Dr. Monika Gibas, Dr. Cornelia Briel, Petra Knöller,
Steffen Held, translated by Cynthia Dyre Moellenhoff, 2009,
Leipzig City History Museum

"Jews in Leipzig: Nationality and Community in the 20th Century,"
Robert Allen Willingham II, dissertation, May 2005, University
of Texas at Austin

"The Family in the Third Reich, 1933–1945," Lisa N. N. Pine,
PhD thesis, Department of International History,
LSE http://etheses.lse.ac.uk/1410/1/U084457.pdf

"Inter-generational diachronic study of the German-Jewish Fein
family from Leipzig," Rico Langheine, 2014, University of Sussex

Fein Family Papers, Sussex University Library Special Collections

Fein Family Collection, 1872–1990, Leo Baeck Institute

Mein Kampf, Adolf Hitler

The Perfect Nazi: Uncovering My Grandfather's Secret Past,
Martin Davidson

Let Me Go, Helga Schneider

Germany: Memories of a Nation, Neil MacGregor

A Time to Speak, Helen Lewis

The Third Reich: A Chronicle, Richard Overy

I Shall Bear Witness: The Diaries of Victor Klemperer 1933–41,
Victor Klemperer

To the Bitter End: The Diaries of Victor Klemperer 1942–45,
Victor Klemperer

A Child of Hitler: Germany in the Days When God Wore a Swastika,
Alfons Heck

East West Street, Philippe Sands

Lebensborn, Jo Ann Bender

Seduced by Hitler: The Choices of a Nation and the Ethics of Survival,
Adam LeBor and Roger Boyes

"Leipzig 1937," Historiche Adressbücher

SONG TRANSLATIONS

"Lieder, totalitarianism, and the Bund deutscher Mädel: girls'
political coercion through song," Rachel Jane Anderson,
thesis, July 2002, McGill University, Montréal, Québec, Canada,
source: Library and Archives Canada/OCLC 57575010 ▶

A Select List of Sources *(continued)*

JOKES

Dead Funny: Telling Jokes in Hitler's Germany, Rudolph Herzog, 2011
Lifehack, Erik Lund
"Werner Finck, Anti-Nazi Jokes,"
    evanfleischer.com

FICTION

The Reader, Bernhard Schlink
Reunion, Fred Uhlman
Alone in Berlin, Hans Fallada
Little Man, What Now?, Hans Fallada
The Boy in the Striped Pajamas,
    John Boyne
Yellow Star, Jennifer Roy
All the Light We Cannot See,
    Anthony Doerr
The Book Thief, Markus Zusak
Schindler's List, Thomas Keneally
Fatherland: A Novel, Robert Harris
Maus: A Survivor's Tale, Art Spiegelman
The Silver Sword, Ian Serraillier
Slaughterhouse-Five: A Novel,
    Kurt Vonnegut
The Zookeeper's Wife, Diane Ackerman
Once, Then, Now, Morris Gleitzman
When Hitler Stole Pink Rabbit, Judith Kerr
Bombs on Aunt Dainty, Judith Kerr
A Small Person Far Away, Judith Kerr ໑